Truck You

A Hate to Love Small Town Romace

The Mutter Brothers
Book 1

Aria Bliss

MISADVENTURE
PRESS

Copyright © 2023 by Aria Bliss
Written by Aria Bliss
www.ariabliss.com
aria@ariabliss.com

Published in the United States by Misadventure Press, Gainesville, FL.
www.misadventurepress.com
info@misadventurepress.com

Book Layout, formatting, typesetting and cover design by
Angelique's Designs, a Misadventure Press Author Service
https://misadventurepress.com/author-services/

FIRST EDITION
ISBN (Original paperback): 978-1-948169-82-0
ISBN (Special Edition paperback): 978-1-948169-83-7
ISBN (eBook): 978-1-948169-81-3
Printed in the United States of America

Books by Aria Bliss

The Mutter Brothers Series

Truck You: A Hate to Love Small Town Romance

Truck Me: A Grumpy-Sunshine Small Town Romance

A Drunk Love Contemporary Romance Series

Not for Me: A Fake Dating Romance

Let Me Stay: A Friends to Lovers, Best Friend's Sister Romance

Lead Me Here: A Grumpy-Sunshine Romance

Aside From Me: A Roommate to Lovers Romance

Make Me Go: An Age Gap Romance

Hearts of Watercress Falls Series

Healing Hearts: A Second Chance at Love Small Town Romance

Trusting Hearts: A Single Dad Small Town Romance

Falling Hearts: A Secret Marriage Small Town Romance

Laughing Hearts: A Best Friend's Sister Small Town Romance

Forgiving Hearts: A Hate to Love Small Town Romance

Standalone Novels

Good Wine & Bad Decisions: A Sexy Romance

An After-Hours Affair Series

In Charge: Book 1

One Drink: Book 2

You're Mine: Book 3

Charm Me: Book 4

Stuck Together: Book 5 (A Holiday Romance)

Trigger Warnings:

This series deals with some heavy themes including abandonment, anger and rage, physical and mental abuse, fear and helplessness, growing up too young, guilt, loss of childhood, jealousy and hatred, substance abuse, emptiness and inadequacy, self-harm, neglect, self-loathing, self-doubt, low self-esteem, domestic violence, and poverty. While all themes are not presented in every book, there may be hints to them throughout the series. However, this is still a romance and a happily-ever-after will be delivered with a heavy dose of humor along with all the big feels you expect from an Aria Bliss novel.

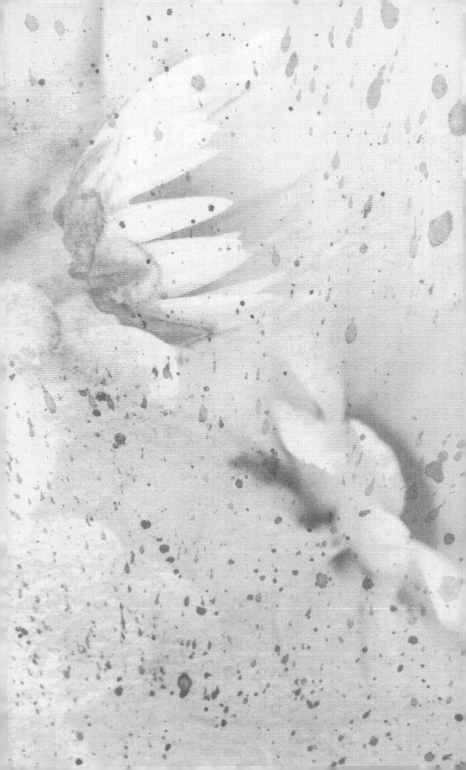

Chapter 1

Apples aren't the only things that are red.

Mac

There's an energy in the air that feeds my soul and sends a buzz of excitement through every bone in my body.

I love this time of year. The temperatures are cooler, the leaves are changing colors, and before long, there will be snow on the ground. I might have to wait a few more months for that, but it's coming. Racing ATVs in the snow is one of my favorite activities.

But for now, there's still a warmth that draws people out to enjoy good food, silly games, and *mostly* safe carnival rides.

Because it's festival season.

My brother Ash and I step into a local tavern in downtown Jackson, a small city close to where we grew up racing and fixing cars in the hills of southern Ohio with our five older brothers. Many of whom should be here soon. We'll grab a couple of beers before we head out to enjoy the opening night of Jackson's locally famous Apple Festival.

"Yo, jackass! What are you drinking?" Ash yells across the noisy bar.

I cup my hands around my mouth and call back. "A Bud's fine."

He nods while I claim a pool table in the back corner. I'm surprised to find one open considering how busy this place is tonight. It's always crowded in here during the Apple Festival, and playing pool typically isn't an option.

I'm racking the balls when someone jumps up on my back and hollers in my ear. Normally, I'd stiffen and ready myself for a fight, but not tonight. I know it's my dumbass brother Chase. I can pinpoint his fancy-ass cologne anywhere. Plus, he's always doing shit like that.

"Get off me, motherfucker." I jab my elbow in his ribs before I turn around and secure him in a headlock. I tousle his hair, knowing how much he hates it.

"Off the 'do, man." He shoves against me and runs his fingers through his hair, attempting to put each strand back in place.

"Aw, did I mess up the pretty boy's hair?" I tease and rush to the other side of the pool table before he can retaliate.

"Mac, stop razzing your sister," Liam, our oldest brother, teases as he drops onto a stool at a neighboring high-top table. It's good to hear him joking around. He's always so serious and acts like he's our dad most of the time instead of our brother.

Chase glares at him, but the jab doesn't stop him from fixing his hair.

"Who's up first?" Ash asks as he sits two bottles of Budweiser on the table next to Liam and keeps one for himself. Another one of my brothers, Christian, hands a bottle to Chase while taking a long pull on his own.

I stare at Christian and Chase and shake my head at how different they look. Sometimes I can't believe they're identical twins.

Chase is clean cut, in a nice button-down shirt and crisp jeans, while Christian looks like he just stepped off the set of *Sons of Anarchy* in his ripped-up jeans and black leather jacket. Chase's dark brown hair is perfectly styled, and Christian looks like he just rolled out of bed.

Their personalities are just as different as their appearance. Chase is fun-loving, playful, and charming. But Christian has perfected the silent bad boy, damaged soul demeanor. It amazes me how much the chicks dig it. He gets more tail than any of us.

"Babies first," Chase says with a grin. Good thing he's on the opposite side of the pool table or else I'd mess up his hair again.

By *babies first*, he means Ash and me. We're the youngest of the Mutter brothers, with me being the actual baby, as they love to remind me *all the fucking time*. Not that we're all that young anymore. I'm twenty-seven, and Ash is a year older. Maybe when we hit our thirties they'll shut the fuck up.

One can hope.

"Where's Garret?" Ash asks. He brushes his dark blond hair out of his eyes where it swoops down into his face. If he'd go get a haircut, that wouldn't happen. He's the only one of us that has dark blond hair and blue eyes. The rest of us Mutter brothers all got our dad's exact shades of brown hair and brown eyes. Which, if you think about it, is pretty fucking amazing since we don't all have the same mom.

Liam shakes his head and sighs. "Couldn't get him to come out."

Garret's the third oldest of seven, and a recluse. I swear he'd never show his face in public again if he didn't have to work.

We all live on our family's property in Beaver, a tiny ass village in the middle of nowhere. It's so small, it's barely a map dot.

But the Mutters have owned over sixty acres in the surrounding countryside of Beaver for almost a hundred years, so that's where we all live.

All of us except our brother Warren. He moved away for college sixteen years ago and never moved back. He lives somewhere in North Carolina designing racecars now. At least he's doing something with his life that we can relate to. He's the smartest of all of us. Earned his PhD and everything.

Garret got himself one of those tiny houses and put it on his eight acres. The rest of us still live in the main house with Dad and Grams. It's a huge Victorian-style house that's seen better days, but it's home, and we all like living close. Maybe one of these days we'll each settle on our inheritance like Garret did. Until then, it's happy, noisy bliss on the Mutter homestead.

"We never should have let him put that garage by his hut," Chase says around a drink of his beer. "Fucker never comes to the shop anymore."

"Don't think that would've mattered." Liam adds. "He spends most of his time running around the county fixing broken appliances. I can't even recall the last time he worked on a car."

"I don't get it. Working with us is fun." I frown. The time I spend working with my brothers at the garage we own is the best part of my day. Between building custom racecars and racing them on local tracks, my days are a blast.

"And that, baby brother, is the problem." Chase slaps me on the back before he ducks into the seat opposite Liam. "Fun and Garret don't mix."

"Come on, break the rack already so we can get a couple of games in before we eat. I'm already starving." Ash glares at me from the opposite end of the pool table. I'd tell him to go first, but it wouldn't do any good.

In our family, it doesn't matter what we're doing, the youngest always goes first. Whether it be a game, fixing our plate at dinner, or taking a damn shower after a long day in the garage. It's always youngest to oldest in the Mutter household.

I chalk up the end of my cue stick, place the cue ball near the outside rail, and prepare to break the rack. I take my shot and the rack breaks beautifully, knocking three solids and one stripe into a pocket.

After studying the layout in relation to the cue ball, I make my call. "Five ball in the corner pocket."

It glides into the pocket with ease. I take two more turns before I miss.

Ash is a much better player than me, so I know I'm toast. Knowing him, he'll end this game in a single turn.

Put me behind the wheel of a car, however, and I'll leave everyone within a fifty-mile radius in my dust. Racing stock cars is where I excel. Hell, if I hadn't had a near fatal accident that broke my leg in several places two years ago, I'd be dominating the Sprint Cup by now.

But shit happens, and it happened to me.

"Well, well, well. Look what we've got here. A couple of little girls thinking they can play pool like the big boys."

I growl because *shit* just walked in the door.

I turn around and come face-to-face with none other than Tanner Koch, one-fifth of the offspring of our sworn mortal enemies. Unfortunately, the other three-fifths of the male offspring are right behind him. They look like they're itching for trouble.

"Girls, my ass." Ash puffs his chest out. "I think I hear your momma calling. Your bottles are ready."

Tanner cuts his glare to Ash, but before he can step forward, Liam steps between us, effectively pushing Ash and me back.

"What do you want?" Liam crosses his arms over chest and straightens his spine, making him look taller than he already is.

All the Mutters are at least six feet or taller. Not only is our height an advantage over the Koch brothers, but so is our strength. Not a one of them reaches five-feet-ten, and they're all softies. That's what happens when you work desk jobs.

Tanner gives him a broad grin and matches his stance. "Cool your jets, man. Just wanted to make sure you all got the invitation to the high-stakes poker game next month. We hope at least one of you will buy in."

Liam laughs and shakes his head. "Hell, no. We're not as stupid as your ancestors."

Tanner's nostrils flare, and he takes a step closer to Liam. "You chicken?"

"Nah, man. Just smart." Liam smirks. "Nothing you say or do

will ever goad us into putting the homestead up for grabs. Give it up."

It's been a longstanding battle between the Kochs and the Mutters over the rightful ownership of *our* property.

Over a hundred years ago, their great-great-grandfather lost the homestead to our great-great-grandfather in a drunken hand of poker. They've been trying to get it back from us ever since. But the deed is ours, and there isn't a damn thing they can do about it.

Not wanting to ruin my good mood or the fun I plan on having tonight, I toss my cue stick down on the table and push past my brothers.

"Come on," I wave them on as I head toward the exit. "It's time to eat greasy carny food."

"Let me get that for you." Chase wipes his thumb across my chin in the same way a mother would do for her child with a dirty face.

I slap his hand away. "What the fuck, man?"

"You had a little mustard on your chin." His eyes roam over my face like he's inspecting it for something else to wipe off.

I give him a shove and fight the urge to roll my eyes. "Just tell me next time. I can wipe my own damn face."

"Where would the fun in that be?" He grins before he sprints in the direction of the water gun game that Liam, Ash, and Christian are already playing. Well, Liam and Ash are playing. Christian is leaning against the pole, smoking a cigarette like he's bored out of his mind. At least he's here and trying. That's more than I can say for Garret. He's probably at home, alone in his tiny house, brooding.

Not interested in shooting water guns at a small target, I head over to the skeeball tent. I buy myself a bucket of balls and settle in front of an open lane.

I'm just about ready to toss my third ball after swishing the first two right down the hundred-point ring when a loud squeal causes me to stumble. Glancing around, I freeze when I find the source of the noise a few lanes over. A young woman about my age is bouncing on her toes and clapping after successfully hitting the hundred-point target with all nine balls, earning herself the top score.

But her score is not what's captured my attention.

It's her.

With a bright smile, fair skin, and fiery red hair, she just might be the most beautiful woman I've ever seen. She looks ethereal and yet tough as nails in her tight-as-fuck jeans and knee-high boots. Her features are soft and delicate, but there's something about the smile she's sporting and the way she carries herself that screams *badass*.

She turns to face the carny who's providing her with a selection of prizes to choose from, and the light hits her face. Her eyes are the color of the sky on a cloudless summer day. She has a scattering of freckles over her nose and cheeks that I want to trace with my finger. Her peach-colored lips are full and plump and begging to be kissed.

She's fucking adorable, and I need to know who she is right now.

Jackson is a bigger city than the small village I'm from, but I've lived in this area my whole life. Everyone knows everyone in these parts. I can't imagine someone as strikingly beautiful as her could live here this entire time without me seeing her before.

Movement out of the corner of my eye pulls my eyes off her. Tanner Koch is watching her with lust-filled amusement. He says something to one of his brothers and moves in her direction as if he's going to act on his wicked thoughts.

A possessive growl grumbles out of my chest like I have some claim to this gorgeous stranger despite knowing full well that I don't.

But that doesn't stop me from taking the first step toward her. My strides are long and quick, and I reach her before Tanner even gets within twenty feet of her.

He glares at me like he's itching to start a fight, same as he did in the bar earlier tonight. I shift my stare to the redhead that drew me over. She's looking back and forth between us with raised brows before they finally settle on me.

"Do you know that guy?" she asks.

"Yeah." I wave him off like he's unimportant. "Just some guy from my hometown."

She watches me with a careful gaze as if she wants to ask me more. Clearly, she clued in on the tension between Tanner and me. I could tell her more, but I don't want to scare her off before I even get her name.

"So, I take it you're not from Jackson?" She rests her hands on her hips and tilts her head to the side as she looks up at me. She's not exactly short, but if I were to guess, I'd say I have a good five to six inches on her. I'm not as tall as some of my brothers, but at six feet, I'm taller than most people around here.

"Nope." I give her my best smile. The one that always makes the girls swoon. "I live about fifteen miles west of here. How about you? I've never seen you around here."

"New in town. Just arrived this afternoon." She glances around as if she's seeing all the booths and games for the first time. "I did not know I was arriving at the start of a local festival. This is awesome."

"It's pretty cool. We southern Ohioans love our festivals."

Her eyes narrow slightly, she adjusts her stance and studies me. Her eyes dart around my face before a puzzled look takes over her expression. I raise a brow as if to question why she's inspecting me so carefully.

Then her eyes widen, and her jaw drops before she covers my mouth. "Oh, my God. You're Mac Mutter."

My smile widens. "You've heard of me?"

She nods emphatically. "I'm a *huge* racing fan. I've followed your career for years."

"Really?" Suddenly, this red-headed bombshell just got a whole lot more interesting. "I guess you'd have to be if you know who I am. I never made it to the Sprint Cup."

She shrugs as if that doesn't matter. "I watch more amateur and ARCA races than I do Sprint. I think those drivers sometimes have more heart."

I press my hand to my heart and look to the heavens. "Jeez, Red. Are you trying to make me fall in love already?"

She laughs and scrapes her foot across the ground like it's a nervous habit. "Sorry to disappoint but racing already owns my heart."

I mock being hurt, but really, I'm thrilled. A girl that loves racing as much as me is a rare find. Assuming she's being truthful and not just saying all that shit to fool me. It wouldn't be the first time.

"You know, I was really bummed you got knocked out a couple of years ago." Her expression turns serious and a little solemn. "I would have loved to have seen you dominate the Sprint Cup. You planning a comeback?"

Huh, so she's not lying. If Red knows about that, then she *knows* racing.

I shrug, suddenly uncomfortable with this conversation. I hate talking about the accident. I still race, but that accident messed me up more than I want to admit.

"Maybe." I finally answer. "I'm racing again. Taking it slow. An accident like that can really make a man reevaluate his priorities."

She nods and scans the surrounding area, looking at anything and everything except me. I hope my truth about racing didn't make her uncomfortable. My brothers give me enough shit about me getting back in the game. I don't need it from a stranger too.

Then she lifts her bucket of balls and smiles. "Do you like skeeball?"

My smile returns and I point over my shoulder at where my bucket still sits. "I love skeeball. It's my favorite carny game."

Her smile grows, and her eyes sparkle with mischief. "Care to wager?"

I cross my arms over my chest and take a step closer to her. "Are you challenging me?"

She pats my arms and grins like she thinks *I'm* being adorable. "You bet your ass I am."

And just like that, she draws me in even more.

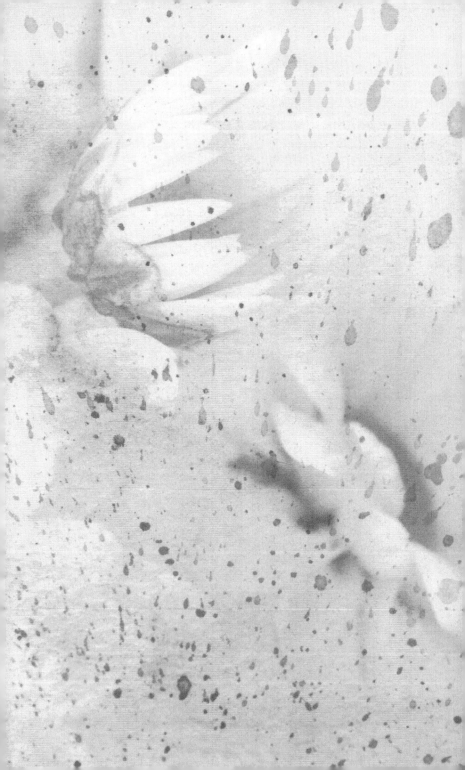

Chapter 2

Caramel apples aren't the only thing I find irresistible.

Sophia

Could I gawk more? I must look like a crazed fan with the way I keep staring at Mac.

Oh, my God. Mac Mutter.

Meeting him was bound to happen at some point this week, but I didn't expect it to be on my first day in town. I'm not even in *his* town. Or rather, village. I'm in the closest city that had a vacant room in a hotel because there are no hotels in Beaver.

Because there's nothing in Beaver. From the research I did, there's only one gas station, a small family-owned grocery store, and one restaurant. That's pretty much it. Everything else in the area is scattered throughout the hills, at least a good ten-to-fifteen-minute drive from Beaver.

And yet here he is in all his handsome glory.

The TV didn't do him justice. He's much taller than I imagined, with broad shoulders and thick arms. His biceps flex with every move he makes, causing a riot of sensations to swirl around in my belly. Those strong, muscled arms look like they could lift me up as if I were as light as a feather.

He's wearing a black t-shirt that fits snug across his chest, revealing every ridge and valley of his defined chest and abs. His waist is narrow, but I can't see his hips or ass because he has his jacket tied around his waist. He's wearing a worn pair of light blue denim with holes all over the legs that look like they came from hard work and not because it's a design feature.

I look back up at his face to see he's watching me check him out. The grin he's sporting causes my face to warm. *God, Soph. Don't blush.* With my fair skin, my face turns beet red when I'm embarrassed, and I am definitely embarrassed right now for being caught gawking at him.

But his smile is bright, and his dark eyes lighten just a tad at my perusal. His face looks just as good as the rest of him. A powerful, sharp jawline, freshly shaved, a smile that probably melts panties all over the country, and chocolate brown, playful eyes that look like they're currently imagining what I look like naked.

Thank God I'm wearing a long sleeve shirt. My arms are probably all red and blotchy from how flustered I feel. Damn Irish genes.

He takes another step toward me. His body is almost close enough to touch mine. Then he lifts his hand and brushes a strand of my long, probably frizzy, red hair behind my ear.

"Are you checking me out, Red?" He smirks as his eyes settle on my mouth.

I suck my lips into my mouth and curl them between my teeth. *Did it suddenly get hotter outside? My body is on fire.*

I take a deep breath and do my best to smile like a sane person and not someone who's crushing on a man she just met. "Just sizing up the competition."

He lets out a deep, throaty laugh that causes my body to zing with excitement. What in the hell is happening to me? I never react this way to men, no matter how damn cute they are.

He narrows his gaze, but his smile remains. "You expect me to believe you're thinking about the skeeball challenge right now?"

"Yep." I nod. "I'm a very competitive person."

He leans forward until his lips are almost close enough to touch my ear. "What do I get if I win?"

I suck in a breath from both his words and the husky sound of his voice. "What do you mean?" I ask, my voice way too breathy and weak.

He stands up straight and shrugs, looking smug and sure of himself. "If I win, what do I get?"

I narrow my eyes, a bit of my composure returning. He thinks he can beat me. "What do you want?"

"To spend time with you," he says without hesitation.

I chuckle. "Aren't you currently spending time with me?"

The full force of his smile returns, and my damn belly does acrobatics that nearly knock me on my ass. His smile is dangerous. "Maybe I want to see you again after tonight."

"You don't even know my name."

"I would if you gave it to me."

I stare at him for a moment, debating my next move. He's cocky, for good reason, and I want to spend time with him, too. But I have no clue what I'd ask him for if I win.

I hold my hand out, offering it to him for a shake. He takes it. A jolt shoots up my arm, causing my lungs to constrict and struggle for oxygen. Based on the way his lips twitch, he feels it too. "I-I'm Sophia."

"Nice to meet you, Sophia." His voice is rough and scratchy, like it's a struggle for him to get his words out.

"Skeeball," I say in a rush because I need to refocus my brain before I do something really stupid like jump his bones in the middle of this crowded street. "Loser buys the winner a caramel apple."

"Red, I'll buy you a caramel apple regardless of if you beat me." He winks. "But if I win, I get a date."

"A date?" I square my shoulders and place my hands on my hips like I'm going to challenge him. I'm totally open for a date, but

I don't want to look too eager. "What if tonight is my only night in town?"

"Is it?" He quirks a brow.

My shoulders deflate just a tad. "Well, no."

"Okay, then. If you win, I buy you a caramel apple. If I win, you go out on a date with me. Not exactly a fair arrangement, but I accept."

I narrow my gaze as his smile grows. Cocky isn't a strong enough word to describe how sure of himself he is. "Fine. It's a deal."

TWENTY MINUTES LATER, AND I'M GLOATING. WE PLAYED five rounds, and I beat him four out of five. He totally owes me a caramel apple.

The best part is, he doesn't seem the least bit upset about it. He's grinning from ear to ear like he knows something I don't.

"Come on. Let's play the ring toss game." Mac points to the booth next to us.

"How about I watch this time?"

He gives me a side eye. "What's the matter? Scared?"

"Nope." I smile and step up next to a father trying to win a stuffed dog for his daughter. "I know my strengths and weaknesses. Ring toss is *not* a strength."

"In that case, let me show you how it's done." Mac pays the teenager manning the booth. "You may have kicked my ass at skee-ball, but I'll win you a stuffed animal. Watch and be amazed."

I chuckle and roll my eyes. "You think you're that good, huh?"

He gives me a wink, and my belly does a cartwheel. "I know I am."

He tosses ring after ring, completely relaxed, like he does this every day. Every single ring lands exactly where he wants. Right around a bottleneck. He doesn't miss a shot.

"Daddy! Why can't you do that?" The little girl beside us frowns up at her dad, who's only made two out of the six rings he's tossed.

"Sweetie, it's harder than it looks," the man says.

"He made it look easy." The girl points at Mac.

"It's not. Trust me." Mac smiles and kneels down next to her. "Don't get upset with your dad. He's trying. It took me a long time before I got this good."

"But I want the doggy." I don't know how it's possible, but her frown deepens.

Mac looks up at me and shrugs. "How about you take the doggy I just won? I bet my girl won't mind. Will you, Red?"

I swallow hard at how he called me *his girl*. I just met him, but I like the sound of that. "Of course not. I bet you'll take better care of him than me anyway."

The smile that covers the little girl's face is totally worth it. She bounces on her toes and looks up at her dad. "Daddy, did you hear that? He's giving me the doggy he won."

"I did, sweetie." The man smiles at his daughter before looking at Mac. "I appreciate the offer, but you don't have to do that."

"Nah, don't worry about it." Mac takes the doggy from the carny and passes it over to the little girl. "I know she'll love this doggy more than either of us."

The girl squeals and hugs the doggy close. "Thank you!"

"You're welcome." Mac beams at her, and I swoon. "Enjoy the rest of your evening."

He takes my hand as we say our goodbyes and leads me down the street, past the other game booths. His strides are long, and I find I have to walk double time to keep up.

I also don't miss how good his hand feels wrapped around mine. His skin is rough to my soft. His fingers are long and thick, swallowing my hand as if it's a tiny delicate flower.

My body is alight with anticipation and heat and something I've never felt before.

I see a food truck with the words *CARAMEL APPLES* painted in big bold red letters across the side, but he doesn't lead me to it. Instead, he veers off down a side street away from all the food trucks and toward a ticket booth.

"Where are you taking me?" I ask, a little breathless from walking so fast.

He grins at me again and winks. *God, that wink.* I swallow a moan at how sexy he looks when he does that.

This man needs a warning label.

"We're going to hit some rides first," he says, like that's the most logical thing in the world two strangers would do when they meet at a small-town festival at random on a Wednesday night.

"Okay," I say. Because what else can I say? I want to spend more time with him. I want to see if there's more to this man than his good looks, racing abilities, and sense of humor. Plus, he makes my belly do weird things no guy has ever done to me before.

We hit the ticket stand line and have to wait because it's at least ten people deep. There's a family at the front with four kids who are all crying that they want to ride different rides. Their dad looks equal parts stressed and irritated that they can't seem to agree on anything. It makes me smile.

But that smile is short-lived when my phone buzzes in my back pocket. There's only one person I can think of that would call me tonight. I debate on ignoring it, but Mac raises his brow as if silently asking me if I'm going to answer it.

I pull it out and fight to hide my frown when I see it is indeed my mother.

Swiping to answer, I say in the sweetest tone I can muster, "Hey, Mom. How are you?"

"Don't *how are you* me. Why didn't you call me?"

"Didn't you get my text?" I say with an innocent air I know she'll hate.

"I asked you to call me when you arrived. That was at least a two-hour drive." She lets out an audible huff that's loud enough to hurt my ear.

"That's not very far, Mom. Plus, traffic was light. I'm here, checked into my hotel, and will let you know how Saturday goes."

I lift my eyes to Mac to see if he's listening to my conversation. If he is, he's acting like he's not. I'm not sure I'm ready to tell him the *real* reason I'm in town. I kind of like him, and I don't want to chase him off by telling him what I do for a living.

She harrumphs like my words are the most ridiculous thing she's ever heard me say. "What is all that noise I hear in the background? Are you at a bar?"

"Mom! No, I'm not at a bar, and even if I were, it's not like you can stop me. I'm twenty-five."

"Then where are you?"

"There's a festival in town. I checked it out rather than staying in my hotel room. In fact, I should go. I'm in line to get food, and I'm up next."

"Well, okay, dear. If you're sure you're fine."

"Yes, Mom. I'm perfectly fine. I'll call you this weekend. Give Dad a hug and kiss for me. Bye!" I hang up before she can say anything else to drag out the conversation. Talking to Mom about my life choices is the last thing on my agenda for the night.

When I look up, Mac is staring at me with a confused look on his face.

"What?" I ask.

"You lied to your mom."

I sigh. "Yeah. I never would have gotten off the phone with her if I told her the truth."

"And what *is* the truth?" His eyes roam down my body. The heat of his gaze is so intense, it's like flames lick my skin.

"Umm." I nibble on my bottom lip and squeeze my eyes closed. I don't need a mirror to know my cheeks are bright red. "That I'm in line for carnival rides with the first man who hit on me because I think he's cute."

His lips turn up in a wicked grin. "You think I'm cute?"

I roll my eyes and give him a playful shove. "You know you're cute."

He grabs my hand, wrapping it in his before he holds it close to his chest. "I think you're cute too, Red."

My face flames up again, and I drop my head toward the ground. I don't know if he's calling me that because of my red hair or for how often he can make me blush.

The line moves, and he tugs me forward. "So, what'll it be first? The Zipper, Bumper Cars, or the Ferris Wheel?"

"Duh, Bumper Cars. Do you really have to ask?"

His smile widens, and I swear a sparkle lights up his dark eyes. "Something tells me you and I are going to have a lot of fun tonight."

———

"I WANT THE RED ONE!" I YELL AS I RUN TO GRAB THE BUMPER car of my choosing. Mac laughs from behind me, walking slowly, as if he doesn't have a care in the world.

"Why the red one?" he asks. "Is it because of your hair or the way you turn bright red when you're blushing?"

I hide my face from him as I feel my cheeks heat just at the mention of how much I've blushed around him tonight. "Neither. I just like red."

He chuckles as if he knows how much his comment is making me blush again. Apparently, I have no control of my body's reaction to him.

He climbs into the green car next to me as nothing but little kids, no more than nine or ten years old, pile into the remaining cars.

"How much you want to bet I can beat you around the track?" I ask.

He gives me a challenging stare. "You really want to race with all these kids around?"

"Are you scared?" I tease.

"Not in the least." He waggles his brows. "Few people can beat me in racing. Not even in bumper cars."

"We'll see about that." I grin, put both hands on the wheel, and hold my foot over the peddle. Moments later, the buzzer signals the start and our cars come to life.

I quickly maneuver my car away from the pile of kids, who are all stuck in an endless circle of bumps and twists as they all turn the wheel too sharp in one direction. It takes Mac a moment to extract himself from the mess of kids as one after another bumps into him, knocking him back every time.

While he looks frustrated, I can't help but laugh. I slow down slightly, giving him a chance to catch up. This won't be fun unless we start on an even playing field.

"It took you long enough." I glance over my shoulder and give him a playful grin. "Are you ready to get your ass handed to you by a girl?"

"You know I race professionally, right?" The slightest hint of guilt hits me at his statement. This would be a great time to tell him I race cars too, but I don't.

"Is that supposed to intimidate me?"

"No, it's just a fact."

We come up on a turn, and I take it on the inside, effectively cutting him off as he tries to pass me. I look over my shoulder and smile. "Then why I am leading?"

He narrows his eyes at me and tries to hide the smile threatening to take over his face. We come up on a straight stretch, and he pulls up beside me. I knock my car into his, pushing him into the wall. He curses as I speed ahead of him and secure my lead around the next corner.

Before he catches up to me, three kids push their way in front of Mac, trapping him in the middle of their entanglement. He tries to move around them, but they keep knocking into each other, making it impossible for him to escape.

Meanwhile, I loop around the track, passing him with a teasing wave.

By the time the buzzer sounds, signifying the end of the race, I've passed Mac twice while he fought to get away from the group of kids. The kids continue to laugh and tease each other like their little pile-up was the most fun they've had all day. But Mac glowers as he climbs out of his car and stalks toward me.

I bite down on my bottom lip as I fight back the urge to laugh. He's doing his best to act like he's pissed, but I can tell it's all for show.

We exit the gate just as a group of guys yell from across the track. "Hey, Mac! Way to lose to a girl."

Mac flips them off, but a chuckle escapes him just as he reaches me.

I lift a brow. "Friends of yours?"

"You could say that." He smirks. Then he tosses me over his shoulder, causing me to cry out in surprise.

"Mac! What are you doing?"

"I haven't decided yet." His large hand squeezes my thigh, and I can feel the heat of his skin through my jeans. My heart rate kicks into overdrive. My mouth runs dry, and I'm suddenly wondering what his hand would feel like if he moved it a little further up my leg. "You know, you're really crushing my ego here, Red. You've beaten me twice now."

"It's not my fault. I'm better than you."

He grabs me by the hips and slowly lowers me back down. My chest brushes against his as my feet meet the ground. Our eyes lock and I'm hit with the full force of his intense and heated gaze.

For a moment, I think he's going to kiss me. Instead, he takes my hand and leads me toward another ride. "Let's see how you handle the Zipper."

I eye the ominous rotating boom with individual rotating cages with reluctance. This is one of my least favorite rides and the last thing I want to do after the high I just got from beating Mac at bumper cars.

"Do we have to?" I ask, my voice low and hesitant.

Mac squeezes my hand and tugs me close to his side. "Not if you don't want to."

I shake my head. "Not a fan of rides that go upside down. I mean, I love a good thrill, but that one, not so much."

He nods, and to my relief, he doesn't push the point. "How about the Ferris Wheel instead?"

"The Ferris Wheel is perfect."

The line is short, and we're able to hop right on without waiting. Within minutes, we're at the top, looking out over the city. The sun is just starting to set, and from up here, the sunset view is stunning.

The sky is shifting from pale blue to deep oranges, yellows, and hints of purple. The colors match the changing leaves I can still see in the distant hills beyond the city limits.

"Yo, Mac!" A male voice cuts through my thoughts. When I look down, I see the same group of men that called out to him as we were leaving the bumper cars. "Who's your girlfriend?"

"Wouldn't you like to know?" Mac calls back as we sweep down and start our round and round cycle.

"Who are those guys?" I ask.

"Just my brothers. They like giving me shit every chance they get. Curse of being the youngest child."

I glance over my shoulder and count at least four men. "Wow. So you're from a big family."

He nods. "And two of them aren't here tonight. I'm the baby of seven."

I smile at how affectionate and proud he sounds. "Are you close?"

"Oh yeah. Very." His brothers yell something else at us as we pass by, but I can't make out what they're saying. Mac grins and shakes his head before he looks at me again. "Our family owns a lot of acreage, and all but one of us still lives on the land. We all work together too."

"Must be nice. My siblings are cold and distant."

He frowns at me. "How many do you have?"

"Just two. A brother and a sister. I'm the baby, same as you."

"That sucks." He leans back in his seat and stretches his arm across the back. He doesn't touch me, but it still feels like an embrace. "I can't imagine my life without my brothers. I mean, we fight and stuff, but we're always there for each other, no matter what."

"It's always good to have family you can count on. I may not have that in my siblings, but I have a couple of cousins I can count on."

His smile is back. "Yeah, I'd hate to think what life would be like if I were alone."

He eyes me for a moment, like he's studying me. "What? Is there something on my face?"

He shakes his head. "I'm just wondering where you're from."

"Oh." I brush my hair behind my ear, and his eyes track the movement. "Cincinnati. Born and raised. But I went to college in upstate New York."

"What did you study?"

I wrinkle my nose and force myself to maintain eye contact. Just because most people judge me for my career aspirations doesn't mean he will. He practically has my dream job. "Automotive engineering. Well, technically mechanical engineering with a focus on automotives."

His eyes widen. He stares at me like I'm an anomaly, and if he blinks, I might vanish. "Are you serious?"

I nod. "What can I say? I love cars. I love racing them and fixing them. Though I'm not that good at fixing them yet. But I want to learn. And I want to take a stab at building them someday. Cars are my passion."

He blinks—and blinks again—before he shakes his head and presses his hand to his chest. "I think I'm in love."

"Oh, stop it." I give him a light shove just as the Ferris Wheel operator begins to make stops to unload this round, and revel in the fact that he doesn't seem to be judging me for what I just told him.

A few moments later, we're on the ground. He stares at me. I stare at him. And things feel awkward and weird for the first time since we met.

He shoves his hands in his pockets, and his gaze shifts to my mouth. It's too dark out now for me to see the shift in the color of his eyes, but if I were to guess, I'd say they're dark and heated based on the way he's staring at me.

He takes me by the hand and starts walking backward, dragging me along with him. He doesn't stop until we're standing alone in the shadows of a dark alley.

"Mac?" I glance over my shoulder at where a crowd of people are waiting in line at the Ferris Wheel. "What are you doing?"

He rubs a strand of my hair between his fingers. There's just enough light that I can see he's looking at me.

"I want to kiss you." His voice is rough and gravelly, like that admission hurt him to say it.

I swallow hard. "You do?"

"Yes." The admission rumbles from deep in his chest. I wait for him to say more, but he doesn't. Is he asking me for permission or simply admitting to me what he wants? This entire experience with him is new and surreal and exciting.

"Okay," I finally say.

"Okay, as in ..." His voice trails off as he cups my cheeks. He runs his thumb over my bottom lip, and I swear he sucks in a breath like that action caused him pain. "Tell me I can kiss you."

My heart feels like it's being revved up to over seven thousand RPMs, and if I don't take off now, my engine will blow. I lift my hands and wrap them around his wrists as I take a step closer. "Yes, you can kiss me."

His eyes slide closed as he lowers his mouth to mine. The moment his soft lips brush across mine, my heart takes off. Every nerve ending in my body fires off in an electrifying sensation that leaves me feeling light, like a falling leaf floating in a light breeze.

He moves his lips slowly, as if he's savoring the moment just as much as he's savoring me.

Then he tilts his head to the side and parts his lips. His tongue swipes across my bottom lip and I groan.

The next thing I know, he presses my body against the brick building and his mouth devours mine. Gone is the slow, tentative, savoring kiss, and in its place is a deep, claiming kiss that has me grasping at his shirt and pulling him closer.

I lift my leg and wrap it around his thigh, causing him to grind into me. When I feel his solid erection press against my center, my body erupts into flames. We're too far apart and there are way too many clothes between us. I want to feel him, touch him, kiss him everywhere.

His hands slowly rake down my body and settle around my waist, just below my chest. His thumbs brush the underside of my breasts, and I moan at the erotic sensations it arouses in my body.

Jesus, this is crazy. I can't believe I'm making out with Mac Mutter in an alley at the Apple Festival.

My eyes fly open as my mind focuses on what's really happening here. "Mac," I mumble against his mouth, "we need to slow this down."

He freezes, then he jumps back and throws his hands in the air like he was just caught trying to steal a cookie from the cookie jar. "Oh, shit. I'm sorry. That really escalated."

I reach for his hand and waffle his fingers with mine. "It's okay. I'm just as much to blame."

"Fuck, Red. I just wanted to kiss you. I didn't mean to maim you in a dark alley." He steps closer and runs a finger along my jaw. "Can I see you again?"

I nod. "I'd like that."

"How long are you here for?"

I cringe. It's an innocent question, but one that reminds me I haven't been completely open with him. I'm not sure I'm ready to be that open. He may not have an issue with my degree choice, but I'm not sure he's ready for all my truths. "That depends. I have a job interview on Monday. If it goes well, I might be around for a while."

His smile grows. "Let's hope it goes well then."

"Yeah," I mumble because that's all I can seem to muster.

He presses a quick kiss to my lips before he steps back and adjusts himself. Then he takes my hand and tugs me back toward the crowd. "Come on. I believe I still owe you a caramel apple."

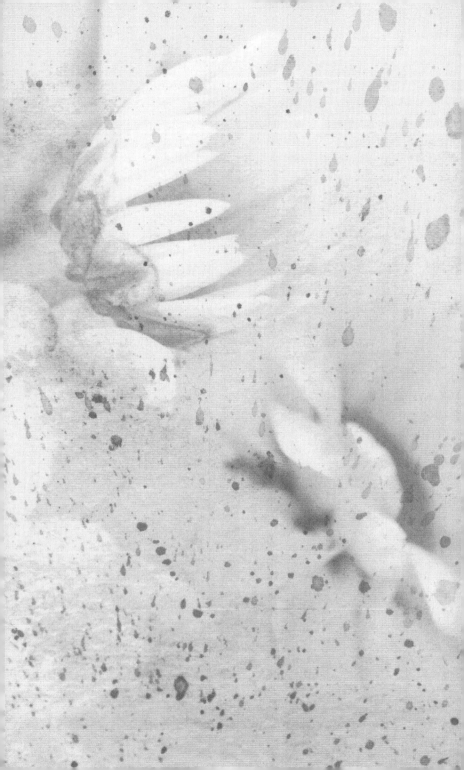

Chapter 3

Gearheads and farm boys are surprisingly a good mix.

Mac

A loud creak rings in my ears, followed by a bang. My eyes slowly blink to open, and I shift my head toward the window. The sun is up, which means so is my family.

There's no such thing as sleeping in at the Mutter house. My bedroom is on the first floor, just off the kitchen, so as soon as someone is up, I hear every noise they make.

Besides running the garage, Mutter Truckers Auto & Racing, we farm some of our acreage. Or, I should say Chase does. He's the only one of us that enjoys farming. We endlessly tease him about being the prettiest farmer around. We also help him when he asks, but he mostly tends to it on his own.

It's a small farm that makes us some money, but nothing like the garage. We manage a few acres of crops and a few more with livestock.

Our large Victorian house sits close to the main road, and the garage is next to it. It has seven bedrooms and three large bathrooms. Plus, the master bedroom, which is now Liam's, has its own bathroom.

This house has been in our family for five generations. Grandpa built the garage before I was born. Before that, the

Mutters were just farmers. Grandpa brought the love of cars and trucks into our family.

Unfortunately, I didn't get to know him before he passed. I was only three and barely remember him. But Grams always tells us he'd be so proud of us following in his footsteps.

I toss my covers back with a yawn, then check the time. It's just before seven in the morning. Knowing Chase, he's already milked the cows, gathered the eggs, and fed all the farm animals. He's done with the crops for the season, which means he has more time to help in the garage. That's always a plus.

I grab a pair of sweatpants and a long sleeve Henley before I head to the bathroom. By the time I'm done relieving myself and brushing my teeth, the smell of sugar and cinnamon wafts through the air. I smile, hoping Grams is cooking this morning. She makes the best cinnamon rolls in the state. Hell, everything she makes is incredible.

We may have gotten the short end of the stick when they were handing out mothers and fathers, but our Grams is the best.

Heading back to my bedroom, I open my sock drawer to grab a pair and my eyes land on the red ones sticking out from around the mostly gray and black socks I own. My mind is instantly assaulted with memories of the gorgeous redhead that charmed the socks of me last night. Gorgeous isn't even a strong enough word to describe her. Stunning. Magnificent. Exquisite. Ravishing. I could go on and on with descriptors and still not capture her beauty.

And those plump, peach lips. So sweet and skilled.

If she hadn't stopped us in the alley, I may have fucked her right there.

Who am I kidding? I totally would have fucked her. Her body was too tempting. So soft and firm in all the right places.

I grab my phone from my side table and pull up her number. It's probably way too soon to text her. I'm sure it makes me look desperate, but I don't give a shit. I like her.

MAC
Any chance you're free Saturday night?

I smile when I see the three little bubbles instantly pop up, indicating that she's messaging me back.

SOPHIA
Maybe. What did you have in mind?

MAC
There's a bonfire party at the Meadow. Wanna come?

SOPHIA
What's the Meadow?

MAC
Just a big open field where half the town hangs out occasionally. It's fun.

SOPHIA
Can I get back to you? I have some things going on during the day on Saturday that could interfere.

I frown at her response. It's cryptic and non-committal and I don't like it.

MAC
Okay. So you'll let me know?

SOPHIA
Yeah, should know by late afternoon if I can make it.

MAC
I look forward to hearing from you.

I plug my phone back in and head toward the kitchen. Grams is standing at the stove. I step up behind her and kiss the top of her head. She's a petite woman, only five-foot-three, with a head full of completely silver hair. "Morning, Grams."

She smiles up at me and pats my cheek. "Morning. I hear you met someone last night."

I groan and glare at my brothers sitting around the table. Liam is at one end pretending to read the paper, Ash is sitting back in his seat grinning like he knows a secret, and Chase is pretending to be cool, acting like he doesn't have a clue what Grams is talking about.

"You shit." I knock Chase upside the head, knowing damn well he's the one that told her.

He laughs and jerks away before I can pull him into a head-lock. "What? You were awfully sweet with that redhead. You ditched us and everything."

"She's new in town. I was just being friendly."

"Is that why you dragged her into a dark alley?" Ash mumbles under his breath. I narrow my gaze in warning, and it only makes his smile grow. I should have known they saw me do that.

These fuckers know the rules. We never discuss our hook ups with Grams. Not that I hooked up with Sophia, but it's a strong possibility that it will happen. Maybe even as soon as Saturday night.

"I was just being *nice*." I ground out.

"You two looked pretty cozy on the Ferris Wheel." Chase teases. "But I particularly loved the way she kicked your ass on the bumper cars. That was the highlight of my night."

I flip him off before I grab a mug from the cabinet and pour myself a cup of coffee. Maybe if I ignore him, he'll shut up.

Thankfully, the back door opens, and Garret's entrance distracts my family. He heads directly for Grams and gives her a hug and kiss before he takes a seat at the table next to Liam as if this is a normal thing for him. It's not normal. He never joins us for breakfast.

While we're all staring at him like he's a mirage, Grams smiles and sets a plate at each of our seats. She smiles at Garret and says, "I take it you got my message?"

He grunts and nods but doesn't use actual words. That *is* normal for Garret.

Neither one of them elaborate but based on the way Garret digs into his cinnamon roll the second Grams puts it on his plate, I think it's safe to assume that's what got him to the house. None of us can resist Grams' baked goods. Not even a grumpy recluse like Garret.

"Haven't seen Rayne lately," Grams says. "Have you?"

This is directed at Garret. Grams will try anything to get Garret to talk and Rayne is usually a good way to do that.

Rayne Weber is the ten-year-old granddaughter of our next-door neighbors, Jim and Lois Weber. They've raised Rayne since she was a baby. Her mom, their youngest daughter, Carol, died of pregnancy complications shortly after giving birth.

Rayne's a good kid. She's always upbeat and cheerful even though she has good reasons to be mad at the world. She has no clue who her dad is and probably never will, and she lost her mom before she ever got a chance to know her.

For reasons none of us can figure out, Garret enjoys having her around.

Their house butts up next to the property line, close to where Garret put his tiny house. Rayne is always stopping by and chatting with him. Well, Rayne talks, and Garret listens with the occasional grunt.

Garret shakes his head without a word. Then he digs into his cinnamon roll, making it clear he has no interest in talking.

We're all eating in silence when the back door opens again. This time it's Dad that walks in. "Mornin' boys. The car's loaded up for you."

I tip my head in his direction. "Thanks, Dad."

"Of course, son." He gives me a tight smile before he refills his coffee mug and heads back outside.

To say we all have a strained relationship with our dad is an understatement. He's a decent man if you don't consider his poor parenting skills. He's fathered seven kids from four different women. He only married one of them, Susanne—Liam's, Warren's, and Garret's mom. I think it's also safe to say she's the only woman he ever loved too.

Unfortunately, she was diagnosed with cancer shortly after she found out she was pregnant with Garret. She opted to forgo treatment in favor of the life growing inside her. Dad fought her hard on that. But Susanne couldn't be swayed. She died within hours after Garret was born.

Dad never got over the loss, and he blames Garret for her death. Well, blame might not be the right way to put it. Garret didn't cause her to get cancer, and Dad knows that, but he's never been able to look Garret in the eyes. Ever. Seeing Garret is a constant reminder that Susanne chose Garret over herself. Admirable if you ask me, but Dad couldn't handle it.

No wonder Garret's a grumpy recluse.

Despite Dad's grief, it didn't take long before he had another woman in his bed. In fact, for the first several years after her death, his bed never went empty.

First it was Christina. She's probably the worst of the lot. She was on drugs when Dad met her, and she's still on drugs to this day. The only time in her life when she went clean was when she was pregnant with Chase and Christian. Though it's unclear if that's true.

She left right after they were born, but not before she did her fair share of damage. Still too lost in his grief, Dad didn't see how abusive she was to Liam, Warren, and Garret. Even now, she still fucks with Chase and Christian. She lives locally, and rumor has it, she's the reason Christian got wrapped up in drugs in the first place.

As far as we know, he's clean now. But he relapses often, and we all worry how bad the next time might be.

Next was Monika, Ash's mom. She wasn't as bad as Christina, but she's still not a winner. She stuck around just long enough to give birth to Ash, then left without a word. No one had heard from her for years, then one day she showed up with a toddler on her hip. She dropped off this little girl, Alvara, like she expected Dad to raise her. It wasn't his kid, but he took her in anyway. Or rather, Grams did.

A few years later, Monika showed back up and to collect Alvara like it was the most normal thing in the world to do. Dad and Grams didn't stop her despite how much we all protested. We didn't care that she was only blood-related to Ash. As far as we were concerned, Alvara was our sister too.

Then there's my mom, Heidi. She was Dad's rebound for Monika. Got her pregnant almost immediately. Ash and I are only eleven months apart in age.

My mom stuck around longer than the others. I was five when she left, and it completely caught me off guard. I thought she loved me. At least she told me she did every single day. But that was a lie. Just like how she told me she'd be right back the day she left to go grocery shopping. She didn't go grocery shopping. I was too little and didn't pick up on the fact that her car was loaded down with all her belongings.

Mom was the first woman to lie to me. She's the reason why it's hard for me to trust women, and the reason I can't handle it when people lie to me.

Seven sons with four different women over the span of seven years, with me being the youngest at twenty-eight, and Liam being the oldest at thirty-five. Needless to say, we've been the subject of lots of village gossip over the years. Most of it being lies.

But there's one universal truth in all of it. Paul Mutter is a shitty dad. He left most of our upbringing to Grams, and never really took part in anything we did as kids.

But he's still here, so I guess that's something.

"Hand me the larger wrench. This one's too small," Ash says from where he's stretched out underneath my racecar.

I have a huge race this weekend, and if I win, I'll gain back a lot of the momentum I lost after the accident a couple of years ago. My sponsors are getting antsy. They want to support a winning team, not a mediocre one.

"Is this the one you need?" I slide it under the car to him.

"Yep. Thanks." Ash tinkers under the car for a few more minutes before he slides out. I'm not sure what he's doing under there. I trust my brothers to keep my cars running safe and fast. Ash and Chase build them, and I drive them.

I know just as much about cars as they do. Maybe not building racecars from the ground up, but I can fix anything that goes wrong under the hood. I just don't love it as much as them.

My passion is the actual racing.

Which is why it sucks that the accident is still messing with my head after all this time. I was at the top of my game. Winning race after race. I'd met all the requirements in the ARCA (Automobile Racing Club of America) series and earned my place in the Sprint Cup.

That was over two years ago. I should have made my comeback by now. I should be able to get behind the wheel without having anxiety. But every day is a struggle. Every day I have to pump myself up to do the thing I love the most. No amount of internal pep talks seems to do any good. I still get nervous when I step up to my car. My hands still shake when my fingers grip the steering wheel. And my heart beats so fast it feels like it's trying to win the race.

Every day feels like a setback, and I'm not sure how much more of this I can take before I have a complete meltdown.

My brothers will support me in whatever I decide, but there are others that would be relentless with the jabs. I can hear them now. *Poor baby Mac. Too scared to drive a racecar.*

I'm not fucking scared. I'm just ... It's hard to ... Oh, hell. I don't know what's wrong with me anymore. All I know is my heart still wants to race, but my mind is being a bitch about it.

Just goes to show you how quickly things can change.

"Hey, you okay?" I look to my side to find Liam watching me with a concerned look on his face.

"What's that?" I ask.

"I asked if you were okay. You're in a daze and haven't responded to any of my questions."

"Oh, sorry." I push off from the wall where I had been leaning and shake my head. "Just thinking about the race and who's in it."

"Should be an easy one for you. It's not a big one. Plus, you have more experience than half the entries combined. I don't even recognize most of the names."

"Yeah." I nod. "That's what worries me. I don't want to get taken out because some new kid isn't experienced enough to handle his car. That would suck."

Liam watches me closely for a beat too long. His eyes narrow and his chest heaves, almost as if he can read my thoughts. But then he sighs and shakes his head. "No one's going to take you out. You're too skilled a driver to let yourself get tangled up with someone that inexperienced."

"I know." I do my best to shrug it off like I wasn't just contemplating my demise as a racecar driver. "Still, it's good to mentally prepare myself for anything."

"Sure, I get it." He squeezes my shoulder and smiles.

"So, what did you need?" I ask, hoping to change the subject.

He looks at me for a moment as if he doesn't know what I'm talking about. Then he shakes his head. "Oh, I asked if you talked to Warren yet."

"I did. He was very non-committal. He doesn't sound happy, but he also didn't sound eager to come home either."

A low grumble escapes from my brother's mouth. "We could really use his help. I wish he'd come home."

"Have *you* tried calling him?" I ask. Warren has been gone for a long time, and I suspect it has a lot to do with a disagreement he and Liam had a few years after Warren left for college. The two of them have never gotten along. Grams says it's because they're so close in age. Warren is less than twelve months younger than Liam.

I'm not convinced Grams is right. There's only eleven months between Ash and me too, and we get along fine. Maybe it's because we have different mothers.

Liam pinches his lips and shakes his head. "He doesn't want to talk to me."

"How do you know if you don't call him?" I push. "Maybe if he hears from you, he'll come home."

Liam pins me with a glare. "I'll probably have better luck getting Christian to help more."

I chuckle. "Yeah, right? He's unreliable and only wants to work on custom motorcycle builds."

"It's worth an ask." He argues.

"You can ask, but you're wasting your breath, and you know it. Christian only does what Christian wants to do."

"Well, someone is going to have to help us out around here or else there will be no garage. We can't keep up with the workload."

"I told you I would help."

"You need to focus on racing if you want to get back to where you were before. Chase has the farm. He can help us through the winter, but come spring, he needs to step back. Ash's time is split between the garage and keeping your cars running. I can't manage the garage and do all the work. We need help."

"Then I'll help!"

We're both yelling now, and too focused on making our point rather than hearing what the other is saying. We've had this conversation one too many times and haven't worked out a solution yet.

"I thought you were interviewing someone on Monday?" Ash says from beside us. I glance over my shoulder. Has he been standing there the entire time?

Liam sighs and pinches the bridge of his nose. "I am. But

there's no guarantee he'll take the job or that we'll like him. Plus, I'd rather keep it in the family."

I lean forward and squeeze Liam's shoulder. He's only trying to do what's best for the family business, and we all appreciate it, but he has to stop being so stubborn about this. "Then either call Warren yourself or let me work."

"Outside help isn't a bad thing." Ash chimes in. "Think of it as growth. A lot of family businesses hire outside the family. Nothing wrong with that."

"Yeah, we'll see." Liam lets out a deep breath before he heads to his office. I shake my head and grab a pair of coveralls from the hook near the bathroom. Might as well get some work done, since there's no one else around to do it.

Liam can yell at me about it later.

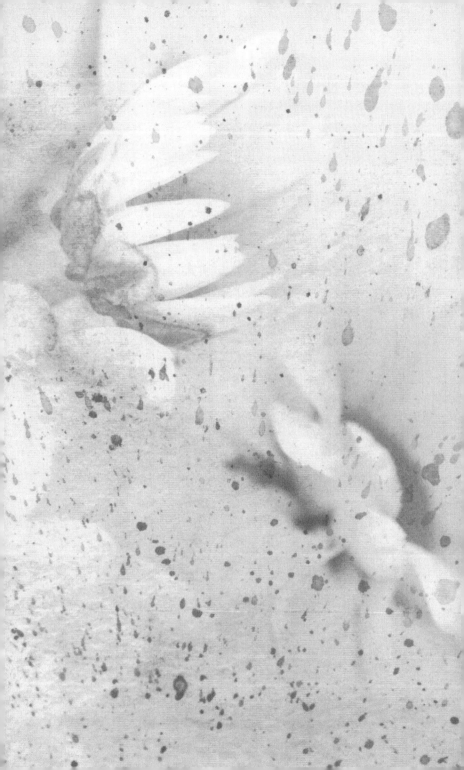

Chapter 4

Family feuds fed by apple pies and bad attitudes.

Sophia

Apparently, honesty in advertising doesn't apply when hunting for a place to live in southern Ohio.

I'm walking through the fifth rental house of the day —and I use the term house loosely—and just like the last two I looked at, it's nothing like described. Large open concept kitchen means a previous tenant knocked the interior wall out. Private lot on a lake means off a dirt road next to a pond in the middle of nowhere, where no one will find your body should Jason from *Friday the Thirteenth* come crawling out of said lake. And my favorite is onsite security. Translation—a dozen dogs that bark at every leaf that falls from the surrounding trees.

Every rental property I've looked at within a ten-mile radius of Beaver is a rundown trailer that looks like it's barely holding together.

Have these people ever heard of apartment complexes?

I smile at the elderly lady that was kind enough to show me around and tell her I'll think about it. More like I'll have nightmares about those dark stains on the carpet in the living room. Someone needs to buy her a steam vac.

At least the hotel I'm staying at is nice, but if I get this job, I'll need to find a long-term solution to my living arrangement. The hotel is too expensive, not to mention I don't want to drive that far to work every day.

The job. Why didn't I tell Mac the truth on Wednesday?

Because you're a chicken shit. That's why.

I learned a long time ago that people handle what I do for a living better after I prove myself rather than telling them up front that I race cars and am an obsessed gearhead.

That never seems to go over very well. Especially not with men who also race cars and are obsessed gearheads. So, I didn't tell Mac the truth.

I didn't *exactly* lie to him. Not really. I just omitted the real reason I'm in town. I always omit my truths to strangers. Although can I really call Mac a stranger after the way he kissed me in that dark alley?

Leave it to me to complicate matters by letting him kiss me. I feel my face heat at the thought of his lips pressed against mine and his rough hands gripping my neck. A shudder runs through me at the memory.

After shutting the car door behind me—and locking it for my own safety—I look in the rear-view mirror and press my hands to my cheeks. My face is bright red just from thinking about Mac.

I start the car up and get out of there as quickly as I can. I'm ready to forget this day ever happened.

Thankfully, the drive back to Jackson is uneventful. There's not much in the way of traffic on these roads. I truly am in the middle of Nowhere, Ohio.

That is, until I enter Jackson.

The streets of Jackson are even busier tonight than they were when I arrived on Wednesday. I thought opening night of the Apple Festival was busy, but that has nothing on a Friday night. I'm forced to drive around the hotel parking lot several times before I finally snag a parking spot.

I debate between going back to my room and eating the leftovers from last night's dinner or hitting the food trucks at the festival. The spicy aroma from the steak sandwich with fresh-cut fries truck assaults my nose for the hundredth time since I've been here, and the festival wins.

It's still early for dinner. It's barely past four o'clock, so I decide to walk around before grabbing some food. If I'm going to eat greasy carny food again, I could use the exercise.

At the end of one street, there's a stage that's gathered a large crowd. The stage is empty, but in front of it are several tables lined up with pies. Lots and lots of pies.

My eyes land on the hand-painted sign just off to the side that reads *The Apple Festival's Annual Apple Pie Baking Contest.* An apple pie baking contest? I just died and went to heaven.

I'm not a huge eater of sweets, but I can't resist apple pie. It doesn't even have to be a good apple pie. I'll still eat it above anything else.

There are seven contestants, each has at least a dozen pies on their respective tables, with a placard that says buy it by the slice. I let out a low groan. Best. Festival. Ever.

The contestants are busy cutting their pies while people gather around their tables. I see a large blue ribbon hanging on the edge of an elderly woman's table that says first place in big, bold gold letters.

"Would you like a slice, dear?" Her sweet, slightly raspy voice draws my attention away from the pies I'm drooling over and to the woman standing behind the table. She's a few inches shorter than me with bright silver hair that's cut short and spiked on top, making her look like the coolest grandma ever. She has kind eyes and a gentle smile. The deep crinkles around her eyes and lips suggest she's spent a lifetime smiling.

Even if I wasn't a lover of apple pie, I couldn't say no to that smile. "Um, yes. Of course."

She grabs a paper plate and starts to scoop up a piece.

"Wait." I reach my hand out to stop her. "Can I have that piece?"

I nibble on my bottom lip as I point to a piece where the pie juices and sugar spilled over the edge while baking, making the crust extra crispy and extra sweet.

Her smile grows. "I like a woman who can recognize the best damn piece in the dish."

She winks before she scoops it up and hands it to me in exchange for three dollars. As soon as the sweet scent of baked apples hits my nostrils, I can't get the first bite in my mouth fast enough.

"Oh, my God." My eyes fall shut as a deep, and somewhat embarrassing, groan escapes me. "How much for an entire pie because this thing is heaven?"

I don't know how it's possible, but the woman's smile grows. "That's sweet dear. Why don't you just take one? I don't do this for the money."

"Of course you just give it away," a harsh, angry voice says from behind me. I turn around to see a woman who looks to be about the same age as my mother, glowering at the sweet grandma who just offered to give me pie. "Why would a thief need money?"

The older woman sighs, "Now, Johanna, you know I'm not a damn thief."

"You're a liar as well." Johanna crosses her arms over her chest and narrows her eyes. "What's it going to take to get you to admit your family stole my great grandmother's pie recipe?"

"No one stole anything." There's a flicker of annoyance in the woman's eyes, despite the fact that she's still smiling. "This is my recipe. One that I perfected based on my own baking secrets."

I slowly take a few steps back, clearly having stepped into something I don't want to be a part of. When I turn around, I run into a young woman about my age standing behind me. She's got long, straight brown hair that hangs just past her shoulders and dark-rimmed glasses that sit low on her nose. She's wearing jeans with a light blue cardigan over a white-collared blouse. Despite her glasses, I can see she has large dark blue eyes. She's beautiful, although I suspect she does nothing to highlight her appearance. She looks like she should be standing behind the counter of the public library.

"Sorry. I didn't see you there."

She smiles and waves me off. "Don't worry about it. I snuck up on you, coming to rescue you from the Great Pie War."

"The Great Pie War?" I raise a brow, hoping that encourages her to elaborate.

"It's so silly." She points to the woman named Johanna. "Johanna Koch insists Grams," she points to the older woman who offered me free pie, "stole her great grandmother's apple pie recipe and that's the only reason Grams wins every year. But I highly doubt it's true. The Koch family will find any reason they can to hate the Mutter family, even if they're wrong."

"The Mutter family? As in ... Mac Mutter?" I ask, hoping this doesn't draw too many unwanted questions about how I know Mac.

She nods her head quickly. "Do you know Mac?"

"Not really. I love racing, and I've followed his career."

She tilts her head from side-to-side like my answer makes perfect sense, then she holds her hand out. Her arm is stiff like she's not used to introducing herself to others. "I'm Clara, by the way. I baked pies this year too, but I didn't win anything. No one can beat Grams when it comes to pie. Although I keep trying."

"I'm Sophia." I accept her hand. "So, this is your grandmother?"

"Oh, heavens no. I grew up with her grandkids." She adjusts the glasses on her face with a slightly awkward smile. "Everybody calls her Grams though."

"Really?" I give her a quizzical glance. "Even though she's not your grandmother?"

Clara rests her hands on her hips and looks at me like she's confused about why I'd ask such a thing. "You're not from a small town, are you?"

I chuckle with a shake of my head. "I grew up in Cincinnati."

She lets out what I can only describe as a disappointed sigh. "That explains a lot."

"Hey, Clara Bell!" A handsome man with dark blond hair comes up behind us and wraps his arm over Clara's shoulder. "How did you do?"

Clara cuts him a sideways glare, but I don't miss the way her hand trembles when she brushes her hair behind her ear. "How do you think I did? Your Grams was competition."

"Well, it is hard to beat perfection." He gives Clara a huge grin and a side hug before he releases her and steps around the table. "Hey, Grams. Got any of that award-winning pie for your favorite grandson?"

"Now, Ash." Grams cups his cheek. Her smile is so wide and bright it makes me wish I had a grandma just like her. Unfortunately, all my grandparents passed long before I was born. "You know I don't pick favorites."

"Don't worry, I won't tell the others." He winks. "Now, how about that pie? Clara won't let me eat any of hers."

"I never said that." Clara huffs and points a scolding finger at him. "I said you had to wait until after the competition."

Grams chuckles. "Did you run over to her house and try to eat her pie last night after I kicked your ass out of my kitchen?"

Ash presses a hand to his chest and acts wounded. "I would never do such a thing."

"Sure you wouldn't." Grams shakes her head in disbelief before her eyes land on me. "You seem to know these two, but we've not been officially introduced. I'm Mila Mutter, but everyone calls me Grams."

"Hi." I take the hand she holds out for me. "I wouldn't say I know them, we just met moments ago. But I'm Sophia. It's nice to meet you."

"You're Mac's girl, aren't you?" Ash's smile doesn't fade as he narrows his eyes like he's studying me.

"Oh, no." I wave him off. "I'm nobody's girl. I just arrived in town on Wednesday."

"So you have met Mac," Clara says like I've committed some small-town crime.

"Yes. We met briefly on Wednesday."

Grams eyes me up and down, causing me to shift on my feet. "Is this the young lady you were teasing Mac about yesterday?" Grams asks as her smile turns mischievous.

"It sure is." Ash grins like the cat that caught the canary.

"Well, then." Grams rushes out from behind the table and pulls me into a tight hug. My body stiffens and my arms hang tight to my sides. My own parents don't hug me like this, let alone a stranger. "It's about damn time one of my grandsons finally found someone. You'll have to come to the house for dinner sometime. I love cooking for my boys even if they are little shits that don't deserve it."

"Oh, no, no, no." I wave my arms nervously after she releases me. "I am *not* Mac's girl. I hardly know him."

"Is that why you let him drag you into a dark alley on Wednesday?" Ash taunts in a low voice, but it's still loud enough for Grams and Clara to hear. He follows it up with a silly kissing face.

My eyes widen and my mouth drops at how easily those words fall out of him. I've no doubt my face is bright red, along with my neck and arms. Hell, I'm so embarrassed right now. Every inch of my body is burning hot.

"Ash!" Grams swats Ash's arm. "That's no way to talk to a young lady. You apologize right now."

Ash's smile fades, and he lowers his head. "Sorry, Sophia. No disrespect intended."

"It's okay." I take a couple of tentative steps back and point over my shoulder. The urge to run is strong. Not just because of Ash's teasing, but because of the reminder of how easily I gave in to that kiss with Mac. I'm not that kind of girl. "I'm going to go get myself some dinner. It was very nice meeting all of you."

"Don't go!" Clara reaches for me, a look of panic on her face, and rests her hand on my arm. "Don't let this ogre chase you away. He's really trying to pick on Mac, not you. Which should tell you how unintelligent he can be, considering Mac isn't here tonight."

"Hey! I'm not unintelligent." Ash wraps his arm around Clara's neck and puts her in a loose headlock. "Take that back."

Clara giggles and jabs her elbow into his stomach, forcing him to release her. "Only if you promise to be nice to Sophia. I like her."

"I promise." He tosses his hands up in surrender and gives me a pleading look.

"And you have to buy both of us dinner." She adds.

"Fine, play hardball." Ash turns back to Grams and pulls her in for a hug and a kiss. "Bye, Grams. See you at home."

After a quick round of goodbyes and another hug from Grams before she hands me a boxed-up pie, we head off in search of dinner.

"So what will it be?" Clara asks. "Corn dogs, tacos, hamburgers, bad stir fry, the options are endless."

"I was thinking steak sandwiches and fresh-cut fries." I add. "The smell from that food truck has been tempting me for three days."

"Ah, good choice. I love fresh-cut fries with vinegar." Clara holds her hand out to Ash. "Give me some cash. We'll get sandwiches and fries. You go get us fresh squeezed lemonades."

He lets out a grumbling noise that might be some sort of protest, but it's not clear. Then he leans in close to Clara and whispers, "Woman, you aggravate the hell of me sometimes. You know that."

Clara simply shrugs with a *what are you going to do about it* attitude. "Yep. That's what friends are for."

Ash slaps a couple of twenties in her hand and heads in the opposite direction of the steak sandwich truck. Clara turns to me and grins, waving the money in the air. "Let's go get some food."

As we're standing in line waiting to order, I notice Clara keeps looking over her shoulder in the direction Ash went. I can't get a good read on those two and their relationship. Are they just friends or something more?

"How long have you known Ash?" I finally ask, hoping to get more information about the family from her.

"Practically since we were babies. We're the same age and grew up together. My dad is good friends with Ash's dad."

"So ... You two ever date?" I ask, curious if the attraction I sense from her is real or just my imagination.

"Oh, God. No." She lets out a nervous chuckle. "I'm more like the annoying sister he never wanted. Although he does have a half-sister. She's a lot younger than us. She lived with them a while when she was little but ended up back with their mom after a few years. She hasn't been back in a long time. Ash always goes to visit her. Anyway, I'm rambling. Ash and I are just friends. Best friends actually."

I nod, doing my best to hide my smile. I'm pretty sure the attraction vibes I'm getting from her are correct, but I don't want to push away the first friend I've made since moving here. I like Clara. She's a little quirky, but nice.

I look around at the crowd, and the number of people crammed into the blocked off streets is impressive. We have street fairs in Cincinnati, but nothing like this.

"Is the Apple Festival always this busy?" I ask.

Clara nods. "It's the biggest festival in the area. Been going on for close to ninety years now. Plus, Friday nights are always the busiest with the pie contest and the concert. People come for miles to eat the pies. Of course, the feud between the Mutters and Kochs always attracts attention. Just you wait until it's dark out. It'll be nothing but elbow room close to the stage."

I wrinkle my brow, suddenly filled with more questions than answers. I want to ask her more about the feud, but opt to hold off on that one for a bit longer. "There's a concert tonight?"

"Oh, yes. Us southern folks love our country music. This year we got Mark Chesnutt. He's always been popular around here. The streets will be filled with drunk, dancing fools in no time."

"Sounds like fun. Can't say I've ever experienced anything like this before. I've never even been to a concert, let alone one that takes place in a city street."

"What?" Clara gasps. "Never? Are you not a fan of music?"

I shrug. "I like music just fine. I listen to it, but I don't fangirl over any artists. I can't even tell you the name of popular songs or artists."

"Don't let Mac hear you say that. That man loves music. He can sing too." Clara wags a finger at me as she steps up to the counter and orders three sandwiches and three cups of fries. She gives the guy her name and pays before we step to the side and wait for our order to come up.

"Um, Clara." I turn to her, feeling way more nervous than I should. Probably because the words I'm about to say feel like a lie. "There's nothing going on between Mac and me. I just met him Wednesday night while playing skeeball. We hung out for a bit. That's all."

She stares at me for a moment, her expression completely unreadable. Then she smiles. "Do you want to go to a party with me tomorrow night? It's in Beaver, so about fifteen miles from here. I can pick you up or you could meet me at my house. Whatever works best for you. It'll be lots of fun."

"A party? What kind of party?"

"A bonfire party. It's at this place we call the Meadow, which is just a large open field in the valley between a couple of hills. There aren't a lot of places to hang out in Beaver, so we make our own fun. Usually outside somewhere. But it would be a great way for someone new to town, like you, to meet more people. And I promise, I'm not some crazy person trying to drag you out to the middle of nowhere and abandon you. I just think you'd have fun."

I chuckle and nudge her shoulder with mine. "I didn't think you were trying to drag me out to the middle of nowhere to abandon me. I'm just asking questions. A party sounds fun. I'd love to join you."

She lets out a long breath and a look of relief smooths her expression. I'm relieved, too. I have a feeling this is the same Meadow that Mac invited me to. Knowing my luck, after tomorrow, he'll rescind his invitation. This way, I still get to go.

"Great. It'll be nice to have another girl around. Especially one that I suspect can hold her own around the Mutter brothers."

Before I can comment further, the guy inside the food truck calls her name. We grab our food and head in the direction Ash went. We run into him halfway with drinks in hand.

I didn't know what to expect when I arrived on Wednesday, but this wasn't it. I expected to feel like an outsider, but so far, everyone I've met in this town has made me feel welcome. Like I've always been here.

Hopefully, I still get this warm of a welcome after tomorrow's race.

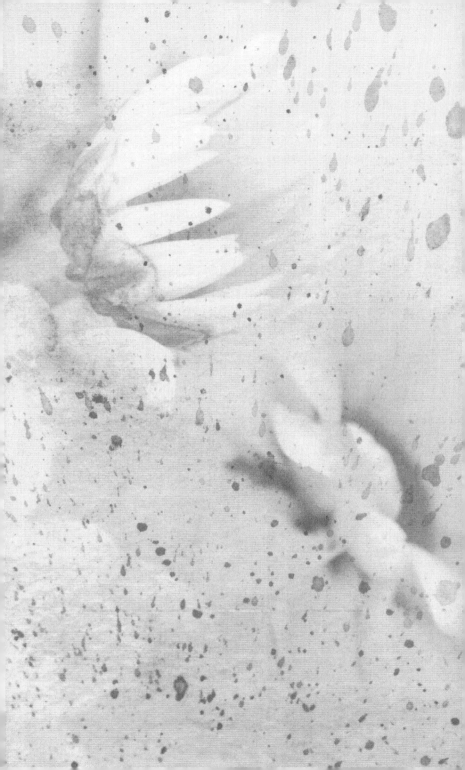

Chapter 5

Losing never felt so good.

Mac

Breathe in. *Breathe out.*

I remind myself for the hundredth time since crawling behind the wheel of my car. My grip on the steering wheel is so tight, my knuckles are white. I have to force myself to peel them off one at a time and shake them out at my sides. I've held on so tight for the past few loops, my hands ache.

It wasn't always like this.

I used to live for racing. I still do, but it's not the same. Nothing is the same anymore. Not since my accident.

The smell of rubber burning on the track used to excite me. It got my blood pumping and my energy level elevated in ways nothing else could. The sounds of engines revving and crowds cheering used to feed my soul.

Now, it gives me anxiety.

Every time I hear tires squeal on the pavement, I tense. I wait with bated breath for the sound of crunching metal to follow. Then the lightness in my stomach from the car rolling in the air, making my body feel weightless.

All the sounds and smells I used to love, now feed my nightmares.

It was one accident. *One*. I've been racing since I was old enough to reach the pedals, and I've had one accident in all that time.

I've seen countless drivers get in accidents over the years, and every one of them always walked away no matter how bad it looked.

Hell, even I walked away. Well, the rescue crew carried me away because I broke my leg. But I survived. This is racing. Accidents are inevitable. They're not an *if*, but a *when*. They're a certainty.

So why can't I shake this?

It's been two years, and I still hear the sounds of the crash as if it happened yesterday. I feel the seat belt cutting into my chest as I dangle upside down in my car. I smell the smoke billowing around me as the fuel leaking from my engine burns.

But it's the panicked cries and terror-filled faces from my brothers that haunt me the most.

Liam was the first to reach me. The rescue crew had to tackle him to the ground to keep him from dragging me out of the car and causing more damage. Thankfully, Chase and Ash calmed Liam down enough so the EMTs could do their jobs and save my fucking life.

I thought their cries were bad. That was nothing compared to the frantic looks on their faces. You would have thought I was already dead with how grief-stricken they looked.

As soon as the doctor cleared me of any brain or spinal damage, my brothers did what anyone would do in this situation. They laughed and joked and downplayed the what ifs and moved the fuck on as if nothing had happened.

But not me. I can't move on. I can't get it out of my head. And this anxiety is killing my performance.

I close my eyes as the next turn gets closer, silently telling myself to breathe in and breathe out. I used to love the corners, but not anymore. The accident happened on a corner.

"Mac!" Chase's voice calls through my headpiece. "Why are you slowing down? The car okay?"

I shake my head and refocus my eyes on the track and the cars close to me. I didn't even realize I'd let my foot up off the gas. *Get it together, asshole.*

"The car's just fine." I answer.

"Then get your ass moving. The new guy is gaining on you."

"Which new guy? Miller?" There are a lot of newish drivers in this race, but Bo Miller is performing better than the rest of them. I'm by far the most experienced, probably too experienced for this level of race. But it's what I need until I get my head on straight.

"No. The *new*, new guy. Becker," Chase says, almost as if he doesn't believe it.

"What? Isn't this his first race?"

"As far as I can tell. But I didn't research the guy. For all we know, he's been racing for years in some other part of the country."

"Fucking great," I mumble.

One reason I've continued entering these smaller races is because I felt safer. Not completely safe, but experienced enough that I can avoid inexperienced drivers that can cause accidents. I'm not prepared for actual competition.

I shake my head and focus on the road in front of me. I'm still in the lead. As long as I keep my head in the race, I've got this.

I take the next corner with ease and accelerate hard when I hit the straight stretch. I just have to put some distance between me and them.

"Mac, you're looking great." Chase's voice is calm, like always, but I sense a hint of hesitation. "But that's not enough to lose this guy. He's right on your tail."

"I'll lose him on the next turn. There's no way he can pass me on the outside."

I make the next corner with ease, but I'm sweating way more than normal. It's not because it's hot in here—which it is—it's because my nerves are getting to me. The tension settling in my body has my hands clenching around the steering wheel and every muscle in my body aches.

My breathing increases and I can hear my heartbeat ringing in my ears. I blink a few times and try like hell to slow my air intake, but I'm fading fast. My vision is blurring and my head hurts.

I just want to pull over and get the fuck out of this car.

"One more turn, Mac, and you've got this." Chase's voice soothes. "Stay with me, bro."

I blink again, trying to focus on the road. If I can just forget there's another driver on the track, I can do this. It's just me and the open road.

"Mac!" Chase says, a little louder this time. "Focus on my voice. Keep your foot on the pedal and steer that car to the finish line."

"Where's Becker?" I ask.

"Don't worry about Becker. You just drive like I know you can. It's just you out there."

I cringe at his words. I thought I'd done a good job of hiding my anxiety, but he knows I'm struggling.

Taking a deep breath, I ready myself for the last turn. The finish line is right around the corner.

Breathe in. Breathe out.

Then I catch movement on my right side. "Fuck."

Becker is right beside me. If he takes me on the outside, I'm screwed.

I shake my head again. I've done this a thousand times and nothing bad happened. *Focus on your skill, on the car, on the road. Accelerate and maintain your lead. That's all you have to do.*

Instead, I do the opposite. I hesitate, and Becker slings past me and takes the lead.

I hear Chase's muffled curses through my headset, and I know I've lost.

I lift my foot off the pedal and let my momentum push me over the finish line. While Becker takes his victory lap, I glide into the pit and stop next to my crew. Turning off my headset, I don't bother getting out right away. There's no reason to. Plus, I don't want to hear my brother's criticism.

Chase is the first to approach. He likely told the others to stay back. He knows me too well. Even if I was in top condition, my temper gets the best of me when I lose. But I'm not losing my temper today. Whatever is going on in my head it isn't feeding my anger. I feel lost, and not because of the race.

Chase leans against the car and pins me with a stare. "You okay?"

I nod and lift my helmet off my head. "Let me out of here."

He steps back so I can climb out. I may hate the fact that I lost, but I'm not a sore loser. I always congratulate the winner.

Once Becker's car stops, I make my way toward him, along with a crowd of others. His crew surrounds his car, and they practically drag him out of the car in excitement. They don't even give the guy a chance to take his helmet off first.

I grin. How could I not? I remember what it was like winning a big race for the first time. This may not be the ARCA series, but the first-place prize money is still a good chunk of change.

Hell, I'm still getting paid well for second place.

Becker gets to his feet and lifts his helmet over his head. I freeze when a mop of long, red hair falls down his back. Or should I say *her* back?

Becker slowly turns around as if she knows someone is gaping at her. When her eyes meet mine, my jaw drops.

My Sophia from Wednesday night just handed my ass to me —*again*—only this time racing stock cars.

Instead of shaking her hand like I always do with the winner of a race, I spin around and head to my tent. Betrayal and mistrust overwhelm me. She had every opportunity to tell me she'd be racing today, but she kept it from me. Why? Did I give her reason to think she couldn't be honest with me?

I liked her, and she lied to me.

My walk turns into a sprint as I bypass the tent and head to my truck instead. I'm blinded by fury and anger, and I have to get as far away from her as possible before my temper flares.

Win or lose, I always enjoy the afterparties we hold at the Meadow. What's not to love about an open field, fresh air, a bonfire to beat all bonfires, Bacardi 151, loud music, all my favorite people—and a few I don't like—an endless supply of beer, and mud running through the logging trails?

Sometimes we even get a local band to come out and play. Those are my favorite nights. Nothing soothes my troubled thoughts better than good country music.

Unfortunately, tonight I have to do with the sound system and my favorite playlist. It gets the job done, but I prefer live bands.

We arrived about an hour ago, and I've been keeping to myself. Chase keeps eyeing me like he wants to talk, but so far, he hasn't said anything. I'm pretty sure he's the only one that knows I'm struggling to get my head back in the race.

The rest of my brothers are leaving me alone—for now—because they think I'm sulking in my loss. I'm not sulking—*much*. At least not about the loss. I've lost countless races over the years. And if I keep racing, I'll lose a lot more.

I'm pissed at myself. I just don't know how to get out of my head.

I'm also pissed at Sophia. Way more than I probably should be. I'm not mad she won the race. Good for her. She drove like a pro. It's the secrets that are bothering me. I feel like she lied to me, and nothing gets under my skin more than a woman who lies.

Thanks to my worthless piece-of-shit mother, I have trust issues where women are concerned. It doesn't help that every example of a woman my dad brought home was also untrustworthy. He's picked some real doozies over the years.

So the fact that Sophia didn't tell me the real reason she's in town rubs me the wrong way. She had to know I'd find out. Hell, there's no way she didn't know I was in the race today.

Since she knew exactly who I was, she deliberately didn't tell me.

Headlights crest the treeline, and I don't need to see the truck to know who it is. Only one person in this town has blinding spotlights on the roof of his truck. Tanner Fucking Koch.

I don't like any of the Koch brothers, and not just because of the feud they insist on maintaining, but because they're all assholes. But Tanner is the worst.

He's flashy and cocky and has zero respect for anyone outside his family.

He pulls up next to Linden's truck. Linden's the oldest of the Koch brothers. He's the same age as Liam, and by far the quietest, but also the meanest son-of-a-bitch I've ever met. Rumor has it he doesn't like anyone, not even his own family.

Aaron Koch is a necessary evil we all have to deal with sometimes. He's the only doctor in a twenty-mile radius. Sometimes we have no choice but to see him in emergencies.

The youngest Koch brother, Jason, doesn't cause much trouble for us. He went to school with Ash, and Ash says he doesn't care about the feud. As far as I can tell, that's true. Jason never takes part in his brothers' antics. Overall, he seems apathetic to all of us.

As does their only sister, Amelia. She's always been friendly when we see her around town. She's one of those people that likes everyone no matter their flaws and seems to be liked by everyone as well.

Tanner hops out of his truck and zeros in on me immediately. The grin on his face screams he's ready to cause trouble. Normally, I'd be ready to give it right back to him, but tonight, I want to be left alone.

"Heard you lost to a girl." Tanner calls over the low rumble of voices. He's loud enough that everyone heard him, and all conversation immediately stops.

"Are you suggesting women can't race as well as men?" I retort.

His smile fades slightly. "Not at all. Just pointing out that you lost to one."

I take a long pull from my beer before I narrow my gaze at him. "I've lost plenty of races to plenty of talented drivers. Today is no different. I don't see why it matters if the driver has a dick or not."

Tanner puffs his chest out and steps toward me. I feel the presence of every one of my brothers behind me. Even Garret is here tonight.

"Are you suggesting that I don't think women can race cars?" he asks.

I mimic his stance. "You said it, not me."

Tanner eliminates the remaining space between us until his face is in mine. I fight back a smirk because he has to lift his chin high to do it since I'm a good four inches taller than him. "I don't like what—"

"Tanner. Enough." Amelia grabs his arm and tugs him back a few feet. "Stop trying to start shit. Leave 'em alone."

Tanner glares at his sister, then pulls his arm from her grip. "Stop sticking your nose where it doesn't belong, Lia."

Christian steps up next to me and flicks his cigarette at Tanner. It hits his pant legs before it falls to the ground. Tanner lets out a low growl but says nothing. Probably because of the death glare Christian is giving him.

Christian may not be the biggest of us—that honor falls to Garret—but he is the toughest and the dirtiest fighter. It's the company he keeps. He spends a lot of time with a local motorcycle club. There's even been rumors they've tried to induct him as a member.

Thankfully, Tanner walks away. Amelia gives me an apologetic look before she turns her gaze on Christian. Her eyes soften, and his nostrils flare before he says something under his breath and walks away too.

I hate this fucking feud. It's stupid and an unnecessary annoyance. Maybe if the Kochs weren't such sore losers, this thing could end once and for all. But something tells me they're never going to stop trying to get the house and property back.

My eyes flicker past Amelia and land on the one woman I *was* excited to see tonight. Sophia Becker is standing next to Tanner's truck, gaping at us. Has she been there long? And who in the hell told her where to come tonight? I sure as hell didn't.

Tanner sees her and rushes to her side, instantly turning on the charm like he didn't just insult her to God and everyone within hearing distance.

I clench my fists and growl at how close Tanner leans into her. I want to rush over there myself and teach him what happens when he messes with something that's mine. Only she's not mine. Not now. Not after what she did.

Instead, I head to the back of my truck. I refill my beer from the keg and hop up on my tailgate.

"You okay?" Chase asks as he hops up next to me.

I nod, but don't speak. I'm not sure if he's referring to the altercation with Tanner, the fact that Tanner is now flirting with Sophia, or that I lost the race. The race is the last thing I want to talk about right now.

"Dude, I can't believe your girl from Wednesday night races cars. How fucking cool is that?" Ash's grin is a mile wide as he steps up next to us. "I liked her before, but now she just might be the perfect woman."

I glare at Ash and bark out my response. "Why would you say that?"

His smile fades slightly. "Say what?"

"That you like her. You never met her."

His smile turns mischievous, and he waggles his brows. "Yeah,

I did. Hung out with her last night at the Apple Festival. Had dinner together and everything."

A low growl rumbles out of my chest. My first instinct is to kick my brother's ass. How dare he take a woman that I've already touched, kissed, and fantasized about to dinner?

"Ash, stop being an ass." Clara rushes to stand between us before she turns a gentle smile in my direction. "It wasn't like that, Mac. I ran into Sophia at the pie contest. We hit it off and hung out for the night. Ash just happened to be there."

The tension in my shoulders instantly releases its hold. I study Clara's face. She's telling me the truth. "You invited her here tonight?"

"I did." She glances over to where Sophia is laughing at something Tanner said. My body instantly tenses again. "I like her. It's not often I meet a girl I get along with. I hope you don't mind."

I let out a deep huff. There's a part of me that wishes Sophia weren't here tonight. I'm not in the right headspace to deal with her. But I'm also glad to see her again. I turn to Clara and shake my head. "Of course not."

"Great." She smiles. "Let me go rescue her from the Kochs before they steal my new friend."

I can't deny Clara a friend. Making friends has never been easy for her. Growing up, she preferred to play in the mud with Ash over playing with dolls. She was a tomboy as a kid and grew up to be an awkward book nerd.

A moment later, Clara returns with Sophia on her heels. "For those of you who haven't officially met her," Clara starts, "this is Sophia. Sophia, you've met Mac and Ash, but let me introduce you to the rest of their brothers."

Garret grunts his hello. Chase gives her one of his typical charming smiles. Christian nods with an apathetic expression.

But Liam smiles like he knows a secret. Then he reaches his hand out to offer her a shake. "S. Becker, huh?"

I narrow my gaze at him, confused by the way he's greeting her. Then I remember that's how she listed her name for the race today.

Sophia gives him a sheepish smile and says, "Yeah, that's me. Using my initial has become a necessity. Unfortunately, most people respond like Tanner did when they find out a girl can race cars." She shifts her eyes to me briefly before looking back at Liam. She heard our exchange. "It's the only way I can ensure I'm given a fair chance. It sucks being rejected before I even start simply because I'm a woman."

"Well, we're not sexist at Mutter Truckers Auto & Racing. Prove you've got skill, and it's all good."

Liam glances at me and winks. I raise my brows, completely lost over the direction this conversation took.

"Good to know." Sophia smiles and turns to Clara. "Any chance I can get a beer?"

"Of course." Clara's shoulders relax. She looks relieved that my brothers have accepted her into our circle. I'm not sure how I feel about it. She and I still need to talk about how she lied to me.

"You better drink fast," Ash says before he cups his hands around his mouth and yells. "It's racing time!"

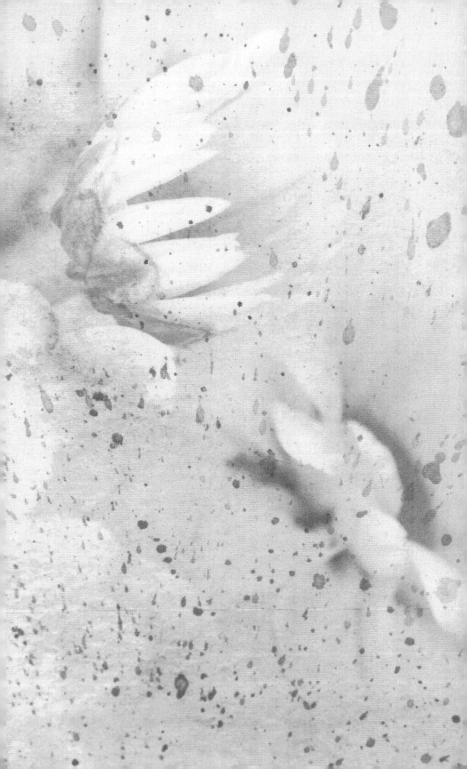

Chapter 6

God made dirt, and dirt don't hurt.

Sophia

Before I can wrap my head around what Ash said, everyone runs to a truck and the sound of engines revving echoes through the open field.

Mac and Chase jump off the tailgate, shut it quickly, and run around the sides. Mac hops into the driver's seat while Chase opens the passenger door.

Garret hops into the driver's seat of a neighboring truck with an extended cab. Clara slides into the back seat while Liam sits in the front. Ash jumps into the bed of Garret's truck while Christian jumps into the bed of Mac's truck. They both grab onto a bar affixed to the roof of the trucks like they're preparing to go water skiing.

"Come on!" Chase waves me over to where he's still waiting by the open door.

I take off in a sprint toward him, sensing the urgency in his voice. I hop in and slide over next to Mac before I even think to ask why.

Shaking my head, I turn back to Chase, who's now sitting next to me buckling his seat belt. "What's going on?"

"Buckle up, sweetheart." Chase gives me a huge grin and I hear a grunt come from Mac. "It's mud racing time."

"What?" I glance between them, not entirely sure what's going on. It was dark by the time I got here. Maybe I missed the track when I arrived.

My eyes settle on Mac's smiling face. It's the first time he's smiled since I got here. He hands me my seat belt and winks. "You better put this on. It's about to get rough. This is nothing like the tracks."

"What's not?" I ask, but neither of them answers me.

Glancing around, I see several other trucks lined up next to us, all with someone standing in the bed hanging on, just like Ash and Christian.

Then a sound fires and all the trucks take off.

I press my hand against the dashboard and gasp as we head straight for the treeline. "What are you doing?"

Chase laughs and Mac presses harder on the pedal, speeding toward the trees so fast there's no way he'll be able to stop before we hit them.

"Don't worry, Red. I know what I'm doing." Without warning, he jerks the wheel to the right, cutting off the truck next to us, and darts into an opening between two trees. We're instantly enclosed under the canopy, racing along a rough and muddy trail.

The truck jerks and bobs up and down as Mac maneuvers us down the path. Mud flings in every direction, including through the open windows on either side of me. A large clump of mud hits me right on the cheek, causing me to yelp.

"Oh my God." I wipe it off my cheek and laugh. This is insane but thrilling.

I look at Mac, and he peers at me through the side of his eyes. He's got a serious expression on his face. He's concentrating on the trail while also trying to gauge my response.

I wipe the mud on my hand down the side of his face, smearing as I do. "I think this is meant for you."

He chuckles and wipes some mud off his arm and onto mine. Before I can retaliate, he jerks the wheel to the left and we plummet down a steep hill. The truck slides through the mud, but Mac maintains control like an expert.

Loud whoops and hollers have me spinning my head around, suddenly remembering Christian is in the truck's bed. He's gripping the bar with one hand in the air and a huge smile on his face. This might be the first time I've seen him smile.

With every drop and dip and bob of the truck, Christian's body sways. A few times, his feet bounce off the bed, sending his body into the air. But he never loses his hold on the truck.

"Is he okay back there?" I yell above the rumble of the engine and the music blaring through the speakers.

"He's fine," Chase answers me. "We've done this countless times."

Right after he says that the truck tilts to the right, lifting us up on two wheels. On instinct, I grab a hold of Mac's arm to keep me from falling into Chase. I squeeze my eyes closed and send out a prayer to the universe that I will not die today. Flipping over and rolling down a forested hill is not the way I want to go.

Mac jerks the wheel, and we fall back onto all fours. Christian's cheers grow louder, as if he's having the time of his life. Meanwhile, my heart feels like it's struggling to keep beating. This is wild and intense.

I glance at Mac, and the smile on his face is pure magic. Despite how scary and insane this is, he's in complete control and happy. He's having the time of his life. I can't deny this is a rush I enjoy, but a part of me is terrified for my life.

A wave of relief washes over me when I see the flicker of flames appear through the trees, then an opening. We bounce off the forest road and back into the open field mere seconds after another truck. The windshield is too filthy to tell who it is.

We race through the field, neck and neck with the other truck.

I glance around and realize all the trucks have exited the forest and are hot on our trail.

Just ahead of us, I see a long line of lights on the ground and a short podium in the center. Someone is standing on it, waving a glowing flag in the dark.

Mac hits the gas, trying to take the truck next to us, but he doesn't make it. Whoever it is beats us by a few seconds.

"Dammit." Mac hits the steering wheel as we come to a stop. "That fucker always beats me."

Chase reaches behind me and playfully punches Mac in the arm. "You may be the best behind the wheel of a racecar, but no one can beat Garret on the logging trails."

Mac turns the truck around and heads back to where he was parked near the bonfire when I arrived. He climbs out of the cab, then turns to offer me his hand. I stare at it like it might jump out and bite me.

I meet his gaze, and the look in his eyes causes me to suck in a breath. Desire and anger are tangled up in his heated stare.

He still hasn't called me out about the race earlier today. I expect him to be mad that I didn't tell him, but the way he came to the defense of women drivers to Tanner gave me hope that maybe that wasn't the case. Now, I'm not so sure.

I accept his offer to help me out. When our hands join, a jolt of energy shoots up my arm and warms my entire body. I know my face just turned bright red. I can feel it as my body heats. Thankfully, it's dark out and he can't see my blushing skin.

"Dude, that was awesome!" Ash hops out of the bed of Garret's truck and jumps up on Mac's back. "Those trails are always the best after a hard rain."

Ash wraps his arm around my shoulder and hugs me tight. He's covered in mud and makes no apology for getting it all over me.

I look down at myself and frown. "Glad I didn't wear my good jeans tonight."

Ash chuckles. "Yeah, it's best to wear old clothes when you hang around us. You never know what we'll get into."

"Clearly. I've got mud caked in my hair too. I don't think I've ever been this filthy."

"That's too bad." Ash waggles his brows. "It's fun getting filthy."

"Har, har." I push him off me and step back to run my fingers through my hair. With my long curly locks, it's going to take forever to wash all this out.

"So what? You can race cars, but you don't like a little dirt on you?" Mac says from beside me. His voice is low and gravelly.

I snap my eyes to his. "Not at all. As my dad always says, God made dirt, and dirt don't hurt. It just would have been nice if someone would have warned me before shoving me inside the truck."

"A warning huh?" He crosses his arms over his chest and narrows his eyes. "I could say the same thing about today's race."

My shoulders sag, and I sigh. "I didn't tell you because—"

He holds up his hand to stop me. "No need to explain. I get it. You didn't trust me enough to be honest with me. Good thing I'm used to dishonest women or else I'd be hurt."

He turns to walk away and then stops, glancing back over his shoulder with a deep scowl on his face. "For the record, I would have been fine with it. In fact, I think it's pretty fucking cool."

He grabs himself a clean cup and heads for the keg before giving me a chance to defend myself.

Liam walks past me with a huge grin on his face. "See you later, S. Becker," he says with emphasis on the S.

Mac glances back at his brother with a confused look on his face.

Oh, boy. This is going to be fun.

THE DRIVE TO MAC'S FAMILY GARAGE HAS MY NERVES ON HIGH alert. I can't remember the last time I felt this anxious.

I woke up with a tightness in my stomach that made it next to impossible to eat. I hoped a shower would help, but it didn't. I've spent the entire twenty-minute drive from Jackson to Beaver talking myself down from what feels like a nervous breakdown, but it hasn't helped.

I should have told Mac the truth. The moment I recognized him, my gut screamed at me to tell him why I was in town, but the starry-eyed girl in me with the crush on her favorite racecar driver took over my mind, and I kept my mouth shut.

It wasn't because I didn't want him to know. It's not like I would have been able to keep it a secret at the race on Saturday. He was always going to find out.

I just didn't want to be disappointed in the man I've admired for years when he looked at me like I was crazy. Or said something chauvinistic like *women can't race cars.*

It's happened to me more times than I care to recall. Who can blame me for protecting myself from another display of male superiority?

Maybe Mac wouldn't have responded that way. Maybe he would have surprised me. It's happened a time or two over the years. But from my experience, it's best to downplay my gender when entering races until I've proven myself. Only then will people take me seriously.

And it's not just men. Sometimes women can be worse. More wives and girlfriends have approached me to tell how I ruined their husbands' or boyfriends' chance at qualifying because I won the race.

The number of times I've been told I need to learn my place is exasperating. Careers should not be gender specific. It should be about skill and knowledge. If a person is capable and performs well, then who cares if it's a man or a woman?

I'm a damn good racecar driver, and that's what I wanted Mac to see before he found out why I was really here.

Maybe I should have trusted him. Did he really mean it when he defended women drivers to Tanner, or did he say it because of what happened between us on Wednesday night?

I may never know the truth behind that.

My GPS on my phone calls out that my next turn is coming up in a quarter of a mile. I shake my head and focus on where I'm going. I've never driven on backroads like this, and I don't want to get lost.

The minute I turned off the highway, I felt like I entered an entirely different world. It's a paved road, but it's narrow. Passing other cars on it seems next to impossible. Especially with all the trees lining each side. There isn't even room to pull over to let someone pass.

There's a bend up ahead, and the road opens up after I take it. An open field comes into view, with a large house sitting close to the road. Just past the house is a sign that says Mutter Trucker Auto & Racing.

The house looks like it's over a hundred years old. It's massive, with traditional Victorian architecture, complete with a wrap-around porch with a swing in each corner. The house's white paint is peeling and a little rough for wear in a few places, but it's still beautiful with its black shutters and planted window boxes.

The landscaping is tidy and simple. The shrubs that surround the porch probably stay green all winter long. There are several flower beds that are dying with the cooler weather we're getting. I bet it's bright and cheery in the summer. If all goes well this morning, maybe I'll find out next summer.

I pass the house and pull into the entrance for the garage. It's much larger than I expected. Not that I knew what to expect. The Mutters are successful auto mechanics. They're known for their custom builds—both motorcycles and racecars—and racing, but they also provide basic auto services to their community.

The garage has four bays that look like they go two cars deep. The first bay is open, and from what I can see, it looks clean.

I park my car near the customer entrance and take a deep breath. By the time I get out, Christian—or is it Chase?—has stepped out of the open bay and is staring at me in confusion.

I study him for a moment—messy hair, frown, tired eyes, a harshness to him that screams bad boy. This is definitely Christian. If it were Chase, he'd already be charming my socks off.

"Sophia, isn't it?" His voice is rough and groggy, like he hasn't talked much since he woke up this morning. "Are you here to see Mac? He's at the tracks if you are. I can give you directions."

I shake my head. "I'm here to see Liam. Is he around?"

"Liam?" He furrows his brows, then opens his mouth like he's going to say something, but then stops. He points his thumb over his shoulder through the open bay and says, "He's in the office. I can show you back."

"Thanks." I follow him through the bay door. My eyes widen as I take in the inside of their garage.

The bay on the far end has two racecars on lifts, each, I assume, is a custom build. The next one is empty, but based on the equipment I see, it looks like it's used for tire changes and alignments.

There's a motorcycle in parts in another spot, and the open bay has a car in each spot, like they're waiting to be worked on.

Tool cabinets line the walls along with every specialized equipment known to man.

If I get this job, I will learn a lot of practical knowledge that the classroom can't teach.

"Liam." Christian's voice bellows through the garage as if he's put out by my interruption. "You've got a visitor."

"Okay, thanks," he calls from the open door.

Christian nods to me, then heads toward the mess of motorcycle parts and gets back to work.

I stand there unsure if I should stay put or head to the office. Liam didn't tell Christian to send me in. I glance around and see a row of chairs in the adjoining room. I assume it's the waiting room.

Not wanting to be rude and interrupt him if he's in the middle of wrapping up some work before my interview, I turn toward the chairs. I only make it a few steps before he calls my name.

I spin around to find Liam walking out of his office with his hand offered for a shake. "Thanks for coming in. I'm looking forward to chatting with you."

I accept his handshake, nice and firm, just like my dad taught me. "Thanks for agreeing to meet with me. I hope I didn't throw you for too much of a loop."

"Oh, you did." He chuckles. "But that's okay. I understand why you did it. It's not like you lied or anything."

I let out a nervous laugh. "I'm not so sure your brother sees it that way."

"Who, Mac?" Liam waves off my comment. "Don't worry about him. He'll get over it. Come on, let me show you around. Then we can sit and chat."

He spends about twenty minutes showing me around the garage and describing all the equipment to me. Most of it I'm familiar with from an academic perspective. I've worked in auto repair shops before, but only on simple things like oil changes and tune-ups. No one ever let me assist with bigger jobs like engine or transmission rebuilds. If he gives me this job, I hope that changes since they seem to do it all.

"As you can see, we've got a lot going on." Liam says as he leads me into his office. "Christian does all the motorcycle builds. Ash and Chase are our experts with racecars. While they help with other small jobs, it won't be enough. Mac helps us in a pinch, but I'm trying to free up his time to focus on racing. Your resume is impressive, and if you're up for it, I think this could work."

"Really?" My smile grows. "You'll give me a chance?"

"Of course." He smiles in return. "It's clear you know a lot about cars. We won't have to train you on oil changes, tune-ups, alignments, and tire changes. That's what most of our jobs are, and we need someone who can jump right in. Plus, I'm sure Ash and Chase would love to teach you more about building racecars, assuming you're interested in that as well."

"Are you kidding?" My smile grows so wide it hurts my face. "I'd love that. If I'm honest, that's why I want to work for you guys. I'm great behind the wheel, but I want to learn more about what makes a great racecar. I feel like that would make me an even better driver."

"I'm sure it will." He digs around his desk until he finds the folder he's looking for. "Let's get you started on this paperwork so I can get you on the books. When would you like to start?"

"As soon as you want me." I take the paperwork, feeling like everything is finally working out for me, and I finally have the career I of my dreams.

I also hope Liam is right, and Mac will get over my minor deception.

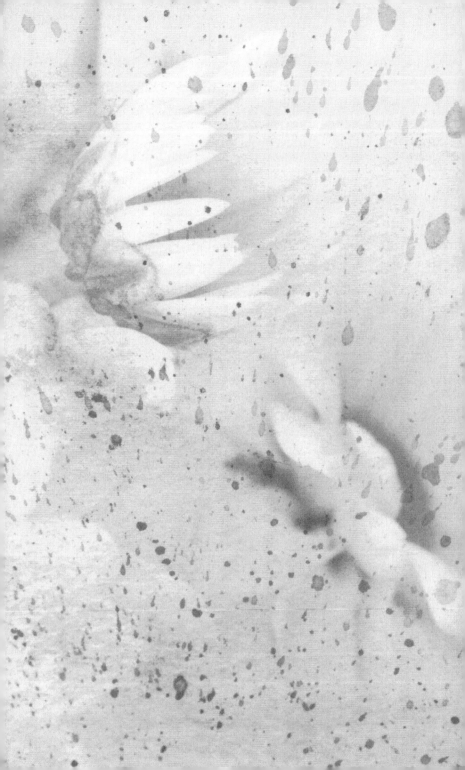

Chapter 7

Control is just an illusion.

Mac

"Rev it up again," Ash yells at me from under the hood. I press my foot on the gas until I hit over seven thousand RPMs. I hold it there until he waves at me to let up. "Kill it."

Once the engine comes back down, I kill the ignition and stick my head out of the window. "Well?"

We've been here all morning testing two cars Ash and Chase built that are finally ready. The first one is perfect—smooth, fast, and tight around the corners. This one, however, shakes when I hit a hundred and fifty miles-per-hour. Something is off, and they've spent the last hour trying to figure out what it is.

"You wanna take it back out? See if it's any better?" Chase leans against the car and studies my face. He's been watching me a lot more closely than usual this morning.

"Shut her up and let's do it." I nod toward the open hood.

Chase holds his gaze on me for a moment longer before he turns to Ash. "Alright, close her up. Let's hope this fixes it."

Ash drops the hood, then walks around to my window. "Take it slow on the first loop. Really listen to the engine and tell me if you hear anything off."

I nod, slide my helmet back, and make sure my headset is on before I start the car. It roars to life as I give it more gas. The deep rumble combined with a high-pitch chirp of a perfectly tuned engine is music to my ears.

"She sounds great." Chase's voice rings through my headset. "Let's see how she does on the first loop. Don't take her above one-twenty."

Without delay, I put the car in gear and squeal the tires as I take off. Dust clouds form around me, and the smell of burned rubber fills my nostrils.

When it's just me, alone on the track, it's a welcomed smell.

No triggers.

No anxiety.

No other drivers in sight.

Just me, my car, and the open track.

The car glides down the straight stretch of the track like a dream. She even turns the first corner tight and fast and smooth. Exactly like she's supposed to drive.

I finish the first loop and call out to Chase. "She feels great. No shaking. Smooth and tight. Ready for me to kick it up?"

"Good," Chase answers. "Open her up and give it all you've got."

"My pleasure." A grin spreads across my face as I take her from one-twenty to one-eighty in a matter of seconds. I hold her there a few seconds, focusing on her sounds and vibrations. Once I'm certain everything is great and I clear the first turn, I max out her speed, easily breaking two-hundred miles-per-hour.

"How does she feel?" Chase asks.

"So far, so good." I shout through my headset. "I'm maxing her out and there's nothing unusual. Whatever Ash did, it seems to have worked."

"Good. Take her for a few loops like this and let's see if it holds."

I don't respond. I just keep driving.

I love being behind the wheel of a fast car on the open road. Nothing can stop me. I feel alive and free. I'm invincible and completely in control of this car and my surroundings. I'm going to cross the finish line and take the prize.

This feeling is why I love racing so much.

This is what I was born to do. It's in my blood and deeply rooted in my soul.

This feeling—right now, right here—is what I'm missing every time I enter a race.

The second other drivers are on the track with me, I tense. I remember what happened two years ago, and I lose my head.

I can control myself and my car, but I can't control other drivers. They're a wild card, a risk that I'm struggling to manage. Until I can figure out how to accept that unknown, I may never race the same way again.

If I'm not racing, then who in the hell am I?

"Damn, Mac." Chase's voice sounds happy, and I shake myself out of my thoughts. "You look fantastic out there. Your time on that last loop was your best yet. Drive like this in your next race, and no one will catch you."

"Keep building me cars like this, and that'll be easy." I smile, because this feels right.

I need to harness this moment and keep it close to my heart, so I'll never forget why I love this sport so much.

Then everything goes to hell.

Bang! A loud noise fills the inside of the car like a metal mallet hitting a gong. The car jerks and veers to the side as if I hit a solid wall. Smoke surrounds me, along with hissing and crackling sounds. I pull the steering wheel in the opposite direction, attempting to straighten out the car, but it does little good. I'm heading right for the inner wall and there's nothing I can do about it.

THE SOUND OF CRUSHED METAL REPLACES CHASE'S VOICE IN an instant. My body jerks forward before it's slammed back into my seat. Everything around me fades to black as all the anxiety and fear I've been fighting for months on end consumes me.

That was not supposed to happen.

Not while I was in control.

I squeeze my eyes tightly closed as reality dawns. I'm not in control of anything. Not this car, my life, or the outcome of any race I ever enter.

Control is just an illusion.

It's a lie we tell ourselves to make us believe we're safe. That nothing bad will happen as long as we maintain control.

"Mac!" Ash is the first to reach me. My eyes are still closed, but I feel his hands on me, tugging on my arm to check if I'm okay. "Mac, man. Loosen up."

I give my head a shake. Slowly, I open my eyes. My hands are still gripped around the steering wheel, and my entire body is stiff with tension. I shift my blank stare to my brother. The panicked look in his eyes is enough to snap me out of it.

"I'm fine." I lie because nothing about how I'm feeling is fine.

I take a few deep breaths, feeling somewhat calmer than I did moments ago. At least it's enough to stave off the anxiety threatening to rule me. I lift the helmet off my head and toss it to the side. The early morning September air instantly cools my heated face.

"Come on. Let's get you out of there." He pats my arm and steps aside.

Chase is right behind him, ready to help me climb out of this car. I meet his gaze, and the look in his eyes reignites my anxiety.

I reach around and grip the roof of the car and pull myself out. I need to get out of here before I lose my shit. But it's too late. One look at the front end, and I tumble into the past to the day I crashed, flipping the car and breaking my leg.

"Fuck," I mumble and turn away. I practically run in the opposite direction.

Today's performance on the track *was* a huge win for me. I've felt more like myself behind the wheel than before the accident. My lap times were the best I've had in ages—if not my entire career —and this one incident just set me back.

Chase knows it too. I can tell by the way he's calling after me.

He reaches me and crosses in front of my path. I try to dart around him, but he's faster than me and grabs a hold of my shoulders.

"Chase, let me go." I bark out and push his hands away.

"Not until you talk to me." He tightens his hold on me and forces me to look at him. "This was no one's fault. Just a fluke. The car has been giving us issues from the start. You know that. *Do not* let this get in your head."

"You don't know what's going on in my head!" I yell.

"Oh, I have a pretty good idea." His tone is firm, almost fatherly, which is unusual for Chase. Even when he's being serious, he keeps it light. There's nothing light about the way he's talking to me now. "Mac, an accident like yours would mess with anyone's head. But you refuse to talk about it. It won't get better unless you talk to someone. Tell me what you're thinking?"

I shake my head and push him off of me. "There's nothing to talk about. I'm fine."

"You're not fine. We all see it, man."

"I'm fine!" I ground out. I point to the car behind me where Ash is still standing, watching us like he has no clue how to handle my meltdown. Because I am definitely having a meltdown.

Closing my eyes, I force my breathing to regulate and run my fingers through my hair before I speak again. "I promise. I'm fine. The car blowing just surprised me. That's all."

I walk away before Chase can call me out on my bullshit. Hearing him tell me how I'm fucked in the head won't do me any good. I already know it.

He can't fix this anymore than I can. If that were possible, I would've done it by now.

THE DRIVE BACK TO THE GARAGE IS SILENT AND AWKWARD. Not only does Chase know I'm struggling, but Ash also knows something's wrong with me. With two brothers knowing about my anxiety, it won't be long before Liam knows as well.

It's not that they'll run to Liam and tell him about my meltdown, but they'll probably talk about it in the garage and Liam will overhear.

Then again, Liam is pretty fucking perceptive. He'll probably sense something's off with me the minute I walk into the garage.

Ash pulls the truck and trailer into the front parking lot. He stops so I can hop out and open the bay door for him. They'll have to rebuild this car, engine and body. It's trashed.

I rush through the open entrance and hurry toward the far side where we work on the custom racecars. I don't see Liam. Hopefully, that means he's got his nose buried in paperwork in his office.

Christian looks up at me from where he's sitting on a stool working on one of his motorcycles. He raises a brow, clearly sensing something is wrong. But he remains silent. He just stares at me for a moment, then gets back to work.

Unfortunately, I don't make it far before Liam calls my name. "Mac, where in the hell have you been? You said you'd be back by ten. It's almost noon."

"Got held up at the track," I say as I hit the button to open the bay door. Ash is already in position to back the cars in. Chase is standing by the trailer to act as a spotter.

"That's a shitty answer. I needed you guys here to help. I can't do the work *and* manage the garage."

"Sorry," I say, barely above a whisper. "It won't happen again."

"Sorry?" Liam crosses his arms over his chest. "That's all you've got to say for yourself?"

This is the moment where he'd threaten to fire us and hire all new employees if he could. But we're all equal owners in the garage and he can't.

I shrug, doing my best to not let his anger affect me. He has every right to be upset. We promised to be back by ten to help with the day's workload. We didn't make it.

"What do you want me to say?"

"I don't want you to say anything." He grumbles something else under his breath, but I can't make it out. "I want you to do what you say you'll do and be here to help when you say you'll be here. Is that too much to ask?"

I look my oldest brother in the eye and his angry expression softens. "No, it's not. I promise to do better next time."

I turn to walk away, but he grabs my arms to stop me. He studies my crestfallen face and sighs. "What happened?"

My gut instinct is to tell him that nothing happened, but he'll know that's a lie the second he sees the crushed front end of the car.

I drop my head and rub the bridge of my nose. "It was a bad morning, okay? One of the cars was acting up, and—"

"What the hell?" Liam's gaze moves past me. His eyes now tracking the trailer being backed into the garage.

Chase stops next to us and sighs. "Engine blew. We think it was a faulty intake valve, but we won't know for sure until we pull it out."

Liam turns to me, his gaze piercing and full of concern. I drop my eyes to the floor. "How fast were you going when it happened?"

"Almost two hundred miles-per-hour," I mumble.

"Shit." He sighs. "You okay?"

"I'm standing here, aren't I?" I say way louder than I should. He's only expressing his concern. But I'm fucking tired of everyone's concern. I just want my head back.

"That's not what I mean." His tone is soft in contrast to mine. "The front end of that car is gone. That had to affect you. Especially since—"

"Don't say it." I hold my hand up and glare at him. "I don't need you or anyone else reminding me of the past. I'm dealing with it. Now drop it."

"But you're not dealing with it, Mac," Chase says.

"I said drop it."

I turn on my heel to leave, but stop when I see a familiar redhead standing at the opposite end of the garage, staring at us with wide eyes. She's pulled her hair back in a ponytail, and she's wearing a pair of baggy overalls that look three sizes too big for her frame.

"What the fuck are you doing here?" I bark.

She opens her mouth like she's going to respond, but then looks to Liam instead. I follow her gaze and stare at my brother, waiting for him to answer.

"So, yeah." Liam rubs the back of his neck nervously. "Sophia is going to be helping us out around the shop."

"What do you mean, she's helping us out?"

"I told you I was going to hire someone. I can't keep this place running by myself."

"You're not running it by yourself. You've got us."

"It's not enough!" Liam yells. His frustration is getting the best of him. "Today is a perfect example of that. You're too busy racing. Ash and Chase are busy building your cars, and Christian has more motorcycle builds than he can handle on his own. I can barely keep up with the invoicing and scheduling, let alone work on the cars too. I had to hire someone to help."

"And *she's* who you hire?" I point behind me to where Sophia is standing.

"What's that supposed to mean?" Sophia yells out, sounding offended.

I glare at her because I didn't mean that the way she took it. She could be the best mechanic in the fucking world, and I still wouldn't want her working here.

"Yes, Mac. I hired Sophia. And thank God she was ready to

start work today, cause I needed the help." He rests his hand on my shoulder in that stern, fatherly way he sometimes does. "It's my job to keep this place running. She knows her shit and has a lot of talent."

"A lot of people know their shit and have talent. Why her?"

He narrows his eyes at me. "Do you have a problem with Sophia?"

"Yes. Isn't that obvious?"

"Then help me understand why, because she's done more to help this morning than you three put together." He points at Chase, Ash, and me. "I want to give you guys the freedom to focus on racing. But to do that, I need to hire help."

Liam pushes past me and heads toward his office. Chase and Ash are unusually quiet, and Christian does what he always does. He works quietly and pretends none of us are here.

"She's a liar." I call out. "I don't like liars."

"Mac." Sophia lets out an exasperated sigh. "I didn't lie to you."

I point at her and growl. "An omission of the truth is still a lie."

I rush through the open bay door, needing to put distance between me and everyone else in that garage. I'm being a total ass right now, but I don't care. She shouldn't be here. I have enough problems messing with my head. I don't need her too.

"Mac, please." She calls from behind me. "Can we just talk about this?"

I spin around, and she runs right into me. I didn't expect her to be this close. Her sweet scent immediately assaults my senses. Strawberries and vanilla mixed with grease.

It's pure fucking heaven.

I stumble back a few steps, not trusting myself to be this close to her. I may be pissed at her, but my body doesn't seem to understand that. All I can think about is pressing my body against hers and kissing her again like I did last week.

"Look," I say. "I'm sorry. But I have enough complications in my life. I don't need another one."

"How am I a complication?" She steps toward me. So close, her chest almost touches mine. I want to grab her. Wrap my arms around her. Feel her skin against mine.

Her hand brushes against mine where it hangs stiffly at my side. The light touch sends a shock wave of desire through my entire body.

"I didn't intend to lie to you," she whispers. "I didn't even expect to meet you last week. We had fun, and I really like you. Can't you understand how my truth scares me? I didn't want it to get between us before we even got to know each other."

I let out a low huff. "Open your eyes, Sophia. It got between us anyway. Now I guess we'll never know what could have been."

"Mac, don't do this."

But it's too late. I spin around and rush out of the garage without a look back.

What is it with the women in my life? First my mother. Isn't a mother supposed to love her child unconditionally? What a fucking lie. She left just like my brothers' mothers. They all leave. They all lie and hurt and cause pain to those they're supposed to love the most.

Why should I expect Sophia to be any different?

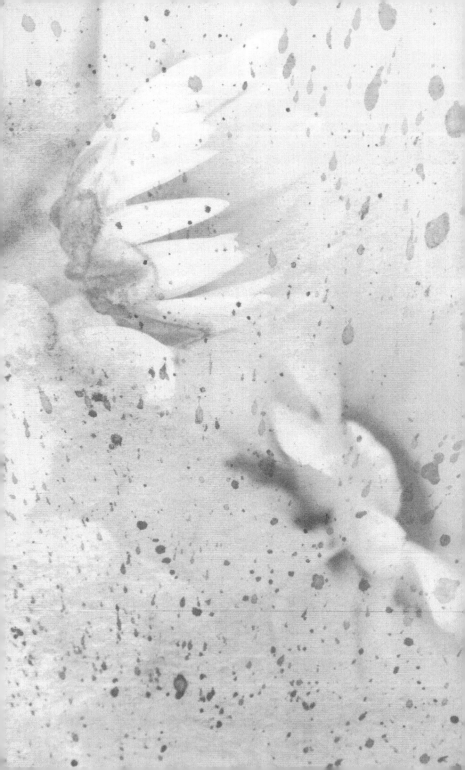

Chapter 8

Small towns are weird.

Sophia

"You have to loosen the lug nuts first," Mac growls from where he's been standing over me like a sentry for the last three hours.

I glare at him. "No shit, Sherlock."

The furrow in his brow deepens. "Then why are you putting it up on the lift already?"

"Do you see the lift rising?" I place my hands on my hips and stare up at him. When he's standing like that, he looks so tall. And mean. He hasn't smiled once all week.

Every day has been the same. He hovers over my every move as if I'm going to make a critical mistake. Sometimes he says nothing. Just grunts or hums, making it known that he doesn't like what he sees. And other times—like now—he tries to tell me I don't know what I'm doing.

I've yet to make a single mistake. Although he'd never admit that.

"No." He finally answers. "But you're setting up the lift. You're not ready for that."

"I can do my tasks in any order I see fit. I've got this. You can go." I grab the torque wrench and turn back to the car I'm working on. Changing these brake pads will go a lot faster if he'd stop watching my every move.

I pull the wheel lock key from where I stashed it in my pocket and affix it to the wrench. My hand slips, and it slides from my grip and bounces on the floor. I scrabble to grab it, but it rolls out of my reach. When I stand to look for where it went, Mac is standing closer to me with his hand held out.

His stare is hard and fierce, as if he's trying to burn a hole right through me. If I weren't so pissed at him, it might actually scare me, but there's no bite behind his bark. He's just being a big baby.

I reach for the wheel lock key, but he closes his hand around it. "Need some help?"

"No, I don't need your help." I growl at him, and he snorts his disbelief.

"You look like you could use it." His words are laced with contempt. It makes me want to junk punch him.

"Just give me that." I grab his wrist and hold his hand still so I can pry it open, and I hate how my body vibrates with need from this simple touch. I want to hate him, not want him.

Thankfully, he doesn't resist. He's way stronger than me, and if he wanted, he could make sure I never got this back from him.

"You two bicker like you're a couple, you know that?" Ash teases from the other side of the garage. "It's cute."

He and Chase have been working on the car Mac crashed on Monday. They have to rebuild the engine—something I hope they let me learn from—and the body damage is severe. It's going to take a lot to get that car operational again.

"He wishes we were a couple." I huff.

"The hell I do." Mac's gravelly retort sends a tremor through my body. I glance up at him, and he's way too close. The gold flecks in his deep chocolate brown eyes catch the light like tiny little twinkle lights. His lip twitches, and God help me, I want to kiss him.

"Then why are you hovering over me like I need your protection?"

"I'm not *protecting* you." He scoffs. "I'm *watching* you."

I poke him in the chest with my finger. His behavior is irritating and infuriating and annoyingly hot all at the same time. I hate him for it.

"And *why* are you watching me?" I retort.

He takes a step closer, crowding my personal space, and my body instantly heats. *Please don't let my skin turn red. Please, please, please.*

I hate that my body is attracted to him. How did we go from making out in a dark alley at the Apple Festival to growling and bickering like rivals?

"Because I don't trust you." His lip curls up on one side, and it's the sexiest thing I've ever seen. Why? I don't know because he looks really fucking angry.

Pressing up on my tiptoes, I get right in his face. "You're an idiot. You know that?"

"I may be an idiot, but at least I'm not a liar." His face is so close to mine, our lips almost touch. The slightest bump or movement and we would be kissing.

"Should we leave and give you two some privacy?" I jump back at the sound of Christian's voice. It's rough and raspy, like it hurts for him to use it. He so rarely speaks, it probably does.

Mac straightens and clears his throat. He shakes his head, and his eyes look a little dazed, like he just now realizes how close he was to me. Then his expression turns back to armored steel.

"Why would we need privacy?" he asks. His voice is devoid of all emotion, and for some reason, that pisses me off even more. I want him to feel everything I'm feeling so he can be just as confused as me.

"Oh, I don't know?" Clara's sweet, teasing voice cuts through the tension building between us. "Maybe because you two looked like you're about to have a tongue war. I could be wrong, but most people prefer to do that in private."

"Clara!" I gasp. "When did you get here?"

She gives me a sheepish smile and shrugs. "Just before you two started your little face-off."

"Hey, bestie." Ash slides up next to Clara and wraps his arm around her shoulder. "Shouldn't you be at work?"

She adjusts her glasses as she looks up at Mac. "Planning period before my lunch break. I don't have class again until one."

"Class?" I ask, realizing I have no clue what Clara does for a living.

"I teach high school English."

"Oh." A slow smile spreads across my face. "That's very fitting."

I don't know Clara that well, but being an English teacher seems like the perfect job for her. I can easily see her standing in front of a class talking about her favorite books or instructing them on how to structure the perfect term paper. Plus, she's got that sexy librarian look about her.

She gives me an awkward smile and pushes her glasses back up her nose. She suddenly seems nervous and all the playfulness from a moment ago is gone. "Um, I wanted to ask ... Um, do you want to grab lunch?"

She says it so fast that her words run together. She averts her eyes like she's nervous about my response. Her confidence was evident when I first noticed her, but now she seems shy and unsure of herself.

"I'd love to," Ash says, his smile growing wide. "Give me a minute to clean up."

"Not you, you goof." Clara pokes him in the side and he jumps back. "I'm asking Sophia."

Ash presses his hand to his heart like he's hurt. "What? You mean you're not here to see me?"

Clara laughs and pats his arm. Ash's playfulness seems to relax her. "Sorry, not this time. But I'll bring you something back."

Ash's smile grows, and he kisses Clara's cheek. She lets out a soft sigh that I don't think Ash notices. "That'd be awesome. I'll take a footer with sauce and mustard."

"You got it." She pats his chest. "How about you, Christian? Do you want something?"

"If you don't mind."

"Of course not."

He gives her a small smile, and I think it's the first I've seen since I started working here. "I'll take a cheeseburger and some onion rings then."

"Oh, I want some onion rings too." Ash adds.

Then she turns her friendly, slightly more confident smile on me. "So, what do you say? Lunch?"

"I'd love to." I turn my smile on Mac. "That is if Mr. Sentinel here says it's okay."

Mac's frown deepens. "Why would I care?"

I snort-laugh and shake my head. "Oh, I don't know. Maybe because you've been watching my every move like a hawk. Heaven forbid I step out of line and injure your sense of trustworthiness."

Mac's stare hardens, and his hands clench into fists at his side. Then he shakes his head like he's trying to clear his mind of all thoughts, turns on his heel, and walks away.

I turn a victory smile to Clara. "That's a definite yes to lunch."

TWENTY MINUTES LATER, WE'RE PASSING A LARGE HAND-painted sign that says *Welcome to the Village of Beaver*. It even has a smiling beaver painted on one side.

I've passed by so many of these little villages while traveling to races, but I've never actually stopped in one before. There's never much to them—a few buildings and houses, maybe a gas station or small family-owned market.

I've been here for less than a week, and this is my first time within the limits of the village. I expect it to be similar to the ones I've passed through before. That is, until we stop at a red light at a three-way stop.

I glance around, and we're the only car on the road. We don't have to wait long before it changes to green, but then we're immediately stopped at a second red light not two hundred feet up the road. It's also at a three-way stop.

I glance over at Clara. She's tapping her finger on her steering wheel like there's nothing odd about the lights. I shake my head and ask, "Why are there red lights here?"

She shrugs. "Dunno. They've been here for as long as I can remember."

"But there's no traffic." I glance over my shoulder to make sure there's no one behind us, and there's not. There's not even a car coming down the connecting road. "Does rush hour traffic hit later in the day or something?"

She laughs. "Rush hour traffic in Beaver? That's funny. Occasionally two or three cars pass on this road at the same time, but it's rare."

"And that level of traffic requires not one, but two red lights?"

"Probably not."

"Does everyone stop for them even though there's no need for them?" I ask, knowing that I'd have a real hard time with these lights myself.

"Oh yeah. Trust me, you run these lights, and Elvis will chase you down."

"Elvis?" I raise a brow.

Clara chuckles. "Officer Ricky Warner, aka Elvis, our local law enforcement. We call him Elvis on account that he wears his hair in that big swoopy way Elvis always did. And he dresses up like him and sings all Elvis's hit songs at the Oktoberfest every year.

Sometimes he even comes out for karaoke night at Posey's Lounge if he happens to be off duty."

I blink several times as I process what she just told me. "Beaver has an Elvis impersonating officer protecting its streets?"

Her shoulders shake with silent laughter. "Yeah, when you put it that way, I guess it is kinda funny."

I tilt my head to the side. "It's original. I'll give you that."

The light changes to green without a single car ever passing by. Clara takes the next right and pulls into the parking lot of a tiny diner with a sign at the corner that reads Frank's Frosty Kreme.

"Oh good. We're early enough that we can get a table." Clara grabs her purse and steps out of her car. I do the same and take in the cool, fresh air.

It's not exactly warm out, but it's not cold either. It's one of those fall days where a light sweater or jacket is necessary, but you won't freeze without it. The sun is bright, and the sky is clear. There's even a light breeze blowing the fallen leaves across the paved road.

Aside from a few cars parked next to the neighboring building on the back side of the parking lot, we're the only car here. I only see two picnic tables. One is under a small overhang on the back corner of the building and the other is occupying a parking space in the back.

"Come on." Clara calls out to me. "I don't have all day."

I turn to see she's holding a glass door open for me to enter the restaurant. Although, I don't think restaurant is the right word for it. The inside is nothing more than a waiting area. There are no dining tables or servers ready to take our orders. It's carry-out only.

Clara walks up to the window that reminds me of a receptionist's window like I'd see in a doctor's office, not a restaurant.

"Well hello, Clara Bell." An older gentleman, who looks like he could be our grandpa, greets her with a smile. "Don't usually see you here at this time of day."

Clara smiles in return. "Hi Frank. I snuck out for lunch today.

I'm entertaining a new friend." She turns her smile to me. "This is Sophia Becker. She's new in town. Just started working for the Mutters."

"You don't say." Frank turns his friendly gaze to me. "Well, aren't you a pretty thing? My Rosie May had red hair just like yours. Miss that woman every day."

"Thank you, sir." I give him a wave, feeling my face warm from his complement. "Who's Rosie May, if I may ask?"

"Oh, she was my wife." The sparkle in his eyes fades slightly, but he's still smiling. "Married thirty years before she passed. Heart attack. But I don't suppose you young ladies came here to listen to my sorrows. What can I get you?"

"Any idea what you want?" Clara looks at me. "Everything here is good."

I study the menu that's on the wall above the counter. They serve a little of everything, from ice cream and milkshakes to hot dogs, burgers, subs, and pizza.

"I'll have a cheeseburger and maybe some fries."

"I can do that," Frank says. "You want all the fixins on that burger?"

"Um, just lettuce and mustard."

"You got it. And what can I get you to drink?"

"Can I get a caramel milkshake?" It's a little cool outside for a milkshake, but it sounds too good to pass up.

"Of course you can." Frank scribbles my order on a little green notepad before he turns to Clara. "And for you, dear?"

"I'll have the same, but make my shake strawberry," Clara says. "And I have an order for Ash and Christian, but do you mind waiting about twenty minutes before you make it?"

"Anything for you." Clara gives him Ash's and Christian's order while a young girl behind the counter makes our milkshakes, and an older man makes our food.

I pull some money out and hand it to Clara, but she shoves it back at me. "This is on me."

"Thanks." I put my money away. "Next time you'll have to let me pay."

Frank sets our shakes on the counter and tells us he'll bring our food out to us once it's ready if we want to wait outside. We take our shakes and sit at the covered picnic table.

I take a sip of mine and groan. "Oh my God. I don't care that it's too cold for milkshakes outside. This is so good."

"Right?" Clara takes a long sip of hers until her nose crinkles. She presses her palm to her forehead. "Gah! Brain freeze."

Once it seems to pass, we both laugh. "I really hate when that happens," she says. "I always drink my shakes too fast."

"Maybe if these shakes weren't so good, it'd be easier not to." I suggest.

"Maybe, but knowing me, I'd—"

"Oh, yoo-hoo. Clara, dear." We both look up to see an older woman crossing the street and waving her hand in the air. She may be calling Clara's name, but she's looking at me.

"Oh great," Clara mumbles. "Prepare yourself for Mrs. Engle. She does not know the meaning of mind your own business."

"I'm so glad you're here. I wanted to ask you about your cake entry for the competition next month."

"I don't have a cake entry for next month," Clara says.

"Well, that's what I'm trying to tell you. I haven't received your entry forms, and the deadline is coming up. I'd hate for you to miss it."

"Mrs. Engle, I'm not submitting anything this year."

"But!" Mrs. Engle presses her hand to her chest and gasps like Clara's news physically hurts her. "I don't understand. You always enter something for the Oktoberfest."

Clara shrugs. "Maybe next year."

Mrs. Engle looks like she's going to object further, but then turns her gaze to me. "Well, aren't you going to introduce me to your friend?"

"Of course. Where are my manners?" Clara struggles to hide

her eye roll. "This is Sophia Becker. She's new in town. And this is Mrs. Engle. She runs the hair salon right across the street."

"I run the *only* hair salon in Beaver," Mrs. Engle says with forced exaggeration as if it's important for me to know her salon is the only one. "And what brings you to our lovely town?"

"Um, I ... I race and work on cars. I took a job working for Liam Mutter to learn more."

"Why on earth would a pretty girl like you want to do that?"

My hackles rise, and my need to defend myself is on high alert. "I don't see what my looks have to do with anything."

"But racing and cars is a man's job. I don't understand why—"

"Mrs. Engle." Clara puts her hand on Mrs. Engle's arm to get her attention. Then she nods across the street. "It looks like your next appointment has arrived. You best be getting back to your salon. I know how you hate to make people wait."

Mrs. Engle glances over her shoulder and sighs. "Right. Thank you, Clara." She looks back at me with a frown but doesn't push me further about my choice in a job. "I guess I best be going."

Just as she turns to leave, Frank brings us our lunch. "Here you girls go. I'll give you about ten minutes, then I'll get the rest of your order underway."

"Thanks, Frank," Clara says. "I appreciate it."

We eat in comfortable silence for a few minutes before someone else walks up to us and interrupts our lunch. This time it's a man by the name of Billy Schwartz. He pretends he needs to ask Clara about his daughter's reading assignment, when really, it's to find out who I am.

After he leaves, Mr. Schroeder, the committee chair for the upcoming Oktoberfest, interrupts us. He, too, asks Clara about her lack of an entry for the cake baking competition. But we both know it's just an excuse to meet the new stranger in town.

"Is everyone around here so nosy?" I ask once we're alone again.

Clara chuckles. "Girl, you have no idea. Just wait until people figure out Mac has a thing for you."

"Mac *does not* have a thing for me." I give her a pointed stare. "I think it's safe to say he hates me."

She snorts. "That man does not hate you. He may not know what to do with you or how to process his feelings. He *is* a man, after all. But he *definitely* has a thing for you."

"Well, I have too many other things to worry about besides his struggles over his feelings."

"Like what?"

"Like finding a place to live. I can't stay in the hotel forever, and everything I've looked at has been ... Well, let's just say unlivable."

"I have a spare room."

"You do?"

She nods. "Yeah. I moved into my grandma's house when she moved in with my parents. She needs constant care. It's just me. There's plenty of room."

"Really? How much?"

She shrugs. "I dunno. Never thought about having a roommate before. The house is paid for, so I don't have a mortgage or rent. If you split the utilities and groceries with me, I'd be more than happy for the company."

"Okay." I smile, finally feeling a little better about my move to this small town. "You've got yourself a roommate."

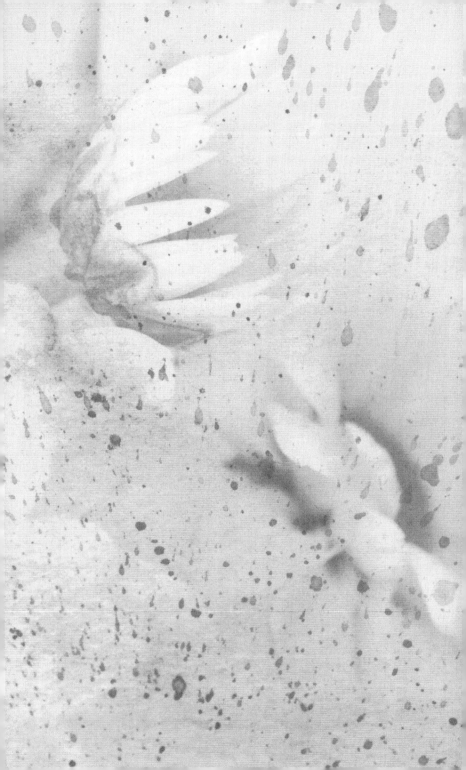

Chapter 9

Beauty and the Dare Devil.

Mac

It's been two weeks since Sophia started working at the garage and invading my life.

More like invading my every thought.

When I'm not at the racetrack with Chase and Ash, I'm in the garage watching her every move. She acts like it annoys her, but secretly, I think she likes all the attention I give her.

Okay, maybe I do annoy her. But she deserves it.

I don't like secrets and lies, even those by omission.

Though if I'm being honest with myself—which I'm not—I shouldn't hold her lie of omission against her. I get why she did it. It's hard to break out and get noticed in racing even if you're a man. For women it's next to impossible.

I should cut her some slack, but I'm enjoying our banter a little too much. I enjoy fighting with her, which is weird because I don't typically like fighting with anyone. Except for the Koch brothers, but they don't count. I like to play and have fun.

Rather than being my usual annoying self today, I skip the garage. Instead, I hide in my bedroom watching old races to study my competition for my next race.

It's something I used to do all the time before the accident. I stopped because every time a car rubbed another one, I tensed up. It fed my anxiety.

But this morning it's been helpful. I feel better about my upcoming race. I even have a strategy in mind to help me win. There isn't a driver entered that I haven't beaten before. I know their weaknesses and their strengths.

I'm ready for this. I can do this. No amount of anxiety can keep me from winning.

I turn off the TV and toss the remote on my bed. This helped. A lot. Maybe if I do this a little every day—like I used to when I was at the top of my game—I'll be ready by race day.

My stomach rumbles, reminding me it's time to grab something for lunch. Checking the time, it's later than I realized.

When I reach the kitchen, I only find my dad and Grams sitting around the table. Dad's reading the paper like he always does, and Grams is peeling potatoes.

"There you are." Grams looks up at me and smiles. "I was about to hunt you down. It's not like you to miss a meal."

"Sorry, Grams." I kiss the top of her head. "Watching old racing footage and lost track of time."

She gives me a knowing nod of approval. I might like to think no one knows my head is a little fucked up from the accident, but everyone's noticed my change in habits. I'm just in denial.

"I made you a sandwich. It's in the fridge." I smile, loving that she didn't say anything about me watching races. With Grams, we don't always need words.

"You didn't have to do that." I open the fridge and pull out the sandwich wrapped up on a small plate.

"Of course I did. I always feed my boys," Grams tsks with a hint of annoyance. It makes me chuckle. She loves cooking and will feed anyone who gets within eyesight of our house like it's her job.

I set the plate down on the opposite side of the table, grab myself something to drink and a bag of chips from the pantry before I take my seat.

I eat in silence, feeling Grams' eyes on me. When I glance up, she's watching me. Her expression is serious and knowing.

"What?" I ask, even though I know I'm going to regret it.

She continues peeling the potato in her hands before she speaks. "I really like Sophia. She's a delightful addition to the garage. Smart, strong girl. Kind of badass if you ask me."

I keep my head down so she can't see the way my lips turn up at how she called Sophia a badass. Grams has never shied away from cursing. She's sweet as pie ninety-nine percent of the time, but when she wants to make sure her point is known, it's hard to tell what will come out of her mouth.

"When did *you* meet Sophia?" I know damn well Grams met Sophia at the Apple Festival. Sophia may not be eating her lunch with us in the house, but I know that Grams has been making her lunch every day just like she makes ours and having it delivered to her in the garage.

When Grams doesn't answer me, I glance up at her. She's giving me one of her knowing stares. "So that's how you're going to play it, huh?"

"Play what?" I frown.

But Grams doesn't get a chance to answer because there's a knock at the door. I wipe my face with my napkin and push up from my chair. "I'll get it."

"We're not done talking about this," she says as I walk away. I glance over my shoulder to catch her smiling at me.

Grams is way too perceptive and way too eager to see her grandsons settle down. She only had one son, and to say Dad is a disappointment to Grams when it comes to women is an under-statement. His choice in women is largely why all of us have remained single for so long.

Whoever is at the door knocks again before I reach it.

"I'm coming!" I call out.

We don't get many visitors at the house. People drive out here for the garage, not to socialize with Dad and Grams. That's what the new community center in town is for.

A few years ago, the local school district won a huge grant from the state to build a new school complex. The new complex combined three smaller schools into one. Once it was complete, they tore down the old high school, but the elementary schools are now community centers that offer arts and craft fairs, workshops, bingo, and other activities for the elderly in our community. Grams goes there at least twice a week to hang out with her knitting friends.

I swing the front door open and frown. I'm greeted by a tall woman with long dark hair with streaks of silver throughout. She's dressed in clean, crisp jeans and a black leather jacket. The hard wrinkles on her face suggest she's close to my dad's age. But it's her piercing blue eyes that cause me to pause. There's something oddly familiar about this woman, but I can't pinpoint what.

"Mac," she whispers my name.

I narrow my eyes, studying her face. I'm almost positive I've never seen this woman before, but she's looking at me with tear-filled eyes like she knows who I am.

"I'm sorry. Have we met?" I ask.

She nods and chokes back her tears. "It's been a really long time. So long, in fact, I'm not surprised you don't remember me."

There's something in her voice that triggers a memory. I stare at her eyes again. I see it, but I can't quite reach it. Searching my memories, I latch on to one from so long ago, it feels like another lifetime. It's one that I try to forget exists, but with a trigger standing in front of me, it's impossible to keep it locked up tight.

It's a memory of a five-year-old little boy waving goodbye to his mom with a huge smile on his face. He's smiling because he has no clue that she's never coming back again.

Anger fills me as recognition dawns. I cross my arms over my chest and square my shoulders. The shift in my demeanor causes her to take a slight step back, but then she smiles.

"Aren't you going to invite me in?" she asks.

"No!" I huff. "Why should I?"

"Because I'm your mother."

The dry laugh that escapes me says it all. She may have supplied half my genetic code, but she is not my mom. If anyone has earned that role in my life, it's Grams. This woman is not welcome here.

"Is that right?" I ask. "Just tell me why you're here and then leave. You know what?" I hold my hand up to stop her from answering me. "Better yet, just skip to the part where you leave. I don't want to hear anything you have to say."

I go to shut the door, but she presses against it with her hand. "Mac, please. I know I should have come back for you a long time ago, but I was really messed up back then. I've been clean for years."

"I don't care. It's too late for whatever it is you hope to get out of this visit. Now leave!" I yell that last part so loudly, Dad and Grams rush from the kitchen to join me.

"Heidi? Is that you?" Dad asks.

I turn to see a slight smile on his face.

"Dad!" I yell. "You can't be serious? She's not welcome here."

He turns his gaze to me and immediately drops his smile. "I'm just surprised to see her. That's all."

"Well she's leaving. So don't get your hopes up." I step outside and slam the door shut behind me.

Dad has zero control where women are concerned. It never mattered how poorly they treated him or his kids. He always took them back. Knowing him, if Heidi said she was here because she missed him, he'd let her stay.

"Mac, please just listen. I'm not here for Paul. I'm here for you."

"You're twenty-two years too late for that, don't you think?" I charge toward her. She steps back until she's off the porch and standing in the driveway. "You said you were going to the store.

You lied. Do you have any idea how long a five-year-old will sit by the front window waiting for his mom to come back? *Too fucking long.* It's too late. I don't need anything from you now."

"Please!" she pleads. "If you'd just—"

"No!" I growl out so loudly my entire body shakes with anger.

"What the fuck are you doing here?" Liam's voice bellows from behind me. Liam, Ash, Chase, Christian, and Sophia are watching us from outside the garage. I squeeze my eyes closed, hating that Sophia is witnessing my angry outburst.

"I just want to talk to him," Heidi says.

Liam shakes his head as he approaches. He squeezes my shoulder and nods at me, letting me know he'll get rid of her.

He grabs Heidi by the arm and leads her to her car. He opens her car door and pushes her inside. They exchange a few more words, but I can't hear them. I'm not sure I even care what else she has to say. I just want her gone.

AS SOON AS LIAM SLAMS THE CAR DOOR SHUT ON HEIDI, I spin around and run toward the garage. I need to get out of here.

Chase grabs my arm to stop me, but I push him off me.

"Mac, stop," he calls after me.

But I don't. I keep running.

I run through the open bay on the front of the garage and out the open door on the back.

I head straight for the separate building behind the garage where we store our personal vehicles.

Once inside, I grab the keys to one of our ATVs and my helmet off the shelf.

"Mac!" Liam calls after me. "You're too upset to go riding. She's gone, and I told her to never come back."

I ignore him, clip my helmet into place, and mount the ATV. I start it up, give it a little gas, then look up. Liam, Ash, Chase, and Christian are lined up, elbow-to-elbow, blocking my exit.

"Move!" I yell out above the sound of the engine. None of them respond. They just stare at me like they're daring me to run them over.

And I dare.

I give the ATV a little gas and it jerks toward my brothers. They don't flinch.

"Get out of my way." I demand.

"You're going to have to run us over if you want out of here," Liam says.

I glare at him. If that's the way he wants to play it, so be it.

I give the ATV a little more gas and slowly approach them. I almost knock into Ash when Sophia yells out.

"That's enough." We all look in her direction. She's clipping a helmet in place as she approaches me. Before any of us can object, she swings a leg over the back of the ATV and slides in close to me.

"Get off!" I growl.

"Nope," she says. It sounds like she's smiling and that makes me even angrier. "If you're going, so am I."

"No, you're not," I say through clenched teeth.

"Yes, I am. If you're going to be dumb enough to risk your life, then you're risking mine too." She wraps her arms around my waist and presses her chest against my back. I hate how much I like how it feels. "Let's go, hot stuff."

I shake my head, wanting to argue with her, but lacking the energy or the words. When I look up, my brothers have stepped aside. They're staring at us in surprise and maybe even a little awe.

I get it. And as much as I hate to admit it, Sophia is an exceptional person. Grams is so right about her. Sophia is a badass, and she puts up with my shit like a champ.

I've been nothing but an ass to her for two weeks, and yet she hopped on the back of the ATV with me, ready to make sure I'm okay.

I don't deserve her kindness, but she still seems ready to give it to me.

Something tells me she's going to ruin me for all other women.

I take off out of the garage without a glance back at my brothers and head for the forest trails. I don't take them nearly as fast and hard as I want to. I still drive like a wild man, just dialed back a notch or two.

But Sophia doesn't know that. Every time I go barreling down a steep hill faster than I should, she tightens her hold around my waist and yells at me to slow down. I don't.

Mainly because I really like how she clings to me. I like how her hands feel pressed against my abdomen. It causes my chest to tighten and my dick to thicken.

When we reach an opening in the woods, I veer the ATV off the trail. It's a secret path I've taken many times before, but not enough that it's easy to see the trail. The ground is rough, and the ATV jerks from side-to-side, making it a challenge to stay upright. But I know what I'm doing.

Despite Sophia's pleas, I keep pushing forward until I reach the spot where the trees open up to a grassy bank near a small creek that runs through our property.

Before I even get the ATV turned off, she hops off and pulls her helmet off her head. "What in the hell is wrong with you? That was some crazy driving, not to mention reckless!"

"I didn't ask you to come with me," I say, my voice devoid of all emotion. "You're just gonna have to take me as I am. Besides, I took it easy on you."

"You call that easy?" She lets out an incredulous laugh. "You almost flipped us at least a dozen times."

I climb off the ATV, take my helmet off, and set it on the seat before I turn my gaze to her. She looks pissed, and it makes me laugh. "We were in no danger of flipping over. Trust me."

She shakes her head and lets out a deep breath. "You're the one with the trust issues. Not me."

"I didn't want you here," I say, not wanting to address her trust comment.

"Clearly." She gives me a *you're a dumbass* look. "But I'm here. So talk to me."

"No."

She rolls her eyes and it makes me want to kiss her. I don't know why because it's not a good look on her. She looks like a brat.

I push past her to the small rock wall that hides a small cave I found years ago when I explored these woods as a kid. I climb up the edge and around the small ledge that hangs over the creek below. When I reach the opening of the cave, I sit and let my feet dangle over the edge.

A few moments later, Sophia sits down next to me and takes in a deep breath.

I dare a glance at her and fight a smile. Her eyes are closed with her head tilted toward the sky like she's trying to soak up all its warmth. The sun beams down on her, making her red hair glow like flames. She's so beautiful. All I want to do is pull her into my arms and stare into her big blue eyes.

Her eyes fly open and dart to mine like she knows I'm watching her. Our eyes lock and there's a heated exchange between us that causes my stomach to bottom out. Or maybe that's just hunger. I didn't eat much of my lunch before Heidi showed up.

She looks out over the water, a small smile on her face.

"This place is beautiful. Do you come here often?" The softness of her voice is in complete contrast to the way she was just yelling at me moments ago.

"Yeah." I lean back on my hands and do my best to look at anything but her.

I hate how much I want to hold her, kiss her, touch her, have all of her. I'd prefer it if I really disliked her. It's the real reason I lash out at her. Everything I do is to make her hate me the way I want to hate her. It's easier that way. One day she'll leave. A mutual dislike protects my heart.

"How old were you the first time you raced a car?" she asks.

"Huh?" Her question surprises me.

She turns her soft, sweet smile to me, and I swear my heart falls out of my chest. I don't deserve that smile. "You heard me."

"Question surprised me, is all." I close my eyes, mostly so I won't stare at her before I answer. "Seven. Dad took me to a race, and I instantly fell in love with the sounds, smells, and all the fast cars going in circles around the track. He knew one of the drivers and took me to meet him after the race. The guy let me sit on his lap. He pressed the pedals while I steered. I was hooked."

"That sounds like a great memory."

"It was." I open my eyes to find her staring at me. The longing I see staring back makes my mouth run dry. Something tells me that if I pulled her to me and kissed her, she wouldn't stop me. Instead, I clear my throat and turn her question around. "How about you? When was your first time behind the wheel?"

Her smile falters, and a sadness washes over her features. "Believe it or not, I was younger than you."

She tears her eyes off mine and looks down at the creek below. There's a vulnerability in the way her shoulders sag that I haven't seen on her before. It makes her look younger, almost like a little girl who's been told she can't have something she desperately wants.

"My dad is a mechanic," she whispers. "He would always take me to the garage he worked at when I was little. I was such a daddy's girl and loved watching him work. While other little girls were playing with dolls, I was playing with Matchbox cars. I was four the first time he let me sit on his lap while test driving one of the cars he was working on. I felt like such a big girl. I was instantly hooked. At the time, my parents just thought I was a little girl who idolized her dad. I was, but it was more than that, you know?"

She looks at me, and her eyes are wet with emotion. I nod because I do understand.

She lets out a long sigh and looks away. "As I got older and my love for fast cars and racing intensified, my mom discouraged me from going to the garage with Dad. I became a car-obsessed girl who dreamed of racing cars for a living, and she hated it. They don't support my choices. They would prefer I do something more appropriate for a girl."

"That sounds tough," I say, because I don't know what else to say. My mom may have abandoned me, but my family supports what I do.

"It is." She gives me a sideways glance. "But I know they love me, and I guess that's more than a lot of people can say. I hid my dreams from my parents for so long, it's become second nature. I never tell people I just meet what I do. It's a habit."

Our eyes lock, and I finally understand. Her parents are the reason she didn't tell me. It's her secret pain. It's the why behind everything that defines who she is, and the strength that propels her forward.

"Come on." I push to my feet. "We better head back before Liam yells at me for today's workload not getting done."

But what I really mean is we better get back before I do something really stupid like kiss her until I'm the only man she ever thinks about again.

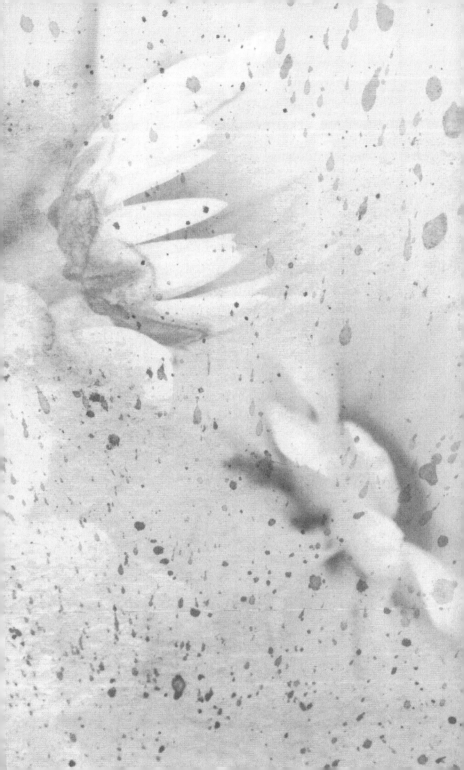

Chapter 10

I touched you first, therefore you're mine.

Sophia

Black grease coats my hands, my back aches from laying under cars all day, and my knee still hurts from when I banged it against the corner of a toolbox. But I can't stop smiling.

I've gained more valuable experience these past few weeks working for the Mutters than I have from my last three jobs combined. They take me seriously and go out of their way to teach me new things.

This week, Ash has been rebuilding the engine from one of Mac's racecars. In between oil changes and tune-ups, he's let me help him. He takes the time to explain to me what he's doing. He's even guided me through some steps so I can get hands-on experience.

"You coming out tonight?" Ash leans against the sink where I'm attempting to wash the grease off my hands.

"To the Oktoberfest?" I ask.

"Yeah. We all go every year. You should come out."

"Clara mentioned it earlier this week. I'm going with her."

Ash smiles and taps his fingers on the edge of the sink before he backs away. "Good. It may be a small event, but we always make it fun."

"So I've heard." I chuckle.

Clara told me all about Beaver's Oktoberfest. It's Beaver's one and only annual event. They close the entire stretch of Main Street, which isn't that much area. Main Street probably isn't even a tenth of a mile long.

There will be arts and craft booths, along with food trucks, games, baking contests, and a center stage where live bands and various performances will take place. There will even be a few rides set up on the old elementary school's—now turned community center—former baseball field.

It sounds like a lot of the same things I saw at Jackson's Apple Festival, just on a much smaller scale.

When I look up from drying my hands, I catch Mac staring at me again. He quickly diverts his gaze. He's done this a lot since the day he drove the ATV out to the cave.

It's been a week, and he hasn't really spoken to me since. I get the occasional hi or a grunt. But we haven't talked. He's been distant, maybe even a little cold toward me.

Every time I catch him watching me, he grumbles something under his breath that I can't hear. Then he walks away. He's making it quite clear he doesn't want me here.

Which is sad, because I thought we had a breakthrough sitting by that cave. I shared something personal that I thought helped him better understand me.

I guess I was wrong.

I stick my head in Liam's office and say, "I'm done for the day. See you later tonight?"

"Sure thing. Thanks for all the hard work." He smiles and waves as I walk out.

I wave to Chase and Christian, who are both still working on a motorcycle, and they wave back. Chase with his usual grin, and

Christian with his typical stoic expression. Those two couldn't be more different for identical twins.

"Hey." Ash calls before I exit the main door. "You wanna have a few beers with us before you head out? Bring Clara along."

"Can't. The rest of my stuff arrived, and I wanna get some of it unpacked tonight."

"Unpacked?" Mac's eyes shoot to mine. He's wearing a scowl that confuses me even more.

"Yeah. At Clara's house," I say.

"Why?" His question sounds accusatory, and I don't like it.

I cross my arms over my chest and glare at him for asking me questions he knows he has no business asking. At least he has the decency to look regretful.

"Clara is renting me a room. The rest of my things from Cincinnati arrived yesterday, and I need to unpack. Is that okay with you?"

He nods but doesn't say anything else. He turns his attention back to the racecar they've been working on all week and acts like I'm no longer there.

I roll my eyes and try not to let my frustration get the best of me. I don't think I'll ever understand that man.

It takes me about fifteen minutes to get to Clara's house. Everything takes about fifteen minutes to get to in Beaver. The only things within the limits of the village are a small grocery store, the smallest post office I've ever seen, Frank's Frosty Kreme, a gas station, a doctor's office, the community center, and, of course, Mrs. Engle's hair salon.

The small village doesn't even have a bank or an ATM. I have to drive the twenty minutes to Jackson every time I need cash.

According to Clara, there was a small bank in Beaver in the 1950s, but someone robbed it. They closed it down and one never opened back up.

This antiquated village brings new meaning to small-town life.

I pull into Clara's driveway and smile. The house sits off the road at the top of a small hill surrounded by open fields. The driveway is lined with birch trees, which she says are her grandma's favorites, and there are three large oak trees next to the house. One in the front yard that shades the entire front of the house, and two in the backyard.

It's a pale yellow, two-story, three-bedroom house with white shutters. There's a swing on the front porch and empty flower beds waiting to be replanted when spring arrives. It's cute, and I'm happy to call it home for the foreseeable future.

THE MOMENT WE ARRIVE AT THE OKTOBERFEST, SOMEONE stops Clara and won't stop talking. It's one of the older women who clearly loves to gossip and has an opinion on everything. If it were me that got stopped, I would have ended the conversation before now, but Clara is being too nice.

Deciding to let her talk, I excuse myself to walk around. Clara gives me an apologetic look and mouths *sorry*.

The first few booths I pass are selling handmade items—knitted socks and scarves, and quilted blankets. Two booths down, I glimpse Grams and make my way over to say hi.

As soon as she sees me, she rushes out from the booth to give me a tight hug. "It's so good to see you, dear. Did you come alone?"

I shake my head. "I came with Clara. She got held up talking to someone. I think it might be her boss or something."

Grams gives me a knowing smile. "That'd be Mrs. Hoffman, the principal of the high school. That woman sure can talk."

"I noticed." I glance around her booth and my eyes widen as I take in all the baked goods and jars of jam. "Oh, wow. Did you make all of this?"

"Of course, dear. Been baking nonstop for the past two weeks, and I started canning the jams this summer as soon as the fruit was ready. Chase produces it all for me. He's quite the farmer. But I don't suppose that's the grandson that interests you."

I snap my eyes to her. "What do you mean?"

Her smile turns mischievous as she slides her arm through mine. "Oh, I do believe my youngest grandson is smitten with you. Although that damn boy is too stubborn for his own good. He'll deny it if you ask him. But my Mac likes you all the same."

Even though I doubt the truth of her words, they make me all warm and fuzzy inside. I want Mac to want me. More than I probably should.

Wanting to change the subject, I pat her arm and turn my attention to her baked goods. "So, any of these recipes up for ownership debate?"

She harrumphs, and it makes me chuckle. "Now don't you go listening to the Kochs. All my recipes are mine. Ain't nobody stole a damn thing. That family is riddled with jealousy, and jealousy is like a raging fire. Once it takes hold, you've got to let it burn itself out."

"I can't imagine it's a healthy reason to fuel a rivalry between two families."

"No, it certainly is not." Grams smiles up at me. "Let me bag you up some of my chocolate peanut clusters. They're Clara's favorite."

I gladly take the candies as a gift, stuff them into my purse, and say a quick goodbye before I glance around for Clara, but I don't see her. Hopefully, that means she got away from Mrs. Hoffman.

"If it isn't my favorite female racecar driver," Tanner Koch's voice has me turning around.

"I'm pretty sure I'm the *only* female racecar driver you know," I say with a forced smile.

"That's why you're my favorite." He grins.

I roll my eyes. "Tanner, that is not a compliment."

"I guess I need to try harder." He wraps his arm around my shoulder and tucks me into his side.

"No, you really don't." I push against his chest, but he doesn't budge.

"How about we get you a drink?" he asks. "Do you like beer?"

"Yes, I could drink a beer." I glance around at the nearby food trucks. "Where's the booth?"

He tosses his head back in laughter. "Sweetheart, this village is dry. There is no booth."

"Dry?" I furrow my brows.

"Yeah, you know? When it's illegal to sell alcohol within the village limits."

"I know what dry means." I push against his chest again, and this time I manage to extract myself from his embrace. "How is it a German village with an Oktoberfest is dry? I thought Germans loved their beer."

He shrugs. "I didn't make the rules, but I know where we can find the beer so we can break them. Come with me."

He takes my hand and leads me off the street and onto the sidewalk behind the row of booths. He doesn't stop until we reach a house with a sign out front that reads Family Practice, Dr. Aaron Koch.

"Are you related to this doctor?" I ask.

He nods. "Aaron is my older brother. He makes sure to have the Beer Garden stocked every year during Oktoberfest." Tanner opens a gate to the fence blocking off the yard next to the doctor's office. "Normally this is BYOC, but since you're new in town, I got you covered."

"BYOC?" I raise a brow.

"Bring your own cup." He winks and his flirty smile returns.

"HERE, YOU CAN USE THIS CUP." TANNER HANDS ME A BLACK tumbler with a lid. Unless anyone gets close enough to smell what's inside, they'd think I had coffee in here.

"Um, thanks." I give him a tight smile. "Will this get me in trouble?"

He tilts his head and gives me a quizzical eye. "Why would it get you in trouble?"

"You said Beaver is dry. What if someone catches us out there with beer? Isn't that like breaking the law?"

"Nah." He winks at me again. "Everyone knows we drink it. We just can't sell it."

He takes my arm and leads me toward a wall of kegs along the fence. I glance around, and the Beer Garden is just a fenced-in backyard. The patio doors on the back of the house are open, revealing a tidy kitchen and dining area. It looks more like a house than a doctor's office. Maybe his brother lives here as well.

Plastic furniture litters the yard and patio area. Several people I've never seen before occupy the chairs. There's a grill on the patio, tables filled with food, and people laughing and drinking in almost every open space.

"It's all Budweiser. I hope that's okay?" Tanner says as he fills the tumbler to the top.

"Sure." I take the beer and glance around again. "Who are these people?"

Tanner smiles and steps closer to me. "Friends of ours. By hanging out with the Mutters, you've missed out on meeting some of the best people in town. Have you met my brothers?"

"Not officially, but I know who most of them are." I point to where Linden and Aaron are talking with an older man who looks like he could be their father. "Those two are your older brothers, right? Linden and Aaron?"

"Yep." He points in the opposite direction where a younger version of him is sitting with a group of girls. "And that's Jason. He went to school with Ash. Everyone says he's the nicest, but I think they're wrong."

"And that's your sister over there, Amelia?" I point toward the dark-haired beauty who's staring at me with a worried expression on her face. "She doesn't look pleased that I'm here."

Tanner waves off my comment. "She worries too much. Always trying to keep the peace. Where's the fun in that?"

His smile widens as his gaze fixates on something behind me. Then he wraps his arm around my shoulders and tugs me closer. His action catches me off guard, and I stumble over my feet, drop my beer, and face plant into his chest. I grab at the skirt my dress, tugging it down to make sure my ass is still covered.

"Tanner! What are you doing?" I regain my footing and jerk out of his hold, only to fall into another very hard body.

A deep growl startles me, and I whip around.

If looks could kill, then Mac's angry glare would put Tanner in an early grave.

"Mac." His name is a whisper from my lips.

His eyes dart to mine, and the lightning I see spark in his dark eyes has me taking a step back.

"You don't belong here." The harsh tone of his voice rolls over my body like thunder.

Before I can defend myself, he lunges toward me, lifts me up, and slings me over his shoulder like a caveman. A cool breeze blows up my dress, and I hope that doesn't mean I'm flashing everyone here.

"Mac!" I yell and slap at his back. "What in the hell are you doing? Put me down!"

He grunts and marches out of the Beer Garden with his hand splayed possessively over my ass. I'm pissed and oddly turned on at the same time.

I hear catcalls and whistles from the crowd we've left behind and even a few innuendos suggesting the Koch brothers could do it better. I don't even want to acknowledge what they think is happening between Mac and me. Because this man hates me.

Moments later, I'm surrounded by darkness and the loud calls of the crowd have faded to a low rumble. He pulls me off his shoulder and pins me against a wall of what I assume is a neighboring house or business.

"What are you doing?" I push against his chest, but he doesn't budge.

He places his hands on either side of my head and leans down until his eyes are level with mine. "What in the hell were you doing with Tanner?"

My frown deepens. I want to equal parts knee him between the legs and pull his lips to mine. The battle going on in my body is giving me whiplash.

"That's none of your business." I say through clenched teeth. For now, my anger is winning the war. "You've made it quite clear you don't want me around."

The thunderous growl that rumbles out of his chest is so intense and fierce I feel it throughout my entire body. "What I don't want is to find you hanging out with Tanner Koch. You work for us!"

"What does it matter?" I fist my hands in his shirt when I should push him away. "Tanner was just showing me where to get a beer."

He shakes his head and steps closer, caging me in like a wild beast ready to eat its prey. "He had his hands on you. He's not allowed to touch you."

"Excuse me?" My eyes widen and my heartbeat rings in my ear. "You don't get to dictate who I hang out with or who touches me. Stop acting like a jealous boyfriend."

"Oh, but I am a jealous man." His words are eerily calm. "And I don't appreciate you giving me reasons to be jealous."

"You have no reason to be jealous of anyone where I'm concerned. I don't belong to you."

"Yes. You. Do," he roars, and it's so feral and intense I swear my ovaries flip in excitement. I should be pissed, but my treacherous body seems to love this possessive side of him. Every nerve ending in my body is on fire with desire.

"W-what?" I mumble through my fog of need.

"No man gets to lay a finger on you. Not after I had my hands and mouth on you. Is that understood?"

"Why do you even care? You don't like me!" I cry.

Then his lips crash into mine.

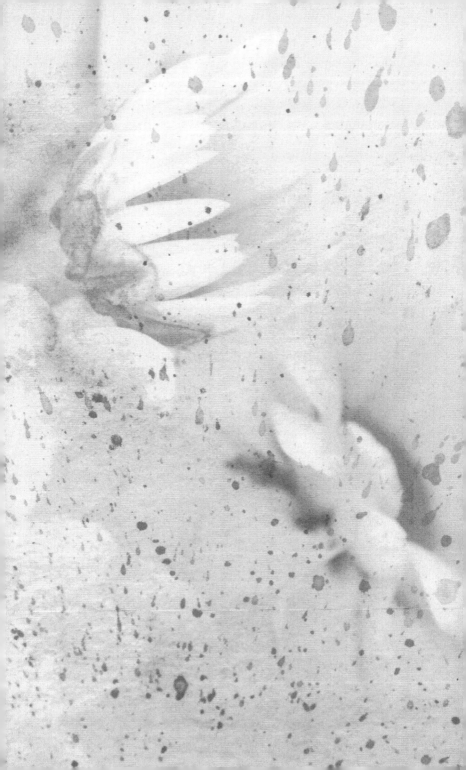

Chapter 11

A wall works just fine.

Mac

I'm losing my fucking mind, and it's all this woman's fault.

It's her smart mouth and her red hair and the smattering of freckles across her nose. And her damn pouty lips. They've taunted me. Day and night.

All I've wanted since the night I met her is to taste her and feel her body next to mine again. I've both craved to have her close to me and desperately wanted her to go the fuck away.

My need to kiss her, taste her, and feel her, won.

I shove my hands into her long fiery locks and tilt her head to the side so I can devour her mouth with mine. She doesn't resist as I thrust my tongue between her lips and swipe it against hers. She tastes like something sweet with a hint of spice.

Her hands slip around my neck, and her fingers glide into my hair. When her nails scrape against my scalp, I groan.

I slide my hands under her ass, lift her up, and press my throbbing cock between her legs. The whimper that escapes her drives me wild.

I need more.

Pulling my mouth off hers, I roughly kiss down her neck and between her breasts—her gloriously plump and pert breasts. I shove her jacket to the side and bite down on one of her breasts through the thin fabric of the dress she's wearing.

Of all the nights for her to wear a dress, it had to be tonight, when my control snaps. Nothing short of her telling me no is going to stop me from taking her right here, right now.

"Fuck, Red." I grumble against the soft skin of her neck. "I want you. Please, tell me yes."

I feel her head nod, but she doesn't speak. "I need words."

"Yes," she whispers as she pulls my mouth back to hers. She kisses me hard, our tongues warring for dominance. "Please fuck me."

The storm building inside me converges with my desire, and my chest roars with a triumphant cry. "When you say it like that, how can I refuse you?"

She wraps her legs around my waist and squeezes them tight like she's trying to snap me in two. My cock aches to be inside her and my hands itch to touch every inch of her.

I press my body against hers, using the wall behind us to hold her up. Then I pull her dress down to reveal a pale pink lace bra covering her breasts. At least I think it's pink. It's hard to tell in the shadows of darkness. But it's not too dark to hide her rose-colored nipples through the thin fabric.

I suck a nipple into my mouth through the fabric, and she writhes. Her hot center presses into my cock, causing my eyes to roll back in my head. I can't wait another minute to be inside her.

Releasing her, I place her feet on the ground and step back. My eyes roam down her body, enjoying the way her chest heaves and her legs tremble. Her hair is disheveled, and her dress is hanging off her shoulders. If there were more light, I'd bet money that her pale skin is flushed a pretty pink just for me.

She's wearing sexy, knee-high boots that spur all sorts of erotic images of her spread out before me in nothing else but them.

I drop in front of her and slip my hands under her dress. She gasps as I wrap my fingers around her panties and slide them down her legs. Once they're off, I stand and rub them between my fingers. They're wet with her arousal, and I can't stop myself from smelling them.

"So fucking sweet." I let out a low groan before I stuff them in the front pocket of my jeans. "These are mine now."

She doesn't speak. She just stares at me through lidded eyes.

I retrieve a condom from my wallet before I unzip my pants and pull my cock out, giving it a rough squeeze. Her eyes widen as she takes me in. I'm not a small man, and I'm going to enjoy spreading her open with my cock.

"Tell me something, Red." I say as I roll the condom down my iron-hard shaft. "Are you a screamer?"

She blinks several times, like she's trying to understand what I asked. When realization dawns, she whispers, "No."

A smirk lifts my lip as I stalk toward her. "Well, you're about to be."

"Mac, we're in public. Someone might hear us."

I lift her up, and she immediately wraps her legs around my waist. My cock finds her entrance like he knows exactly where he wants to be. Grabbing her hands, I hold them above her head, effectively pinning her body against the wall.

"You should have thought about that before you let Tanner Koch put his hands on you."

I slam inside her in one quick thrust, completely filling her up. Just like I wanted, she lets out a high-pitched cry.

My own thunderous growl joins hers. We're so loud, in fact, that anyone within earshot can hear us.

I still as my body adjusts to the feel of her wet heat around me. She's so tight. My head is spinning with dizziness, and if I move, I'm going to blow my load before either of us enjoys this. I haven't felt the urge to come this fast since my first time when I was a teenager.

She rocks her hips against me, and I groan.

"Don't," I growl.

"I need you to move." She pants.

I shake my head before I bury it in her neck. "I need a minute. You feel too good."

We're both breathing heavily as I slowly pull out, leaving just my tip inside her. I plant soft kisses on her neck and up to her ear that are in complete contrast to how I want to fuck her. Once I'm certain I've got control of my dick, I whisper in her ear, "Are you ready to be fucked?"

"Oh, Mac. Yes!" she moans.

This time I don't hold back as I slam inside her over and over until she's crying my name. Her already tight heat clenches around me like a vise. She's close, which is a damn good thing because I'm not going to last long.

"Mac!" she screams just before her core squeezes around me, triggering my orgasm. I pump my hips harder and faster, wanting to drag this out because it feels so fucking amazing to be inside her.

We both moan. Our bodies collapse into a puddle of pleasure and contentment. Her legs are still around my waist with my dick buried deep inside her, and I still have her arms pinned above her head. I lift my head and meet her heavy gaze.

She's never looked more beautiful than she does right now. Sated and exhausted from my dick. A heaviness settles over my chest, and the storm that's been raging inside me for months brews again. Suddenly it's hard to breathe, and the urge to run is strong.

I release her hands and untangle her legs from around my waists. My cock aches in protest as I slowly slide out of her. I already miss the soft warmth of her body, and I haven't even left her side.

I'm so fucked.

I scrub my hands over my face as I put some distance between us. I tie off the condom and stuff it in the wrapper I tossed on the ground before I right my clothes.

When I finally look at her, she's fixed her dress and is running her fingers through her hair. I want to kiss her again and mess her up. I like her messed up.

All my fears and insecurities surface, and the high from my release wanes. All I can think about is how I shouldn't have touched her. That I can't be the man she deserves. That she'll lie to me about something else—something more significant. Or that she'll end up leaving anyway, because that's what women do. They lie, and they leave.

"Shit, I'm sorry." I blurt out. "I shouldn't have done that."

Her eyes widen as they dart to mine. "What? Did you seriously just say that to me?"

"Yeah, I mean ..." I sigh and run my fingers through my hair because I don't know what I mean. I just know that this was the best sex of life and it's freaking me the fuck out. "I don't think this is a good idea."

"Oh my God. You're unbelievable." She charges toward me and shoves me with both her hands on my chest. I stumble backward. "Then why did you barge in there, practically club me over the head, and then demand that I belong to you?"

My chest heaves with anxiety because I don't have a good answer for her. "Because I'm an asshole. I'm sorry, but I've gotta go."

I turn around and bolt. I'm out of earshot before she speaks. I'm sure whatever she said isn't good, but also well deserved.

But I can't be near her right now. I'm too damaged, too fucked in the head, and too jaded where women are concerned.

I need to be alone.

I HEAR ONE OF MY BROTHERS CALLING AFTER ME. A TINGE OF disappointment washes over me that it's not Sophia. Which is stupid since she's the person I'm running from. Yet some deep-rooted and sick part of me wants her to follow me.

I want her to call me out for being a dick.

I want her to fight with me and refuse to take my shit.

But why would she? Not after what I just did.

When I saw Tanner lead her into the Beer Garden, I lost my shit. He touched her. The man put his arm around her. And he flirted with her, making her laugh.

He did it because he knew it would piss me off. The moment he saw me arrive, he went straight for her.

And worst of all, she let him do it all.

I hear my name again, but I don't stop. I don't want to talk to anyone right now.

When I reach my truck, I start it up before I even get the door closed. Gravel flies out from under my wheels as I slam on the gas and speed away from town.

I don't have a destination in mind. I just drive. My head is spinning with images of Sophia's face as she came. She looked like perfection with the way her eyes rolled back and her mouth hung open. I want to put that look on her face every day.

But I made sure that will never happen again. Because that look vanished when I told her it was a mistake.

What in the hell is wrong with me?

"Fuck!" I slam my hand down on the steering wheel as I whip the truck around the next corner and into the Meadow. I didn't even realize this is where I was headed until I turned the corner.

I back my truck up to the fire pit and hop out. I doubt anyone has been out here since our last Mud Run a few weeks ago. Dropping the tailgate, I reach for the cooler I stocked with beer before I left the house earlier.

I pop the top of one and guzzle half the bottle down before I hop up on the bed and lay back to stare up at the sky. It's a clear night and I can see all the stars without obstruction.

The fireflies twinkle in the trees, and if I wasn't in such a shit mood, I'd enjoy the way they flicker and dance. When I was little, I loved catching fireflies and putting them in a jar. It was one of the things Mom did with me. I'd set the jar by my bed and watch them until my lids grew heavy and sleep took me.

I was such a happy kid. Why can't I be that happy now?

Shifting to my side, I pull the letter that came in the mail today out of my back pocket. It's the real reason I'm in such a shit mood and bailed on Sophia after I fucked her.

I stare at the name above the return address. Heidi Winkler. Why won't she leave me alone? I thought I made it clear that I wanted nothing to do with her when she showed up unannounced. Now she's sending me fucking letters.

I debate on what to do with it. I'm not sure I care what she has to say. Burning it sounds way better than reading an apology or reading about her regrets and mistakes. None of that matters to me.

Sighing, I pull my phone out and turn on the flashlight app. Then I rip open the envelope and pull out the single piece of paper. When I unfold it, I'm surprised by how short the letter is.

Mac,

Since you refuse to let me speak to you in person, I guess I have no choice but to do it in a letter. It pains me that you're so angry with me. I don't blame you. I deserve so much worse than anger. I abandoned you, and for that, I don't expect forgiveness.

But you should know, I got married a year after I left your father. I'm still married to that man today. He and I have three kids. Two girls and a boy. You have more siblings. I should have told you about them a long time ago. I don't know why I didn't. I guess because I was afraid.

I recently told them about you, and they would

love to meet you. If that's something you're open to.
Millie is twenty and finishing up her last year in
nursing school. Greta just turned sixteen and passed
her driver's test. My youngest, Ben, is fourteen.
He's excited to finally be in high school.

Anyway, now you have my address, and I listed
their phone numbers at the bottom. If you want to
meet them, they're waiting.

Mom

I CRUMPLE THE LETTER, HOP OFF THE TRUCK, AND SCREAM. I
scream and scream and scream until my throat hurts. Then I fall to
the ground and beat my fists into the dirt until my knuckles bleed.

I don't know how long I sit there before headlights illuminate
the field. I'm vaguely aware of the truck that pulls up next to mine.
I should probably look to see who it is, but I don't care.

Maybe it's one or all the Koch brothers, and they've come to
kick my ass. I could use a good ass-kicking. The pain would be a
welcome sensation.

"What the actual fuck, Mac?" I close my eyes in disappointment at the sound of Ash's voice. "Please tell me you didn't just do
that to Sophia."

"I don't want to talk about it," I mumble under my breath.

"Well too fucking bad. If she quits because of you, I'm gonna
kick your ass."

"I'll apologize to her," I say, but there's no emotion behind my
words. I can't actually feel anything right now.

"Man, snap out of it." He grabs my shoulder and forces me to
look at him. When he sees my expression, some of his anger dissi-
pates. "What happened?"

I don't answer him. Instead, I hold up the letter from Heidi.

"What's this?" he asks as he takes it from me.

"Just read it."

He watches me for a moment before he smooths out the paper and uses his own phone as a flashlight. He's silent as his eyes roam over the letter. When he reaches the end, he lets out a low curse.

"Whoa. Three more siblings. That's heavy."

All I can manage is a nod.

He says something else, but my mind shuts down. All I can think about is how little I meant to her. She never cared about me. If she did, she would have come back.

Instead, she made a new family and forgot all about me. She had three more kids and never told me. More lies. More hate. More pain.

More reason to never trust a woman with my heart.

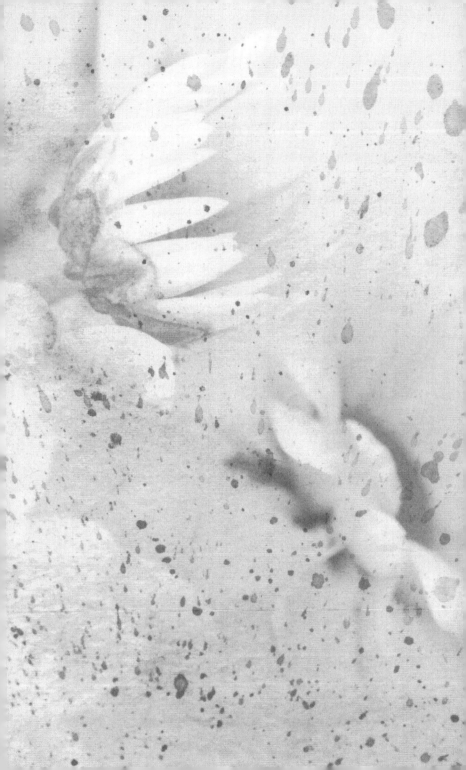

Chapter 12

Not all history lessons are boring.

Sophia

Rolling over in bed, I hide my head under the pillow to stifle my groan. Mac Mutter gets under my skin like no one ever has before. And for reasons I can't explain, I have zero control around him.

So much so, I can't believe I had sex with him—a man who *acts* like he hates me—out in the open, where anyone could walk up and catch us.

And his hatred toward me is definitely acting. No man—I don't care who he is—would ever barge into enemy territory like Mac did last night if he didn't have feelings for me.

The way he tossed me over his shoulder was so primal and hot.

It infuriated me and turned me on at the same time. Clearly, since I let him fuck me against a building no more than a block away from Main Street, where all the festivities were taking place.

I don't even want to think about how many people heard us.

His brothers heard us. I know that much. After Mac ran off, Ash followed me. He tried to talk to me and make up some sorry ass excuse for Mac's behavior. I didn't want to hear it.

Instead, I found Clara and told her I needed to go home. She gave me her keys and said she'd get a ride from someone else. How did I get so lucky to make a friend like her?

Deciding I need to repay her, I toss the covers back and climb out of bed. It's still dark outside, but the sun will be up soon.

I put on a pot of coffee, then dig around the refrigerator and pantry to see what we've got to make for breakfast.

There's a package of maple sausage links and everything I need for pancakes. *My favorite.* I'd eat pancakes for every meal if they were available. I hope Clara likes pancakes too.

While the coffee is brewing, I fry up the sausage and mix up the batter. By the time I'm ready to cook the pancakes, the sun is up and glaring through the small kitchen window above the sink.

It's so bright, it's blinding, but I like it. There's something about it that leaves me with a feeling of ease and comfort. It's like a welcoming friend greeting me as I start my day.

I also like the quiet. Living my entire life in a big city, I got used to the constant hum of noise. There is no noise in the country. I hear an occasional tree branch creek when the wind blows, but otherwise it's just me, the sizzle of the sausage, and my thoughts.

Though, I'm not having much fun with my thoughts today.

I plate up the sausage and cover it with foil to keep it warm as I flip the pancakes. I'm almost done, and Clara still isn't up, so I turn the oven on low heat to keep the food warm.

Her kitchen is old, but large. It's so open there's room for a center island if she ever decides to remodel it.

It's got one of those ceramic farmhouse-style sinks I always thought were cool. The cabinets are solid wood, but could use refinishing, and the countertops have seen better days. They're laminate with chips throughout where it looks like someone dropped stuff on it over the years.

But the hardwood floors are gorgeous. Rustic and dark, they extend throughout the entire house.

An arched entryway leads to the dining room. The walls are covered with China cabinets and buffet tables. The China cabinets are stuffed with more dishes than any one person needs. It looks like her grandma collected salt and pepper shakers based on how many sets there are.

The table is big enough to seat ten guests. I wonder if Clara ever entertains that many people. The only friends I've seen her talk with are the Mutters.

I set the table on the side closest to the kitchen. Plates, flatware, syrup, butter, and glasses for orange juice. When I turn back to the kitchen, I smile when I see Clara yawning and watching me with confusion.

"Good morning." I smile.

"What are you doing?" she asks.

"I made breakfast. Please tell me you love pancakes. They're my favorite, and I'm not sure our friendship will survive if you hate them."

She chuckles. "Then it's a good thing I love pancakes."

I let out a dramatic sigh and run the back of my hand across my forehead, feigning relief. "Thank God. I really didn't want to have to look for a new friend." I tease. "Coffee?" I hand her a mug. "It's just the way you like it. Two sugars and a dash of cream for color."

She takes the mug, holds it up to her nose, and breathes in deep. "Perfect. Thank you."

"Go ahead and sit. I'll bring everything in."

While Clara takes her seat, I grab the sausage and pancakes from the oven. After double checking that everything is turned off, I join her at the table. She's staring at the plate in front of her with wide eyes and an odd expression on her face.

"Everything okay?" I ask, hoping I didn't do something wrong like set out her grandma's special China that's only used on special occasions. These dishes didn't look special, but what do I know?

Clara snaps her head up and gives me an awkward smile. "Yes, I'm fine." She clears her throat and takes a sip of her coffee. "It's just, I've never really had a friend before that was a girl. Is this what girlfriends do?"

I smile, trying to push back the feelings that arise in me. I feel bad for her, but she doesn't need my pity. She needs my friendship.

"I don't know." I answer honestly. "I have plenty of friends that are girls, but I spent most of my time around cars. Cars are easier to understand than people."

"I can relate to that," she says, and grabs two pancakes.

I do the same. We're silent as we fix up our plates. Once we both have our pancakes buttered and syrup poured over the top, Clara starts again. "It's why I love books so much. Books never judge me. Girls, however, they're mean. I never had an interest in clothes or make-up or doing my hair. Playing outside with the boys or reading a book was always more fun. It didn't help that I grew up with two beauty queens for sisters."

I chuckle. "I bet that was fun. My mom wanted me to be a beauty queen. I was sixteen the first and only time she forced me to wear a ball gown. I went to the garage and changed the oil in my dad's car out of protest. Ruined the dress. She's never forgiven me."

Clara laughs so hard she snorts. "I would have loved to have seen that."

"After that, she realized I was a lost cause. She leaves me alone about girly things but still lectures me about cars."

"I'm grateful my parents never tried to change me. In fact, they encouraged my friendship with Ash."

I take a big bite of my pancakes and groan as the sweet maple syrup hits my taste buds.

"What was it like growing up with the Mutters?" I ask. "I bet that had to be interesting."

She eyes me above the rim of her glasses, a small smile playing across her face. "You mean was Mac always like this?"

I feel my cheeks warm, and she chuckles. "You should see your face. You just turned bright red."

I press my hands to my face, embarrassment taking over my entire body. Even my arms are blotchy with red spots. "I can't help it. My skin hates me. I turn red at the slightest poke."

"I'm sorry. I'm not trying to pick on you."

"It's okay." I take a drink of my coffee before I meet her gaze. "So, what was Mac like? Was he always so hot and cold?"

She eyes me thoughtfully before taking a drink of her coffee. "No, not always. At least not with everyone. He doesn't date a lot, but he's had a few girlfriends over the years. Nothing serious though. He always kept them at a distance. I think that's why he's struggling with you."

"What do you mean? I'm too close?"

She nods. "And he really likes you too. You might be the first girl he's ever liked this much. That makes this harder for him. I know he acts like an ass toward you, but that's his defense mechanism kicking in. He doesn't trust women. Not after how his mom abandoned him. All their moms really. Except for Susanne. That's Paul's first wife. Liam's, Warren's, and Garret's mom. She died right after Garret was born. But none of the other women stuck around for very long."

"So the others all have different moms?"

"Yeah. Chase and Christian's mom, Christina, is a piece of work. She still lives around here. Has a bad drug problem. She plays mind games with the twins. She's also the one that got Christian hooked on drugs."

"Christian does drugs?" I gasp. "He's quiet and broody, but he doesn't seem like he's using."

She shakes her head. "He's clean now. But he struggles with it. Drugs are an issue around here. It's hard to escape them. He's relapsed several times. And every time Christina calls them, tensions rise. She triggers his addiction. Chase runs interference a lot. It's hard on all of them."

"That's awful. I can't imagine."

"Unfortunately, it doesn't stop with Christina. Ash's mom, Monika, isn't much better. She didn't stick around for long after Ash was born. Showed up several years later with a little girl, Ash's half-sister, Alvara. She lived with them for a while. They all took to her and treated her like a sister. Then one day, Monika came back and took her. Paul didn't even try to stop her, even though the boys fought it. Ash still sees them both. He's close with Alvara, but his relationship with Monika is strained."

"And Mac's mom?" My voice is timid. I'm not sure I want to hear this, but my curiosity is piqued. Maybe if I understand his relationship with his mom, his behavior will make more sense.

"I heard she showed up."

I nod. "It was ugly. He didn't handle it well. I tried to get him to talk about it, but he refused."

"Doesn't surprise me. She left when he was five. As far as I know, this recent visit is the first time he'd seen or heard from her in over twenty years."

"I picked up on that fact. I can't imagine what that was like."

"Me either. My parents can drive me crazy sometimes, but I know they love me. And they'd never leave me. That's not the case for the Mutters. They have Grams, and, well, she's awesome. But every one of their moms left. Mac's mom stuck around the longest. I've always wondered if she said something to him when he was little that made all this harder on him."

"And that's why he has trust issues where women are concerned?"

Clara nods with a despondent look on her face. "That's why he sees your omission to why you were really here as a deceit. Not that it is," she adds quickly, "but to him, it was a betrayal of trust."

"I didn't trust him enough to tell him the truth. As if he wasn't worthy to really know me."

"Yep." Clara pops the P at the end before she takes a drink of her coffee.

I push my pancakes around on my plate, and suddenly I've lost my appetite. I really screwed this one up without even trying. My reasons for not telling Mac the truth from the start are because of my issues, not his. I hope I can convince him of that.

Because now my heart is involved, and I want to push past his hard exterior and really get to know the good man I've seen glimpses of underneath.

It's late morning when Liam walks out of his office. It's been quiet for a Monday. I'm three hours into my shift, and I've mostly been alone in the garage.

"Is Christian back?" he asks when he only sees me under the hood of a car.

"Not yet. He left right after I got here. Said he should be back in a couple of hours, but I haven't seen him yet." I shrug, not really sure what else to say.

Liam rubs the back of his neck and glances around the garage. "You okay if I run some errands? I don't expect anyone to stop by until later this afternoon."

"Yeah, I've got this. Do what you need to do."

"K, thanks." His shoulders relax slightly. I'm not sure if it's because he really needs to go on these errands or he's happy I didn't object. "I shouldn't be gone long. If anything comes up, just call my cell."

"Will do."

Once he leaves, I crank up the music and get to work. I have two cars to get done before I break for lunch. One is an oil change, which I'm almost done with, and the other needs new spark plugs and a battery. Both are easy jobs.

I already changed the brakes on a Jeep this morning, and I've got at least one tune-up this afternoon. I'm getting faster on these jobs, and I hope that means I'll get more time to work with Ash on the engine rebuild.

Just as I slide under the car to replace the drain plug for the oil change, the music shuts off.

"Christian? Is that you?" I call out from under the car. I hear footsteps, but no one answers.

"Christian?" I call again. "Or is that you, Liam?"

"No, it's me." I shudder at the sound of Mac's voice. We haven't talked since he bolted on me Friday night. I hoped I'd make it through this day without seeing him too. I'm not ready to deal with all the emotions I have where he's concerned.

I slide out from under the car to find him looming over me with his arms crossed over his chest. He's playing the damn sentinel again.

"What are you doing here?" I ask.

His eyes narrow. "Um, I work here."

I huff. "That's not what I mean. I didn't think you'd be in today."

"Where is everyone?" he asks, choosing to ignore my question.

Pushing to my feet, I wipe my hands before I grab the oil for the car. "Christian is delivering a custom build, and Liam had some errands to run."

"And he left you here alone?" His words sound harsh and accusatory.

"Yes." I bark in reply. "Why are you here? I thought you were at the track with Ash and Chase all day."

"I was, and now I'm here."

"Again, I'm gonna ask you why?"

He scoffs and runs his fingers through his hair. "You drive me fucking crazy. You know that?"

"Well, the feeling is mutual, asshole."

He steps closer to me, blocking the light from under the hood, so I back away. "I think a better question is, why are *you* here?"

I fight the urge to roll my eyes. "Because *I* work here."

"Don't be a smart ass. You know that's not what I'm asking."

"Then maybe I need you to be more specific. Really spell things out for me, so I understand."

"Why are you in *my* town, working in *my* garage? You could have taken a job anywhere. Why *here*?"

I slam the wrench down on the bench and storm at him. "No, I couldn't. Do you have any idea how hard it is to find a garage willing to hire a female mechanic or a racing team willing to let me learn from them?"

When he doesn't answer, I take another step toward him. "No. Why would you? You're. A. Man. No one ever questions *your* ability."

His nostrils flare as he eliminates the remaining space between us. "I'm not questioning your ability. You already proved you can drive and that you're competent under the hood. I want to know why *us*? Why the Mutters?"

"Because I admire you and your work!" I yell, exhausted from going in circles with this man. "Everyone in the business knows your brothers make some of the best race cars on the track. And you?" I poke him in the chest, and it's like poking a boulder. Hard. Solid. Immovable. "You're one of the best drivers I've ever watched. I wanted to learn from you and them. Why is that so hard for you to believe?"

He leans down so he's eye level with me. "Then why did you lie to me?"

"I didn't lie!" I grind out through clenched teeth.

A low rumbling sound rolls up and out of his chest. His eyes shift from mine to my lips. I'm panting from frustration and this sexual tension that's surrounded us since the first night we met.

I want to push him away. Tell him to leave me alone. But I don't.

Instead, I slide my hands around his neck and cover his mouth with mine.

He doesn't hesitate to take control of the kiss by parting my lips with his tongue. It's a deep kiss, yet softer and sweeter than what we shared on Friday night. There's no sense of urgency, but rather a slow exploration and a need to be closer to one another.

He slides his hands under my ass and lifts me onto the bench. I part my legs, making room for him to step between them and press his body to mine. I feel every inch of his hard length against me, sparking memories of how good he felt inside me. I want to feel that good again.

But we can't do this. Not until I know he won't run from me as soon as we're done.

"Mac," I whisper against his lips. "You can't keep doing this."

He sucks my bottom lip between his teeth, lightly nibbling on it, and it causes an intense heat to pool between my legs.

"Doing what?" His words sound so innocent and free of guilt.

"Acting like you hate me, and then kissing me like that."

He pulls back. His gaze is heavy with desire and need. "*You* kissed *me*."

I run my finger along his jaw, then over his bottom lip. I really want to kiss him again, but I need to know where we stand first.

"Yeah, but you kissed me back," I say. "It's confusing."

He holds his stare on me for several beats before he finally nods, like he's acknowledging what I've said.

"I don't hate you."

"You sure as hell act like you do."

He shakes his head and slowly extracts his body from mine. I instantly miss his heat and his touch. "Just the opposite actually. I like you too much, and that's a fucking problem."

I close my eyes, knowing I'm losing this battle. He's not ready to give me more. But I ask my next question anyway. "Why is that a problem?"

He steps back with a mournful expression on his face. "Because me and women don't mix. It never ends well."

Before I can argue that I'm nothing like the women from his past, he turns and walks out the door.

I don't know how it's possible, but somehow, him leaving me now hurts so much more than when he left me Friday night.

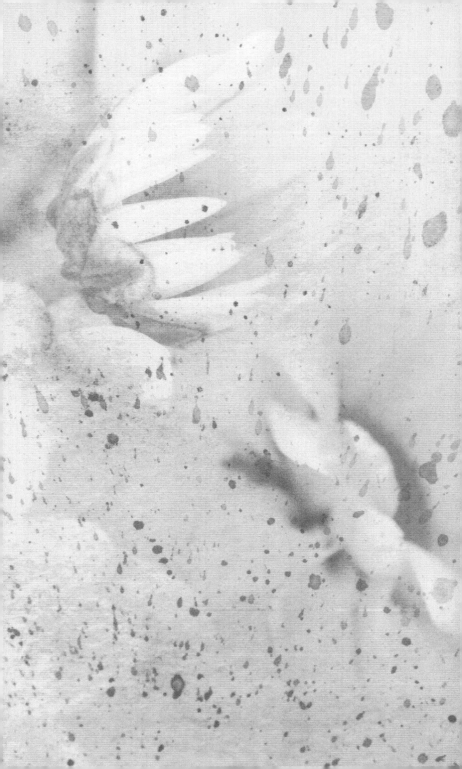

Chapter 13

Trapped in a metal box with temptation.

Mac

Ash double checks the trailer hitch one last time before I pull the truck out of the garage. I park it along the edge of the driveway before I hop out and help him double check all the ties.

My next race is tomorrow afternoon near Beckley, West Virginia. It's not too far from the New River Gorge.

This isn't a big race, or even one that will get me a lot of sponsorship or media attention, but I race it every year. We really go for the outdoor activities. It's a great excuse to spend a few days on the river.

The New River has some great rapids, and whitewater rafting is one of our favorite activities. Even Garret leaves his tiny little house and joins us for this trip.

It's cold this time of year, but we don't let that stop us. That's what wetsuits are for. It also means there won't be a lot of tourists, and we'll mostly have the river to ourselves.

Liam and Christian are staying behind though. Someone needs to run the shop while the rest of us are gone.

Chase exits the garage and tosses supplies into the back of my truck. Then he drops the tailgate and drags the cooler to the edge.

"What are you doing?" I ask. "We're not taking my truck."

Chase tosses me one of his mischievous grins. "We've got one more joining us. Two trucks will be more comfortable."

"Who?" I frown, but he doesn't answer me. Instead, he pats my forearm and laughs as he walks away. "Who else is coming?" I call after him.

I don't have to wait long to find out because moments later, Sophia pulls up.

"Oh hell no. She's not coming with us." I groan.

"Sure she is," Chase says. "She asked to help with the pit crew. She's never seen that side of racing, and she's eager to learn."

"You guys hate me, don't you?"

"Oh, come on. I'd think you of all people would be happy to have her tag along. A pretty girl into cars is hot as fuck. You can't tell me you don't find that attractive."

I growl and turn away from my brother because he doesn't need to see how affected I am by this woman. Not that he doesn't already know. "Don't talk about her like that."

"Like what?" Chase laughs.

I snap my head around and pin him with a glare. "Don't call her hot."

"But she *is* hot." He waggles his brows. "Especially when she's covered in grease and using car terms that most girls have never even heard before. It's enough to make any man hard."

I grab Chase by the shirt and lift my fist. We're the same height, but I'm broader than him. I can easily take him in a fight. "Don't think about her like that."

He laughs like he thinks my reaction is the funniest thing he's ever seen. I know he's just trying to get under my skin, but I don't give a shit. He can take his charm and shove it where the sun doesn't shine.

He can flirt with any girl he wants, except Sophia. *She's mine.*

My body tenses, and I release him from my grip. What the

fuck is happening to me? Sophia is *not* mine. She can't be mine. I spin around, needing space between Chase and me before I do something I'll regret.

"What's his problem?" I hear Sophia ask as I storm around the front of my truck.

"Just you, darlin.'" Chase is still laughing as I slide behind the wheel of my truck and slam the door behind me.

I drop my head against the headrest and take a few deep, calming breaths. I have to get my shit together if she's coming with us.

Chase says something else to her, but I don't make out the words. That's probably for the best anyway, because it would only make me mad.

THE PASSENGER DOOR TO MY TRUCK OPENS AND SOPHIA hops in.

"No!" I hold my hand up before she shuts the door. "You are *not* riding with me."

She rolls her eyes like she thinks I'm a complete idiot. Maybe I am, but that doesn't change the fact that I don't want to spend three hours in the cab of my truck alone with her. This will be pure torture and my brothers know it.

She ignores me and shuts the door. "Chase told me to ride with you. Ash is already sprawled out in the extended cab, pretending to sleep. Garret is driving, and Chase says he needs to stay with the car. Sorry, but you're stuck with me."

She clicks her seat belt into place as if signifying the end of my objection.

I clench my fists around the steering wheel and fight the urge to scream. She can't be here. She's too much of a temptation. A temptation that I cannot resist.

Garret honks the horn, letting me know he's ready to hit the road. He pulls out without checking to see if I'm ready. *Typical.* This is their way of ensuring Sophia rides with me.

I take in a deep breath before I start my truck and follow him out.

I feel Sophia's eyes on me, and when I glance at her, she's frowning at me. "What?"

She pulls one of her legs underneath her and rotates so she's facing me. I try to pretend I don't notice how cute she looks in a pair of black leggings and a bulky oversized sweater. "I'm on to you."

"You're on to me?" I huff. "What's that supposed to mean?"

"You think if you act like an asshole to me, I'll go away."

My jaw tenses at her words because she's not wrong. It's the only way to get her to leave. If she stays, she'll end up hurting me just like all the women in my life.

"It won't work." She adds. Then she turns back to the front and pulls a tablet out of her bag.

A few minutes later, we merge onto the highway. It'll take us about an hour to get to the Ohio-West Virginia line, and another two before we reach the cabins we're renting on the river.

Thankfully, Sophia buries her nose in a book and leaves me alone.

Unfortunately, the silence leaves me with nothing but my thoughts. All I can think about is the way her body felt pinned against that wall while I fucked her. And the smell of her wet panties when I sniffed them. I carried those damn things around with me for two days before I finally stuffed them in a drawer next to my bed.

Flipping on the radio, I tune it to my favorite country music station. An old George Strait song, *The Fireman*, comes on and I crank up the sound. It's one of my favorites. Tapping my fingers to the steering wheel, I belt out the lyrics without holding back.

I don't know if Sophia likes country music and frankly, I don't care.

This is my truck.

A few more songs I like come and go. It isn't until a Kenny Chesney song, *She thinks My Tractor's Sexy*, that she bothers to look up from her book.

"Hey, I know this one." She smiles and hums along while I sing the lyrics.

When we hit the Ohio-West Virginia line, I turn the radio off and glance over at her. She kicked her shoes off and is resting her feet on the dashboard. There's something about the way she looks right now—comfortable and relaxed in my truck—that puts a smile on my face.

"What are you reading?" I ask.

"A book." Her response is dry and clipped.

I glance over at her, and she's still looking at her tablet like I didn't just ask her a question. "No duh. What book is it?"

She huffs and snaps the cover closed on her tablet, then turns to face me. "Why do you care? You've made it clear you don't want me here. So why bother asking me?"

I lift a hand in surrender. "Just trying to make small talk."

"Really?" She sits up straight, and I don't have to look at her to know she's glowering. "Then why did you act like it was such an imposition for me to be here? You made it pretty clear you weren't interested in talking to me."

"Forget I asked." I growl and flip the radio back on.

The music drowns out the silence, but I don't hear any of it. It's just background noise that's doing a piss-poor job at soothing my frustration.

Sophia lets out a loud sigh, then turns the radio off again. "I met a romance author, Alexis Stone, a couple of years ago when I moved to New York City. She's a good friend of my cousin's. I'm reading one of her books."

I quirk a brow. "Romance?"

"Yeah, romance. Something you know absolutely nothing about."

I scoff. "I know plenty about romance."

She laughs. "Sure you do."

"I do!" My voice raises a bit too much in defense.

"Your track record suggests otherwise."

I glance at her before I turn back to the road. She's staring at me with a challenging grin, and I don't fucking like it. Now I have no choice but to prove her wrong.

"What about the Apple Festival? I romanced the hell out of you that night. Almost got you to let me fuck you in a dark alley."

"Fucking me in a dark alley is *not* romantic." She argues.

"I won a prize for you at that ring toss game I played."

She crosses her arms, and it pushes her breasts together. Her cleavage rises above the collar of her sweater and my pants suddenly feel too tight in the crotch.

"You gave my prize away."

"To a little girl whose dad couldn't win. She was going to cry. I saw the way you looked at me after that. You ate that shit up. Because it was romantic."

"No, that was hot. It was hardly romantic."

"Oh, come on. It was too."

She laughs, and suddenly I'm laughing, too. This little debate broke the tension between us, and I finally feel relaxed.

"Sorry, Mac. I'm afraid you're going to have to work harder than that."

I meet her gaze for a moment, then I flip on my turn signal and follow Garret into the parking lot of the restaurant we're eating lunch at before we head out to the cabin. Once I'm parked, I turn to Sophia.

"I hope you're ready, Red. 'Cause I'm going to prove to you just how much I know about romance. Don't move."

I rush around the back of the truck before Sophia can open her own door. If she wants romance, I'll show her romance.

I hold my hand as an offering to help her out. She looks at me like I've lost my mind. "What are you doing?"

"I'm being a gentleman, which most women find romantic."

She rolls her eyes but takes my hand. I ignore the way my body tingles when her hand slides into mine. As soon as her feet hit the ground, we both pull our hands away from each other.

I make sure I'm the first to reach the restaurant door so I can hold it open for her. She shakes her head as she walks past me. Before I step in behind her, I catch Garret, Chase, and Ash watching us from the sidewalk with knowing grins on their faces. Instead of addressing them, I flip them off.

A few minutes later, a hostess shows us to a table. Before Sophia sits, I pull her chair out for her. She glares at me like I'm annoying her. I just grin.

My smile grows when she takes the seat and lets me push her chair in.

When I choose the seat next to her, she looks at me like I'm crazy. I don't care. She challenged me. Now I have to prove her wrong.

"What in the hell happened during that ride?" Ash asks as he sits across from me. "Did you two kiss and make up?"

"I think they did." Chase grins. He sits back in his chair, his eyes darting between us. "Looks like this little weekend retreat is the push they needed."

"There's been no kissing assholes." I pick up my menu and study it. Only my eyes can't seem to focus on anything it says. I'm distracted by the redhead sitting next to me.

"He's trying to prove to me he knows how to be romantic," Sophia says.

"Might help if he stops acting like an asshole," Garret says as he plops into the remaining empty chair.

I wad up a napkin and throw it at him. "I like you better when you don't talk."

The table erupts with laughter. Even Garret's lips turn up in a smile.

Thankfully, the server comes, gives us each a glass of water, then takes our order before anyone else jumps in and picks on me. By the time everyone has ordered, they seem to have forgotten about my bet with Sophia.

"Are you close to your family?" Garret asks Sophia, and we all freeze and stare at him.

She takes a long drink from her water like she's stalling. When she sets it down, she's frowning. "I used to be. I'm close to my cousins in New York, but things have been strained with my parents for a while."

"Is that why you moved here?" Ash asks. "You're from Cincinnati, right?"

"I am, and no. My parents had nothing to do with where I moved to. I wanted to learn from the best, and well, you guys are some of the best."

"Why is your relationship strained with your parents?" Chase asks.

"They don't support my career choice. According to them, I have no business pursuing a *man's* career. They think something is wrong with me because I love cars and racing. And the worst part is my dad's a mechanic. He's the one who taught me to love cars."

"That sucks," Ash says. "What about siblings?"

"I have a brother and a sister. They followed traditional career paths that my parents deemed appropriate. Nora is a teacher, and Roane is a dentist."

I wince and shake my head. "I'd much rather stick my hands under the hood of a car any day over someone's mouth."

"Right?" Sophia chuckles, and my chest tightens. I prefer to hear her laughing over yelling at me.

She adjusts in her chair and her leg brushes against mine. My mouth runs dry as my body recalls how those legs felt wrapped around me.

If I don't put some distance between us this weekend, things are going to get heated really fast.

Something tells me that no matter what I do to avoid Sophia, my brothers are going to push her in my path.

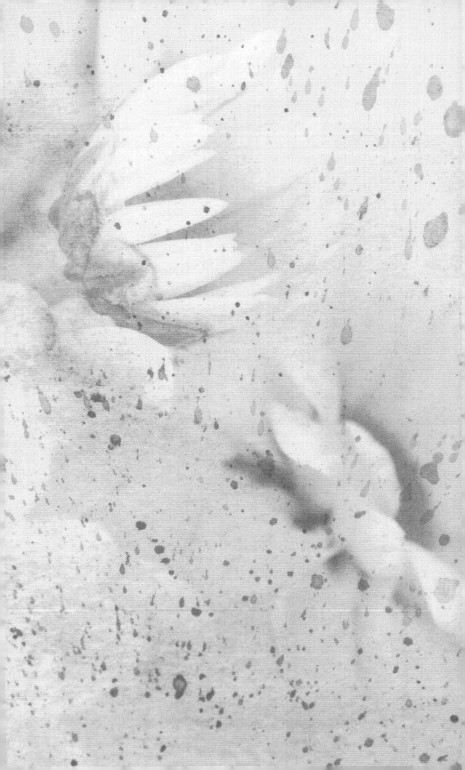

Chapter 14

Small places plus forced romance equals excessive tension.

Sophia

There are two one-room cabins, each with one bed.

There are five of us.

This doesn't quite add up.

I turn to face the men. They're standing in a row like they didn't know this was going to be a problem. I can tell by the looks on Chase's and Ash's faces that they knew this about our sleeping situation before we left Ohio. Garret? I'm not so sure about. Mac, on the other hand, looks genuine in his ignorance.

"So, what are the sleeping arrangements?" I ask.

"Well," Chase gives me one of his flirty grins, "Garret, Ash, and I will share one cabin, and you and Mac can take the other."

I stifle a groan and rub the bridge of my nose. "You're kidding, right?"

"Would you rather shack up with one of us?" Ash grins and waggles his brows.

"No!" Mac's voice thunders, and I can feel the vibrations all the way over here. All three of his brothers laugh.

"That's what we thought." Chase slaps Mac on the back as he heads toward the cabin closest to him. "They're identical inside, so we'll take this one. You two can get *cozy* in that one." He winks at me as he points to the cabin set back in the trees. "Ash, you wanna grab the sleeping bags?"

"Yep, on it." Ash rushes back to the truck to grab the bags. Garret follows to help.

I turn to Mac and take in his worried expression. He stuffs his hands in his pockets and stares at the ground.

"You okay with this?" he asks, unable to look me in the eye.

"Do I have a choice?"

"You could always sleep under the stars." He gives me a sheepish smile.

I know he's only kidding, but it still irritates me. This is his brothers' doing. I'm ninety-nine percent positive Mac didn't know this would happen.

"Or you could," I say with enough venom behind each word that he flinches.

He kicks a rock with his toe and heads toward his truck. "I'll get our bags. Why don't you go check out the cabin?"

He tosses me the key. I catch it one-handed, then stare at the tiny cabin that I have to share with him for the next three days.

It's rustic and cute and *tiny*. It doesn't look like it's much bigger than a standard sized bedroom. But it has a large porch with a swing and a few chairs with great views of the surrounding hills.

Inside is clean and not as cute as the outside. It's bare bones and clearly not meant for multiple guests. There's a tiny kitchenette with a two-burner stove that has seen better days. There's a half sink, about two square feet of counter space next to it, above a double cabinet. The small window above the sink has a direct view of the rolling hills.

There's no table or chairs, but there is a couch, and as promised, one bed. One *twin-sized* bed.

I close my eyes and rub my hands down my face. *You can do this, Soph. It's just three days.*

I open the only door inside the cabin to find a small, clean bathroom. As bathrooms go, it's nice. It has a full-sized shower and tub.

Considering how small everything else is in this place, that surprises me. There's a large mirror over the vanity sink and the thickest, fluffiest white towels I've ever felt. They seem like a luxury and completely out-of-place for this cabin.

When I exit the bathroom, Mac is standing in the middle of the cabin staring at the bed. He looks just as anxious about this arrangement as I feel.

Without looking at me, he says, "You take the bed. I'll sleep on the couch."

"No, I'll take the couch. You have to race tomorrow. You need a good night's sleep."

He shrugs and tosses his bag next to the couch like this discussion is over. "I can sleep anywhere."

He sits down and kicks his shoes off, then stretches his long legs across the couch. It's not long enough and his feet hang off the edge.

"Mac, take the bed. You're too tall for that thing." I insist.

He doesn't address my concern. Instead, he says, "I'm going to take a nap."

I huff, trying to not let my irritation get the best of me. "Why stay out here? Why not stay in Beckley, closer to the track? I'm sure there are some nice hotels that would've been more comfortable for all of us."

"We like the quiet of nature. It's more relaxing, even if I have to sleep on a couch that's too small for me. Besides, the track is only thirty minutes away."

"But it could've been only ten minutes away, and we could've all slept in a bed."

He lifts one eyelid and stares at me. "Are you going to let me take that nap now?"

I hold his stare for a moment before I let out another frustrated huff. "Fine."

I grab my bag, toss it on the bed, and dig out my hiking boots. Once I've changed my shoes and slipped on my jacket, I head for the door. "I'm taking a walk on some of the hiking trails I saw."

I don't wait to see if he's going to say anything. I just leave.

Once outside, I take a deep breath. The afternoon air is warm, fresh, and revitalizing.

There are at least three trailheads close to our cabins. From what I can tell, there are several cabins in this area with access to trails, fishing, rafting, and hunting. I suspect hunters use these cabins more than other guests. They're clearly not meant for romantic getaways.

There's a sign on one trail that says it has views of the river. I've never seen the New River before, but the pictures of it look stunning. I don't know how close the river actually is, but I can hear the rush of water.

The area surrounding us is forested, and the trail I decide to take is hidden within the canopy. It's late enough in the fall that the leaves are looking browner than the initial oranges, yellows, reds, and purples they were a few weeks ago.

Without the direct rays of the sun, a chill surrounds me, so I zip up my jacket. Before long, it'll be too cold for hikes like this.

The sound of rushing water gets louder. I haven't walked that long, so it can't be the river. The trail bends along the side of the hill our cabins are sitting on, then a small rocky creek comes into view. Glancing around, I find the source of the rushing water. There's a small waterfall crashing over a small cave with jagged rocky edges.

After taking a few pictures with my phone, I continue down the trail that runs parallel with the creek. I don't know how long I walk before the trees open up and I'm standing on a rocky ledge that looks out over the New River.

The creek I'd been following empties into the river via a thin waterfall that's more of a trickle down the rocky side than a raging fall.

The view of the river and the bridge is breathtaking. I find a seat on a small rock and watch as rafters guide their rafts toward a small dock near the base of the bridge. There are a few people on the bridge. I squint and hold my hand over my eyes to get a better look. They're base jumping.

Excitement runs through me. I've always been a thrill seeker, and base jumping is something I've always wanted to try. I doubt we have time for me to try it on this trip, but maybe I could come back.

The crunching of leaves catches my attention. When I turn around, Mac is heading toward me.

When he's close enough to hear, I ask, "I thought you were taking a nap?"

"I did. I only need ten or fifteen minutes, and then I'm re-energized. Couldn't stay in the cabin another minute. Guess I took the same path as you."

I turn back toward the river and watch as someone leaps from the bridge. Their body glides through the air with their arms spread wide. Moments later, their chutes open, causing their bodies to jerk and slow.

"Mind if I sit?" he asks.

I shrug. "Yeah, I guess."

I kick my legs out in front of me and lean back on my hands with my face tilted toward the sky. My skin warms from the brightness of the sun.

He sits with his knees bent with his arms resting on them. "Ever done it?"

"Ever done what?"

"Base jumping." He points to the person gliding toward the ground. "You were watching them jump with rapt fascination."

"Oh." I shake my head. "Always wanted to try, though."

"What about whitewater rafting? Ever done that?"

"Nope. This weekend will be a first."

"It's a real rush." He leans back and brushes his shoulder against mine, and my body lights up with anticipation. "You know that feeling you get when you first take off in a car? Your stomach drops and your body feels like it's floating?"

Our eyes meet, and I get that stomach dropping, floating feeling right now. "Yeah," I whisper.

"It's like that, only more drawn out. With every rapid, your body actually flies up from the raft. You have to simultaneously row and hang on for dear life at the same time. It's intense."

"Sounds fun. I can't wait. I love thrill-seeking adventures."

He eyes me for a moment before a playful grin spreads across his face. "And yet you refused to ride the Zipper with me at the Apple Festival."

"The Zipper spins upside down. I hate rides that go upside down."

"But fast and dangerous is okay?"

"Yes. Fast with a *little* danger is a must."

He nudges my shoulder and winks. "Good to know."

Then he lays back on the rock, stretches his body out, and rests his head on his arm. I make the mistake of letting my eyes linger down his tall frame. I can't see his abs because of the jacket he's wearing, but I know they are there.

"When I was little, I loved to look for patterns in the clouds," he says. When I look over at him, he's grinning. "Don't make fun of me, but I still do it. Do you see that one right there?"

He points to a group of clouds right above us, and I lay back on the rock with him so I can see it better. "The one that looks like a mountain?"

He gives me a side eye glare. "That's not a mountain. It's a house."

I chuckle. "How do you see a house? Just because one side has a point doesn't make it a house."

"Sure it does. Look." He scoots closer to me and points at the clouds. "See the straight edges and windows? I can even see an outline for a door with the way the other clouds layer around it."

"Wow, Mac," I deadpan. "I didn't know you had such an imagination."

He drops his hand and it falls next to mine. "Are you making fun of me?"

"Maybe." I smile.

I feel his eyes on me, but I don't look at him. There's something intimate and personal about this moment that I don't want to spoil with lust-filled looks. And I'm pretty sure that's what I'll see if I look at him.

A moment later, he turns his head back to the sky. Then his pinky finger brushes against mine and slowly loops around it until we're linked.

A warmth washes over me, and my breath catches in my chest. It's not much, but it's nice. I might even go as far as to say this is romantic. Unlike the forced romance from earlier today at the restaurant, this feels genuine.

Later that night, when I'm lying alone in bed, I can't sleep because all I can think about is how nice it was to almost hold Mac's hand.

ANOTHER YAWN STRETCHES ITS WAY OUT OF ME, DESPITE HOW hard I fight it. Chase keeps looking at me with a questioning look. I know he's trying to figure out if something *more* happened between Mac and me.

I don't blame him for being suspicious. I'm distracted. I'm supposed to be learning from him and Ash, not daydreaming about Mac. Maybe if I slept better last night, I would be able to focus more.

But I slept like shit. If you can even call what I did sleeping. I tossed and turned with my mind on a constant loop, replaying the way Mac made me feel yesterday.

He can go from being Mr. Asshole to being Mr. Nice Guy in

sixty seconds flat. But after the ride here, he's mostly been nice. I like nice. Nice excites those butterflies in my belly that make me feel light and tingly inside. I like light and tingly.

But Chase doesn't need to know any of that. We have more important things to focus on than the tension linking Mac and me together.

We have a race to monitor. Mac's behind the wheel of a race-car, going close to two hundred miles per hour. Our job is to keep him safe, call out other drivers' positions, and give him a heads up on any obstacles that might pop up.

"Please tell me Mac isn't as tired as you?" Chase finally asks after my thousandth yawn.

I shake my head. "As far as I know, he slept fine. On the couch. Alone."

Chase smirks with his hand still holding the microphone away from his mouth. His headset is linked to Mac's, so they can communicate throughout the race. "Good to know. I want him to keep his first-place position. He needs this win."

I smile as Mac flies past us, completing another lap. "It's looking good. He's a full lap ahead of the second-place car."

But my smile is wiped away by the sound of a loud crash. We rush to the fence to get a better look.

Another driver hits the wall just after the turn Mac is about to make. A second car slams into the first, causing them both to spin out-of-control. Chase's focus instantly shifts to the track and guiding Mac through it without incident. Thankfully, both wrecked cars can still function and pull off the track, so no other cars join them.

Just when it looks like Mac is in the clear, his tire blows. Blowing a tire at any speed is hard to control, but when you're racing, it's one of the scariest things that can happen.

"Shit, Mac!" Chase yells into the headset. "Talk to me."

I can tell from the look on Chase's face that Mac is responding.

A moment later, he turns to Ash. "He hit some debris. He's coming in. Get a wheel ready."

Ash jumps into action, grabbing one of the many spare wheels ready to replace a damaged one. His speed and agility under this stressful moment is impressive. One wrong move could cause a delay that results in Mac losing the race.

"Here." Chase shoves a water bottle at me. "Take him some water."

Seconds later, Mac pulls up next to us. Ash is around his car and working on his tire almost before he stops. I hop over the low fencing with the water bottle and am amazed that Ash already has the blown tire off. *Damn, he's fast.*

I shove the water bottle at Mac, holding the straw so he can easily reach it. He lifts his visor and takes a long sip. I meet his heated gaze and my insides melt. His expression is intense, and I know his focus is on the race, but the want and need sparking between us is undeniable.

Mac behind the wheel of a racecar is hot, and it's doing funny things to my lady parts.

Ash tightens the last lug nut in record time. Without a word, Mac closes his visor and hits the gas. He's gone before Ash and I can even take a single step back.

Okay, that's even hotter.

He's back on the track with plenty of time to spare. He's still at least a quarter of a lap ahead of the second-place car.

"Alright, man. You've got this. Only three more laps to go," Chase says as Mac takes the car back to top speed. "Everything good?"

They exchange a few more words that I don't hear. I'm too focused on the race. He's leading, but just barely. One wrong move and the car behind him could take the lead.

But Mac looks good out there.

He looks in complete control.

He looks better than he has since before the accident.

Two more laps to go. This is always when I get tense watching races. Accidents are always hard to watch, but it's those last minutes, those last few laps, that hit me the hardest. Especially when someone I care about is in the lead.

The last turn approaches and Mac speeds up. He takes it on the inside and glides around like his car has wings. Moments later, he crosses the finish line, and the crowd erupts in cheers.

Chase pulls me in for a hug, then Ash rushes in and wraps his arms around both of us.

Mac takes his victory loop before he pulls off and stops next to us. Every member of our pit crew, and a few from others, surround his car to congratulate him. The smile on his face as he accepts pats on the back and cheers as he pushes his way through the crowd is so big and bright. I want to make him smile like that every day.

Chase and Ash reach him before me, both pulling him in for a hug.

"Dude, you looked great out there," Ash says. "We're already getting messages from big name sponsors."

Ash holds his phone up to show Mac something that makes him smile more. Mac nods and pats Ash's shoulder before his eyes lock on mine.

He ignores the crowd and marches right to me. "Congra—"

He cuts me off when he sweeps me into his arms and presses his lips to mine. His lips are soft yet firm as they move over mine in a closed mouth kiss. It's tender and sweet and ends way too fast.

He sets me back down on my feet and cups my cheek. "I liked knowing you were here."

"You did?" My voice croaks.

He nods, then brushes a stray strand of hair behind my ear. "All I could think about those last few laps was getting back here as fast as possible so I could kiss you."

"It was the water bottle, wasn't it?" I tease, recalling the intense look we shared during his last pit stop.

His smile fades slightly as he shakes his head. "No, it's you."

Then he slides his hand around my neck and pulls me in for another kiss.

I can't help but to melt into him because this kiss feels so good. Maybe a little *too* good. I should still be mad at him for how he's treated me. But I'm not. I kiss him back and try to ignore the voice in my head telling me that this means nothing. This is just part of his plan to prove to me he knows how to romance a woman.

Because this kiss is the very definition of romantic.

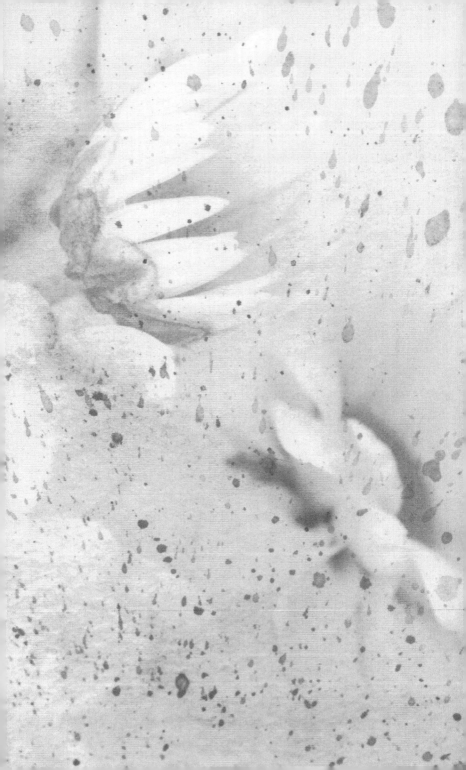

Chapter 15

Sleep is not on the agenda.

Mac

My brothers and Sophia head back to the cabins to prepare a celebration party while I'm stuck at the track, surrounded by reporters, for the past few hours. They pepper me with questions about the future of my racing career the entire time.

This wasn't a big race, but it still gets decent coverage. Plus, it's the best I've driven in two years.

It's the best I've felt behind the wheel of a car in that long too.

I didn't expect sponsors and top performing teams to be watching me though. Two years is a long time to be slogging along without advancing in the ARCA series.

My accident didn't take me out of the ARCA series. I did. Smaller races, like the one today, make me feel safer.

But today, I didn't struggle with anxiety. My mind was too preoccupied with thoughts of Sophia and her plump, luscious lips.

I wanted to kiss her so badly yesterday when I found her sitting on that rocky cliff looking out over the river. And it was pure torture sleeping on that couch when she was so close. All I thought about all night was how much I wanted to touch her.

So I drove my best race and won so I could kiss her.

Dumb? Maybe. But I don't give a shit.

Now I'm in my truck, heading back to the cabins, wishing there wasn't a party so I can have the night alone with Sophia. That's a dangerous thought.

It's not a matter of trust anymore. At least, I don't think it is. I've never met a woman who's affected me like she has, and I don't know what to do with these feelings. Being an asshole to her was easier.

Before I can ruminate on my feelings for too long, my phone rings. I smile when I see the name.

"Hey, Warren," I say after I accept the call. My brother rarely calls.

"Hey, Champ. Great race today." His voice sounds cheerful through my truck's speakers, which is unusual for our calls lately.

"You already heard?"

"Nah, man. I watched it."

"You watched the race? Didn't realize they would broadcast that far away."

"I get access to all the races here. Benefit of working in racecar central." He pauses, and I sense it's not because he's giving me a chance to speak, but because he's choosing his next words carefully. Warren does that. He's never one to rush his thoughts. "You looked good out there. Like you found your groove again."

I smile at his compliment. "It felt good too."

"Does that pretty redhead I saw you kissing have anything to do with it?"

My smile drops. "What?"

"Yeah." He chuckles. "Imagine my surprise to find out on TV that my baby brother has a girlfriend."

"She's not my girlfriend." I growl.

"You sure as hell kissed her like she's your girlfriend."

"Well, she's not." I grind out. I have no idea why I'm arguing this point so vehemently, but I can't stop myself.

"Okay. Okay. I didn't call to give you shit. I wanted to congratulate you."

I let out a deep sigh as I take the last turn back to the cabins. "Yeah, thanks. It's good to hear from you. Give any more thought to what I asked you? We keep getting more requests for custom racecars. The team could really use you."

He's silent for a moment before he answers me. "I have. I'm ... I'm considering it."

"Seriously?" We've been trying to convince Warren to move back home for years, and this is the first time he's hinted that it's a possibility. "Man, that would be awesome if you did."

"Yeah, well. Don't say anything just yet. I haven't made up my mind. But I think I need a change."

There's a hint of sadness in his voice that I don't like. Warren never sounds sad. Angry or aloof, but never sad. "Everything okay?"

"Of course. Just getting bored. You know how I am."

"Yeah, I suppose I do." Which is true to a degree. But out of all my brothers, Warren is the most secretive. He never tells any of us what's going on in his personal life. Hell, he rarely updates us on his career. We have to call and harass him if we want details.

My truck crests the last hill before our cabins come into view, and I slam on my breaks. "Whoa."

"What's wrong?" Warren asks.

"Umm." I clear my throat. "Just arrived back at the cabins and there are a lot of cars here."

Warren chuckles. "It's a party, numbnuts. Go celebrate your win."

I glance around and my eyes narrow in on Liam's truck. A small smile spreads across my face. "You knew about this?"

"I might have spoken to Liam before I called you." I can hear the humor in his words. "He's proud of you. Let him do this for you."

"*Liam* is responsible for the party?" I ask as I pull my truck up next to my cabin and throw it into park.

"The others helped, but it was Liam's idea. They've been planning it for weeks."

I shake my head and stare at the group of people huddled around the bonfire. Liam can be hard on me and act like he's my dad, but he's also the one that cheers me on the most.

"But what if I lost?"

"But you didn't. Now go enjoy yourself and be nice to your girl. I hear she's great."

I roll my eyes even though he can't see me. "Oh, and I supposed you talked to Liam about her too?"

"You know I did. Why do you think I called him first? I needed the scoop."

"Bye, asshole," I say with every intention of it being an insult, but I can't stop smiling.

He must hear the lack of conviction in my words because he laughs. "Talk to you soon."

We hang up and I stare at my phone for a moment before I get out. I hope what he said about moving back home is true because I miss my older brother. He's the only one that's not here, and it doesn't feel right with him being gone.

I catch movement out of the corner of my eye and look to the side. Liam and Christian are approaching. As soon as I hop out of my truck, Liam pulls me into a hug.

"You did it, bro. I knew you'd win."

"Thanks." I pat his back before he releases me. "What are you doing here?"

I glance over Liam's shoulder and wave at Christian. I'd hug him too, but he's not much of a hugger.

"You didn't think we'd miss this, did you? We drove up early this morning so we could watch the race."

My smile grows so wide it hurts. "You guys were here?"

"Of course." Liam squeezes my shoulder and nods toward my cabin. "Now go clean up. You smell like shit."

I shove him off me and walk backward toward the cabin. "You would too if you spent your day sitting in an oven on wheels."

I rush inside, smiling at Sophia's clothes tossed on the twin-sized bed. Grabbing a clean change of clothing, I quickly shower and rush back outside to join the party.

The bonfire is blazing. There are burgers, hot dogs, chips, and several kegs. I make myself a plate and grab a beer. Each of my brothers comes up to me and congratulates me again. As much as I love my family, they're the last people on my mind.

There's only one person I want to see right now. And she's standing on the other side of the bonfire with her cup raised to me and a smile on her face. The blazing fire lights up her hair, making it even more red than it already is. She's stunning.

A little more of the hard shell I've built around my heart cracks. Suddenly, all I can think about is her naked and sprawled out on that tiny bed for me to play with.

Fuck celebrating. Who needs to celebrate with family when there's a beautiful woman with her eyes on me?

Sophia avoids me the entire evening. I drink beers with my brothers, shoot the shit with a few racing buddies that stopped by for a while, and stare at Sophia, wishing she were by my side.

But every time I get close to her, she moves before I reach her. It's like we're playing a game of cat and mouse, only I don't want to play.

It's driving me fucking mad.

I know she wants me just as much as I want her. She's been staring at me just as much as I'm staring at her. The look of longing and desire is evident in every stolen glance.

What I don't know is why she's avoiding me. And now, I don't see her at all. Glancing over my shoulder, the light is on in our cabin. *Did she sneak off when I wasn't looking?*

The party is dying down. The only people still here are my brothers. Garret's already turned in for the night. Liam and Christian put up tents on the other side of Garret's cabin. They even brought an extra one that Ash is going to sleep in.

When no one is looking, I slip away to our cabin. I step through the front door and lock it behind me. The table lamp is on by the bed, but I don't see Sophia. Then the bathroom door opens, and her appearance sucks all the air out of my lungs.

"Fuuuuck." I draw the word out with a low exhale.

My eyes rake down her nearly naked body. Her red hair is down and swept to the side over one shoulder, revealing the soft pale skin of her neck. She's wearing a thin nightshirt—if you can even call it that. It's satin and lace with thin straps that I'm dying to snap in two. The pale pink color combined with the sheerness of fabric hides nothing.

It's short enough that I can see the soft curves of her stomach, and thin enough that I can see the dark outline of her taut nipples.

My body reacts accordingly.

My dick strains against my jeans. Every nerve ending in my body is tingling with desire. My hands are itching to touch her. And my mouth is watering to lick and taste every inch of her beautiful pale body.

I swallow, and it feels like rocks are rolling down my throat.

"You've been avoiding me," I finally manage, but the words come out rough and gravelly.

"Your brothers drove a long way to be with you today. I didn't want to get in the way."

In slow, deliberate steps, I walk toward her. Once I'm standing right next to her, I twirl a strand of her silky hair between my fingers. "You're not in the way. You're stunning."

"Mac," she whispers, and her eyes fall closed. I hear every bit of her hesitation in the way she says my name.

I can't blame her. My issues have driven a wedge between us.

I've been an asshole to her in the worst possible way on multiple occasions.

I've sent her mixed signals.

I told her she was mine, then ran after we had sex. I wouldn't blame her if she never forgave me for that one.

But nothing I've done has changed how I feel. Now it's time to man up.

I cup my hands around her cheeks and lift her face to mine. Worry crosses over her pale blue eyes and her body tenses. I sense her internal struggle to pull away—to protect herself from me.

I brush my lips across hers and relish at how her body trembles. "I want you, and I'm done fighting it."

"Mac." She clenches her hands into my jacket and tugs me closer. "Don't hurt me."

"Hurting you is the last thing I want to do." I hold my gaze on hers, hoping she sees the sincerity in my words. "But I have issues. I won't always say or do the right thing."

She slides her hands up my back and hooks them around my shoulders. "We all have issues. That's life."

Then she presses her lips to mine.

Her lips are soft and tentative, almost like she's afraid to take this next step. I can't blame her. Not with how I've acted.

I want to take the kiss deeper—taste her mouth with my tongue —but I also don't want to push her too fast. Then she parts her lips and flicks her tongue across my bottom lip.

I snap.

I dive into her, thrusting my tongue into her mouth like a wild man. She tastes like peppermint toothpaste and smells like a divine goddess. Hints of strawberries, vanilla, and something I can't find the right words to describe cloud my mind. It's so uniquely feminine and intoxicating. I could smell her all day and never tire of the sensations it arouses in me.

Lifting her into my arms, I flip her around. We tumble onto the bed in a mess of hands and tongues and lips and groans. She's as hungry for me as I am for her.

She reaches for the zipper on my jacket at the same time I reach for the hem of her nightshirt.

"Way too many clothes," she moans. Her hands fumble to unzip my jacket, and I chuckle.

"I'll gladly help you with that." I push off the bed and instantly miss her heat.

She tracks my every move as I strip myself of my jacket and then my shirt. Her eyes fill with heat when she sees my bare chest. I can't help but flex my pecs under her intense gaze.

I reach for the button of my jeans and her eyes flick to mine. I see a hint of hesitation, so I pause.

"Is this okay?"

She nods and then strips her nightshirt off and tosses it aside. The groan that escapes me is otherworldly. Her pale, freckled skin reddens under my gaze. Her curves are soft and her breasts are full. This is the first time I've really been able to appreciate just how perfect her breasts are. My mouth waters in anticipation of sucking on her pert nipples and tasting her sweet skin.

"Fuck, Red. Do you have any idea how beautiful you are?"

She sucks her bottom lip between her teeth with a seductive gleam in her eyes. She looks like a fucking tease, and it makes me even harder. "Why don't you show me?"

Tossing my head back, I growl like the savage beast she's turning me into. I shuck my jeans and boxer briefs before rushing to my bag to grab the box of condoms from my travel bag.

When I return to the bed, she's got her arms above her head with her body stretched out like an offering. I toss the box of condoms next to her and her eyes flicker to it.

"An entire box?" She quirks a brow.

"You didn't think you were actually sleeping tonight, did you?" I grab her legs and tug her to the edge of the bed. Her chest rises and her skin flushes a deep crimson that makes my dick even harder. "But first, I need to taste you."

I rip her panties from her body and drop to my knees by the bed. She spreads her legs and rests her feet on my shoulders without instruction. She knows what I want, and she's here for it.

When I look up at her, our eyes lock. My lip turns up in a smirk as I lean closer to her. But I don't put my mouth on her yet. Instead, I run my finger down her slit and push it inside her. She whimpers and her eyes fall closed.

"Eyes on me," I snap. Her eyes fly open, and she looks surprised by the harshness of my demand. "Close them and I stop."

She pushes up on her elbows and looks down at me. "Is this better?"

My lips turn up in a smirk as I shove my finger back inside her so hard, she flinches. I pump it in her a few times before I pull it out and bring it to my mouth. I suck her wetness off my finger and let out a deep, guttural groan. "Fuck, you taste just as sweet as you smell."

I wrap my arms around her thighs and dig my fingers into her skin. Her eyes flare with excitement when I lean in and lick her from her entrance to her clit. Her body shudders when I suck her clit between my lips and flick it with my tongue.

"You like that, baby?" I ask as I do it again.

"Yes," she says as her head drops back.

I smack her thigh and pull back. She jerks her head up and meets my narrowed gaze.

She glares at me like she's angry I spanked her. "Why did you do that?"

"Do you want my tongue on you?"

"Yes."

"Eyes. On. Me." I growl.

Her breathing increases and her eyes shift from anger to something a little wild and needy. Something very close to how I feel inside.

Just like the first time I fucked her, I feel a storm raging inside me. It twists round and round like a violent wind tunnel waiting to break free. I want to unleash it. I want to let this storm consume us.

Being this close to her—smelling her, tasting her—has the beast inside me roaring for more. He's demanding that I take everything she's willing to give without apology.

I suppress those wild urges because this isn't about speed or complete dominance. I want to own her pleasure and drag every last drop of it out of her in agonizingly slow strokes of my tongue and cock until the only name she remembers is mine.

I force myself to go slowly as I lick her again. I rotate between plunging my tongue inside her to sucking her clit between my lips. Her tight little nub pulses in my mouth and I know she's close every time my tongue flicks it.

"Mac," she whispers as she struggles to keep her eyes open.

"Tell me what you want, baby."

"I want to come."

"Do you want to come on my tongue or my cock?"

"Both."

"Grab a condom," I demand.

Then I smile when she does what I say and rips open the box. I suck on her again. This time I don't calm the storm inside me. I let it loose and lap at her like a squall thrashing in the night.

She fumbles with the roll of condoms and falls back on the bed as her orgasm slams into her like a tidal wave.

It's so beautiful to watch her come. I can't even bring myself to reprimand her for breaking eye contact. All I can do is watch and marvel at her beauty.

I stand, grab the condoms from her, and stroke my aching cock. Her eyes fly open and meet mine. She's breathing hard. Her eyes are heavy and her lips are slightly parted. It makes me want to stick my tongue in her mouth and devour her.

Once the condom is secure, I climb over her and loop my arms under her shoulders. Dragging her up the bed, I rest her head on the pillow, and then part her legs with mine.

"Think you can handle me?"

Her brows furrow, and she spreads her hands over my chest. "I've had you before."

"I'm not talking about my dick inside you," I say as I slowly nudge my tip past her entrance. Her breath hitches and I swear my dick gets harder. "I'm talking about *me*. The man. I'm jealous and possessive. I don't trust easily, especially women, and I'll push you away more than I let you close."

"Oh, that." She smiles. She fucking smiles up at me like she just won a prize, which I know is bullshit. I am no prize to be happy about. She presses her lips to mine and wiggles her hips, taking a little more of me inside her. "I know who you are, Mac. And I'm still here. I can handle you."

I push the rest of the way inside her and we both groan. "Fuck, you're so tight."

"Mac." She runs her hands around my neck and threads her fingers into my hair. When her nails dig into my scalp, I thrust harder inside her.

Her lithe body moves with mine in fast, rhythmic thrusts. Even with my release building quicker than I want, I can't bring myself to slow down. Thank fuck she's close too. Between her soft moans and her body tightening around me, I'm about to go off like a rocket.

"Come, baby." My chest rumbles from the command. "Right. The Fuck. Now."

"Oh God. Mac!" she cries as her orgasm washes over her. She squeezes around me like a vise, and I come tumbling after her.

But I don't stop. My thrusts increase and become more erratic. She feels too good to stop now. I want to drag this out as long as possible. Because this feels so good. So right. Almost too right, and that scares me. Because for the first time in my life, I feel like I'm with the one woman I'm meant to be with.

My movements slow and I collapse on top of her. She wraps her arms and legs tight around me like she's afraid I'm going to bolt like I did last time. Truth be told, the thought has crossed my mind.

"Mac," she whispers. I lift my head and meet her gaze. She brushes her hand through my hair, and I lean into the touch. Then she presses her hand to my chest, right over my heart, and it beats faster. "You've got a good heart. I see it clearly through all your possessive and jealous tendencies. You're so much more than you give yourself credit for."

Her words send an unfamiliar wave of emotion through me. I want to both hold her closer and run at the same time.

Instead, I kiss her. Because when I kiss her, all my worries fade into the background.

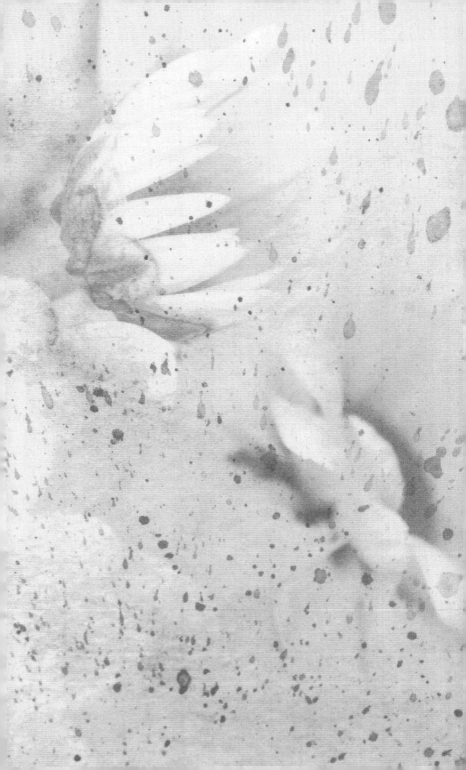

Chapter 16

Up a river with a paddle and no way to turn around.

Sophia

I've always considered myself adventurous, but this might be more than I bargained for. And not for the excitement of rafting down a river, but because of the men surrounding me.

Liam and Christian stayed another day to go rafting with us, which means we're all piled into one raft with a guide.

I'm sandwiched between Mac and Ash. Garret is behind Mac while Christian, Chase, Liam, and the guide are in the row next to us. Every time we hit a rough rapid, Mac grabs onto my arm like I'm going to fly out of the raft and crack my head open on a rock. I guess that's a possibility, which is why I wish he'd stop doing it. It's making me tense.

Besides, with seven men—all experienced rafters—surrounding me, it's not like I'm contributing a lot to this excursion. It's killing the thrill and excitement.

We opted to raft the lower river, which experiences class IV and higher rapids. It's meant for intermediate rafters, but since I'm the only one on our raft that's never been before, our guide said we'd be fine.

Mac seemed fine with that before we left, but once we hit the rapids, he went all growly bear, overly protective of me. I'm more pissed than surprised by his behavior.

Some of these rapids have been intense, but nothing I can't handle. I drive racecars for crying out loud. I can manage whitewater rafting with seven experienced rafters by my side.

There are two other groups with us on this trip. One raft is a group of couples. Some of whom have done this before and some who are first timers like me. After sitting through the quick safety training with them, I was confident we'd all be fine.

The other raft is a group of men who apparently travel the world searching for thrilling adventures.

Our guide calls out that we're approaching some falls. Then he instructs us where to guide the raft. Mac leans forward and yells in my ear. "We've got this if you want to hold on."

I glance over my shoulder and glare at him. "Not on your life."

"Hold on!" His voice rolls through my body like thunder. I may be pissed at how he's acting, but it makes me laugh all the same.

"I'll be fine." I give him an exaggerated eye roll. "Even if I fall out of the raft, I'm in a wetsuit and life jacket. Plus, I'm a strong swimmer."

"Can't swim if you crack your skull open," he grumbles.

I narrow my eyes on him before I turn back around to follow every one of our guide's instructions. Maneuvering the raft through the rapids and falls is challenging. It requires an insane amount of upper and lower body strength, but I'm strong enough to manage it.

Mac is being ridiculous. And kind of cute. He's infuriating, but I like that he cares enough to worry about my safety.

We make it through the waterfall without incident. Mac had to focus on using his paddle to help get us through it without tipping, so he couldn't hold on to me. It's the most fun I've had since we left this morning.

The river calms and we get a reprieve. I turn back to Mac and smile. "Did you see that? I can do this. Will you stop trying to protect me now?"

He leans forward, slips his hand around my neck, and kisses me. "I'll try. But no promises."

Chase says something I can't make out, but apparently the others hear him because they all laugh. Even Garret and Christian. They rarely ever laugh. But Mac growls and glares at his brothers. I can only assume it's a jab at his show of affection.

We continue down the river, safely making it through several class IV rapids and even one our guide says is most likely a class V. Mac didn't grab for me once. I could tell he wanted to, but he resisted. I'm finally enjoying this excursion now that he's let up.

About an hour into the trip, and just when I thought my arms couldn't take another minute of this, the guide directs us to the shore where he says we can relax and do some swimming.

The river is calm, and we're surrounded by several large, flat rocks.

Chase lets out a loud whoop as he jumps up behind Mac. "Race you up the rock."

He runs past us, but Mac doesn't take the bait. Instead, Mac sits next to me by a large tree.

"You don't have to stay with me. Go swimming with your brothers."

"Maybe in a minute." He winks at me with a content smile on his face. "You having fun?"

"Now that you've let up, yes. It's intense but I love it."

"Sorry. I guess you can add overly protective to the list of my annoying qualities."

I laugh at his honesty. "I can handle it as long as you don't actually try to stop me from doing the things I love. Are you going to be able to handle my upcoming race?"

His eyes snap to mine. "You have a race coming up?"

I nod. "In two weeks. It's close to Cincinnati. My last one of the season."

He narrows his eyes. He doesn't look angry. It's more like he's just now realizing that I'm a racecar driver just like him. "Have you been practicing? You know, getting track time?"

I pick at the dead grass next to my leg, tossing the blades in front of us. "Yeah. But I can only afford two or three sessions a week. I usually go after work."

"What about a crew?"

"I pieced a team together over the years. They're all great guys and help me out part-time. It helps that my crew chief is a family friend. He can't be with me all the time when I practice, but he never misses a race."

"Then who helps you when you practice?"

"I always find locals to help. It's not ideal, but it works."

Mac stares at the calm river in front of us. His contemplative expression makes me chuckle. "What are you thinking about?"

He shrugs. "That I'm an ass."

This makes me laugh even harder. "You're just now figuring that out?"

He cuts me a glare. "I'm serious. You've been here for what? A little over a month now? We could have been helping you."

"Your brothers have been helping me." I suck my bottom lip between my teeth as I brace myself for his reaction. "In addition to working with me at the shop, Chase and Ash have come to the tracks with me a few times."

Mac's eyes widen. "For real?"

"Yeah." I wrinkle my nose. "You're not mad, are you?"

"Why would I be mad? Wait," he holds his hand up as if to stop me from replying, "I probably would have been mad before. Now I just feel like a bigger asshole."

I nudge his shoulder. "Don't worry about it. After a lifetime of trying to fit into a man's sport, I'm used to it."

His frown deepens. "But it shouldn't be that way. I'm sorry if I—"

"Don't." I cut him off. "You didn't do anything to make me feel like I shouldn't be behind the wheel of a car. You just didn't want me here."

His smile returns. "True. But I've changed my mind about that." He leans over and gives me a chaste kiss. "You're growing on me."

"Good." I cup his cheeks and he shivers from the chill of my icy hands, but he doesn't pull away. "You're growing on me too."

I press my lips to his for a soft, sensual kiss that is so unlike anything we've shared so far. Mac's kisses are typically demanding and harsh. Everything about this man is typically intense and maybe even a little overbearing. But not this time.

He's letting me see a softer side of him. A side I suspect he hides from everyone, even his family. And it's at this moment that I realize I'm in serious risk of falling hard for this man.

One hot, fun weekend together isn't enough. There's something much more meaningful than a fun time in the sack happening between us. I feel it deep in my bones. But his track record suggests he'll push me away sooner rather than later. Hell, he even warned me that he'd make that mistake again.

I didn't move to Beaver to risk my heart. I'm here to become a better racecar driver, and to learn from one of the best teams around.

I'd do well to remember that.

WHILE MAC AND HIS BROTHERS HELP OUR GUIDE PULL THE raft out of the river and load it on the trailer, I lean against a tree and watch. We ended the trip at the base of the New River Gorge Bridge. It's foggy close to the water, and the sky isn't as clear as it was two days ago when I walked to the ridge above.

Mac was relaxed for the rest of the trip down the river. He stopped acting like I couldn't handle myself and just enjoyed the ride. I like this carefree, fun version of him. Mostly because it means he's letting down his walls and being vulnerable with me.

A vulnerable Mac is even more dangerous for my heart, but I can't bring myself to care about that right now.

"You guys looked good out there. Do you raft this river a lot?" a male voice asks from behind me. I turn to see one of the men from the group of thrill seekers standing just behind the tree I'm leaning on.

"This was my first time, but my friends come here every year." I point to Mac and his brothers.

"It's our first time, too. Which is funny considering two of my friends grew up in West Virginia. Rafted all over the world but not in their own backyard."

I smile. "Isn't that how it usually goes?"

He shrugs, his eyes trained on the bridge. "That's what they say."

"What's the best river you've rafted?"

A slow smile spreads across his face. "The Zambezi, in Africa. Hands down, the best and most beautiful. I also love The Futaleufú in Chile."

"Wow. Sounds like you travel a lot."

"Yeah, my wife hates it, but she loves me, so she doesn't complain too much."

"She doesn't travel with you?"

"Sometimes." He gets a wistful look in his eyes as he watches someone base jump off the top of the bridge. "But it's hard with kids. Especially international travel. I don't travel nearly as much as I used to."

"Yeah, I worry about that too sometimes," I say without thinking. I never talk to others about my hopes and fears about having a family someday. I've always wanted to get married and have kids at some point, but I don't know how that will work with my dreams of racing. I may have missed my opportunity to make it to the Sprint Cup, but that doesn't mean I can't still make a career out of racing in other, less prestigious divisions.

"Do you travel a lot too?" He looks at me for the first time since stopping to talk to me.

I nod. "But not for adventurous activities like this. I'm a racecar driver."

"No shit!" He looks surprised, yet pleased, at my confession. "You any good?"

I shrug. "I do okay. I won my last race. Beat that guy right over there, and he qualified for the Sprint Cup a few years ago." I point at Mac, who looks in my direction at that exact moment. A deep furrow replaces his relaxed expression.

The guy chuckles as Mac strides in our direction. He doesn't look happy, but he also doesn't look like he's going to go all caveman on me again either.

When he reaches us, he leans in and gives me a kiss on the cheek. "Who's your friend?"

I smile at Mac. He's trying to keep his jealousy in check, but I still sense it. "I don't actually know his name." I glance over at the man I've been talking to.

"Oh yeah." He holds his hand out to Mac. "I'm Rob."

Mac takes his hand, and I'm pleased to see it's a civil handshake. "I'm Mac. Sophia's boyfriend."

My eyes snap to his in surprise. He winks with a grin when our eyes meet.

"It's nice to meet you. She was just telling me about how you both race cars. I bet that's quite the rush."

Mac nods. "Nothing quite like handling a car at two hundred miles per hour. But adventures like this are a close second."

"Hey, Rob!" One of his friends calls for him. "You ready?"

He nods before he smiles at us. "Well, it was nice chatting. Enjoy the rest of your day."

He waves before he rushes off toward his friends. I look up at Mac and smile. "Boyfriend?"

He shrugs before he takes a step closer to me. "What would you call me?"

I step out from against the tree and move backwards. My smile grows as I tease him. "My friend."

"Friend?" He quirks a brow.

"Sure." I hold my smile and struggle not to laugh as I say this next part. "It's not like we've talked about being more. Just because we had one night of hot sex doesn't mean we're exclusive."

His nostrils flare, and he stalks toward me. My laughter breaks free at the intensity in his eyes. This only makes him growl like the wild beast he can sometimes be.

I take off at a sprint into the trees. I don't make it far before I hear his feet behind me. He's gaining on me quickly. Not only are his legs longer, but I'm a weak runner. When he catches up to me, he spins me around and pins me against a large tree.

"You enjoy teasing me, Red?" His voice is low and gravelly in my ear. My breath catches in my chest when his hand cups me between my legs. We ditched the wetsuits first thing, and I'm left in nothing but the thin pair of leggings I wore underneath. He might as well be cupping me bare.

"Yes," I breathe.

He grumbles as he lifts his hand to the waistband of my leggings and shoves it inside. His fingers press between my legs and find my entrance. He teases me for just a moment before he shoves two fingers inside me.

"You're already wet for me, Red. Does that mean you already know you're *mine*?"

I let out a shaky breath. "Am I?"

"Yes," he says. That one word holds so much possessiveness and conviction I flinch. "If last night wasn't clear to you, then let me show you again."

He removes his hand from my pants, twirls me around, and pushes my chest into the tree. Then he presses his hard cock into my ass. "You feel that? That belongs to you, and only you. Just like this," he slips his hand between my legs again to touch me, "belongs to me."

"Yes." I can barely breathe. The excitement in me is building fast, making it next to impossible to think straight.

"Yes, what?" He commands as he jerks my leggings and panties down to my knees. Before I can register what he's doing, I hear the crumble of a condom wrapper.

"Mac! What are you doing?"

"I'm reminding you that you're mine. Apparently, you forgot since this morning."

Before I take my next breath, he digs his hands into my hips and thrust inside me. He pulls out almost as quickly as he entered, before slamming back in.

"Fuck, baby," he groans like he's in pain. "This is yours. Only yours. Do you understand?"

"Yes," I moan as he hits that spot deep inside me that makes my legs tremble. He's going to make me come within earshot of everyone on this excursion with us. I know if I looked around this tree, I could see them by the river. It's not like we're in a secluded spot.

His thrusts increase, pushing me closer to the edge. "Tell me you're mine," he demands.

"I'm yours!" I yell, a little too loudly. "Mac, I am *so yours*."

"And we're exclusive. Let me hear you say it."

He slams inside me hard, and I gasp. "Yes. We're exclusive."

He roughly cups his hand around my jaw and turns my head to face him. He kisses me. It's so sensual and loving and in complete contrast to how he's fucking me. "Fuck, Red. You're going to be my undoing."

"Mac!" I cry against his lips. "I'm coming."

He pumps harder as I come around him. "Give it to me, baby. Give it *all* to me."

I come hard. My body slumps against the tree, and I feel like I'm falling. His arm wraps around my waist as he continues to pump inside me, chasing his own release. "I've got you, baby."

His groans join mine as our climaxes mingle, taking us both to new levels of pleasure.

When our bodies finally still, we collapse to the ground. He falls to his back, holding me against his chest.

"Fuck, Red. That was ..." He gasps for air, and his chest rises and falls quickly beneath me. "I can't find the words."

I take a deep breath as I try to calm my racing heart. "Unexpected."

A rough and husky chuckle escapes him, and my insides tingle. "Yeah. It was definitely unexpected."

Now that I'm coming down from the high he just sent me on, my thoughts fixate on what we said. What he demanded from me as he fucked me. I need to know if he meant it. "Did you mean everything that you said, or was that just sex talk?"

He tightens his arms around me and kisses the top of my head. "I meant every word. Tell me you did too."

I struggle to roll over on top of him. My leggings are still dropped around my knees, making it hard to move. But I manage. Once I'm facing him, I cup his face. "I meant it. It looks like you've got yourself a girlfriend."

A sly smile covers his face. "Good."

Then he kisses me like it's the last time he's ever going to get the chance.

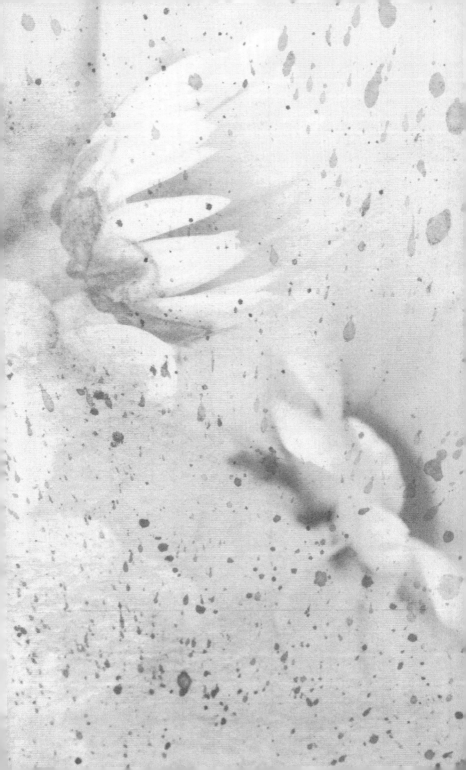

Chapter 17

Costumes, beer, and forks in the road.

Mac

Why did I let Sophia talk me into this? I look like an idiot.

It's Halloween, and it's tradition in Beaver that we dress up and party at The Forks. The Forks being a literal fork in the road in the middle of nowhere. The hills of southern Ohio are littered with unnamed dirt roads. Long before my time, this particular dirt road became a local hangout.

One unnamed and hardly traveled dirt road meets with another in the middle of a forested area on a nearby hill. Hence, The Forks. In all the years we've partied out there, maybe three cars have come up on us, requiring us to move a truck or two to let them pass. No one ever complains about it. I guess it's better than partying in the old school's parking lot in town.

As long as no one gets hurt, no one seems to care where we party. The community's views are the same for the Meadow. Out of sight. Out of mind. And no trouble to be seen.

I pull up outside of Clara's house and grumble as I look down at myself. Sophia begged me to dress up in a couple's costume. I should have waited until she decided what those costumes would be before I agreed. I'll never make that mistake again.

Because I look ridiculous dressed as Steve from *Stranger Things* in his Scoops Ahoy uniform. She's dressing up as his friend, Robin. Also in a Scoops Ahoy uniform.

I can't believe you can buy that shit online and get it delivered in less than three days. Thank God she found a blue sailor's uniform with long pants. I was not looking forward to those shorts with knee-high white socks. No, thank you. This shirt is bad enough with its red and white striped sailor collar and red tie that hangs to my waist. My brothers will never let me live this one down.

With any luck, the cold temperatures will be enough of an excuse to wear a jacket all night so no one will witness this monstrosity of a costume.

A few minutes later, I'm standing on Clara's front porch and knocking. When Sophia opens the door, my heart stops beating. I may look ridiculous dressed up in this Scoops Ahoy sailor costume, but Sophia looks fucking hot.

She opted for shorts—very short shorts—and knee-high socks. Paired with nude-colored tights, her legs and ass look too good for public consumption. She even manages to make the blue shirt with the sailor's collar and red tie look sexy. The growly caveman in me wants to sling her over my shoulder and drag her to her room and show her just how sexy I think she is.

I meet her eyes and her smile is so bright that I falter. *I fucking falter.* As in, I have to catch myself to keep from falling on my ass. What in the hell is wrong with me? Hot girls smiling at me never make me stumble around like a love-sick teenager.

She chuckles and reaches out to touch my arm like that's going to be enough to steady me. It does the opposite. My insides tingle and shudder from need. "You alright there?"

I clear my throat and nod like a damn bobble head toy. "Yep. Totally fine. Why is it you make this costume look hot as fuck, while I look like an idiot?"

"You don't look like an idiot." She's still grinning when she rests her hands on my chest and presses up to give me a chaste kiss. "You're adorable. I like this look on you."

"Adorable?" I frown. "I'm not adorable. Do I need to drag your ass upstairs and show you just how *not* adorable I am?"

She tosses her head back and laughs even harder. "Maybe later. You promised me a party, and I'm in a partying mood."

I tug her flush against me and groan into her mouth as I take her in a deep kiss. She melts against me, making it even harder to back away before this kiss turns into more.

But I manage.

"Fine. Grab a jacket and let's get. We've got a stop to make first."

"Oh! Jackets!" Her smile turns mischievous, and I narrow my eyes. I don't like the way she said jackets. She rushes into the living room and returns moments later, holding two matching jackets. "I found these online. I didn't think they'd come in time, but they arrived today."

She shoves a blue jacket at me that's very close to the same shade of blue as my Scoops Ahoy costume. I groan when I hold it up and see that it has the same damn sailor's collar with red stripes that I was hoping to hide under my racing jacket tonight.

I glare at her. "Do I have to wear it?"

"Yes." She frowns. "It's part of our costume. We can't hide all of this under a non-matching jacket."

She waves her hands up and down her body like she's Vanna White. Now *that* would have been a costume. A sexy formal gown with a slit up one leg, high-heeled shoes, and her hair smoothed in long wavy locks over one shoulder. Not very practical for where I'm taking her tonight, but it definitely would have been hot.

"Hey." She shoves my shoulder, snapping me out of my vision. When I meet her gaze, I can't help but chuckle. She's got the cutest little wrinkle in her brow. "Stop looking at me like that."

"How am I looking at you?"

"Like we're never leaving this house." She shoves the jacket at me. "And we *are* leaving. So don't go getting ideas in your head."

I step closer to her, resting my hands on her hips. "Red, it doesn't matter where we are. I will always have ideas about what I want to do with you."

I lean down to kiss her, but she blocks me by putting her hand over my mouth. I drop my head back and growl. "Woman, you're killing me."

She chuckles and the growl inside me vibrates my entire chest. "Don't be ridiculous. You're not going to die because I make you wait."

My nostrils flare, and my glare intensifies. "What's ridiculous is this costume you're making me wear."

She rolls her eyes at me and shoves the jacket at me again. "Take this. You're wearing it."

"Fine." I snatch it from her and shove my arms in it like a petulant child. "Happy now?"

She beams at me and bounces on her toes. All my frustration over this costume and being denied that kiss melts away. Seeing her this happy is worth looking like an idiot for one night.

"Yes! We're going to look so good together. Let me grab my keys, and then we can go."

She runs into the house, and I hear her moving some things around. Since she doesn't immediately come back, I step inside and shut out the cold. It's supposed to drop to the thirties tonight, and it's already chilly.

Leaning against the door, I call out, "Did Clara already leave?"

"Yeah, Ash picked her up a little bit ago." Sophia answers from the kitchen. It's been a while since I've been in Clara's house, but I remember the layout. When she rushes back, she's a little breathless, and it makes me want to flip her around and kiss her senseless against the door.

Instead, I nod and open the door. "Then let's go."

After she locks up, she follows me to my truck, and I open the door to help her in. Once she's settled, I shut her door and run around the back and hop in behind the wheel.

"Are you going to tell me where we're going?" She rotates in her seat to face me.

"Nope. It's a surprise. But we have to stop at Koch's first and pick up a few things."

She narrows her eyes. "You shop at Koch's? Isn't that against the feud's rules or something?"

I chuckle. "There are no rules to a multi-generational feud, Red. Koch's is the only gas station within fifteen miles where we can buy beer."

Koch's Pit Stop is a gas station and convenience store just off Highway 32. Tanner bought it a few years ago and changed its name. I swear he chose the name Pit Stop just to piss us off. His family doesn't race, and the name is a dig at the Mutter's business.

"Huh," she says as I start the trunk up and pull out onto the road. "I assumed you'd refuse to give him your business."

I shrug. "I can see why you'd think that. But it pisses Tanner off more that we still shop there."

Sophia just shakes her head and turns back to face the windshield. I reach for her hand and lace our fingers together. I relax when she sighs and squeezes my hand with hers. We may have gotten off to a rocky start but being here with her like this feels good. It feels right.

I never saw myself as boyfriend material. Knowing me, I'll probably screw this up five hundred different ways. But there's something about her that makes me want to try. She makes me want to be a better man, and no one has ever made me feel like that before.

I park along the side of Koch's and turn off the engine. I lift Sophia's hand to my lips and kiss her knuckles. "Let's go see if Tanner is working so we can piss him off."

She rolls her eyes and laughs as we step outside. Once I reach her, I immediately take her hand and pull her close. She's mine, and I want everyone in this town to know it. Especially Tanner Fucking Koch.

Sophia hasn't said anything since we left Koch's Pit Stop, but I sense her confusion. I'm driving into the middle of nowhere and still haven't told her where we're going. Since it's already dark out, she can't see our surroundings either. She'll find out soon enough.

Unfortunately, Tanner wasn't working, so I didn't get to give him shit. He's probably already at The Forks. The feud doesn't keep our families from intermingling at community-wide events.

And Halloween at The Forks is a community-wide event. I expect half the town to be there, which means parking will be a bitch. Hopefully we get there early enough that I get a spot I like.

The Mutters and Kochs talk a lot of big talk, but we rarely ever back our words up with violence. It's been years since any of us have thrown punches. I think the last fight was when Chase and Christian were in high school. Of course, it was with Tanner. He's the one that always causes us the most trouble. Linden takes a close second.

Since then, we've mostly been civil. Sort of. If Tanner tries to flirt with Sophia again, our so-called civil streak will be broken.

I pull off the main road and turn up a narrow dirt road that we call the Divide. Why? I don't know. It's been called that since before Grams' times. It's just a dirt road that goes up a steep hill with no trees or houses on either side. At the top, the road takes a sharp right turn into the treeline. From there, it twists and turns for about a mile before we hit The Forks.

I'm about halfway up the Divide when a flash of light comes barreling toward us. I slam on my breaks just before the light veers to the left and into the ditch.

Sophia lets out a loud yelp and clenches her hands to her chest. "What the hell was that?"

"If I was to hazard a guess, I'd say that was Jerry." I put the truck in park and grab my flashlight from the glove box before I hop out. Sophia follows me.

"Who's Jerry?" she asks.

"Gerald Mayer, the town drunk. But everyone calls him Jerry." I shine the flashlight toward the side of the road and right on a man struggling to stand up. "Jerry, are you okay?"

He turns around and shields his eyes from the flashlight. I quickly divert it down and out of his eyes. "Mac, is that you?"

"Yeah." I take a step closer. "Are you hurt?"

"Nah, nothing injured except my pride. Then again, I damaged that ages ago."

He grabs at his bike, but it doesn't move. "Here, let me help you with that."

I step up beside him and instantly rear my head back at the smell of alcohol. Jerry drinks so much I don't know how he's even standing, let alone riding a bike. After I pick his bike up out of the ditch, I set it on the road to make sure it's okay. "Doesn't look like you broke anything, but can I give you a ride?"

He shakes his head and slaps my shoulder. "Nope. I'm headed in the opposite direction. No need to inconvenience you."

"It's not an inconvenience. Happy to give you a lift."

Jerry dusts off his pants before he grabs a hold of his handlebars. "I'm good. Need to get going before the deer get here. Saw a family at the top of the hill."

I glance over my shoulder to where my headlights illuminate the area ahead of us. "I think they're probably long gone. Between my truck and all the noise we're making, I doubt they stuck around."

Jerry grunts. "Not those damn deer. Knowing them, they're hiding in the treeline waiting for you to leave so they can follow me."

I pinch my lips together to stop myself from laughing. Poor Jerry is terrified of deer.

"More reason to let me drive you." I offer again. If for no other reason than to make sure he gets to town safely. He may not slur his words, but he's stumbling a bit. He's too drunk to even ride a bike.

"That's okay. Thanks anyway." He hops on his bike and takes off down the hill before I can argue otherwise. I shine my flashlight in his direction and watch him until he disappears in the darkness.

When I turn around, Sophia is staring at me with furrowed brows. "What was that all about?"

I chuckle. "That's Jerry. He hit a deer a few years back on his bike. Put himself in the hospital for a few days. Even killed the deer. How he killed a deer while riding a bike is beyond me. He's insisted the deer are out to get him ever since. There are a lot of deer in these hills, and we all have to be careful not to hit them. But they're not chasing anyone."

Her eyes widen. "He hit a deer on his bike? Like bicycle, bike? Not a motorcycle?"

"Yep. Crazy, I know. But that's Jerry." I take her hand and lead her back to the truck. "Come on, let's go before the best parking spots are all taken."

We get back in the truck and head back up the hill. I can't help but chuckle when my headlights illuminate the eyes of the family of deer that had Jerry rattled. They're huddled at the top of the hill like they're waiting for me to leave.

"Well, shit," Sophia says. "He wasn't kidding."

"Guess not." I laugh. "Hopefully, they're long gone before Jerry returns, or else he might wreck his bike again."

"Does he live up here or something?"

I nod. "He has a small cabin just around the bend." I point toward the entrance to his driveway once we reach it. "Right back there. I'm sure he'll be fine. Been riding that bike around for nearly a decade now."

"Why does he ride a bike everywhere?"

I give her a sideways glance. "Did you smell the alcohol on him?"

"Yeah, I guess I did. I take it he's always been like that. Drunk, I mean."

"Yep. Lost his license a long time ago. Rides a bike everywhere and insists the deer are evil and trying to get back at him for killing one of their own. He may be a little nuts, too."

She laughs, and it's the sweetest thing I've heard all day. I smile, but inwardly groan. *Sweet?* What in the hell is happening to me?

She's happening. That's what.

The soft glow of lights appears up ahead and Sophia's laughter fades. She leans forward and squints like she's trying to make out what it is. I can't help but smile at her curiosity.

"What on earth is going on up there?" she asks.

"That is where we're headed."

She glances at me, but only for a second, before she looks back to the road. Her eyes narrow and her nose does this really cute thing where it wrinkles like she can't quite make out what she's seeing.

Once we're close enough that she can make out the cluster of large metal barrels in the middle of the road, she snaps her head at me. "The party is in the middle of the road?"

"Yep." I smile. "We call this The Forks. It's another one of our party spots. We don't come here as often as the Meadow, but this is where we always celebrate Halloween."

"But it's literally in the middle of the road?" She turns her frown on me as I pull my truck into the open space next to Liam's truck. "Why would you do this? What about traffic? What do you do if someone drives up?"

"Babe!" I reach for her hand. "Look around. We're in the middle of nowhere. On a dirt road. No one is driving through here tonight. If a car comes up, it's because they're here to party with us."

"But why?"

I grin and kiss her hand. "You'll see. Now let's go find my brothers."

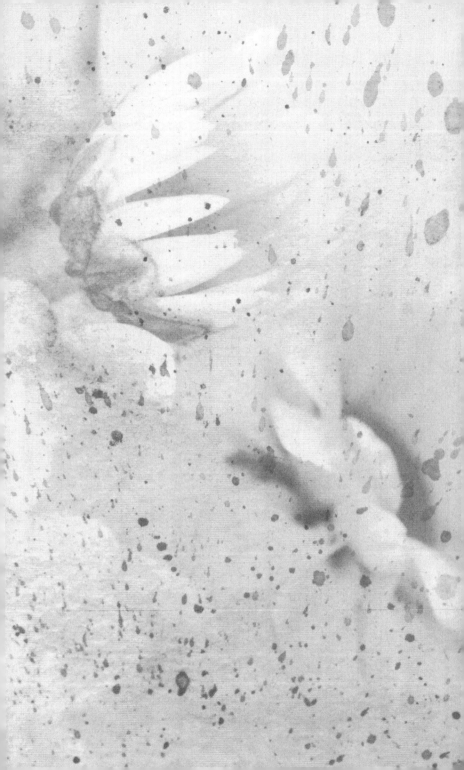

Chapter 18

Silly legends, even sillier country boys, and one weird-ass party.

Sophia

The night air is brisk, the music is loud, everyone is in costume, there's a freaking fire in what looks like three steel drums clustered together in the middle of the road, and everyone is acting like this is all perfectly normal.

There is nothing normal about this.

Mac tugs at my hand, and I shift my eyes to him. While I'm standing next to my door, stunned, he's grinning.

He pulls me against him until my chest is flush with his. My entire body lights up with excitement at the closeness. With a gentle hand, he places his fingers under my chin and lifts my lips to his. It's a soft kiss that makes me melt in a puddle in his arms.

This one feels different. It's slow, sweet, almost reverent. This kiss isn't about falling into bed with each other. It isn't about the physical connection we share. It's deeper, more meaningful on an emotional level.

This one makes me swoon. This kiss is trouble.

Mac may have been the one to insist we're exclusive. He may have been the first to put a label on what we are. But he did that out of jealousy, and that has me a little worried about the safety of my heart.

I want to believe he truly means it—that he wants a relationship with me—but I'm not convinced he's emotionally capable of that kind of commitment. At least not yet.

The man has some serious baggage. We all have baggage, but his is worse. His runs deep into his soul and is attached to it like a parasite sucking the life out of its host.

Mac pulls back from the kiss, leaving me feeling breathless and needy for more. His eyes meet mine as he brushes his thumb over my bottom lip. The look of adoration and longing in his eyes has the same effect on me that the kiss did.

Yep, I'm in trouble.

He looks like he's going to say something, maybe even confess more of his feelings to me, but he doesn't.

Instead, his playful grin returns. "Ready to have some fun?"

"Yep." I nod repeatedly like an idiot because he has me so flustered right now, I can't think straight.

He gives me a quick peck on the lips before he turns and walks to the back of his truck. He opens the tailgate and drags the cooler to the end. Grabbing two beers, he pops the tops and hands me one.

"Feel free to cut loose tonight," he says as he wraps his arm over my shoulder. "I'll go easy on the drinking tonight."

I nod, still a little dazed from that kiss. I feel his eyes on me as I look around, trying to make sense of these feelings inside me.

"Hey." He nudges my shoulder with his. "You okay?"

When I look up at him, his expression is full of concern. "Yeah, of course." I clear my throat. "Just trying to figure out what I'm seeing."

His easy smile returns. "This is The Forks. As I said, it's where we *always* celebrate Halloween."

The emphasis he puts on always causes me to raise a brow in question. I can't shake the feeling that I'm missing something. "And why is that?"

"Look around." He waves an arm in front of him in a sweeping motion. "We're on an isolated, unnamed dirt road that forks in two different directions in the middle of a dark, dense forest. Anything could creep up on us in the forest. What better place is there to host a Halloween party for a bunch of country boys and girls?"

"You say that like Jason Voorhees or Michael Myers is hiding out in the trees, waiting to pick us off one at a time."

He grins down at me and waggles his brows. "Nothing like that, but I like where your mind is going. That'll make tonight that much more fun."

"Okay." I jerk my hand from his and stop. He turns to face me, his grin gone, but his eyes still dance with humor. "You're not telling me something. Spill it."

He tosses his head back in laughter. "There's nothing to spill, Red. Relax. It's a party. Enjoy yourself. It'll be a blast even if I did let you convince me to wear this ridiculous outfit."

I glare up at him, so not convinced by his jovial teasing. There's something going on tonight. I can feel in my bones.

"Sophia! You're finally here!" Clara calls for me from where she's sitting on the tailgate of Ash's truck. She waves us over, and Mac almost too eagerly drags me in her direction.

If I hadn't seen her costume before she left the house, I may not have recognized her. She's dressed up as the girl from the well in the movie *The Ring*. She looks creepy as fuck and perfect at the same time.

"Hey, where's Ash?" Mac asks.

Clara glances around the large group of people like she's looking for him. "He was right over there." She points toward Liam, who's standing on the other side of the fire. I chuckle at his costume. He's dressed up like possessed Billy from *Stranger Things*. He has a curly mullet wig, a fake mustache, and a jean jacket that looks exactly like the one Billy wore. "But I don't see him now."

"I'm going to go look for him." He kisses the top of my head before he releases my hand. "I'll be back in a few."

I nod and slide up onto the tailgate next to Clara.

For an unnamed dirt road, this section is wide. Maybe it's because of the fork, but something tells me they've purposefully widened this spot for their parties. There's enough room for several cars to park along all sides while still leaving room for the three steel drums in the center and so oncoming cars can pass.

A few of the trucks, Ash's included, are backed up around the fire in a circle so people can sit, but most people are standing. It's hard to tell exactly how many people are here. The only light is from the fire that I still can't believe is in the middle of the freaking road. A few cars have their headlights on, but they're parked a good distance away.

The parking spaces in the trees, like the one Mac parked in, look like someone intentionally cleared them so cars or trucks could pull in. Without the fire, the forest would completely hide the vehicles from anyone driving past.

I don't know most of the people here. I recognize a few faces from the party at the Meadow, but I've never been introduced to them.

The Koch siblings are here. They're all gathered on one side of The Forks with what I assume is their group of friends. I'm not sure who they're supposed to be. They're all themed after some sort of horror movie.

In fact, everyone is. Mac didn't tell me this was themed or else I would have picked something different. Then again, we are dressed up as characters from *Stranger Things*. That counts.

I don't see Ash or Chase. Mac is talking to Liam. Christian is standing next to a group of rough-looking men sitting on motorcycles. I assume it's the local MC I've heard he makes most of the custom bikes for. He's dressed in his usual black leather but painted his face white and has fake blood dripping from the corners of his mouth.

Garret is standing next to a pretty girl who keeps looking up at him with dreamy eyes. He's not paying any attention to her. When she speaks, he just nods and grunts. It's clear he's not listening to her.

She's dressed up like a murdered cheerleader, and he looks like he could be the lumberjack that murdered her. Although, based on how annoyed he looks by her presence, I don't think that was intentional.

"I saw it! I swear!" A female voice cries out from the darkness of the road behind us. In unison, all heads turn toward the sound of her voice.

"No, you didn't. It had to be something else." This comes from a man's voice. While she sounds scared, he sounds angry.

"Yes. I. Did." Her voice is louder as they approach. "If you'd just come with me, I'll show you."

"No way. I'm not going anywhere with you."

Once they come into view, Tanner calls out to them. "What are you two bickering about now?"

Clara leans close to me and whispers. "Jojo and Steve. They've dated since high school. Always fighting. No one understands why they're still together."

"We're not bickering!" Jojo yells at Tanner. "I saw another hut and Steve doesn't believe me."

The music cuts off, and it falls eerily silent. The only sound is the crackle of the fire. Everyone is staring at Jojo, and I can't tell if it's from disbelief or fear. My gut is telling me fear.

Tension builds as the silence drags on. I look at Mac, and even he's staring at Jojo with a hint of fear in his expression.

The only person who doesn't look scared is Garret. He still looks pissed.

Tanner takes a hesitant step toward her. "What *exactly* did you see?"

"A hut!" she screams. "Am I not speaking clearly enough for you people?" She points in the direction from which she came. "There is a hut back there in the trees by my car. One of *his* huts."

The last sentence comes out much softer and the emphasis she puts on the word *his* has several people taking a step back.

Clara stiffens next to me like she's trying really hard not to move. I glance at Mac. His eyes flicker to me, but only for a second, before he looks back at Jojo. I stare at him, confused by his expression. It almost looks like he's fighting a smirk.

I look at Clara, and it's as if she's purposefully trying not to look at me.

"What's going on?" I ask.

She doesn't answer me, so I look back at Mac. He, too, looks like he's avoiding my gaze. I narrow my eyes, certain that I'm missing something.

Then a loud, piercing scream fills the silence. The pounding of feet running toward us quickly follows, and then the words, "Orange eyes in the trees!" reverberates through the air.

Several people rush to their cars like they're going to leave, but most of them remain frozen in place.

Again, the silence drags on. I don't know what's going on, but something doesn't feel right. I can't help but sense this is all for show. Please tell me no one is falling for this nonsense?

After a moment, Clara leans close to me, and whispers, "Will you at least act like you're scared?"

"What?" I snap my head in her direction. Before she can elaborate, rustling comes from within the trees, followed by a low, feral growl.

Jojo, along with several other people, scream and run in the opposite direction of the sound. When I look back toward the crowd, Mac is staring at me like he's disappointed.

I raise my brows and ask, "What's going on?"

Clara lets out a long sigh. "This is all for you. You're supposed to be scared."

I frown. "What on earth for?"

She shakes her head and points in Mac's direction. When I

look back at him, he has his arms spread out to his sides. He's frowning, too.

"Are you kidding me?" he asks. "You're not even going to react?"

I glance around, just now realizing that everyone has stopped and is staring at me. "React to what exactly?"

"You're a pain in my ass, Red." He drops his arms and stalks toward me. "Most people are terrified when we introduce them to the Grassman. Should've known you'd be difficult."

"Grassman?" I ask.

But he doesn't answer me. Instead, he picks me up off the tail-gate and tosses me over his shoulder. He slaps my ass and growls, causing everyone to break out into laughter.

"Mac!" I knock my fists against his back. "Put me down."

"I will." The deep timbre of his voice vibrates in his chest, and I feel it all the way down to my toes. "Right after I introduce you to the Grassman."

"Who the fuck is the Grassman?" I ask.

Before he can answer me, a loud roar surrounds us. It's so loud, I can't help but jump in his arms. He drops me to my feet and turns me around. "*This* is the Grassman."

Then he shoves me at a man dressed up in what looks like a Sasquatch costume.

An hour later, Mac drags me to his truck and says we're leaving. Once again, he won't tell me where we're going, only that it's not far.

The party had been fun, but spirits declined when they figured out I don't scare easily. They put on that entire scene just to see me scream. Ash and Chase were both dressed up in Sasquatch costumes. They were hiding in the woods, making noises. The plan was once I was scared, they were going to chase me when I ran. It didn't work out that way.

I turn in my seat to face Mac. "Tell me more about this Grassman character. Did you all make him up to frighten newbies like me?"

Mac gives me a side-eye glance and shakes his head. "I can't believe that didn't faze you in the least. It scares everyone."

"I told you. I grew up watching horror movies. I'm a junkie."

"I know that *now*." He huffs, making me laugh. "It would have been nice to know that beforehand. I would've kicked it up a notch."

"You could have tried, but it probably still wouldn't have worked."

He narrows his eyes and huffs. "You realize we worked with the Kochs to pull this off? You could at least pretend."

"Aw." I reach over and run my hand through his hair. He leans into my touch. "I'm sorry you had to do that for me. Had I known how important this was to you, I would have put on a show myself."

He glances at me, and his lips pull up in a slight grin. With a quick flick of his hand, he unhooks my seat belt. "Get over here. I want you close."

I chuckle but do as he asks. Once I'm next to him, he leans in for a quick kiss before buckling the center belt.

"Hang on," he says. "The road is about to get bumpy."

He takes a sharp turn to the right onto a narrow, unmarked road through the forest. It's one of those roads that unless you know it's there, you'd never see it. The truck bounces on the rough terrain, and Mac has to keep a tight grip on the wheel to keep from hitting trees. His truck barely fits through the path.

But when the road opens up and a small lake comes into view, I gasp. He pulls his truck to a stop on an open grassy area a few feet from the lake's edge. When he kills the headlights, the stars cast a soft glow over the cab.

It's quiet and very private. There's nothing but us and the night sky.

"Oh my God, Mac. This is beautiful." I lean into the windshield to get a better view of the sky. "I don't think I've ever seen this many stars before."

He wraps his arm around my waist and pulls me onto his lap. His mouth is on mine before I can even take my next breath. He bites on my bottom lip before his tongue dives in and tangles with mine. This is a *Mac* kiss. Powerful. Hard. Possessive.

But I don't feel any safer with this kiss than I did with the sweet, sensual kiss from earlier.

I am, without a doubt, falling for Mac Mutter.

He breaks the kiss way too soon. Cupping my cheek, he drops his forehead to mine. We both struggle to breathe. "Making out with you in the cab of my truck wasn't my plan."

I chuckle. "Oh, yeah? What did you have in mind?"

"Let's stargaze." He opens his door and slides out from under me. I stare at him, unsure if I heard him correctly.

"Did you say stargaze?"

He lets out a soft laugh that sends butterflies swirling around in my belly.

"Yeah." He leans in for a quick kiss before he grabs a stack of blankets from behind his seat. "It'll be romantic. We can talk, count the stars, or you know, *whatever*."

He winks and takes my hand to help me out. I know exactly what he means by *whatever*.

He spreads a couple of blankets on the bed of his truck, then helps me up. We stretch out, side-by-side, on our backs. He covers us with another blanket before I snuggle into his side and stare at the night sky.

We're silent for a few minutes before I finally look over at him. "Are you going to tell me about it or not?"

His brow furrows in that same grumpy way it always does, and

I smile. He looks so sexy when he's grumpy and growly. "Tell you about what?"

"The Grassman." I playfully slap at his chest like I'm irritated. "I asked you to tell me about the legend. Is it a local thing or something? Like I have to live here for a certain amount of time before I'm privy to the story?"

"Oh." He chuckles. "No. It's not a local thing. It's an Ohio thing. I'm surprised you've never heard of him before."

"I guess we city kids find other ways to entertain ourselves."

His frown returns. "Like what?"

"Let's see. We go to the movies or go out for dinner. Sometimes, we go out to a bar or a nightclub. There are also comedy clubs and plays. I like comedy clubs. Sometimes they're really funny."

"We have movies, restaurants, and bars," he says like he's slightly offended.

"But you prefer to hang around a bonfire and drink beer in an open field. Or better yet, the middle of the road."

He lets out a deep, throaty laugh that hits me right between the legs. "Yeah, I guess we do."

I shove at his arm. "Now stop stalling and tell me about the Grassman."

He takes my hand in his and holds it over his chest. "Well, there's not really that much to tell. The legend is a lot like Sasquatch, but Grassman is reported to be more aggressive with longer hair. The legend dates back to the Native Americans that lived in these parts. Ohio has a lot of small caves, and explorers have found cave markings they credit to this legend. The Grassman is said to roam the forested areas of southern Ohio. He gets his name from the grass hut he lives in."

I wrinkle my brow. "That's it?"

"Yep. That's it. Ohio's very own Sasquatch. We have fun with it though. You'd be amazed at how many people believe in him. Occasionally, hikers have found long hairs or feces in trees.

They've even sent samples to Ohio State University for testing. Nothing has ever come of it. But legends are fun, so we keep it alive and strong."

"Sounds silly. We never had anything like that in the city."

He lets out a deep, contented sigh before he speaks again. "Will you tell me what it was like growing up in the city with a mom and a dad?"

"Oh, jeez. Let me think." I take in a deep breath. I know what he's really asking me. I know enough about his family dynamics to know he really wants to know what it was like growing up with a *normal* family. But what is *normal?*

"It was good, I guess, if not a little boring. My parents are good people. My siblings and I grew up knowing we were loved. My parents want what's best for us, but they're not perfect. They don't accept my choices. We fight a lot—my parents and me. We didn't used to. I told you about how my dad would take me to work with him when I was little. I thought my life was perfect back then. Then one day, going to work with him became unacceptable."

"But they still love you?" he asks. His voice is quiet, almost too soft to hear.

"Yeah. That's never been an issue. I know they love me and just want what's best for me. But what they think is best isn't what I want."

"They just want you to be safe. That's what normal parents are supposed to want for their kids, right?"

"Mac." I sit up and toss my leg over his waist until I'm straddling him. "You don't think your dad or Grams want you to be safe? Or your brothers? They all care very much about you."

He looks away from me like he doesn't want to hear this. I cup his cheeks and turn his eyes to mine. "Your family loves you. I know you know that."

He nods. "But not my mom. I was never good enough for my mom. Or any other woman, for that matter."

"But you *are* good enough." I give him a quick kiss. "I can't even imagine how her leaving makes you feel, and I hate that for you. But every family has issues, Mac. Even the ones that appear to be normal from the outside. Normal is relative."

"My life isn't normal. That's for damn sure." He lets out a raspy huff before he brushes a stand of my hair behind my ear. "And look what it's done to me. I'm a jealous, possessive man who doesn't trust love."

I suck in a breath. I'm not sure how to take his last statement. *Love.* Is Mac thinking about love when he thinks about me, or is he referring to his mom? Either way, it has my heart racing with excitement.

"I wish you could see what I see. You're so much more than you give yourself credit for."

Something passes over his face that I can't make out. Something deep and meaningful. It's a look that tells me he cares way more for than he wants to admit.

But he quickly replaces it with one of his teasing smiles. "You just like my dick."

"Mac!" I slap at his chest, but he grabs my arms and rolls me over before I make contact. "I like *you*, not your dick."

With my hands pinned above my head, he grinds his thickening cock between my legs. "So you don't want this?" He swirls his hips again, dragging a soft moan from my lips. "If you don't like this, I can keep it to myself."

"You're playing dirty."

A smirk lifts his lips. "I always play dirty, baby. You should have figured that out by now."

His lips crash to mine in an all-consuming kiss. We're all lips and teeth and hands. The heat building between us is so strong, I don't even feel the cold night air. Within minutes, we're both stripped of our clothes. He's sheathed in a condom, and he's pushing inside me.

He moves slowly and deliberately, almost as if he's trying to make me feel so much more than his cock inside me. And oh boy, I feel things I'm not sure I want to be feeling for this man.

He thrusts deep inside me, hitting that spot that causes my entire body to tingle. He does it again and again and again until I'm ready to explode. "Mac. I'm so close."

"Not yet, baby. I want you to come with me." He rolls us over, not breaking our connection, until I'm spread out on top of him. "Ride my cock, Red. Ride me under the stars."

I sit up and roll my hips onto his cock. We both groan when he fills me even deeper than before.

My hair falls forward, and my breasts bounce as I move up and down on him. His hands tighten around my hips, and he thrusts up with every downward move I make.

"You are so beautiful," he whispers almost as if he didn't mean to say it out loud. "And you feel so fucking good."

He slides his hands up my back as he brings himself to a seated position. His mouth clamps around one of my breasts and he sucks hard. My head falls back at the intense sensation. His mouth, his hands, his cock moving inside me all send me closer to the edge.

"Mac!" I cry out as I dig my hands into his hair.

"I feel you, baby. I'm right there with you." He grunts, and his next thrust into me is all it takes to send me over the edge. His movements become more erratic as his release chases mine.

We cling to each other as we come together. Our bodies joined as one, and our hearts pounding fiercely in unison.

"Sophia, Sophia, Sophia," he whispers against my chest. It sends a shiver down my spine that is further intensified by the chilly night air. He so rarely uses my actual name, that I can't help but feel the significance in it now. "What are you doing to me?"

Instead of responding, I squeeze him closer to me. I don't know how to answer that, because I could ask him the same thing.

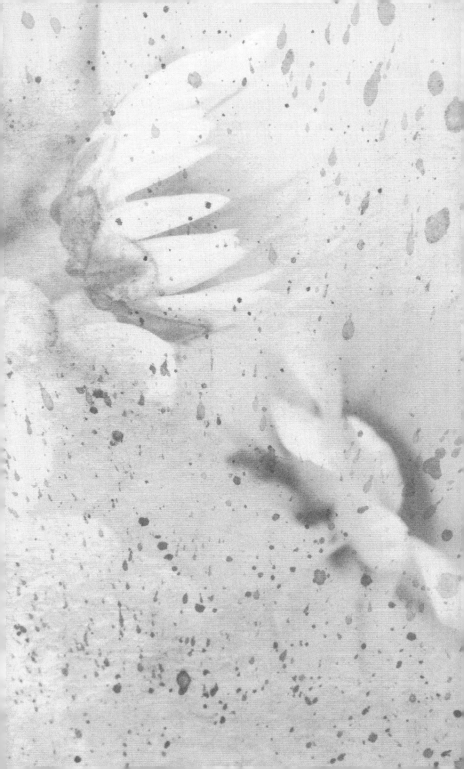

Chapter 19

Once in my head, always in my head.

Mac

My leg won't stop bouncing, so I lean forward in my chair and rest my elbows on my knees. It doesn't help.

Sophia is racing today, and I'm a nervous wreck. Not just because she's the one behind the wheel of a racecar on the track with a dozen other drivers. That has me nervous, but it's not my biggest issue.

She has a great pit crew, and she agreed to let my brothers help. We're all under the tent or at the pit to support her and cheer her on. A part of me wishes I was in the stands where I could see the entire race better, but then I wouldn't get updates from Chase on how she's doing.

I shouldn't worry because she's an amazing driver. She can handle a car better than some Sprint Cup drivers. Her skill is impressive.

But I still can't relax.

"Dude, if you don't calm down, you're going to rattle the screws loose in that chair," Ash says as he drops in the empty seat next to me. "She's fine."

"I know she's fine."

"Then why are you so tense?"

I glance at my brother and shake my head. I'm not sure I'm ready to talk about what has me tied up in knots.

Things between Sophia and me got serious fast. Something shifted between us on Halloween, and I can't shake it. We've spent every day and night together this past week. We've worked together at the garage, sometimes on the same vehicle, and other times on our own projects.

A couple of mornings when we were slow, she joined me at the track and helped Ash and Chase out in the pit. I joined her in the evenings after work, when she'd rented the track to prepare for this race.

We've eaten every meal together, and I've stayed the night with her at Clara's house. We're a full-fledged couple and I'm not the least bit upset about that. I enjoy being with her. I want to be with her all the time.

So, yeah, I'm nervous about her being on the track. I want her safe, and I can't protect her from other drivers any more than I can protect myself. But there's so much more bothering me right now.

I look over at my brother. He's watching me, waiting for an answer.

I take a deep breath and say what's really on my mind. "Her parents are here."

The race is near Cincinnati, about thirty minutes from her parents' house. They may not approve of her life choices, but they still came today to support her.

"Oh, yeah?" Ash stares at me like he's waiting for me to elaborate.

I nod. "I'm supposed to meet them after. She wants me to go to dinner with them."

"Aw, I get it." Ash grins. "Meeting the parents for the first time. That makes this thing between you two pretty serious, huh?"

"It's not that." I lean back in my chair and rub my hands over my face. "I've never met *the* parents before."

Ash narrows his eyes. "What are you talking about? You've met plenty of your girlfriends' parents before."

"No. I've *known* the parents of the girls I've dated before. There's a difference."

His brow furrow deepens. "I'm not following."

I huff, and my leg bounces on the ground again. "With every girl I've ever dated, I knew their parents first. Beaver is small. Everyone knows everyone. Today will be the first time I've ever met the parents after the fact. What if they hate me?"

Ash tosses his head back in laughter. "Oh, man. This is great."

I punch him in the arm and that only makes him laugh harder. "It's not funny, asshole. I really like Sophia. If her parents hate me, how's that gonna work?"

I groan at how stupid I must sound. I've never worried about whether a girlfriend's parents would like me or not. It never mattered before. But Sophia is important to me, and I don't want anything getting in the way of our relationship before we've even had a chance to make a real go at it.

"Mac, it'll be fine." Ash squeezes my shoulder. "Just be yourself. Well, maybe keep the possessiveness under control, but other than that, you've got nothing to worry about."

"Ha," I say with a sarcastic undertone. "That's easier said than done."

"Maybe so." Ash pushes to his feet. "Come on. Get up here and cheer your girl on. She'll be coming in for her next pit stop soon. Let her see your smiling face."

GOD SHE'S HOT.

Like I've-never-seen-a-woman-so-hot-before-in-all-my-life *hot*. It's not just her looks, either. She's a beautiful woman for sure. Perfectly smooth pale skin, with the cutest freckles I've ever seen.

Long, wavy red hair that glows like embers in the sunlight. And her light blue eyes are mesmerizing.

But that's just part of the package that is Sophia Becker. Watching her drive a racecar going close to two hundred miles per hour is a sight to see. She controls that car like she's one with it. She makes it look effortless, gliding around every corner, smooth and easy, like it's the easiest thing in the world to do. No wonder she beat me. She's fucking brilliant with that car.

And I can't believe she's mine.

Now that Ash has helped me get out of my head, I'm able to focus on the race. Sophia is doing great. If she keeps at this pace, she's going to pass the lead car and win. Lord knows, she deserves it.

"I'm already getting calls and messages," Liam says as he steps up beside me. I've been leaning against a pole next to the TV, watching the race from the pit.

"Calls about what?"

Liam grins and holds his phone so I can read a text message. It's one of our sponsors asking about Sophia. They want to know if she's new to our team.

My grin matches his. "I'm not surprised. She's good. What did you tell them?"

"Nothing yet. I don't want to speak for her."

I nod. "That's probably wise. I don't think she'd appreciate that very much."

Liam looks up at me with a hopeful gaze. "Think she'd be interested in joining our racing team?"

I shrug. "Possibly. I know she loves working with us. She's learned a lot from Chase and Ash. She wants to keep racing. Money is her biggest obstacle. If she raced with us, that would ease her financial burden."

"And what about you?" Liam asks, his voice hesitant.

"What do you mean? What about me?"

He looks back to the track and rubs his hand down his beard.

"Mac, you're the only racecar driver we've ever had. We're a team around you. How would you feel about growing our team? And I don't just mean Sophia."

"Oh." I swallow hard and stare at the TV screen. Sophia is still in second place, but one good move and she could swing past the leader. Taking a deep breath, I look back at Liam. He's watching me with a careful eye. "Is that what you want?"

"We've talked about it. But not if—"

"And by *we*, you mean Ash and Chase?" I don't wait for him to finish.

He nods. "It's just been talk. We don't have anyone specific in mind. Well, maybe Sophia now. But we keep making cars for other teams, and those teams are winning. Maybe that should be us."

I wait for the anger and frustration to hit me from learning that my brothers have been talking behind my back about growing the team. But it doesn't come. I feel more relieved than anything, and that reality confuses me.

We have a team because of me and my dreams of being a racecar driver. Had I never pushed to do this as a teenager, Chase and Ash wouldn't be making custom racecars. Even Warren might have followed a different career path had I not been so obsessed with racing as a kid.

Yet here we are. One of the best in the business, and without realizing it, I'm holding us back. If I can't get over my anxiety from the accident and take the team all the way to the Sprint Cup, then I need to open that door for someone else. We've worked too hard to get to this point to not go all the way.

"I think that would be good." I look over at Liam and smile. "If you haven't already done it, we should make a list of young, up-and-coming drivers. If Sophia wants to officially join us, I'm good with that too."

A broad smile lights up Liam's entire face. "Really? You're good with this?"

I slap his shoulder and return his smile. "Definitely. Growth is good, and I think we're ready for it."

He lets out a deep chuckle. "And here I was terrified to talk to you about this. I thought you'd be mad."

"Nah, I'm not mad. In fact, this could be great."

"Hey, get out here," Ash calls to us from outside the tent where he's standing next to Chase.

Chase has a headset on so he can talk with Sophia along with her crew chief. He covers his mic when he sees us approach. "Hey. Number forty-seven is giving her some trouble."

"What's he doing?" I ask, my anxiety instantly returning. I'd calmed down some after my earlier talk with Ash, but now it's back with a vengeance.

Chase turns the screen that's showing the feed from Sophia's rear camera. "He's riding her close. He's even rubbed her bumper a few times, but not enough that it's drawing attention."

"How is she handling it?"

"She says she's fine," Chase says. "I can't tell if it's deliberate, or inexperience on forty-seven's part. Regardless, she's trying to put distance between them. If she passes the leader on this next turn, that should get rid of him."

"Tell me she's being cautious. Don't let her do something stupid."

Chase grins. "Don't worry, bro. She's got this. We've been watching the leader close for the last several laps. He always sticks to the outside. If she can gain some speed before the next turn, she can whip past him on the inside."

I nod. It's a solid plan, but it doesn't make me feel any better. I step back under the tent to watch the race from the TV. Since she's a leading car, the camera is on her.

I see what Chase means. Car forty-seven is on her like glue. The next corner is coming up. Sophia increases her speed, but so does forty-seven. Just like Chase said, the leader takes the outside.

Sophia cuts to the inside. If she's able to put some distance between her and forty-seven, she could take the lead.

But that's not what happens.

Forty-seven also increases his speed, but he overcompensates. He doesn't just rub her bumper. He hits her, causing his car to fishtail. His rear whips around and slams into the back of the lead car. The lead car hits the wall, spins and slams into Sophia.

And I see black as my anxiety consumes me.

———

THE NEXT THING I KNOW, I'M RUNNING FROM THE TENT, pushing past my brothers, and jumping over the fence. I need to get to her now.

Liam is the first to reach me. He grabs hold of me and tackles me to the ground. I shove at him, trying to break free from his grip.

"Let me go!" I yell.

"Mac, you can't go out there. Let the emergency crew do their job."

"Fuck the emergency crew!" I throw a punch at him, but he's prepared for it and blocks me. Before I'm able to break free, Chase and Ash are next to us, ready to help hold me back.

"Did she lose consciousness?" I hear Chase ask, and I stop fighting so I can listen. "Are you sure?" There's another pause. "Okay. We're coming out."

Chase looks down at me and reaches for my hand. "They're letting us ride out. We can meet her at the ambulance."

Chase leads the way to the waiting truck, and we all jump in the back. As soon as we're seated, the truck takes off across the field. All I see are flashing lights through a haze of smoke. I hope that doesn't mean one of the cars caught fire.

The truck stops next to one of three ambulances that responded to the accident. All three lead cars were taken out in that crash.

I hop over the bed of the truck and run around to the back of the first ambulance I see. Sophia is sitting on the gurney inside. As soon as her eyes meet mine, she calls out. "I'm fine!"

The EMT is dabbing at a cut on her hand, and her arm is wrapped in a sling. But it's the blood smeared down her face that sets me off. I feel whatever control I have slip. There shouldn't be blood on her face.

Despite the panic building inside me, my voice is surprisingly calm when I speak. "You don't look fine."

She shakes her head. "This is all just a precaution. It looks worse than it is."

I shake my head and take a few steps back. Glancing around, I scan the area until I find the driver of car forty-seven. He's sitting on the back of the ambulance that pulled up next to his wrecked car.

I charge for him, but I don't make it very far before all three of my brothers cut me off.

"Mac!" Liam presses his hand against my chest. "Calm down."

"He hurt her!" I yell and attempt to shove Liam out of my path. He stands firm and pushes me back.

"Not like this. He's hurt too. Focus on Sophia."

"Mac." Sophia's calming voice breaks through my anger. When I turn around, she's standing outside the ambulance. "Don't."

I instantly deflate and rush to her. Taking her in my arms, I hug her gently, careful not to put any pressure on her injured arm, and whisper in her ear. "Tell me you're okay."

"I'm okay," she answers. "They're insisting on taking me to the hospital. Come with me?"

"Of course."

She takes my hand with her free arm and tugs me toward the ambulance. I'm still angry about her injured arm and the blood on her face, but a lot of that anger dissipated when I heard her voice and saw her standing.

She's going to be fine. And that's what matters most.

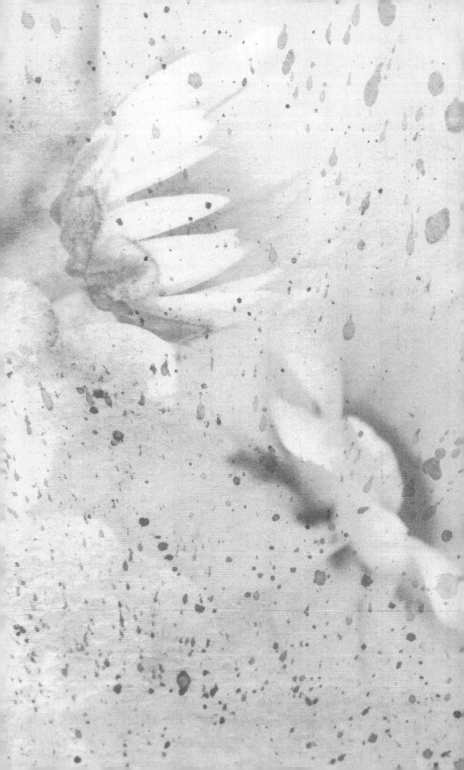

Chapter 20

When everything falls apart, stay calm.

Sophia

D ark, cramped spaces never make me uneasy. I'm not claustrophobic. At least, I didn't think I was. But being forced to lie still inside this dark tube is really getting to me.

My anxiety is high, and I can't seem to calm my breathing.

I know this is protocol anytime someone gets in an accident during a race, but how many tests do they have to run? The X-rays took forever. Then they carted me over to have a CT scan. I thought I was done after that, but I guess the doctor on-call ordered an MRI as well.

I get it. I really do. My helmet cracked. That means I hit my head really hard. But my head doesn't hurt. It's my fucking arm that's bothering me. And being strapped to a gurney for hours unable to move while they run all these tests is only making it hurt worse.

All I want to do is sit up and stretch. Stretching would do wonders for my body right now.

I think being stationary like this for so long is doing me more harm than good. My back is stiff, and my legs are restless. And let's not talk about all the horrible thoughts that keep running through my mind.

What if they find something wrong with me? Just because I don't feel injured doesn't mean there's not something invisible lurking within. I keep telling myself to relax, but it's hard when I've got no one to talk to. If only I could see my friends and family. They'd help keep me calm.

But I haven't seen anyone since being checked in. As soon as we got here, they made Mac stay in the waiting room until I was transferred to my own room. That feels like hours ago. I went from triage to test after test and haven't been carted back yet.

"Sophia, are you okay?" The technician's voice rings through my ears. Why are my ears ringing? I shake my head, desperate to run my hands over my ears, but I can't lift my arms. "Sophia?" He repeats.

"I'm okay," I say, but my voice doesn't sound okay. Not even to me. I sound weak and scared.

"Take a deep breath for me, then try to relax. This will only take about fifteen minutes. Can you hold still for that long?"

"Yeah, just give me a second." I slide my uninjured arm up and rub my hand over my face. It's tight, but the motion makes me feel a little better.

"Do you need to come out for a minute?" he asks.

I shake my head before I realize he can't really see me. "No, I'm fine. Let's get this over with."

I take a few deep, calming breaths and focus on happy thoughts. At least I have lots of them to keep me distracted.

Things these past couple of weeks with Mac have been good. Really, really good. I still sense he's keeping some of his past from me, but our connection is strong. He's trusting me more and more every day. One day, I'll earn all of his story.

I just hope this accident doesn't push him into protection over-drive. He was finally starting to calm down with me. Even his jealous streak hasn't been as bad lately. Last week, I'd managed to have an entire conversation with Tanner when Mac and I were picking up lunch at Frank's Frosty Kreme.

It was obvious Tanner was trying to get a rise out of Mac. But Mac didn't freak out. He sat in the car and waited like a good boy. He glared a lot, but he never got out and did his typical possessive, growly-bear thing that sends shivers through my body.

It's ridiculous how much I love his possessive, growly-bear side. I never thought I'd be *that* girl.

I'm independent and strong-willed.

I don't need a man to protect me.

I protect myself.

But I like Mac's protection. I crave it. It makes me feel wanted and revered in a way no man has ever made me feel.

"Sophia, we're done." The technician's voice interrupts my thoughts. "You did great. I'm letting you out now."

The table I'm on slides out from under the tube. As soon as my head is clear, I lift my hand and rub my face. After lying still for that long, I feel tense and itchy. It's a weird feeling.

"Can I sit up?" I ask.

"Yes, give me a second and I'll help you."

A moment later, he's by my side. He takes my good hand and helps me up. A nurse appears a moment later with a wheelchair. I want to refuse it, but I know it's hospital policy. At least a wheelchair is better than being forced back onto a gurney. I need to sit up for a while.

"Your room is ready," the nurse says. "You have several visitors waiting to see you."

I nod, assuming she means Mac and my parents. *Oh God. My parents.* They saw the accident. I'll never hear the end of this now.

It doesn't take long to head up the three floors to my room. According to the nurse, I'll most likely be held overnight, so I might as well get comfortable.

I barely have time to get situated on the edge of the bed when

Mac barges into the room. He takes one look at me, then sweeps me into his arms. "Tell me you're okay."

I chuckle. "I'm okay. A little stiff from being restricted during all the tests they've run, but otherwise, I feel fine."

He leans back and studies my face before he cups my cheek. "Why did you have so much blood smeared on your face? I was worried."

"I think I wiped my hand on my face after they got me out. I have a cut on it that needed stitches."

My injured arm is no longer in a sling. The doctor determined it wasn't broken but asked that I limit movement until after all the scans were complete.

I look up at Mac. His eyes roam over me like he's searching for missing injuries. The worry he's holding onto only adds to my anxiety. He's been in my position. Car accidents happen all the time in racing, but his was bad. Much worse than mine. My car didn't roll like his did.

"Mac, I'm okay. I promise."

He nods, but I'm not convinced he believes me. The corners of his eyes wrinkle and his lips pinch together as his face tenses.

"I've never felt so helpless in all my life," he says after a few beats of silence. "I wanted to rip this hospital apart to get to you."

I smile. "It's probably a good thing you contained yourself."

He sits next to me on the bed and lifts me onto his lap. "I didn't. Liam and Chase held me back. They wouldn't let me loose."

I wrap my uninjured arm around him and bury my face in his neck. "Thank goodness for Liam and Chase."

"Is this okay?" He tightens his hold around me. "Holding you like this?"

"Yes. Just watch my arm." My injured arm is resting gently on his chest. "I really needed this. I feel better already."

He kisses my forehead before he places a finger under my chin and lifts my lips to his. My insides warm, and the ache I've been feeling in my entire body instantly eases.

"Me too," he says as he presses his lips to mine.

Then he kisses my nose, first one cheek and then the other, before his lips are on mine again. I part my lips and he doesn't hesitate to deepen the kiss. The swipe of his tongue is gentle and slow but the effect it has on me is intense. The fire burning inside me has me wishing we were anywhere else except here.

There's a light knock on the door that causes me to jerk back. But Mac doesn't let me go. If anything, he tightens his grip around me.

The on-call doctor walks in and smiles when he sees me sitting in Mac's lap. "Looks like you're in good hands. How are you feeling?"

"Better now that I can move around."

He nods and looks down at my chart. "I know. Sorry about that. Waiting for all those tests can be hard. But so far—"

"Where is she?" A female voice yells from outside the room. A moment later, the door swings open and my mom's panicked face fills the doorway.

I sigh and bury my face in Mac's chest. This will not be a fun conversation.

"Oh my God. Are you okay?" My mom rushes toward us but stops short when she realizes I'm in a man's arms. I haven't told them about Mac yet. Only that there were some people I wanted them to meet after the race. "We would have been here sooner, but no one would tell us where you were being taken."

"Mom, I'm fine." I give her my best smile and hope that calms her down. "The doctor was just about to give me an update on my tests. You're just in time."

I glance at the door and see my dad staring at me with a worried expression on his face.

"I take it this is your family?" the doctor says.

"Yes. This is my mom and dad, Anne and Lewis."

The doctor nods. "Well, this won't take too long. So far, all your tests have come back clear. No broken bones. Nothing to worry about in the CT scan. Once I get the MRI results and confirm I haven't missed anything, you should be good. I'm still going to keep you overnight for observation. You hit your head pretty hard. Your arm is going to be sore for a few days, maybe even bruised. I can give you something for the pain if needed. Just let the nurse know if the pain gets worse."

"It feels okay so far," I say. They gave me something for pain when I first arrived, even though I said it wasn't that bad.

"If that changes, let us know. There's no need to suffer with pain when we can help with that."

"I will. Thanks."

The doctor smiles at me before he glances around the room. "Any questions?"

"So her head, it's okay?" my dad asks.

"Yes. She's got a mild concussion, but that's to be expected. Her helmet did its job well."

"Thank you," I say quickly, hoping to end this conversation before my parents bombard him with a million unnecessary questions. They worry way more than they should on a normal day. Watching me have an accident probably has their blood pressure ready to pop.

The doctor gives me a smile and nods. "Then I'll leave you alone. I'll be back once I get the MRI results."

The door is barely closed when my mom turns to me with her hands on her hips and a deep scowl on her face. "Please tell me you're finally done with all this racing business."

"Mom, don't start." I sink into Mac, and he tightens his hold on me.

"Of course I'm going to start. This has gone on far too long. The first race we come to watch, and you almost die in an accident."

Mac tenses beneath me. I press my hand into his chest, hoping that will calm him. "I didn't almost die. Nowhere near that."

"But you could have died." She insists.

"And you could have just as easily gotten into a car accident on your way to the hospital. But you didn't. Accidents happen all the time. A racecar isn't required."

"But it puts you at a much greater risk. Why can't you see that?"

"Mom! I've been in hundreds of races and this is my first accident. I was not in danger of dying."

"Well, I still want you to stop."

I sigh and drop my head back to Mac's chest. "It doesn't matter, anyway. I wrecked my car. It's not like I have the money to fix it."

"Baby, don't you worry. We'll build you a new car," Mac whispers, but he tenses even more as if it hurt him to say them. I glance up at him and he looks sincere. Maybe I imagined the tension because I'm expecting more negativity. My parents have trained me to expect the worst from people when it comes to me racing.

"And who are you?" my dad asks. It's the first he's spoken since they arrived.

"I'm Mac. Mac Mutter." He holds out his hand, but my dad just stares at him. "I'm Sophia's boyfriend."

"Boyfriend?" Mom screeches. "Why didn't you tell us you met a boy?"

"Mom." I roll my eyes. I don't have the energy for this right now. If my parents don't calm down, they're going to have to leave so I can rest.

"Don't *Mom* me. Why is this the first we're hearing about this?"

I rub the bridge of my nose with my injured hand and immediately regret it. My head hurts worse than I'm letting on. "It's new. I was planning on introducing you to him at dinner tonight."

"It can't be that new, considering the way you're sitting on his lap."

"Anna." Dad steps up behind Mom and rests his hand on her back. "Calm down. Getting yourself worked up will only make Sophia worse. She needs rest."

My mom lets out a low sigh. "You're right. But we're not done talking about this."

"Are we ever?" I mumble under my breath.

Mom opens her mouth like she's going to say something else but stops herself. Dad may not like that I race cars either, but he's at least good at keeping Mom in check. He'll make sure she doesn't hound me too much until they're sure I'm feeling better.

"Listen," I say. "I'm exhausted. It's been a long day and I need to rest. We can talk more tomorrow."

Mom stares at me like she doesn't like that option, but Dad nods in agreement.

"Alright, pumpkin. We'll leave," my dad says. Mom's head whips around like she's going to object, but Dad squeezes her shoulder, and she stops. "At least give us a hug. This has been stressful for us too."

"Of course, Dad." Mac lets go of me long enough for my parents to hug me. They both hold on to me for longer than is necessary. But I don't complain. They need to know I'm okay.

A few moments later, Mac and I are alone in my room. He pulls me back onto the bed and curls up behind me, spooning his body around mine. He brushes my hair from my face and kisses my temple.

"Are you hungry?" he asks.

"Yeah, but don't get up. This feels good."

He chuckles and digs around in his pocket. He pulls his phone out and starts typing. "I'll get my brothers to bring us something. It's late and you need to eat something before you fall asleep."

"As long as you don't go anywhere, then it's fine."

He finishes typing his message before he rests his phone on the bed in front of me. "Don't worry, baby. I'm not going anywhere tonight."

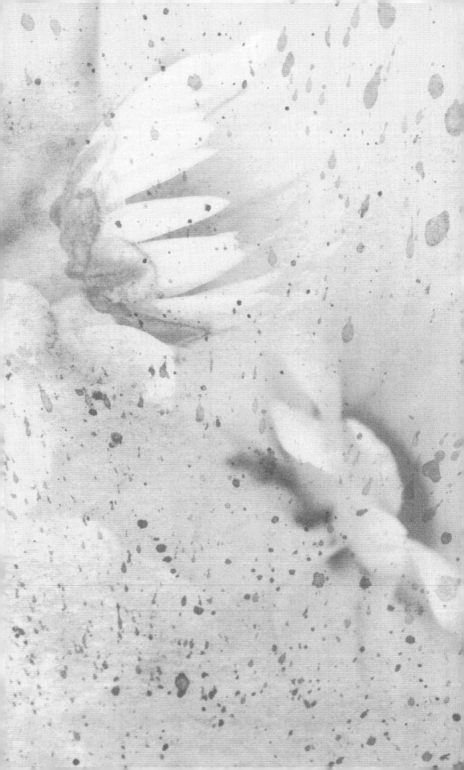

Chapter 21

When you're an asshole, work double time to make up for it.

Mac

My hovering is annoying Sophia. I can't help myself. Ever since her accident, I can't stand to let her out of my sight.

It's only been a few days since we got home from Cincinnati. The hospital kept her for one night. All her test results were good, and aside from her injured arm, the doctor cleared her for normal activity.

She spent one night with her parents before I drove her home. I stayed in a nearby hotel, and it was the worst kind of torture. I hated being away from her so soon after the accident. But she'd insisted one night with her mom and dad would assure them she was okay.

She returned to work today, and I'm being a dick. It's unintentional, but a dick, nonetheless.

I say I'm just trying to help her ease back into her routine slowly. She says I keep doing her job and not letting her work. Help is help. I wish she would take it.

She rolls out from under the car she's currently working on, and I rush over to her with my hand out. She knocks it away. "Mac, you need to stop."

"Let me help you up."

She glares at me. "I don't need help!"

She nudges her foot on the ground and tries to roll away from me, but my leg blocks her.

I lean over her and growl. "Stop being stubborn. Your arm is still sore."

"My arm is fine," she says through gritted teeth.

I ball my hands into fists, attempting to clamp down on my frustration. This woman is infuriating, and I want to yell at her and tell her just how much. Why can't she just let me help her?

Taking a deep breath, I calm myself before speaking again. "Red, it's only been four days since your accident. You need to take it easy."

She just stares at me, blinking rapidly. In fact, she stares quietly for so long I rock on my feet from the agitated energy buzzing between us. She's pissed.

I get that she's independent and wants her life to return to normal, but she's still not back to one hundred percent yet. Besides, it's not like I'm doing anything out of line. It's just help. I don't see what the big deal is.

But I don't say any of that because it would probably just piss her off more.

"Okay, fine. Maybe I've been hovering too much." I concede against my better judgment.

"Too much?" She shoots up to a seated position. Her lip twitches, and she narrows her eyes. If looks could kill, I'd be buried six feet under in the backyard.

I hold my hands up in surrender. "I'll leave. It's almost lunchtime anyway. You want me to bring you something? A sandwich maybe?"

She closes her eyes and takes several long, deep breaths before she looks at me again. "That would be great, thank you."

"Turkey or ham?"

"Turkey with Swiss, if you have it."

"We should." Leaning down to her level, I brace myself over her with one arm and slide my other hand around her neck. I tug her lips to mine. I take her in a deep possessive kiss, letting out all my frustration by sliding my tongue past her lips and swiping it against hers. She instantly relaxes and kisses me back in equal force.

There's so much more I want to do to her right now. Like pull her into my arms, press her against the wall, and bury my cock deep inside her. Or strip her naked and spread her open wide on the hood of this car and lick her until she's screaming my name.

But I can't. Not only is this not the time or place for that, but she's also not up for it yet. No matter what she says, she should still be resting.

When she lifts her hands to cup my face, I break away. With one last kiss to the tip of her nose, I push to my feet, spin around, and head out.

"You're an asshole, Mac!" She calls just before I reach the door.

I turn around and walk backwards for the last few steps. I wink with a huge grin on my face. "I know, baby. You can deny it all you want, but you know you like me this way."

I don't miss the slight uptick on her lips before I turn around and disappear out the door.

I'm still smiling when I enter the kitchen and open the fridge to gather the fixings for our sandwiches. Sophia's lack of concern for her health might irritate me, but I'm still happier than I've been in years. Maybe ever.

My feelings for her still freak me out, but the anxiety and nervousness I feel when I think about how much I care for her is settling into something I can handle. I have no idea where things between us will lead, but I know I want her in my life.

"You look happy." I whip around, surprised to find Grams

sitting at the dining table. I'm so distracted by my thoughts of Sophia, I didn't realize I wasn't alone.

"Hey, Grams. I didn't see you there." I'm impressed with how calm my voice sounds considering my heart rate is speeding. "Making some lunch. Have you eaten yet?"

"Not yet." She looks at me over the rim of her coffee cup. In our house, there's always a hot pot of coffee on. "But don't you worry about me. I'll wait for your dad to return and make us both something then."

I nod and turn to grab the bread out of the cabinet. "Where did dad go?"

"Hardware store. He's going to fix the broken latch on the screen door."

"The one that keeps knocking around at night from the wind?"

She gives me a knowing smile. "That's the one."

The screen door leading to the back patio has been loose for months. No clue why we haven't fixed it yet. It'll probably take Dad ten minutes and less than ten dollars in supplies to do it. It's always the simple jobs that take the longest for us to get done.

"I would've done that for you. You should have nagged me about it."

"I know." Grams waves me off. "Any of you boys would have done it if I asked, but you all work hard all day. Your dad's just sitting around here waiting for orders."

I huff. *Ain't that the truth?* I love my dad, but he's lazy as fuck and hasn't held down a job since I was a toddler. He's helped us in the garage occasionally over the years, but he can't seem to stick with it.

From the stories Grams has told me, he hasn't always been this way. Before his wife died, I hear he had a lot of ambition. Grams always says he and Liam are a lot alike, but I can't see it.

Liam took over the garage when he was in high school because Dad couldn't seem to manage it. He takes care of us. He's the reason we still have a roof over our heads and a thriving business.

Dad may still be in our lives, but Liam has been more of a dad to us than our father ever was.

Dad? He just sits around, drinks coffee, reads his damn paper, and waits for Grams to feed him.

"Besides," Grams continues, "you're too busy taking care of that girl of yours to help an old lady around the house." The teasing tone to Grams' voice has me whipping my head around. The smile lifting her lips matches her tone.

I know what she's thinking. That I've fallen hard for Sophia. She's not wrong. A month ago, I would have denied the depth of my feelings for Sophia as if my life depended on it.

But not anymore. I want Sophia in my life. No. I *need* her in my life, and I think I'm okay admitting that.

But I don't say any of that out loud. Instead, I shrug. "That's what you do when someone you care about gets hurt."

"Yes, it is." She lets out a long, contented sigh. She's watching me with that soft smile Grams always gives us when she's proud of something we've done. "Love is a wonderful thing if you embrace it, Mac. I've waited so long to see one of you boys fall in love. I thought Liam had found it years ago, but I was wrong. Every one of you has fought against love your entire lives. I understand why. It's not like your dad has given you a good example of love. And you never knew your Pops. I wish you boys could have seen how hard he loved me. Maybe then you wouldn't fight it so much."

"Grams, no one is in love." As soon as the words come out, a sour feeling settles in my gut. I've never been in love, and I have no idea what it feels like, but I imagine what I'm feeling for Sophia is damn close.

"Oh, I wouldn't be so sure about that. You don't have to admit it to anyone yet. You don't even have to admit it to yourself. But please don't turn a blind eye to it and pretend those feelings aren't there. You boys are experts when it comes to emotional avoidance. If you let it, love will set you free of all your demons. It will heal your soul and make you whole."

"Grams ... That's a little deep for lunchtime conversation. Don't you think?"

Thankfully, I'm saved from her response when Dad walks into the kitchen with a small bag in hand. I focus my attention on the sandwiches I'm making while he distracts Grams with his rundown of his trip to town.

But the words Grams said hit me hard in the gut. They stick with me while I finish making the sandwiches.

They stick with me while Sophia and I eat together at the small table in the break room.

And they stick with me late into the night while I lie awake in bed, contemplating if they're true.

Do I love Sophia? If I let myself love her, will it heal me of my trust and abandonment issues? Is loving someone and letting that person love me back enough to do that?

It would be nice if it were true, but I can't shake the feeling that it's not quite that simple.

TONIGHT, I'M TAKING SOPHIA ON OUR FIRST OFFICIAL DATE. And by date, I mean dinner and a movie. That's what couples do, isn't it? I've never done this with any of the girls I've dated before, so I hope I get this right.

Grams' words the other day hit me hard, and I need to figure out if she's correct. Hopefully, a real date will be exactly what I need to nail down my feelings for the woman who occupies all my waking thoughts and even some of my dreams.

Besides, I still have to prove to her that I'm a romantic. After tonight, there will be no doubts. I'll still be the possessive asshole that I know she loves, but I'll be a romantic one.

I've showered, dressed in my nicest clothes, and now I'm in my truck, heading to her house to pick her up.

When I park in the driveway, I take one last look in the

rearview mirror before I grab the flowers I ran into town earlier today to pick up. I had to go to Koch's Florist to get them. Not my first choice of florists, but it's the closest one to Beaver. Amelia Koch, the Koch brothers' only sister, was working the counter. Rumor has it she's taking over the florist stop when her mom retires.

She gave me a funny look when I walked in. Rightfully so. It was the first time I'd ever set foot in a florist's shop. But I'm pulling out all the stops tonight. Sophia deserves to be wowed.

Clara answers the door, and she grins when she sees the flowers. "Hi, Mac."

Her eyes peruse my outfit, making her smile grow even wider. By the way she's staring at me, I'd think she's never seen a man dress up for a date before.

I'm not *that* dressed up.

I'm still wearing jeans. So what if they're the nicest pair I own and so dark they almost pass as black dress pants? And is it really that big of a deal that I'm wearing a light blue dress shirt under my charcoal gray wool coat that Grams insists I wear to church on the Sundays I drag my ass out of bed and go?

I don't think so because this is a date. You're supposed to look nice on dates, right?

"Hi, Clara. Is Sophia ready?"

"Almost." She waves me in. "I'll go hunt down a vase while you wait."

As soon as I shut the door behind me, Sophia descends the stairs. My throat tightens and my heart does that thing where it beats faster and harder and rings in my ears. *Fuck.* Just when I don't think she can get more beautiful, she proves me wrong.

She's stunning, wearing a deep red sweater dress with long sleeves and a mock turtleneck that somehow looks sexier than anything I've ever seen her in. Which is amazing since it covers more skin than it reveals.

It's short, stopping high on her thighs. She paired her dress with black leggings and brown leather knee-high boots that are giving me all sorts of dirty ideas of what to do with her in nothing but those boots later tonight.

She's curled her hair, and it lays in soft waves over one shoulder. Her red dress somehow makes her red hair look darker and her fair skin glows more than usual. Just when I don't think my dick can get any more excited about the vision before me, my eyes fall on her luscious lips. The lips that she's painted red to match her dress.

Is it wrong that all I want to do right now is see those red lips wrapped around my cock?

Yes, definitely yes.

"You're ... beautiful." My voice cracks. I clear my throat and lean in and kiss her cheek.

"Thanks." Her cheeks blush and my dick strains against the fabric of my jeans. I shift my hips, attempting to relieve some of the pressure, but it doesn't work. "You look great too." She reaches out and runs her finger along the lapel of my wool coat. "I didn't know you owned anything this nice. I've only ever seen you in your racing jackets."

I can't stop the grin that spreads across my face. "I can clean up nice."

"I see that." Her hand finds its way under my coat. The warmth of it through my dress shirt has my cock thickening even more. If this continues, tonight is going to be very interesting.

"Here. These are for you." I hold the flowers up more as a distraction than anything. She doesn't need to see that I can't control my body around her. Tonight is about romance, not getting in her pants.

Although, I'm not opposed to getting in her pants before this night is over.

Plus, I need to make it up to her for being such an overly protective asshole all week. Sophia is a strong, smart woman. She knows her limits, and I need to learn to respect that about her.

Her face lights up when her eyes land on the flowers. "Oh, wow. They're beautiful."

She takes them, buries her nose in them, and then breathes in deep. Her eyes fall shut as if they're the sweetest things she's ever smelled. The bouquet is a mix of white, deep purple, and pale pink flowers with a lot of dark green leaves in between. I didn't know what to get her. This was Amelia's suggestion, and based on the look on Sophia's face, they're perfect. I'll have to thank Amelia the next time I see her.

Sophia looks up at me and the look in her eyes sends a jolt of nerves through my body. I don't think a woman has ever looked at me with so much awe before.

"I hope you like them," I say, hoping that breaks the intensity of this moment.

"I do. They're perfect. Let me go find a vase to put these in."

"I've got you covered." Clara picks this moment to interrupt. I can't decide if I'm grateful or disappointed. There are way too many emotions passing between Sophia and me right now. Considering our date hasn't even started yet, it's probably best we dial it back a bit.

"Thanks." Sophia hands the flowers to Clara. A look passes between them that makes me think they're having a silent conversation. Have I impressed them both or does that look mean something else?

"I'll set them on the dining table for now." Clara smiles and gives us a wave as she retreats into the kitchen. "Have fun tonight."

"Oh, we will," I say before I reach for Sophia and pull her body flush against mine. I give her a chaste kiss before leaning in close to her neck and breathing in her scent. "You smell so good. Like flowers on a rainy day with a hint of strawberries."

She sighs against me, her sweet breath tickling the skin above the collar of my shirt. "So do you. Are you wearing cologne?"

I chuckle and squeeze her tighter because I can't help myself. She can never be too close to me. "Yes. Is that alright?"

When she looks up at me with that huge smile on her face that I love so much, *I know*. I don't need to go out on a date with her to figure this out. My feelings for her are crystal clear. This woman is it for me.

I am completely head-over-heels in love with Sophia Becker.

"Of course. You smell great. I'm just used to the smell of grease and motor oil on you. Which, by the way, is a smell I also love."

"Good to know, considering I spend most of my time bathing in both."

She drops her jaw in mock surprise and lightly pats my chest. "What a coincidence. Me too!"

Her jovial response makes me laugh. A burning sensation builds in my chest, and it feels like my heart increases in size. Sophia is perfect in more ways than one. She's funny, she puts up with my possessive bullshit, she just might love racecars as much as I do, and she's adventurous in more ways than one. She's almost too good to be true.

But she's here and in my arms. I'd be a fool to let anything get between us and our budding relationship.

She's mine. And I'm going to do whatever it takes to make sure she feels the same way about me.

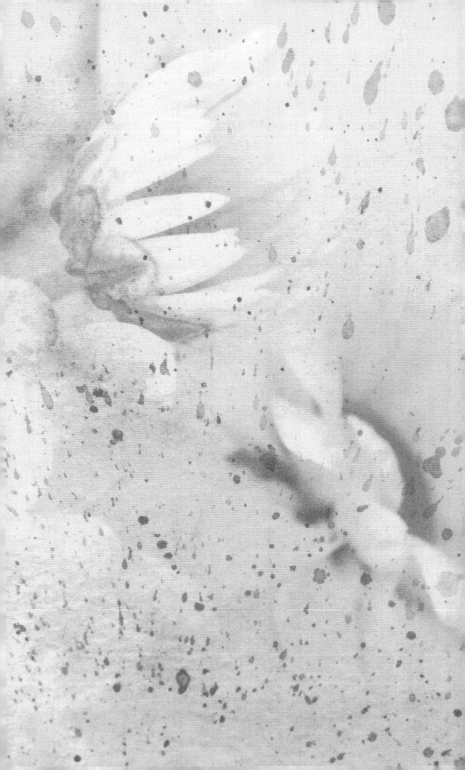

Chapter 22

A perfect first date—dinner, a movie, too much teasing, and a tryst in the woods.

Sophia

"Do you want popcorn?" Mac asks after we enter the theater.

"Do birds fly?" I raise my brows and look up at him with a *duh* expression on my face.

He laughs, that deep bellowing sound that always sets my insides on fire. "So that's a yes."

"Yes!" I clap my hands together and bounce on my feet as I approach the concession counter.

I'm still reeling over the dinner we just had. And let's not forget about the flowers and the sweet way he's been acting toward me since he picked me up.

I'm swooning. Until tonight, I don't think I'd ever experienced honest-to-God actual swooning, but I'm willing to bet all the money in my bank account that this is it.

I still love my growly-bear possessive man that's lying dormant beneath that sexy wool coat of his, but I'm enjoying this side of him too.

As if the flowers weren't enough to make it up to me for being such a pain in my ass all week, he called my mom and asked her for a list of my favorite foods.

He. Called. My. Mom.

Who does that?

Mac, that's who.

I didn't even know he had my mom's phone number. Apparently, she gave it to him at the hospital after my accident.

He took me to this hole-in-the-wall barbecue restaurant where we were seriously overdressed compared to the usual clientele, but the food was phenomenal. Nothing beats good smoked meat and barbecue, and it's always the best from the places that look like dives.

"How about some peanut M&M's®?" Mac rests his chin on my shoulder as he steps up behind me. Just having him this close to me causes my already sensitive nerve endings to tingle and zap like they've been lit by a match.

"I love M&M's®." I spin around and wrap my hands around his neck. "Can I have a blue raspberry slushie too?"

"Baby, you can have anything you want." He plants a kiss on my lips, teasing me with the slight slip of his tongue.

Screw my tingling nerves. That's nothing compared to the ache between my legs. We haven't had sex since before my accident, and I really miss the way he feels when he moves inside me.

God I hope he plans on giving that thing to me tonight.

We order our snacks and head in to grab our seats. We're here to watch a *Friday the 13th* marathon. I'm still in awe that he found a theater showing my favorite movies. They're silly, but some of my best childhood memories start with cheesy horror movies.

The theater is old and looks like something out of a 1950s movie. Unlike modern theaters that can play several movies at a time, this one only has one theater for viewing.

The seats are small, covered in maroon velvet, and smell musty. There's even a balcony that's above the projector room. Of course, that's where I drag Mac.

Once we reach the front row of the balcony, I scan the area below. It's a small theater, and these seats are too close for my liking. Thankfully, we're the only ones here, so we have our pick of the seats.

I take Mac's hand and lead him up a few rows until we're right in the middle of the balcony. The big screen is in the center of our viewing area.

"Perfect." I smile and plop down in a seat.

Mac stares down at me and chuckles. "I thought it was the man that dragged the girl to the most isolated spot, not the other way around."

"Oh, stop. These are the best seats in the house. Besides, every seat in this place is isolated. We're the only ones here."

"True enough." He takes the seat next to me and kicks his feet up on the back of the one in front of us.

The seats predate cup holders in the armrests, so we have to set our drinks on the floor, but the armrests do lift, so I lift the one between us and snuggle up next to him.

"Want some?" Mac holds the popcorn between us, and I take a handful. "You know, I've never seen these movies."

I gasp. "What? How is that possible?"

He shrugs. "Never really watched horror movies. We're more of an action-adventure movie family."

"This is a crime against the classics. Horror movie fan or not, everyone should watch *Friday the 13th* at least once in their life."

"Well, then I'm glad my first time is with you."

"Me too." I have to tamper my giddiness at the knowledge that I get to pop his *Friday the 13th* cherry. "So, I have to ask. Are you the kind of person who makes fun of cheesy movies or appreciates them for what they are?"

"And what exactly am I supposed to appreciate?"

I give him a playful shove. "Oh my God. You make fun of them, don't you?"

"I never said that."

"You didn't have to. I see it in your expression. Word of warning. Do not make fun of *Friday the 13th*. We'll fight."

He waggles his brows. "Maybe I *want* to fight with you."

I narrow my gaze on him, but that only makes him laugh.

"What? I like fighting with you." He places his finger under my chin and lifts my lips to his. "Or should I say, I like *making up* with you."

Just as he takes the kiss deeper, the lights dim, and the projector kicks on. As soon as the sound blasts through the speakers, I grin and pull away.

"Later. The movie is about to start, and you have to pay attention."

Once the opening credits are done, Mac leans close to my ear and whispers. "Did you know this was partially based on a true story?"

My mouth falls open. "No it's not. It's fictional."

"You're wrong. It's actually based on the real-life murders of three teenagers at some lake in Finland. The creators deny it, but the similarities are supposedly eerily similar to those murders."

"How do you know this?"

He shrugs before tossing a handful of popcorn into his mouth. "I Googled it."

"You Googled it? Why did you do that?"

"Because these are your favorite movies. I wanted to learn more about them before I brought you to see them."

Did I mention I was swooning? Totally swooning and lost to this man. "Okay, I'm impressed. So, tell me about this true story that inspired the movies."

"Apparently, these teenagers went camping in tents near a lake. The next day, a carpenter stumbled upon their tents and found them all stabbed to death. Actually, I think one of them was still alive. But they were all stabbed multiple times. But that's not even the worst part."

He pauses like he's not going to continue. I grab his arm and shake it. "Mac! Tell me."

He chuckles. "The lone survivor's description of the murderer was creepy as fuck. He said he was dressed in all black and had bright red eyes. Who the hell has red eyes?"

"You're making that up."

"I'm not. I can prove it." Mac pulls his phone out of his pocket and opens the browser. Within seconds, he's pulled up an article and hands me his phone.

"Oh my God. I can't believe I didn't know this."

The light from his phone is bright enough to light up his face. His expression is one of playfulness and excitement. "And you call yourself a fan."

"Oh, stop. I bet there are things you don't know about some of your favorite movies." I poke him in the side, and he squirms. My smile grows. "Are you ticklish?"

I poke at his side again, and this time he jumps in his seat. "You are!'

He grabs my hand and quickly locks it behind my back before I free it from his grip.

"Don't. Tickle. Me." His voice is rough and deep and sends a vibration of lust throughout my entire body.

"Or what?" I ask, my own voice a little raspy.

"Or I'll have to punish you. Remind you who's in charge." I don't know how it's possible, but his voice drops several octaves lower.

He roughly pulls me flush against his chest. His lips graze the sensitive skin of my neck and I melt. Gone. I'm in a puddle and have no control of my limp body. *This man.*

I want his mouth on more of me—all of me—and now I'm wishing I didn't wear this damn sweater dress. It's one of my favorite outfits, but the mock turtleneck makes it impossible for Mac to put his mouth where I want it.

"Mac," I whisper. "Touch me."

His hand slides down to my leg and teases the hem of my dress. My body instantly lights up with anticipation. But just as he moves his hand further up my thigh, the theater doors below us open with a bang and laughter from a group of teenagers fills the open spaces.

Mac jerks upright and straightens me in my seat. We watch as the group of kids file into the front two rows of the bottom level. Once they've taken their seats, they settle down some, but they're still noisy based on expected movie theater etiquette.

Mac leans close to me, presses his mouth to my ear, and whispers, "Don't think you're off the hook. I'm still going to touch you. Now you just have to be extra quiet."

I PRACTICALLY DRAG MAC BACK TO HIS TRUCK AFTER THE first *Friday the 13th* movie ended. Screw sticking around to watch the other two. I've seen them. I'll make Mac watch them with me some other time when I'm not so worked up because he spent an hour and a half teasing me.

Teasing. Me.

As promised, he put his hands on me. He touched me in all the right places and had me so close to orgasm more times than I can count. But he never let me come.

I spent the last hour and a half growling at him while he silently laughed.

Once we reach his truck, I don't bother to walk around to the passenger side. I slide in through the driver's side and make myself comfortable in the center.

"You better find somewhere private, mister," I say as soon as he shuts the door behind him.

He tosses me that shit-eating grin that I normally love, but right now, I want to kiss it off his face. Okay, maybe *slap* is what I'm thinking, but I'm trying really hard to keep my frustration under control. He relentlessly teased me throughout the entire movie. Frustrated doesn't even begin to describe how I feel right now.

"What's the matter, Red? Something got you all worked up?"

I glare at him, cup my hand over his cock and squeeze. I squeeze hard. He winces and doubles over.

"You know damn well what's the matter. Now drive."

His gravelly chuckle causes my core to clench. "Fuck, baby. You're sexy when you're pissed at me."

"I'll show you pissed if you don't start driving right *the fuck* now."

"Yes, ma'am." His grin fills up the entire cab of his truck. I can tell he wants to tease me more, but thankfully, he starts the truck up and pulls out of the parking space.

It doesn't take us long to get out of the city. Chillicothe isn't that big. It's about a thirty-five to forty-minute drive north of Beaver, and the closest city that provides options for a good night out.

As soon as he pulls his truck off the main road and onto a nondescript dirt road, I shed my coat, unzip my boots, and slide them off. Then I strip my leggings and panties off and toss them in the seat beside me.

"Fuck, Red. You're not messing around." Mac's voice is thick with need.

He presses his foot on the gas and spins his tires in the dirt as we disappear into a treeline. As soon as we're under cover, he slams the truck in park and scoots his seat all the way back.

My hands are on him, and I have his pants undone and pushed halfway down his legs before he takes his next breath. My mouth waters as I take in his hard, thick cock. There's a part of me that wants to return the favor and tease him just like he teased me, but I have to have him inside me, or I feel like I'll die. Dramatic, yes. But that's how I feel.

I fist his cock with my hand as I sling my leg over his lap and straddle him. His hands slide up my thighs, lifting my dress up and over my head. The cool night air hits my bare skin and I shiver. But then he unhooks my bra and sucks my already hard nipple into his mouth, and I completely forget about being cold.

White hot desire licks every inch of my skin where he touches me. His firm hands brace my back as I lift myself up, align his cock with my center, and slowly slide down on his erection. The moan that escapes me as he spreads me open is otherworldly.

"Fuck, baby," he groans out his pleasure. "Condom."

"I ... I want to feel you." I can barely breathe as I slowly move up and down his length, taking him deeper inside me with each movement. He fills me so completely. My vision blurs and my hands shake as I wrap them around his neck. "I'm on the pill."

"Baby," he whispers as he drops his forehead to mine. His arms tighten around me, and his fingers dig into my skin. "Are you sure? I've never done it without one before."

I nod. "Please. I need to feel all of you. Just *you*."

He answers me by lifting me up and slamming me back down on him. The feeling is so intense. My head falls back and the tremor that runs through me makes me feel like I've lost all control. My arms fall limp, and if it weren't for his arms around me, I'd fall back on the steering wheel.

Taking control, he slowly thrusts up. His cock hits that spot deep inside me and that's all it takes to send me tumbling over the edge.

"Mac!" The cry that escapes me is almost as jarring as how quickly my release washes over me. I've never come this fast.

"Fuck," he grunts. "You're squeezing the life out of me."

He doesn't relent. He thrusts hard and fast and keeps pushing my body higher. My orgasm keeps coming, or maybe it spirals into a second. I can't tell.

I've ever felt this good, this high, this satisfied before in my life.

When his lips wrap around one of my nipples, I swear my body explodes into a million tiny pieces of pure pleasure. I didn't know it was possible to feel this good, for an orgasm to last this long, or for another person to make me feel this deeply.

But Mac makes me feel more. More alive. More loved. More needed. More desired. Just more.

He makes me feel everything.

He thrusts faster into me as his orgasm builds. He sucks harder on my nipple and his fingers dig deeper into my hips. Just when I don't think I can take another moment, he grunts out his release.

His body stills as he holds me down on him—his grip tight and possessive. I have no idea how long we sit like that. Me gasping on top of him. Him buried deep inside me with his head resting between my breasts. It could have been seconds or hours.

"Fuck, baby." Mac breathes deeply against my bare chest. "Remind me to tease you more often, if that's what I get in return."

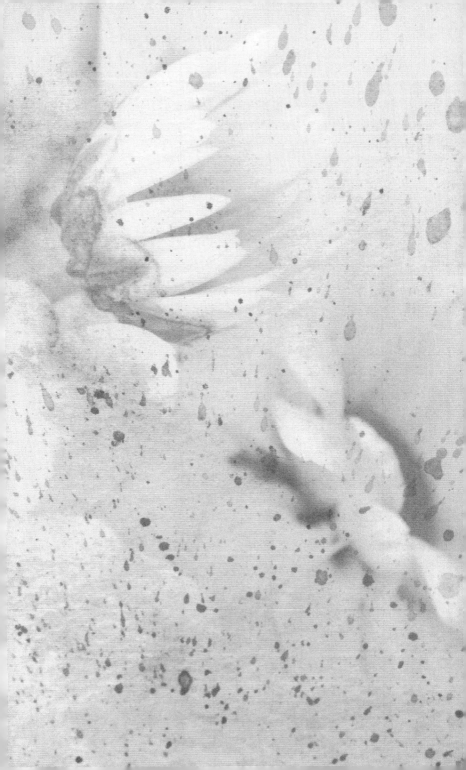

Chapter 23

Throwing a wrench at it doesn't make things better.

Mac

We had our first snowfall last night. It wasn't much, just a light dusting, but the temperature dropped twenty degrees with it. We hit single digits for the first time this season. Something that doesn't happen often in early November.

I hope it's not a sign we're in for a harsh winter. I love the snow, but I hate the cold. Does that make me an oxymoron? Can't have snow in the heat. But if we could, I'd want to live with it every day.

Some of my best childhood memories involve building snow forts with my brothers and then following it up with epic snowball fights. Warren always made the best forts. He was born with a brain for design and structure. I guess that's why he's so successful at designing cars.

But Chase and Ash were the most fun. We'd play until we could no longer feel our hands or our feet. Our faces would be red and chapped and our lungs would burn so badly from breathing the cold air.

Grams would always have hot chocolate with whipped cream waiting for us when we came inside. We'd huddle by a fire in the family room, our hands and feet itching like crazy as they warmed back up. I hated that feeling, but it was so worth it to play in the snow.

I glance over my shoulder at where Sophia is working. She's got a few oil changes lined up today. Nothing she can't handle, but I still want to rush to her side and act as her assistant. She'd probably rip my head off if I tried.

It's been almost two weeks since her accident, and her hand and arm are healing nicely. Her stitches fell out on their own. Her shoulder still has some discoloration from where it bruised, but she swears it doesn't hurt.

She sees me watching her and her eyes narrow. Probably because she can read my overly protective mind. But I just toss her a wink and stick to my side of the garage. I know she can handle herself. I can't help it that every fiber of my being screams at me to protect her—to keep her safe. It's a primal urge that I have to work overtime to keep in check.

We've been busier than normal for this time of year. As the holidays near, folks around here tend to hold off on car repairs and maintenance. They need to save for Christmas, which means come January, we typically have a rush of work that should have been done a month ago.

That's why my racing has been so critical to keeping our business in the black. My sponsors pay well even at the level that I'm currently racing. They're not just paying me to drive cars. They're paying for our brand, too.

Liam is right. We build damn good racecars. We shouldn't be selling them to other teams. We should build a team around our brand, not just around me.

Besides, I'm not sure how much longer I want to race professionally. I love racing. It's in my blood. But my head hasn't been right since the accident. Oddly enough, I think I'm okay with that. I think I'd be pretty damn good at managing a team. Maybe even training new drivers and helping the next generation find their path.

It's something that's been on my mind for a while now. I just have to find the courage to talk to my family about it. I know they'll support whatever decision I make. But it's just a scary change.

The back door to the garage slams, and I whip my head around. Christian strolls in with his head down and his shoulders slumped. He always looks pissed at the world, but this morning he looks more dejected than usual.

I check the time. It's a little after eleven. He's never one to arrive to work at eight like Liam wants, but he's never this late either.

"Hey, man. You feeling okay?" I ask, knowing that could be a trigger question.

His eyes snap to mine, and I fight the way my body tenses. His eyes are bloodshot. He's got dark circles under his eyes and his skin is pale. Even behind his scruffy beard, I can see his sunken cheeks. I've only ever seen him look this bad when he's using.

Christian has struggled with sobriety most of his teenage and adult life. He's been in and out of rehab more times than any of us care to count. The last time he started using, we almost lost him. He'd been on a three-day bender after having gone eight months sober. He took a hit of heroin that nearly took him from us.

That was fourteen months ago. If he's using again, Liam might kill him.

My expression must give me away. He shakes his head and waves me off.

"It's not what you think." His voice is rough and groggy as if he just woke up.

"And what am I thinking?"

He grumbles something I can't make out and heads toward the bike he's working on. I watch him carefully. His hands are steady, and he's not stumbling. That's a good sign, but I'm still worried.

I wipe my hands clean and walk over to him. Once I'm next to him, I look him in the eye. He looks like shit and smells like he drank way too much last night. Christian can still drink alcohol in moderation without relapsing. But from the way he smells, moderation went out the window last night.

"Where were you last night?" I ask, keeping my voice firm and devoid of emotion. We learned a long time ago that Christian responds best to directness rather than tiptoeing around his issue or getting overly emotional.

He lets out a deep sigh but doesn't look at me. "I was at Posey's Lounge. Had a few drinks, then came home."

"How many is a few?"

His eyes snap to mine, and all I see is rage. My interrogation is pissing him off. *Good.* He needs to get angry. It forces him to feel rather than hide behind his addiction.

"Three," he barks through gritted teeth. "Three fucking drinks. Okay?"

I square my shoulders and force myself to remain calm. Losing my temper with him won't do any good. "You don't smell like you *only* had three. You reek, Christian."

He steps into my space and nudges his chest against mine. "Why don't you say what you're really thinking?"

My eyes dart in Sophia's direction. The car she's working on is jacked up on the front and she's currently under it. She may not see what's going on, but I know she can hear every word of our exchange.

I drop my voice so only he can hear me. I don't want Sophia thinking ill of Christian. He may have a shady past, but he's still a good guy. "You smell like you drank the entire bar dry. How much did you really have?"

"Whatever, asshole." He turns away from me and heads toward the bench by his workstation.

I sigh and run my hands over my face. "Christian, I'm not

trying to be an asshole. You can't blame me for being concerned when I see you like this."

"There's nothing to be concerned about!" he yells. His anger elevates with every word that passes between us. "Leave me the fuck alone."

"Everything okay out here?" Liam asks from the doorway. He's standing just inside the garage with Ash and Chase on either side of him.

Chase's shoulders are slumped, and he looks like he's ready to break. It's never easy for any of us to see Christian like this, but it's so much harder on him. They may be opposites, but as twins, they share a bond the rest of us don't have.

"Great. Are you three going to give me shit, too?" Christian asks, his tone harsh and accusatory.

"I'm not giving you shit." I reach for his arm, but he jerks away. He stumbles, trips over his own feet, and falls backward. He slams into his workbench. It tips over, sending his tools flying in all directions.

My eyes follow a wrench that's spinning in the air and heading directly toward the car Sophia is under. It hits the release bar on the jack just right, and the jack falls. The car crashes to the floor with a loud creak. An even louder yelp escapes from Sophia, where she's now trapped under the car.

"Sophia!" I rush toward her, but my brothers are closer, and they reach her first. Ash and Chase lift the car while Liam pulls her out from under it.

"I'm fine! I'm fine!" She calls out before they even have her free.

When I reach her side, I drop to my knees. "You're bleeding!"

The same anxiety I felt after her car accident surfaces. My chest feels tight and every nerve ending in my body feels overly sensitive. My skin tingles and my hands itch.

Her eyes widen when they meet mine. She must see the panic

in them because she grabs at my hand and shakes her head. "Mac. I'm fine. I was low enough it barely grazed me."

"You're not fine. There's blood on your face."

"Mac." Liam gently touches my arm like he's trying not to excite a wild animal. "It's just a scratch. It doesn't even look like it needs a bandage."

"Fuck!" I push to my feet and spin around. The first thing I see is Christian. His expression is remorseful, but the urge to punch him is strong.

If he had nothing to hide, he didn't need to act out like that. If he's using again, then he's out of control and needs help. Either way, he's responsible for hurting Sophia. I want to hurt him in return.

"Fuck! Fuck! Fuck!" I yell. I can't kick my brother's ass, no matter how much I want to. But I have to get rid of all this pent-up anger and anxiety inside me.

I push past my brothers and rush out the back door. All of them call after me, but I don't stop. I need to get away before I do something truly stupid.

Rushing into our private garage, I grab the keys to one of the ATVs. I have it started, and I'm out the door before any of my brothers reach me.

I just need some space. Once I clear my head of this anxiety, I'll be fine.

THE GROUND IS HARD AND SLICK. RIDING ATVs DOES NOT MIX with a light dusting of snow followed up with sleet and freezing temperatures. A full-fledged snowstorm with several inches? Sure. ATVs can be a blast in six to twelve inches of white, fluffy snow.

But this? This is stupid.

Enough water and moisture gathered to create ice patches in strategic locations. And not strategic for my safety. The exact opposite, in fact. Every dip and low spot on the trail is nothing but ice. Add in the canopy of the trees, and the temperatures are probably ten degrees colder here than in the open where the sun is shining.

The trail will not get better.

I should turn around.

I should head back to the garage and face my anxiety.

Ever since my accident, my fears have become crippling. Sophia's accident only made it worse.

Fuck. Sophia. I should be with her. It should be me tending to her wound and making sure she's okay. Not my brothers.

She *is* okay.

She has to be.

Losing Sophia is not an option. Not anymore. I'm in too deep. But my anxiety and deepest fears show their ugly heads.

But women always leave. Your mom left. Your brothers' moms all left.

Women don't stay.

"Shut up!" I yell at the voices in my head.

The very idea of Sophia leaving me turns my stomach into knots. I feel sick. My heart aches and my chest feels so tight it's hard to take in air.

What the fuck is happening to me? Why am I even thinking like this? I have no reason to think Sophia is going to leave me.

Is it because I love her that much?

If this is the other side of love, I'm not sure I want it.

What was it that Grams said to me?

Love will set you free. It will heal your soul and make you whole.

Bullshit. I don't feel free, and I certainly don't feel whole.

I'm a fucking wreck.

Love *doesn't* set you free. It fills you with jealousy and feeds your insecurities and fears.

Before I can sort out all the feelings swimming around in my head, the ATV slips on an ice patch. I go sliding sideways toward a large tree. I try to correct for the angle and straighten myself out, but the trail is too slick.

I'm at the top of a hill and heading directly for a large tree. If I hit it, one of two things could happen. I could come to an abrupt stop. It would trash the ATV, and my body could slam into the tree. That would hurt like hell, but it would put an abrupt end to this accident. That's a much better outcome than option two.

Option two could cause me to spin out of control when I crash. If I spin out of control, then I will tumble down this hill, rolling the ATV over me. There are countless trees—both small and large—scattered along this hillside. If I roll, I will get clobbered.

Fuck, I didn't grab a helmet.

I try again to straighten and alter my direction. I need an option three.

Option three is to not fucking crash. If I can just stay on the trail, I'll be fine.

Nope. There is no option three because I can't stop from sliding on this ice.

When I look up, all I see is the dark rough bark of the large oak. I'm slamming into it no matter what I do.

I brace myself, gripping the handlebars and ducking my head.

Please don't let me hit my head.

I hear the loud crash and crumple of metal before I feel the jerk from the impact. Then the worst thing that could happen happens.

Option two.

When I come to, I'm face down on the ground and every inch of my body hurts.

I'm also cold. Very, very cold. I also didn't bother to grab my jacket when I ran out of the garage. My long sleeve t-shirt is not enough to keep me warm.

I lift my head, slowly blinking until my surroundings come into view. My eyelids are heavy, and everything is blurry. But not because my eyes won't focus. There's something on my face.

Moving one limb at a time—first my arms, then each leg—I slowly push myself up. Fuck, I hurt. But I don't think I broke anything.

Blinking, I still can't get my eyes to stay open. Did I hit my head too hard? Wiping my face, I quickly discover the problem. Blood is dripping down my face and over my eyes.

Using the hem of my shirt, I wipe my face. It helps, but the cut on my head is a gusher and a stream of blood immediately replaces what I wiped away.

The ATV is only a few feet away from me. It's upside down and propped against a very large tree. I may feel like death from rolling down the hill, but it's a damn good thing the tumble threw me from the seat. Something tells me I'd be in worse shape if the ATV trapped me between it and that tree.

Pushing to my feet, I find my bearings and continue down the hill to home. Thankfully, I didn't make it that far into the woods before I wrecked, and it only takes about ten minutes before the house comes into view.

I pick up my pace, eager to get out of the cold and bandage my head. I can't keep the blood out of my eyes. Plus, every inch of my body aches. The warmth of the fire I know Grams has lit is enough to keep me moving.

Sophia is the first to see me when I open the back door.

"Mac!" She jumps up from her seat and rushes to me. "Oh my God. You're bleeding!"

"I'm fine." I wave her off the same way she did to me, even though I know I'm not fine. The throbbing in my head is reminiscent of my racing accident. It's not quite that bad, but it's not good either.

"You're not fine." She takes my arm to help me into the kitchen. "And you're freezing. Will someone grab a blanket?"

I have no clue who responds, but moments later one of Grams' hand-knitted wool blankets is around my shoulders before Sophia shoves me into a chair. Between it and the warmth of the house, I instantly feel better.

"We need to get you to the hospital," Sophia says after she gets a good look at the cut on my head. "This needs stitches."

I shake my head. "I'm not going anywhere."

"Mac. It won't stop bleeding unless it's closed up. This cut is deep."

"Bandage it up. It'll stop." I insist. My tone is too harsh, and she winces.

"No!" Liam barks. "You're going to the hospital."

I shove Sophia's hand away from my face and push to my feet. "Not going. I'll bandage it up myself."

"You will sit back down in that chair, young man." Grams' strong voice cuts through the tension and I freeze. "Not another damn word. I'm calling Dr. Koch."

I fall back in my chair without argument. I don't have to argue. My brothers do it for me.

"Aaron is not welcomed here," Liam says. "I'll drive him to the hospital."

"You'll do no such thing. Forget the damn feud for a moment and think about your brother." Grams waves him off. Her phone is already in her hand and ringing. "Hi, Dr. Koch? This is Mila Mutter."

Her voice trails off as she heads into the living room. As soon as she's out of earshot, my brothers all turn and start on me. With all of them talking at the same time, I can't follow what they're saying, but from the tone, none of it's good.

"Enough!" Sophia yells, and they all quiet. With her hands on her hips, she narrows her eyes on me and I wince. She may be worried about my injuries, but she's still pissed.

She shakes her head and marches past me toward my room. "I'll get you a clean shirt."

"What happened?" Chase asks. I glance up and Liam, Chase, and Ash are staring at me with concern. But Christian isn't looking at me. His head hangs low as if he's hiding his shame.

I let out a deep sigh. "I'm a dumbass, that's what."

"Clearly," Ash says. "Be specific."

"I hit an icy patch on the trail. Spun out of control, then hit a tree that caused me to spin even more out of control and I rolled down the hill. The ATV crashed into a tree after I was flung from the seat. It's probably totaled."

Liam opens his mouth, then quickly closes it. He stares at me for another beat before he spins on his heel and leaves the room. I hear his footsteps retreat up the stairs.

Yeah, I fucked up but good this time.

"Dr. Koch isn't happy about it, but he's on his way." Grams points at me with a horrifying look in her eyes that says I'd be grounded for life if I weren't a twenty-seven year-old adult. "You're going to let that man stitch you up without saying a damn word. Am I clear?"

"Yes, ma'am." I grit my teeth and keep my eyes down. I may not be happy about this, but I know better than to argue with Grams.

"Here." Sophia steps up next to me with a clean shirt. "Put this on and then I'll make you some hot tea."

"I don't like hot tea," I say, avoiding her eyes.

"You're still shivering. You need to warm up."

"I'm not drinking any damn tea." I snap.

Grams whips around and slams her hand on the table. "You'll drink whatever hot beverage that girl gives you, and you'll like it. And show her some damn respect!"

"It's okay, Grams." Sophia's words are laced with frustration. "If he wants to suffer, let him."

"No." It's not a reply, but a command. When Grams makes her mind up about something, there's no changing it. "If he would've stuck around and taken care of you like he should have, this wouldn't have happened. It's his own damn fault he has to drink hot tea."

Sophia tosses the shirt at me. I half expect her to leave. It's what I deserve with the way I'm acting. But she doesn't. She grabs the tea kettle and fills it with water.

I guess I'm drinking tea.

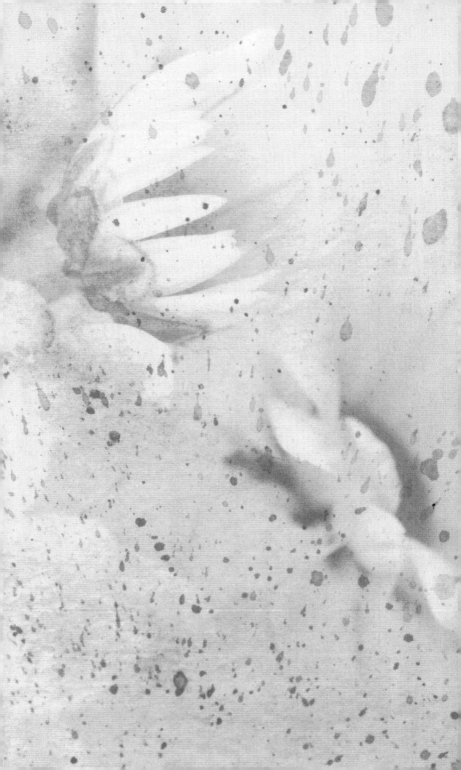

Chapter 24

When a drink isn't just a drink.

Sophia

Mac's being a dick. Well, partially a dick, but still a dick. It's been a few days since the double accident. How he escaped that tumble down the hill with nothing more than a cut on his head is a freaking miracle.

The ATV? It didn't survive. It's not even worth attempting to salvage. Mac is a very lucky man that he walked away with all his bones intact. Hell, he's lucky to be alive.

Me? I barely have a scratch on my head from the jack falling, and he's acting like I'm the one that could have died. He's back to trying to do my job for me rather than letting me work.

Hence, a dick.

But then he gives me unexpected hugs and kisses and little touches that lets me know he cares. It's really not fair because it makes me forget how much of a dick he's being too. He's really perfected the balance between an overly protective, possessive asshole and a sweet, loving boyfriend.

He makes it hard to stay mad at him.

And I *really* want to be mad.

Like now. I'm at the sink washing my hands and he just slipped his arms around my waist and rested his head on my shoulder. "Mac, what are you doing?"

"Hugging you." He plants a light kiss on my exposed neck.

"You hugged me thirty minutes ago. Let me work."

"I am letting you work."

I turn the water off and spin around to face him. I'm staring at him with raised brows and a frown while he's smiling. When he smiles at me like that, he makes it hard to stay mad. I want to be mad.

He leans closer to give me a kiss, but I lift my hand. He kisses my fingers instead. "You need to stop. You're overbearing."

He sighs and drops his forehead to mine. "I'm sorry. I can't stop worrying about you."

"Mac." I cup his cheeks and force him to look me in the eye. "You're allowed to worry about me all you want. I just need you to let me work. I can't get my job done if you're constantly touching me or interfering."

"But I like touching you." He presses his lips to mine before I can respond. I can't deny that I love it when he touches me and kisses me like this. He's a hard man to resist.

"I like it too." I wrap my arms around his waist and hug him close. I love the feel of being engulfed in his hard body and strong arms. "But there's a time and a place for that. Work is not it."

He nods but doesn't say anything. Instead, he kisses me again. This time swiping his tongue along my bottom lip. I instinctively open up for him and let him kiss me more deeply. My body comes alive with desire and need.

I grumble against his lips, and he chuckles. "This is why you're an ass. You know that?"

"You know you wouldn't change a thing about me," he says with nothing but confidence. It irritates me that he's right.

"Will you two knock it off?" Ash calls out as he walks through the side entrance. With how cold it's been this past week, we've left the bay doors closed.

"Gladly." I give Mac a teasing shove. "Just tell your brother to keep his hands to himself."

"I doubt he'd listen." Ash smiles, and it isn't until he steps aside that I realize he's not alone.

"Clara! What are you doing here?"

"Just got off work. I wanted to catch you before this guy monopolizes your time tonight." She points at Mac, but her eyes stay on me. "A group of us from work are going out to Posey's Lounge tonight. They do karaoke on Fridays. It's a good time. You should come."

I wrinkle my nose. Karaoke is not something I enjoy. "As long as I don't have to sing."

"What? No!" Clara's smile fades and her shoulders sag. "Karaoke is only fun if everyone takes part. You have to."

I shake my head and chuckle at how much she looks like a toddler who's just lost her favorite toy. "I do not sing. But I'll gladly watch others make a fool of themselves."

"Who said anything about fools?" Mac crosses his arms over his chest with a furrowed brow. "I can sing just fine."

"Good for you, but I can't. I am not about to deliberately embarrass myself."

"Fine." Clara huffs. "You don't have to sing, but will you still come?"

I glance between her and Mac. She looks hopeful. Where he looks like he's up to no good. His brow is still furrowed, but there's a hint of mischief behind his gaze.

"Okay, fine. I'll go. But the first sign of any funny business and I'm leaving." I wave my finger between them. "Understood?"

Clara's smile returns. "Of course. I promise I won't make you sing."

I hold Mac's stare and he looks like he wants to argue with me. But then he nods. "Fine. I'll pick you up at seven. We'll grab some dinner beforehand."

I shake my head. "No. I'm going to have dinner with Clara

tonight. It's been too long since she and I hung out. Give us a couple of hours with just us girls."

The wrinkle in his brow deepens. "You don't want to hang out with me? I know I've been an asshole again, but I promise, I'll—"

I cut him off with my hand over his mouth. "This isn't about you being an asshole. I just want to hang out with Clara for a bit." I step into his space and lean in close to his ear so only he can hear me. "Meet me at the bar later. I promise to make it worth your while."

The growl that leaves his lips makes me chuckle. "You're so going to pay for this later."

"I'm looking forward to it." I kiss his cheek and undo the top button on my coveralls. "I think I'm going to go ahead and call it a day. Clara, can I get a ride home with you since Mac drove me in this morning?"

"Of course." She's bouncing on her feet and clapping her hands. "This is going to be fun. You coming too, Ash?"

Her eyes light up as she looks up at him. His smile grows. "I wouldn't miss it. I'll make sure Mac doesn't come too early. Just promise to stay out of trouble."

Clara rolls her eyes. "Since when do I cause trouble?"

"Not you." He tousles her hair like she's his little sister and her smile wavers. Can he really not see how she looks at him? "I'm talking to Sophia. She's the troublemaker."

"Hey!" I scoff. "I don't cause trouble."

"Bullshit, Red." Mac sweeps in behind me and spins me around. "You've been nothing but trouble since the day you walked into my life."

I shrug with a grin before I wrap my arms around his neck. "Yeah, but you like it."

"Never said I didn't." Then he presses his lips to mine.

POSEY'S LOUNGE IS A HOLE IN THE WALL. I DON'T EVEN THINK it's nice enough to qualify as a dive bar. Sure, it's filled with locals and is the only bar within a ten-mile radius of Beaver, but it's a dump.

The floors are rough wood and unfinished. If I fell, I've no doubt my hands would be filled with splinters from bracing my fall. There's a stage opposite the entrance that's currently dark with a small dance floor in front of it. Clara mentioned they bring in cover bands on Saturdays, but Fridays are reserved for karaoke. Based on the clientele, I'm having a hard time picturing this group singing karaoke.

The bar is along the right wall, every seat taken by someone who looks like they belong to the local motorcycle club. A few even have jackets on with the name Unholy Ghosts embroidered on the back above what I can only describe as a screaming, terrified face. If those guys sing karaoke, color me shocked.

The rest of the bar is open and filled with tables. Several of them are empty, but the ones filled with patrons cause me to pause. There's an even mix of leather-wearing men, girls dressed in sparkling tops like they're at a nightclub, and a small crowd dressed in business attire. I'm assuming those are Clara's coworkers, since they're waving us over.

There's a separate room between the bar and the stage that I couldn't see until we walked further in. It looks like a game room. There are several pool tables and dart boards. The room is full of more men and women dressed like bikers and nightclub goers.

My gaze catches on a familiar pair of brown eyes. Christian is hunched over a table. He nods his head in greeting before he turns back to the man he's talking to. It's an older man with a light dusting of gray in his dark hair and beard. He's handsome for sure but carries an air of darkness around him. My brain immediately chants *danger, danger, danger* on repeat. He's wearing a similar leather jacket as the men sitting at the bar. I can't see the back of it, but I wonder if it has the same emblem for the Unholy Ghosts.

"Come on." Clara tugs at my arm and pulls me away from the game room.

I follow her, but I can't help but wonder what Christian is doing with them. After the conversation between him and Mac that resulted in the jack falling accident, I can't help but worry.

I like Christian, and I don't want anything bad to happen to him.

He may be quiet and broody, but I haven't noticed anything about his actions that indicates he's using again. But there's something about the man he's talking to that draws concern.

"Sophia, these are my coworkers," Clara says as we approach a table with a group that looks close to our age. "This is Trevor." She points to the only man in the group. He's got dark hair with a mess of curls on top. Even sitting down, he looks tall. He smiles and the cutest pair of dimples pops out. Paired with his dark-rimmed glasses, he's perfected the cute nerdy look. "He teaches calculus and geometry."

He offers his hand, and I shake it. "Nice to meet you." The deep timbre of his baritone voice makes me smile. If he sings, I bet it drives the girls wild.

"This is Karla, the PE teacher and head softball coach." She points to the petite blonde next to Trevor. "Don't let her size fool you. She's a badass."

"From what I hear, Sophia's the badass." Karla beams up at me. "Anyone who can outrace Mac wins the badass title."

"Thanks." I laugh.

"And this is Tide." My brows involuntarily lift as Clara introduces me to the gorgeous brunette who looks like she just walked away from a beauty pageant minus the fancy dress and tiara on her head. But if she were wearing one, it wouldn't look a bit out of place. The woman just smiles and shrugs.

"I know. My name is odd." She says with a slight twang to her voice that gives me Southern Belle vibes. "But it gets even better.

My last name is Waters. If my parents didn't love me so much, I'd swear they wanted to ruin my life with a name."

"It's not odd. Just took me by surprise is all," I say quickly, feeling like an ass for letting my reaction show.

"Eh, it's fine. No need to lie." Her smile is genuine as she offers me her hand. "I've heard nothing but good things about you. I teach music and drama."

"She's the reason we're here tonight," Clara says. "If it weren't for her, we wouldn't have karaoke night."

"Oh, so it's your fault." I smile, hoping she catches the teasing tone of my voice. Based on how she laughs, I think I'm safe.

"Guilty as charged!" She holds her drink up with a nod before taking a sip.

Clara and I settle into our seats, and a server comes by and takes our drink order. Not long after we arrive, the stage lights up and someone wheels a karaoke machine out on a cart. Tide is the first to jump up and pick a song. She sings a beautiful rendition of Dolly Parton's *Jolene*.

The entire bar silences the second her voice projects through the speakers. Even the people in the game room stopped and stepped into the main bar area to listen to her voice. She's remarkably talented and much too good to be stuck in this small town. She could easily take the world by storm with her voice.

"Damn." Trevor takes a large gulp of his drink. "No way I want to follow that up."

"Oh, come on, Trevor." Tide teases as she plops down in her seat. "You have a great voice. Get your butt up there."

"Ha!" He shakes his head. "No way. Let someone else ease the crowd back down to reality. Besides," he turns his gaze to me, "I want to hear more about Sophia."

"Oh yes!" Tide claps her hands. "Me too. Please tell me how you snagged one of the most eligible men in Beaver."

I chuckle. "Not sure I snagged him. It was more of a mutual claiming."

"Whoa." Tide fans herself off. "Do tell. Mac can be rather territorial. Is he the same way in his relationships? Oh God. Don't tell me. He goes all sexy, caveman on you, doesn't he? I bet it's so hot."

I pinch my lips together, trying my best not to laugh. There is no way I can admit just how right she is about him. Instead, I down the rest of my drink and stand. "I'm going to go get a refill. Anyone else need one?"

"Way to avoid!" Clara calls after me as I slowly back away. When no one calls out a drink order, I spin around and head to the bar.

Thankfully, the crowd is focused on the next person on stage singing. I'm not entirely comfortable here. This feels like one of those places where newcomers aren't welcomed with open arms. Unfortunately, the bar isn't big enough to fly under the radar, so the singer is a welcome distraction. Most eyes are on her and not me.

She's young, definitely early twenties, and dressed in black leather from head to toe. Her voice isn't as good as Tide's, but she's still okay. She's got a raspy voice like Joan Jett.

"Hey you." A familiar voice calls from behind me. I turn around and smile when I see Tanner walking toward me.

"Hey. Long time no see." My instinct is to lean in for a hug, but I stop myself. While I don't have a problem with Tanner, he's still Mac's mortal enemy. I didn't think he'd ever calm down after being forced to allow Aaron Koch to stitch up his head. I don't want to think about what he'd do if it got back to him that I hugged Tanner Koch.

"Too long. Mac must be keeping you locked up." Tanner glances around the bar like he's searching for someone. "He here?"

I roll my eyes. "Not yet. He'll be here soon."

His grin grows and turns a little too flirtatious. "Too bad. I was hoping to steal a dance. Or maybe even sing a duet."

"Tanner Koch." I place my hands on my hips. "Are you trying to cause trouble?"

He winks as he leans in close. "Now, why would I do something like that?"

"Same reason you did it at the Oktoberfest. You like pissing off the Mutter brothers."

"Nah, I just can't resist pretty girls. And you, darling, are a very pretty girl."

I shake my head and take a step back. "I'm going to go get a drink. Enjoy your night, Tanner."

I do my best to slip away, but the man follows me. Thank God Mac isn't here to see this, or he'd lose his shit.

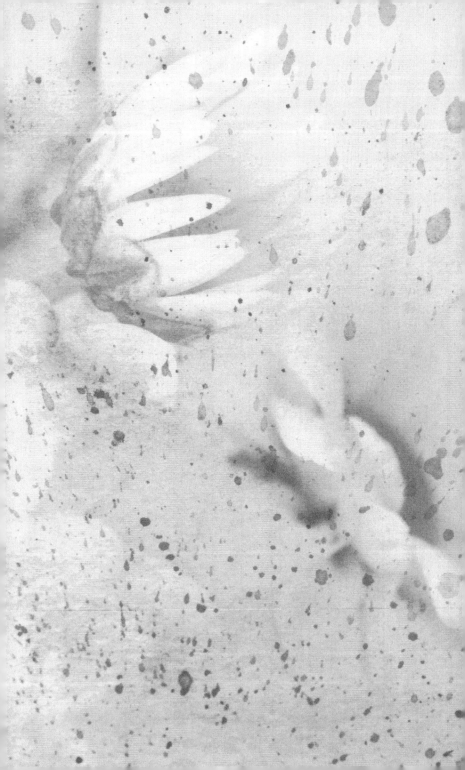

Chapter 25

Being a dumbass is one thing. But being an asshole is unacceptable.

Mac

My brothers are determined to piss me off. I'm already on edge, and I don't need them pushing me over it.

Things between Sophia and me have been tense these past few days. I may be completely to blame for that tension, but my behavior is driven by something real. Something so deeply rooted inside me that I'm not sure how to extricate it from my body.

I've never been in love before, and I'm scared. I'm so fucking scared, and I don't know how to handle it.

I'm scared of fucking things up with Sophia, and scared I'll lose her. Relationships are new to me, and I've no clue what the hell I'm doing. But I want *this* with her. I want *her*.

I'm scared she doesn't care as much for me as I care for her. Sometimes I catch her looking at me in ways that give me so much hope. Those brief looks of longing and want. I like those looks, and I want them to mean something so much more than primal desire. I want her soul to want mine the same that my soul wants hers.

I'm scared she'll wake up one day and decide I'm not worth it. That I'm too much work. That my growly-bear possessive behavior is too much, and she'll realize she deserves someone better than me.

I'm scared of the trust I'm putting in her. Trusting anyone outside my family is risky, but especially trusting a woman.

"Fuck," I say under my breath. I feel so out of control that I can hardly sit still. My knee keeps bouncing, and I'm fidgeting with whatever I can get my hands on.

To make matters worse, my mom showed up here again today. Thank fuck no one else was around to see her. It's bad enough that I have to deal with my emotions over her sudden appearance in my life. I don't want to deal with my brothers' worry over her showing up, too.

She pushed me again to reach out to my half-siblings. I want to —I really do—but again, I'm scared.

I'm so fucking scared of so many things, and I've no clue how to handle it. It's feeding my anxiety and driving me a little crazy. *Literally.*

I pick up the remote and flip through the channels. I've been watching a comedy show on Comedy Central. Well, more like it's been on, but I haven't picked up on anything being said. My mind is too distracted.

I pause on ESPN. College football replays are on. I should change the channel cause this is only going to make me feel worse. Ohio State lost again last week to that school up north that shall not be named.

We've lost for two years in a row. For almost twenty years, we beat the Wolverines. Every. Single. Time. Now it feels like we're on a goddamn losing streak to beat all losing streaks.

Losing sucks, especially to our lifelong rivals.

As much as I want to believe we'll never lose to Michigan, it was bound to happen at some point.

Just another example of how losing is inevitable.

And now I feel even worse.

Because all I can think about is how I'm going to eventually lose Sophia.

One day she's going to wake up and realize I'm not worth the trouble. She'll find someone better. Someone without my issues or possessiveness or insane jealous streak.

That day will suck.

"Dude!" Ash says as he plops down on the couch next to me. "Why are you punishing yourself? Turn that shit off."

He reaches for the remote, and I let him take it. He changes the channel back to the comedy show I had on earlier.

"What's got your panties in a bunch?" he asks.

I cut him a side glare. "Nothing. Just tired."

He snorts. "Liar. Is it because Sophia went out with Clara without you? They're expecting us to come. You know that, right?"

"Of course not." I scoff, already feeling the frustration inside me amplify. Ash has been the worst at poking the bear. "She can go out with her friends whenever she wants."

"Anyone ever tell you you're funny?" he chuckles.

"Shut up, asshole."

"Why are you so pissy?" Chase says as he walks into the room with Liam right behind him.

"I'm not being pissy!" I bark, knowing damn well I'm in a bad mood to beat all bad moods.

"Could've fooled me." Chase grins.

"Well, maybe if you all stopped asking me, I wouldn't be. Ever think about that?"

My brothers exchange glances before they all look at me and say, "No," in unison.

I sigh and push to my feet. "Let's just head to Posey's already. Maybe then you'll leave me the fuck alone."

"Not just yet." Liam steps in my path, stopping me from leaving. "I want to discuss the business first."

My shoulders instantly lift and my back goes ramrod straight. "What about the business?"

I've been waiting for this conversation. My brothers won't let me ignore my anxiety about being behind the wheel of a racecar forever. They've spent two years ignoring it, and it's hurting our business.

It felt good to win my last race. I needed that win to prove to myself that I've still got it. I may still have the skill, but mentally, I'm not in it. If I'm not in it, something has to change.

"I want to ask Sophia to join our team. Maybe even scout for a couple of young hopefuls. And ..." He rubs the back of his neck and scans around the room, looking at anything except me.

"Just spit out," I say.

"What are your plans for racing?" The words rush out of him.

I open my mouth to tell him that my plans are still the same. That all I want to do is race my way into the Sprint Cup, but I stop myself. That's my stock answer that I always give. It used to be the truth before the accident. But now, I'm not so sure that's the direction I want to take.

"Man, it's okay if your goals have shifted." This comes from Chase. His expression is serious and there isn't a hint of playfulness in sight. It's rare to see him like this. "We'll support you no matter what you decide."

My eyes meet his. We still haven't talked about it, but he knows I struggle. He's with me at every single race and sees my anxiety even when I think I'm doing a great job of masking it.

I let out a deep breath and scrub my hands over my face. I have two choices. Lie and insist I'm fine. That I want to continue racing and my goals haven't changed. Or I tell them the truth. I no longer want to pursue the Sprint Cup. I've hardly let myself think those words, let alone say them out loud. It's like admitting failure. I don't want to be a failure.

"I don't want to do it anymore," I whisper before I talk myself out of it. My brothers deserve my honesty. This is their business as much as it's mine.

The sigh that leaves Liam is loud and heavy. I can't tell if it's disappointment or relief that I've finally said it. He lifts his gaze to mine, and all I see is love and concern. "Can you elaborate on that?"

"I don't want the Sprint Cup. Hell, I don't even want the ARCA series." The silence that fills the room lights a fire to my anxiety and I wish I'd kept my mouth shut. I've been thinking about this for a while, but saying the words out loud has my nerves tingling with regret. Their continued silence makes me antsy, and I shift on my feet. "I'm sorry. I just can't get my head back in the game after the accident. I've tried. I really have. I love racing. I need it in my life, but it also has to change. I've been thinking of training. Maybe. If we decide to bring on more drivers, I could work with them. Teach them everything I know. We could grow a winning team."

The smile that lifts Liam's face surprises me. I braced myself for disappointment and even anger from my brothers, but that's not what I see from any of them. I see pride and relief. That should make me feel better, but it doesn't.

"I think you'd make an excellent trainer. Maybe even a team manager if you think you're up for it." Liam's words instantly calm me.

I glance between my brothers. I should be relieved at how calm and accepting they look. And I am, to a degree. Regardless of my inner turmoil, I need to know they're okay if I shift roles. But I still can't shake this fear in my gut. "You guys really okay with this?"

Liam steps toward me and squeezes my shoulder. "Mac. We want what's best for *you*. Don't force yourself to do something you no longer want to do for us. We're Mutters. We adjust and adapt to change better than anyone. Plans change. Dreams morph into new ones all the time. When that happens, we rally behind each other in support. No matter what."

I nod, struggling to keep my emotions in check.

No matter what. The Mutter brother saying of support.

When we were kids, anytime we were faced with adversity, we'd rally behind each and pledge our support. *No matter what.*

We're a unit. We may not always agree, but we'll never let a brother down.

Meeting Liam's gaze, I smile. "No matter what."

"Alright!" Chase pushes to his feet. His typical playful grin is back as he claps his hands. "Let's head to Posey's. I need a drink and want to cackle at my brothers while they sing karaoke."

"I'm not singing." Liam insists.

"But you have to. It's, like, a rule." Ash adds.

I chuckle at the abrupt shift in demeanor. We talked. Maybe not to the full extent I probably should talk to my brothers, but it's good enough. From here, we'll formulate a new plan and business model. That's what Liam does best. He'll make sure we don't fail.

Just like that, we're back to being us.

WHATEVER HINT OF A GOOD MOOD I'D FOUND BEFORE WE LEFT the house is gone now. Not that I was in a good mood. But I at least felt better than I did before Sophia left with Clara.

White hot anger consumes me as I watch Tanner Fucking Koch lean in close to Sophia to whisper something in her ear. Then he has the fucking nerve to rub a strand of her hair between his fingers.

She takes a small step back from him, but she doesn't exactly stop him. In fact, she's smiling at him, and I hate it.

I take a step forward, but Ash's hand stops me. "Don't do it, man. He's not worth it."

I glare at my brother, shove his hand away from my chest, and barge across the room like a bull charging a matador.

I don't want any man getting that close to what's mine, but especially not a Koch brother.

Sophia sees me first. As soon as her eyes meet mine, her smile fades and her shoulders slump. "Mac. It's not what you think."

I step between them and give Tanner a hard shove. He stumbles backward and into the table behind him, spilling several drinks.

Spinning around, I crowd Sophia's space and get in her face. "And what do I think?"

She pushes on my chest, but I don't budge. "I think you're jumping to conclusions. You barge in here like I'm doing something wrong, and I'm not."

"If you have to say it, then chances are you're in the wrong."

Before Sophia can respond, someone grabs me from behind and jerks me around. Tanner grabs a hold of my shirt and growls. "What the fuck, man? I was just talking to her."

"You were doing a hell of a lot more than talking, and you know it. Stay away from her. She's mine."

He lets out an incredulous laugh. "Yours? Sure, man. Whatever you say."

I know he's trying to get under my skin by acting like a douche, and I hate that it's working. "You know we're dating. Stop flirting with my girlfriend."

He tightens his grip on my shirt, and I wrap my hand around his wrist, ready to rip it off me. "I didn't make her talk to me. She did that all on her own. Looks like you need to do a better job of keeping your girl in check."

"Fuck you!" I lift my fist and jerk it back, but before I can throw the punch I'm aching to hit him with, our brothers tear us apart. Ash and Chase grab me by the arms and pull me back while Jason and Linden grab a hold of Tanner.

"I told you, he's not worth it," Ash whispers in my ear. "He's trying to get you riled up, and you're feeding right into it."

I knock Ash off me, ready to lunge at Tanner again. I don't care what he's doing. I've had enough of his shit and plan on ending it right now.

Sophia steps in front of me before I reach him, and I halt. "Mac, don't do this."

"Don't do what?" I growl.

"Start a fight because you're scared."

I freeze and take a step back. "What the actual fuck, Red? I'm not scared."

She tilts her head with raised brows. "Really?"

"Yes, really. I'm pissed. At both of you. How do you think it makes me feel to walk in and find *my* girlfriend flirting with Tanner Koch?"

"I wasn't flirting with him. We were just talking!"

"That looked like a lot more than just talking. You two were awfully cozy."

"Oh my God. Stop! Stop right now! This has nothing to do with me *talking* to Tanner. You're sabotaging our relationship because you're scared. You've been on edge ever since my racing accident, and it's only gotten worse after the jack fell on me. You have got to relax. I'm fine. We're fine. We just—"

"No." I don't let her finish. "We're *not* fine. I can't do this anymore. I don't know why I thought I could do it in the first place."

All the anger in her face vanishes and is replaced with disbelief. "What are you saying?"

"I'm saying we're through. Flirt with whomever you want. You're not mine to worry about anymore. I was an idiot to think we could make this work."

I spin around to head toward the door, but she grabs my arm. "Mac. You don't mean that."

I jerk my arm away and take a few steps back. "You're wrong. I do mean it. Goodbye, Sophia."

I take off for the door before anyone else can stop me.

I know I'm overreacting. I should give her a chance to explain herself or at least listen to what she's saying. But I can't.

I just can't right now.

I need to get out of here, and fast.

Between my anxiety, my mom's random appearances in my

life, the siblings I've never met, Tanner fucking with me, and my inability to keep Sophia safe, I can't see things clearly.

As soon as the cold night air hits me, my breath catches, and I know I've made a huge mistake.

I should go back in there and apologize to her. I should take her in my arms and hold her close. I should tell her that she's right.

I *am* scared. I'm fucking terrified. And not for the reason she thinks.

I love her, and I just walked away from her because I'm terrified she'll leave me first.

I'm such a fucking asshole, and this is one more example of why I don't deserve her.

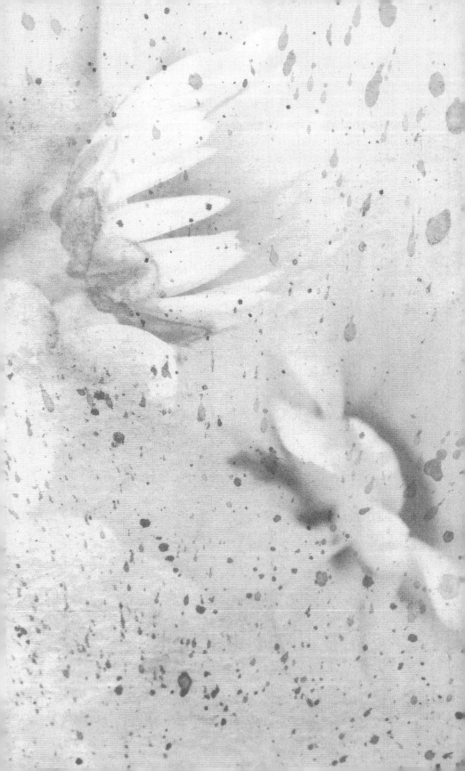

Chapter 26

I'm not fine. We're not fine. Nothing. Is. Fine.

Sophia

Four days. Four heartbreakingly painful days.

It's as if Mac vanished into thin air after he stormed out of the bar on Friday night. Not a word or the slightest peek of him at the garage. If it weren't for this giant hole inside me, I'd swear he never existed.

Even with his absence, work has been awkward for the past two days. No one mentions him, and they all keep looking at me like I'm going to break.

Newsflash. I'm stronger than that.

Yes, I'm hurt and confused and miss him far more than I should. It's not like we've been dating for years. It's been two months since we met at the Apple Festival. That's not long enough for me to feel this empty inside from us breaking up.

But I am empty, and every hour and minute that passes without hearing from him makes it harder for me to fight the urge to break down.

I haven't cried yet. I've wanted to, several times actually, but I've fought it like a badass bitch refusing to admit she's hurt.

I've spent much of my life protecting myself from men who won't accept me for who I am. Men who say women can't or shouldn't race cars. Men who don't think I have any business working on cars. Men who think I'm weird because I'd rather be covered in grease instead of make-up. I prefer coveralls or jeans and a t-shirt over fancy clothes or dresses. Sure, I like to get dressed up on occasion, but it's not my preferred attire.

Mac accepted all of that about me. He never questioned my skills or doubted my abilities. Overprotective for sure, but that had nothing to do with my career choice. He made me feel beautiful and sexy behind the wheel of a racecar. No man has ever done that before.

"Morning," Clara's voice drags me away from the kitchen window where I've been staring at the snow falling since I woke up.

"Morning. I think the coffee is done." I glance over at the pot I made when I got up, realizing I was so lost in my thoughts that I didn't hear it beep.

"Still nothing?" she asks as she grabs two coffee mugs from the cabinet above the pot. While she pours the coffee, I grab the creamer from the refrigerator for her.

"Nope. At this point, I don't expect to hear from him. He's made his choice, and it's not me."

"Soph, it's only been a few days. Give him time. He'll come around."

I shake my head. "He's done with me. I need to accept that and move on."

"No, he's not." Her words are firm and maybe even a little scolding. "Listen to me. I've known Mac my entire life. He's got a lot of issues, especially where women are concerned. All the Mutter brothers do. He loves you. I know he does."

"But not enough," I whisper, more to myself than to her.

"Yes, he does. Cut the guy some slack. I'd bet my last dollar this is the first time he's ever truly loved someone outside his immediate family. Plus, you were flirting with Tanner. That's on you."

"*I* wasn't flirting. *He* was flirting, and I was trying to get away.

Every time I took a step back to put some distance between, he stepped forward. What was I supposed to do?"

"Tell him to fuck off." My eyes widen at Clara's words. She never curses and hearing her say the F-Word is a little shocking. "Oh, don't look at me like that. When it comes to the Koch brothers, cursing is appropriate."

"Hey." I lift my hands in understanding. "I was just trying to be friendly, but I get it now. No talking to Tanner. At least, not friendly talk."

"And you need to apologize to Mac," Clara says right as I take a sip of coffee.

"What?" I spit my coffee out and it goes running down my chin. I grab a paper towel and wipe my face and shirt. "Why am I apologizing? He's the one that acted like a total ass, refused to listen to me, and then broke it off."

"None of which would've happened if you hadn't been flirting with Tanner."

"I. Wasn't. Flirting!"

She shrugs as if the loudness of my voice has no effect on her. "Let me rephrase. It *looked* like you were flirting. It's no wonder he jumped to conclusions."

Balling my hands into fists at my sides, I try hard not to let my anger boil over. I shouldn't be surprised her loyalty lies with Mac. We may be friends, but we've only known each other a couple of months, but she has it all wrong.

"You say that like you think I did it on purpose. If you think for one second, this is what I want, you're wrong. I lo—" I stop myself and take a deep breath before I voice my true feelings. I can't say those words out loud. Not now. Not after how he broke my heart. "The last thing I want to do is hurt Mac. What do I have to be sorry about when it's his misunderstanding?"

"I'm not trying to upset you. I consider you a friend, and I'm just trying to help. The Mutters are an odd bunch and require a little finesse when it comes to relationships. You and Mac are good together. Great actually. I want to see you work through this and come out together on the other side. Maybe suggesting you apologize isn't the right thing to say, but you should at least reach out to him. Show him you care."

"If he doesn't know I care, then he's an idiot."

She pins me with a stare. "This is Mac we're talking about. He *is* an idiot."

This makes me chuckle. She may think of the Mutters as family, but she'll still call out their bullshit, same as she's calling out mine. I have to respect her for that.

"I'll give it some thought. To be honest, I keep hoping he'll show up at the garage, but he hasn't been in all week. If he continues to hide, I may not get a chance to talk to him before I leave for Thanksgiving."

Her brows furrow, and a deep frown etches her face. "I thought you were staying in town?"

"I was, but now I'm thinking about going home. If Mac doesn't want me here, I don't want to intrude. I might head out on Saturday."

Her shoulders slump and her expression shifts to disappointment. "It's not just about Mac. *I* want you here. And I know his brothers do, too. His entire family loves you."

Her insistence makes me feel slightly better. I've grown close to Mac's brothers. Working for them has been great, and they've offered me so much advice and help in racing that I'll never be able to repay them.

I want to be here. I do. But I'm not sure I can handle it now that Mac and I are no longer together.

"If he's still not talking to me, it'll be awkward. That won't be fun for anyone."

"Then talk to him sooner rather than later. Work this out. Trust me when I say he loves you. He's just as stubborn as he is possessive. You're going to have to nudge him along."

I nod, not really sure what to say to that.

Does he really love me? There have been moments when I thought he might. The longing looks he gives me when he thought no one was looking, not even me. The way he kissed and touched me when we're together. There was always a hint of possessiveness about it, but it had become so much more. Sometimes I felt like he was worshiping me.

My eyes sting. I quickly squeeze them shut because I do not want to cry. And thinking about Mac in the past tense is too much for my wounded heart.

I don't want him to be my past. I want him to be my present and my future.

Maybe Clara's right. Maybe I should reach out to him. Would that be enough to get him to talk to me?

I guess there's only one way to find out.

I STARE AT MY PHONE WITH MY THUMBS HOVERING OVER THE keypad.

It's a slow morning, and I'm alone in the garage. Liam is running errands. Christian had to drive to Kentucky to pick up a bike he agreed to restore, and Chase and Ash are at the track testing a new engine they just finished rebuilding.

I have no clue where Mac is. I've not asked, and his brothers haven't offered any news. We're all avoiding the topic of our breakup.

If I wanted to talk to Mac in privacy, now is the time. Assuming he responds to my messages. Messages he can't read unless I send them.

"Staring at it won't make it do anything." I jump at the sound of Grams' voice. My hand jerks and my phone flies up. I scramble to catch it before it falls on the hard concrete floor. Once it's secure in my grip, I press it to my pounding chest.

"You startled me."

A wide grin covers Grams' face. "I see that. Been standing here for a few minutes. You're lost to yourself. Wanna talk about it?"

My mouth gapes open as I stare at her. Grams never comes out to the garage. Like ever. Her grandsons always go to her, not the other way around.

"I'm fine. There's nothing to talk about." Even I hear the lie in the sound of my voice.

Grams scoffs. "Well, if that isn't the worst line of bullshit I've ever heard. Anyone with eyes and ears can see you're not fine."

My eyes widen and my head jerks back at the fierceness of her words. I open my mouth to speak, but nothing comes out. She's not wrong, and I can't bring myself to tell another person I'm fine when I'm nowhere near fine.

She lets out a deep sigh. "Deary, you don't have to tell me. I know what my grandson did. What I want to know is what you plan on doing about it?"

"Me?" I point to myself. "Why does everyone expect me to fix this? He broke up with me. Not the other way around."

She waves her hand at me like what I said is meaningless. "Believe me when I say he regrets it. Boy's been an intolerable bear ever since."

Now it's my turn to scoff. "What's new? He's always an intolerable bear."

Grams tosses her head back and laughs like I just told the funniest joke she's ever heard. "Ain't that the damn truth? Then again, most of my grandsons are intolerable bears. The fact that you know and accept that about Mac is why we have to fix this."

I sigh, ready to concede. "If I knew how, I would. If he'd show his face and give us a chance to talk, it'd help. But I haven't seen him. He's hiding."

"Yeah, he's good at that. Love is wonderful, but it's also the seed that feeds the worst pain we can feel. And that boy is in some serious pain. Pain I'm not convinced he's ever felt before, and he's struggling. And that's saying something because his pain runs deep and spans a lifetime."

"I know about his mother," I whisper.

"Then you understand his heart." She pauses as if she's waiting for me to respond. I nod and that's all the confirmation she needs to continue. "And it's not just his mother. It's all their mothers. My grandsons have only ever seen broken love. I lost my love before any of them could see a good example. Lord knows my Paul hasn't given them one. Sadly, it's left all my grandsons afraid of love. Especially Mac. His poor heart is trapped and suffocated by his fear. Not that he'd ever admit it. I'm afraid his heart doesn't know what to do with this excess love he's been getting from you."

She walks up to the car I've been working on and picks up the busted fuel injector I removed this morning. "Think of him like this car you're working on. The engine can't burn all the excess gas it's getting because of a bad fuel injector. Fix the fuel injector and the engine can breathe just fine again. My grandson's the same way."

"I'm not following. I mean, I get the flooded engine to a flooded heart analogy, but what represents the fuel injector?"

Grams smiles, and it's the sweetest, most genuine smile I've ever seen. She steps up to me and cups my face. "You, my dear. You're a perfectly working fuel injector and exactly what my grandson needs for his heart to find balance."

My breath catches. She thinks I'm perfect for Mac. She's telling me the one thing I hope is true.

Does this mean she thinks I can fix him? Well, not fix him in the traditional sense of a woman fixing a man, but rather help mend what's broken inside him. And do I want that?

"Deary, I see the conflict in your eyes. It's never easy loving a Mutter man. Trust me. I know firsthand. But I also know that you'll never find a man more worthy of your love. Or more loyal. One of you has to be strong, and if it's not you, well ..." She lets out a deep sigh. "Then I'm afraid there will be no hope for you and Mac."

I nod because words fail me. And also because I know if I speak, the hold I've had my tears might slip. I don't want to cry. Not in front of her, or anyone, for that matter.

She gives me one last pat on the cheek before she turns around and walks out of the garage. I stare after her as if I'm transfixed—barely able to breathe, let alone move.

First Clara, and now Grams. Two people who know Mac far better than I do, and they're both telling me the same thing. It's up to me to make the first move. Although Grams' delivery was much softer, which is surprising since she rarely holds back.

I take one last look at my phone and debate on texting Mac. The tension and fear I'm holding onto are intense. The surrounding air is heavy, and I ache all over. My body feels like it's being crushed in a compactor.

Before I can change my mind, I open the message thread with Mac and type. I don't say much—texting isn't how I want to have this conversation—but I'm at least going to initiate the conversation. After this, the ball is in his court.

SOPHIA

Can we talk?

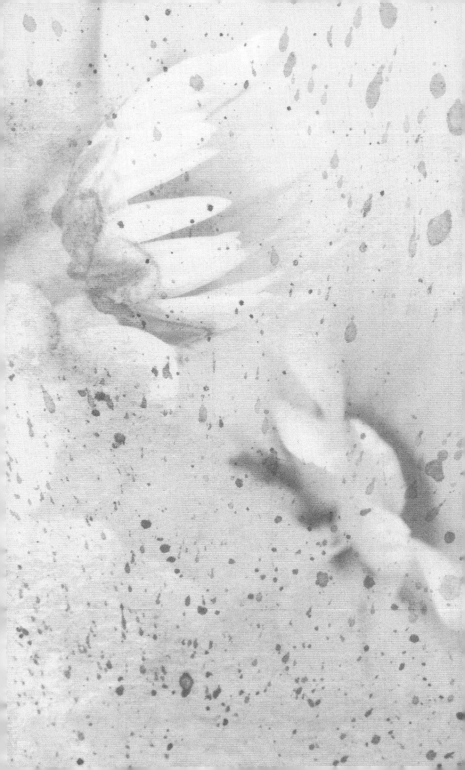

Chapter 27

Once a fool, always a fool.

Mac

Three little words. It's a simple question, or at least it should be, but nothing about it feels simple. It feels ominous. Like I'm about to be reprimanded for bad behavior.

Newsflash, Mac. You behaved badly, and she has every right to be pissed.

SOPHIA

Can we talk?

Yes, please.
I beg of you.
Talk to me.
Don't hate me for being an asshole.
Give me a chance to make it up to you.
I'll do better next time. I promise. Just please take me back.

My mind is overloaded with the things I want *and need* to say to her, but I can't get my fingers to type out a single letter.

I overreacted, and I know it. Everyone who was there to witness my reaction to Tanner talking to her knows I overreacted. Even Tanner.

If my brothers hadn't been there to stop me, I would have kicked Tanner's ass. Then his brothers would have gotten involved, and I would've been screwed. I can't take on three guys by myself. I would've gotten my ass kicked instead.

Not to mention, I would have made the rivalry between us worse. We don't need more fuel to feed the fire that's been smoldering between our two families for generations.

But I wasn't about to lose Sophia to the likes of Tanner Koch. He was too close. Flirting with someone he knew was taken. I had to make a statement.

Yeah, but you didn't have to take it out on her and break up. Ass meet hole.

It should be me reaching out to her to ask to talk. But nope. Not only am I an asshole, I'm also a fool. Instead of responding to her or heading over to the garage to talk to her, I'm hiding in my bedroom, staring at her message.

I haven't gone to work for the past three days, and that makes me feel even worse.

It makes me feel like Dad.

The last person I want to be like is Dad. He let women control his life, his every action, the downfall of his career, and his involvement in his sons' lives. Or should I say lack of? Losing Susanne destroyed him. His inability to overcome that loss fucked up seven kids' lives.

I can't let myself be like him.

Resolve pushing me into action, I pocket my phone and head out to the kitchen to grab some lunch. After a quick bite, I'll head to the garage and talk to her. I'll make this right with Sophia and work my ass off to never act so foolish again.

Because I love her, and it's past time I tell her.

"He lives," Grams says from her seat at the kitchen table. Avoiding her is another reason I've hidden in my bedroom most days since I broke up with Sophia. She's had some choice words for me, as have all my brothers. They've all been quick to tell me all the ways I'm an idiot.

I grunt and open the refrigerator. I stare at the choices. There's leftover chili from Sunday dinner, some fried chicken and mashed potatoes, or I could make a sandwich. I'm hungry, but nothing sounds good.

"Mac!" Grams says with so much frustration, I can't stop myself from turning around to look at her. "Stop being a stubborn ass. Sophia is a good girl. She's good for you. Go make this right."

"I'm working on it." I turn back to the refrigerator and grab the chili. I love Grams' chili. Maybe once I eat, it'll make me feel better.

"And how exactly are you working on it? You're hiding. Trust me when I say hiding will only drag you down more."

"I know!" I say a little too loudly. I scoop some chili in a bowl, cover it, and pop it in the microwave. "Just ... Stop lecturing me. Please. I know I fucked up. I'll fix it."

I feel her eyes on me, but I don't turn to face her. I don't need her disappointment on top of my own. I'm beating myself up enough. I don't need any help in that department.

I brace myself for more berating, but it doesn't come. As the silence drags on, I finally look over my shoulder. Her head is down and focused on her knitting. From the look on her face, it's as if I'm not even here.

I sigh, about to speak, when there's a knock on the door. I tense, wishing I were still hiding in my room so I wouldn't have to deal with whomever it is.

Maybe if I ignore it, Grams will get it instead. Then I can sneak off with my chili and hide some more while I decide on what I'm going to say to Sophia to earn her forgiveness.

"Make yourself useful and get that, will you?" Grams says. I cringe, searching for an excuse to get out of it.

"I'm not presentable. Nor am I in the right frame of mind to welcome a guest. Let Dad get it."

"Your father isn't here. He went to town with Liam."

I drop my head back and groan before I leave the kitchen and head for the front door. I won't argue with her. When Grams asks me to do something, I always do it. It's the respect she deserves.

But when I open the door, for the first time in my life, I wish I defied her.

"Hi, Mac," my mother says.

"Why? Why do you keep coming here?" I yell. "What do I have to say to you to get you to leave me the fuck alone?"

"Oh, don't be so melodramatic. You have no one to blame for my constant reappearances except yourself."

"Me? I'm not making you drive all the way down here to see me. Go away and never come back."

I go to slam the door in her face, but she pushes against it. The action catches me off guard and the door goes flying open.

"This isn't about me. Did you even read my letter?"

"I did." I bark.

"Then you know you have siblings that want to meet you."

"Well I don't know if I want to meet them. I have six siblings that have always been here for me. I don't need more disappointment in my life."

"Mac, don't be selfish. They had nothing to—"

"Are you for real? You're telling me not to be selfish. I'm not the one that did the abandoning. That was you. You show up here after over twenty years of zero contact and expect me to just do as you say? Fuck you. Get out of here and—"

"Mac!" Grams calls out from behind me. "That's enough. I'll deal with Heidi."

I spin around, the anger inside me at a near boiling point. "I can handle this, Grams."

"You call this handling it? If you keep yelling like that, you'll pop a vein. You need to calm down. You've had a rough week. Let me take care of this."

"Fine. You deal with her. Just make sure she never comes back."

I push through the front door and head straight for my truck. But I don't make it far before I realize I don't have my keys.

I can't go back inside because now Grams is in a heated conversation with my mother. Instead, I head to the garage. But as soon as I cross the yard, I spot Sophia standing outside, watching me with concern etched all over her face.

My first instinct is to run to her and take her in my arms. Holding her close, feeling her arms around my waist and her soft, warm breath against my neck sounds like the best thing in the world right now.

But she's not mine anymore. I ruined that by acting like a jealous fool. I have to fix what I broke first, but I can't do that when everything inside is raging like a thunderstorm ready to unload a F5 tornado.

If I try to talk to her now, I'll only make things worse.

I dart between the garage and the house to make a clean escape, but she calls after me. "Mac, please. Don't run from me."

I shake my head and keep walking.

But she doesn't let that stop her. I feel her hand wrapping around mine before I hear her next to me. I jerk it away and spin around. "Not now. I just ... I can't."

The hurt that takes over her expression makes me ache inside. "Talk to me. Let me be here for you. Please."

The way she says please is almost too much for my damaged soul. That one word is filled with so much anguish and desperation. It's almost enough to crack my hard exterior and unleash a lifetime of abandonment and neglect issues that I keep locked up tight.

She's close enough that I can see the light freckles that dot her nose and cheeks. I want to trace them with my finger and follow my touch with kisses. I want to hold her close and pretend my life isn't one fucked up mess after another.

But in true Mac-is-a-complete-fool form, I take a step back and another and another until her freckles fade into the shadows of her face. Then I turn around and leave her standing alone.

IT's EARLY AFTERNOON, AND THE SKY IS CLEAR. THE SUN beams its warmth down on me, but it's not enough to push back the chill in the air. Thankfully, I'm wearing a thick sweatshirt with pockets, but my coat would have made this impromptu walk through the woods much more bearable.

This is what I get for having a hair-trigger temper. If I could've calmed down just a little, I would have had enough sense to go inside and grab my coat before I took off into the woods on a chilly November afternoon.

Hell, I could've even grabbed my keys. Then I'd be in the warmth of my truck instead of outside shivering to death like a fool.

And I am a fool.

Because a smart man would have turned around by now and gone back to the house. But not me. I keep pushing forward like I have something to prove. Or maybe it's more like self-inflicted punishment for the way I treated Sophia.

It's probably for the best, anyway. She deserves better than me. I'm not good enough for her. Even my own mother didn't want me. That has to say something about me.

With my head down, I stuff my hands deeper in my pockets and keep pushing forward. I didn't head into the woods with a destination in mind, but my feet lead the way, nonetheless.

Soon, I reach the break in the trail that leads to the small cave I took Sophia to not that long ago. She eased my pain and anger that day. Without her, I feel lost and sink further into my self-loathing. As much as I wish she were here to be the same calming balm my soul needs, this is for the best.

The forest is quiet. It's too cold even for animals to be out and about. There's nothing to distract me from my innermost thoughts, fears, and flaws. Maybe this time alone will help me figure my shit out.

When I reach the cave, I climb up the rocky side and sit on the ledge, same as I did with her. I lay back on the rock and stare up at the sliver of sunlight breaking its way through the canopy.

I'm immediately assaulted with memories of a little boy walking through the forest with his mother. Memories of when I thought she loved me. We'd walk hand-in-hand for hours through these trails. She'd tell me the names of all the trees and plant species she could identify. Then she'd squeal when I caught bugs and brought them to her like presents.

Then she left. She told me she'd be back, but that was a lie. One of many I later figured out she'd told me. A part of my heart hardened that day, and I've never fully allowed myself to trust another woman since.

But I started to trust Sophia. Even worse, she trusted me.

I destroyed it all with one jealous outrage.

I close my eyes and let the isolation of the forest feed my loneliness. After all, this is what I deserve after the way I've acted.

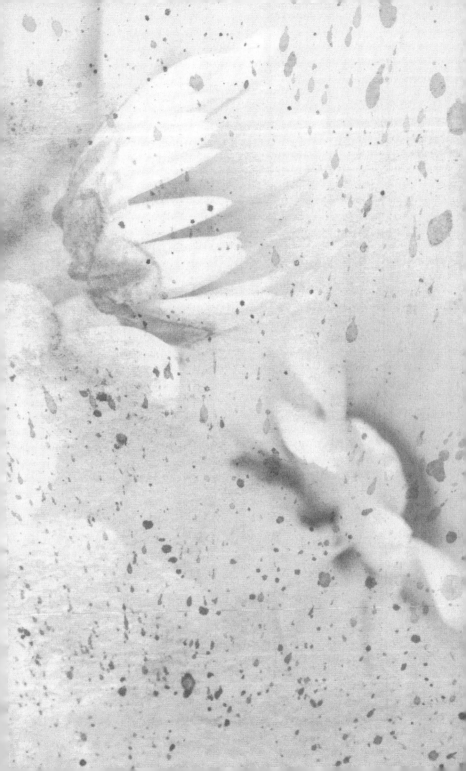

Chapter 28

If you want it ... Fight for it.

Sophia

I've never been more ready for a day to end. Seeing Mac and the way he ran off without talking to me stung worse than our fight at the bar.

The bar fight didn't make me cry. He was irrationally angry that night. But today he was hurting.

Today I saw just how much pain he holds inside himself. All I wanted to do was hold him close and promise him it would all be fine. That I'd make him happy if he'd just let me in.

Today, I cried.

It took me a good ten minutes hiding in the bathroom before I got myself under control and could get back to work. Thankfully, Mac's brothers hadn't returned to the garage yet, and I had a little more time to regain my composure.

It's been about an hour since Liam and Christian returned, and so far, so good. But I'm pretty sure Christian knows something is wrong. He keeps watching me.

At one point, he even walked up to me and stared at me like he could read my deepest thoughts. His intense, knowing stare was almost enough to make me cry again.

He even went as far as to ask me if I was okay. He spoke to me.

Christian rarely speaks. Thankfully, he didn't push when I told him I was fine. He didn't believe me, but he didn't force the issue either. We both went back to work like he never asked me a thing.

At least Chase and Ash aren't back. They'd definitely push. Those two don't know the meaning of the word boundaries.

"Sophia," Liam calls out for me, making me jump. I'm so lost in my thoughts. I've blocked out all background noise. "Got time for one more oil change before you leave?"

I inwardly groan. I'd just finished up what I thought was my last job. There's still forty-five minutes left in my shift, but I was hoping to sneak out early. I need a drink. Maybe lots of drinks.

"Sure thing," I hear myself say, despite how much my inner turmoil is screaming no.

"Thanks." He steps up beside me and narrows his eyes. "You okay?"

I nod, quickly turning away because my eyes sting at his question. I refuse to let any of them see me cry.

He hesitates, and I sense he wants to ask me more, but he doesn't. "Alright. Mr. Bevins is a regular, so we do our best to accommodate him. He's a hoverer. Asks tons of questions, but he's a good man. Try not to let him get to you."

I force a chuckle. "I'll be fine. I've dealt with hoverers before."

He squeezes my shoulder, and it feels so much like something a caring big brother would do to let me know he has my back. Again, I fight the damn tears. I don't cry in front of people.

"While you prep, I'll pull his car into the bay. He's particular about who drives it."

He hands me the clipboard before he walks away. I scan it for the make and model and chuckle. At least this time it's a real laugh. Mr. Bevins drives a 1980 Buick Regal, and he only has twenty-two thousand miles on it. Looks like he's not just particular about who drives but also where and how far.

By the time I return with the oil and filter, the car is in the bay and up on the jack. Liam is standing beside a man who looks old enough to be his great-grandfather. He's thin and frail, and I'd bet money a strong wind could blow him over.

But when he speaks, nothing about him sounds frail. His voice is strong and playful. "Well, who do we have here?"

Liam smiles. "Mr. Bevins, this is Sophia. She joined us a couple of months ago. She's a great mechanic and will do an excellent job on your car."

Mr. Bevins's eyes light up. "A female mechanic. I've never met one of those."

While there's no judgment or malice behind his words, they still make me cringe. Liam notices and quickly jumps in to assure me it's fine. "We only hire the best. Sophia will take good care of you."

"Oh sure." Mr. Bevins beams. "That's why I only bring my car to you."

Liam gives me a nod before he says goodbye to Mr. Bevins and lets me get to work.

I quickly slide under the car before Mr. Bevins engages me in conversation. Not because I can't handle talking to him, but because I want to get out of here as soon as possible.

Once the oil is draining, I slide out, and he's right there next to the front bumper, staring down at me like I'm the coolest thing he's seen in ages.

"You're a pretty thing." His smile is bright and wide. "I hope you don't mind me saying that. You have the prettiest blue eyes. Reminds me of my Anne."

I raise a brow. "Anne?"

A sadness glints in his eyes, but only for a moment. "My wife. Lost her over fifteen years ago. She had the most beautiful light blue eyes. Just like yours."

I can't stop the smile that lifts my lips. "Thank you."

He nods. "How long have you been a mechanic?"

"Not long. Just since I started working with the Mutters. But I grew up in a garage though. My dad is a mechanic. So I learned a lot from him growing up. I also have a degree in automotive engineering."

Mr. Bevins's eyes widen. He looks at me with both surprise and pride. It's a look I wish I'd get from my own dad. "Wow, that's impressive. If you don't mind me asking, why work as a mechanic if you have such a fancy degree?"

"I wanted practical experience. In college, I learned a lot about theory, history, and design. While I had labs, it's not the same as getting my hands dirty working on cars. Plus, I love racing. Who better to learn from than the Mutters?"

"Ain't that the truth? And little Mac sure is a great racecar driver. I bet he can teach you a thing or two."

I smile at the way he called him little Mac. He probably knew all the Mutters from the time they were babies. I wonder what a little Mac was like before the reality of his abandonment sunk in. I bet he was playful and jovial like Chase. That side of him is still present, but it gets masked by his pain and jealousy. None of which makes me love him any less.

"Sophia?" I look up at the sound of my name. Mr. Bevins is watching me expectantly.

"I'm sorry. What did you ask me?"

"I asked if you've seen Mac race."

"Oh, yes. I watched him for years before I moved here. Even had the pleasure of beating him recently."

"You don't say." His smile grows. "Well, you must be a talented and skilled young lady if you can beat Mac. He almost made it to the Sprint Cup. Did you know that? But he had an accident a few years ago that took him out. He's not quite made it back yet."

"Yeah, I watched that race. I was rooting for him."

"That was a sad day around here. Then again, things tend to happen for a reason. Just means he's destined for a different path. But we all hope that path still takes him to the Sprint Cup."

"I guess we don't always have a say in how life turns out. No matter how hard we work to achieve a goal, we don't always get it."

As soon as the words are out, I feel worse than I did before talking with Mr. Bevins. That same idea works with regards to my relationship with Mac. Just because I want him doesn't mean I get to have him.

God, that's so depressing to even think. Because I really, *really* want him. I know that beyond a shadow of a doubt. And I'm pretty sure he wants me, too. We just need to talk. Work through this ridiculous fight we had.

It's not going to be easy. Of that, I am positive. But I'm going to fight like hell to get him back.

———————

THE PHONE RINGS THREE TIMES BEFORE MY DAD PICKS UP. "Hey, pumpkin. I didn't expect to hear from you tonight."

"Hey, Daddy," I say in the most cheerful voice I can muster, but as soon as the words are out, I hear my mistake. I only ever call my dad, Daddy, when I'm upset.

"Uh oh. What's wrong?"

"Nothing. I just miss you." I try to cover up, but my dad knows me too well. He's not going to buy it.

"While that may be true ..." He lets out a soft chuckle. Not a joking or playful one, but more of a ha-nice-try-you're-lying-to-me chuckle. "That's not why you're calling me. Let me guess. The boy?"

I sigh and fall back on my bed. He's the one I always talk to about boy troubles, not Mom. I've always been closer to Dad than Mom. Even with the lack of support I get from him with my career choice, we're still close.

I debate with myself for a split second about lying to him again, but it won't do any good. Dad can always see right through me.

"Mac and I had a fight," I say. It's not a lie. We did fight. But I'm not ready to say the words *we broke up* out loud. Especially not to my dad. If Mac and I get back together—which is my hope—I don't want anything to make Dad dislike him.

He's silent for a moment before he speaks. "Well, fights happen. All couples have moments where they disagree. Some bigger than others. The cause of the fight isn't important. It's how we deal with them after the fact that matters most."

My shoulders relax, and I feel slightly calmer than I did before I picked up the phone. Dad is such a wise man. I've heard my parents argue plenty of times growing up. While they've always been very loving and supportive of each other, they aren't perfect. Fights happen. As much as they tried to make sure they never fought in front of us kids, it still happened on occasion.

"You're right. I guess I've never really been in this situation before. I feel a little lost."

"You really like this boy, don't you?"

I nod before my brain catches up with my body and I realize he can't see me. "Yes. I think I love him, Daddy. Is that even possible? We've only known each other a couple of months. I can't say I've ever been in love before, so I'm not sure if that's what this really is."

"Pumpkin, there's no time frame on falling in love. Some people fall in love in a day. For others, it takes years. Look at you and cars. You fell in love with cars the very first time I took you to the garage with me and let you peek under the hood. I swear there were stars in your eyes. Your mom still blames me for your career path. I know loving cars isn't the same as loving another person, but it's still love. I knew I loved your mother after a week of dating her. We may drive each other crazy at times, but she's mine for better or worse. Nothing will ever change that."

My eyes are hot with tears, and my chest is tight. I nod again because I'm struggling to form words, and I need a moment to collect myself before I speak. While Dad has seen me cry many times, I don't want to cry anymore. I want to fix this. I want Mac back. Tears aren't going to cut it.

"Thanks. I needed to hear that."

"Anytime. You know you can always talk to your old man. No matter what it is. I may not like it, but I'll always be here for you."

"I know, and I appreciate that."

"You still planning on staying there for Thanksgiving?"

"I don't know. I'm debating on coming home this weekend, but maybe I should stay. Like you said, it's what happens after the fight that matters. If I leave, I think that will make things worse."

"Yeah, you don't want it to look like you're hiding or running. We'll miss you. Your mom isn't happy about it, but she's trying to accept that you're all grown up and following your own path."

"This is really hard for her, isn't it? And I don't mean Mac and me or me not coming home for Thanksgiving. I mean my racing and career choice."

"It is. But it's not easy for me either. We're both coming around. Be patient with your parents. We'll get there. We just want you to be happy and safe."

"God, Dad." My voice cracks, and my tears break free. "You're killing me. I think that's the first time you've said that to me."

"Shame on me. I should have said that to you years ago. I should have supported you and made your path to racing easier, not harder. I'm sorry for that."

"It's okay. It may have frustrated me, but I always knew you still loved me."

"Maybe so, but I'm not proud of how we handled it."

A loud knock on the front door has me jumping off my bed. "Hey, Dad. I need to go. There's someone at the outside."

"This late?" I check the time and it's almost nine o'clock.

"Yeah, it might be important. I'll call you and Mom this weekend, okay?"

"Okay. Love you, pumpkin."

"Love you, too." I hang up the phone and toss it on the bed before I head downstairs. Clara is already there and opening the door. A frantic Liam is standing on the other side.

"Hey, Liam. Everything okay?" Clara asks.

"If you tell me Mac is here, then yes. If not, no." Liam looks past Clara and meets my worried gaze from where I stand at the bottom of the stairs.

I shake my head. "He's not here."

"Shit," Liam mutters. "Any idea where he might be?"

"I still haven't talked to him since the fight at the bar. I saw him just after lunch today. His mom showed up again, and he was upset. I tried to stop him, but he took off."

Liam curses under his breath. "Took off where? His truck is at the house. He's nowhere to be found. All the ATVs and other vehicles are accounted for. If he's not with you, I have no idea where else he'd be."

"In case you missed it, he broke up with me." My voice cracks. *Do not cry. Do NOT cry.* I swallow hard and turn my gaze to the floor before I completely lose it.

"I know," Liam whispers. "I'm sorry to even bother you about this, but I'm worried. He's never disappeared like this before. Did you happen to see where he went?"

"He headed toward the trail in the forest. The one ..." My voice fades off, and I close my eyes. "The cave."

"Cave?" Liam questions.

"Yeah. There's a cave deep in the woods. He took me to it once. Remember the first day he got all pissed off about something? He was about to take off on one of the ATVs, and I jumped on behind him."

Liam nods.

"He drove us out to this small cave next to a creek. It's off the main trail and relatively hidden. He said he likes to go there when he needs to clear his head and think."

"But it's freezing outside."

I rush across the foyer and grab my coat and scarf. "More reason to get out there sooner rather than later. If that's where he went, he doesn't have a coat on."

A growl similar to the ones I've heard come from Mac when he's frustrated leaves Liam. "I'm going to kill that boy."

"Do you need me to help search?" Clara asks.

Liam shakes his head. "No, you stay here just in case he shows up. Call me if you see him."

She nods. "If you find him, call me."

I give her a hug before I rush out the door. I squeeze my eyes close and send out a prayer to the universe. *Please, let him be okay.*

I can't lose him. Not now.

Not ever.

If there was any doubt about how I felt about him before, it's gone now.

All I want to do is hold him close and tell him just how much I love him.

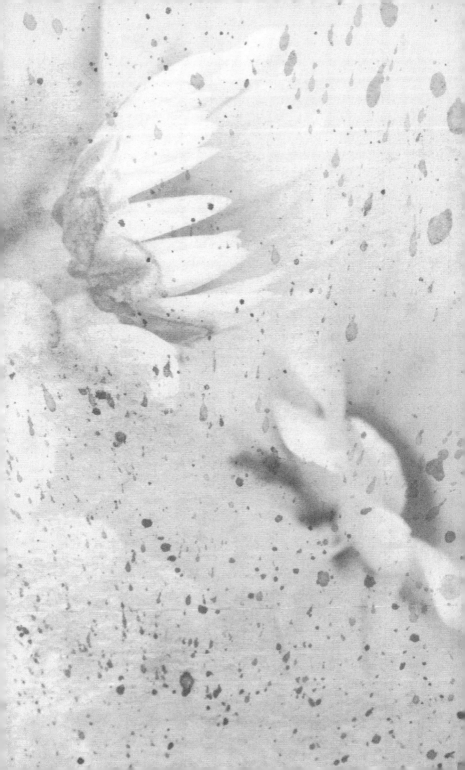

Chapter 29

When you get a second chance, take it.

Mac

The cold wind cuts through me, but the brightness of the sun is enough to make being outside with my family worth it. There are moments when the sun is so bright that the glare makes it impossible to see Sophia's position. If only the sun would warm my body, then today would be perfect.

Sophia turns her smile on me and calls my name. At least I think she says my name. Her muffled voice is hard to hear, and it sounds like we're in a tunnel. But all I see is the wide-open space of a snow-covered field with a thick dusting of snow falling to the ground.

Her bright red hair glows against the white background, as does that of the little girl standing beside her.

It has to be her little girl. They look just alike.

Since when did Sophia have a daughter? I step closer to get a better look, but they fade into the brightness.

"Sophia?" I call out, but I'm met with silence. I wait and listen until the faint sound of giggling comes from somewhere to my right.

The little girl is now alone and running in circles around a snowman.

"We're building a snowman, Daddy. Help us." Her laughter warms my insides and pushes away the chill.

"Daddy?" I whisper, more to myself than anyone else.

The little girl stops and stares at me in confusion. "Are you okay?"

I shake my head and rub my eyes. She doesn't look to be over two or three, but her voice suddenly sounds so grown up. When my eyes refocus, she's no longer alone. Sophia is back and they're wearing matching frowns.

"Mac? You're so cold," Sophia says.

I glance around. My eyes linger on the falling snow before I say, "Yeah, I guess I am. But I can still help you." I look down at the little girl who's smiling broadly up at me. "And what's your name?"

She giggles again and covers her mouth. "Daddy's being silly."

I feel my brows furrow as I stare down at her. Does she think I'm her daddy? I don't have any kids. I don't even have a girlfriend anymore because I'm too much of an asshole to keep my temper under control.

I glance up at Sophia and the tears in her eyes cause me to stumble. I trip and fall backward onto my back. My entire body jerks when I hit the ground.

"Mac!" My body shakes. "Can you hear me? Please, Mac. Wake up."

The panic in Sophia's voice is almost too much to bear. I reach out for her, but she's no longer there. The brightness fades into darkness and a chill unlike anything I've ever felt before causes my entire body to seize.

I blink, and Sophia's tear cover face looks down at me. When our eyes meet, a sob escapes her. "Mac!"

Lifting my hand, I cup her cheek. She feels warm against my frozen hand.

"Sophia?" My voice croaks and it hurts to speak.

"I'm here. Can you get up? We need to get you warm."

I shake my head, and my eyes fall close. "I'm fine now that you're here."

"Mac, please. I need you to get up."

When I open my eyes again, there's a bright light behind her, along with another voice. A familiar man's voice, but I can't quite place it. The light behind her makes her hair glow, just like it did when it was snowing.

"You're so beautiful. So, so beautiful." I struggle to keep my eyes opened and focused on her. "I'm so tired and cold." I manage before everything goes black again.

"Mac, look at me." She demands.

But all I can manage is a small smile. "After I sleep, Red."

She buries her face in my neck and cries. She cries so hard her tears warm my cold skin.

"Aw, don't cry," I say. "Everything will be fine. I promise. I love you, Red."

Then everything fades into silent darkness.

———

Cozy warmth.

That's what I feel now. No more frigid temperatures or cold air that cuts through me like a knife. Just warm comfort.

Even the air I breathe in warms my insides.

And I'm not alone. There's an equally warm body curled up next to me. My eyes slowly blink open, and when I look down, Sophia's head is resting on my chest. Her red hair is spread out behind her and draped over my arm. I instinctively squeeze her closer.

A soft moan comes from her lips, and the warmth of her breath dances across my bare skin. My girl is back where she belongs, and I've never felt more content in all my life.

She stirs and glances up at me. "You're awake."

I nod. Instead of saying all the words she needs—and deserves

—to hear, I roll us over until she's on her back, and I'm hovering over her.

Our eyes lock and so much passes between us with this one look. No words required.

I'm sorry.

I miss you.

Never leave me again.

I need you.

You're my everything.

"Mac, I—"

I silence her with a chaste kiss. "Give me a minute."

She nods and slides her hands around my neck and into my hair. When her nails scrape across my scalp, I moan. God I've missed her touch.

"You're here," I whisper and trace a line between her freckles with my finger. "In my room. I've never had a girl in my bedroom before."

Her eyes are glassy as she smiles. "Grams insisted I stay with you. To make sure you're okay. But I think she has ulterior motives."

"Sounds like Grams." I squeeze her hip with one hand while I'll cup her cheek with the other. "I had a dream about you. About us."

She smiles and runs her fingers deeper into my hair. A tingling sensation starts at my head, runs through me, and settles in my cock. My eyes fall shut, and I groan at how good her touch feels.

"Was it a good dream?" she asks.

I nod. "We were playing in the snow. It was freezing, but the sun was bright. Your hair glowed like a beacon calling me home. And ... And ..."

I drop my head into the crook of her neck, unsure if I can admit this next part. It's deep. In my dream, we were together, maybe even married, and we had a daughter. I don't know if she wants something like that with me. She's here now, but that doesn't mean she'll stay.

"Mac, you can tell me. Anything. I'm not going anywhere."

I look up at her. "Do you mean that?"

She lifts her head and presses her lips to mine. "Yes, Mac. I'm yours."

The growl that escapes me is positively feral. Hearing her say those two little words stirs something so primal and instinctive inside me that I can't stop myself from kissing her more deeply.

When her lips part, and her tongue swipes along my bottom lip, my cock thickens. I grind against her, aching for the friction of our bodies moving together.

She tastes divine, like sunshine and cookies and everything I've always wanted in my life.

Our tongues tangle for control. Both of us kissing the other like it's not enough. We're not close enough. We need more. More touching. More kissing. More holding. Just more ... Everything.

"Sophia." I break the kiss and drop my forehead to hers. "We should talk."

She nods. "Yeah, talk."

Her voice is raspy and so full of need that it makes my already hard-as-steel cock strain even more against the tightness of my sweatpants.

"Finish telling me about this dream?" she asks once her breathing has slowed.

"There's not a lot to it. It was just you and me and ..." I take a deep breath before I brush her hair behind her ear. "And a little girl with the same red hair as you. She called me Daddy."

She sucks in a breath. "You had a dream about our future?"

"I did. And it made me finally admit to myself that I can't live without you. I need you, Sophia. I need you so much. I'm so sorry for how I acted. There's no excuse for losing my temper like that. I wish I could promise you that I'll never do it again, but I know me. I'm an asshole. I get mad—sometimes irrationally so. I'm jealous, and I will be jealous of any man who dares to talk to you. Even my brothers. But I'll try to do better. For you. I'll try to keep myself in check and not act so possessive over you. I love your strength. It's one of the first things that attracted me to you. I don't want to do anything that masks who you are because I love you. All of you. Your strength. Your sense of humor. Your kind heart. Your tenacity. And I want that dream to be real."

"Mac." Her voice cracks. "Are you saying what I think you're saying?"

"I'm saying I love you. I want you. Always. One day, when the time is right, I want more with you. No woman has ever made me feel like this before."

"And how do I make you feel?" Tears stream down her cheeks, and I wipe them away.

"Whole." I press a light kiss to her lips. "For the first time in a long time—hell, maybe even ever—I feel whole when I'm with you."

She sobs as she tightens her arms around my neck and hugs me close. Her lips brush across my ear as she whispers, "I love you too. I'm yours, Mac. Always."

"Oh, baby. Those are the best words I've ever heard in all my life."

She chuckles as I press my lips to hers and claim her mouth with mine. I settle between her legs, my hard cock pressing against her center. She wraps her legs around my waist and lifts her hips to meet mine.

"Baby, I need to be inside you. I need to feel you."

"Yes," she whispers, and that's all I need to hear.

I push up off the bed and rush to my bedroom door to make sure it's locked. When I turn around, Sophia is leaning up on her elbows, her red hair draped across one shoulder. She's so beautiful. Seeing her like this in my bed for the first time makes me ache all over with anticipation and need.

"Strip," I demand as I reach behind me and pull my t-shirt over my head. She doesn't hesitate. By the time I'm crawling over her, we're both naked. My cock bobs between us, swollen and throbbing. I fist my hand around it and tug. It's enough to relieve some of the pressure, but my need to be inside her is too much.

"Are you ready for me? I don't think I can wait." I run the tip of my cock along her center and growl when her wetness coats me. "God, baby. I'm desperate for you. I promise to take my time with you later."

"Mac, please." Her soft moans make me even harder. I press my tip at her entrance but don't push inside her. Not yet.

"Please, what?"

Instead of answering me, she runs her hands down to my ass and squeezes. She lifts her hips at the same time she pulls my body into hers. I need to feel her so badly that I don't fight her. My cock slowly slides inside her, and we both groan.

"This. I need this," she says all breathy and needy. "I need to feel you too."

"I'll give you whatever you want. All you have to do is ask."

She thrusts her hips up to meet mine. "This. I want this. I want you."

Our lips crash together, and we devour each other. I've never felt so close, so united with another person before. Every inch of me is touching and claiming every inch of her. She meets me thrust for thrust until we're both coming. My head spins, and I feel like I'm floating in a sea of love and peace and belonging.

This is where I belong. With her.

Not wanting to disconnect myself from her, I brace myself on my elbows and stare down at her. She gives me a soft smile before lifting her lips to mine.

"Promise me one thing, Mac." Her voice is soft yet commanding. It makes my cock twitch back to life inside her.

"Anything. Just ask."

"Don't ever push me away like that again. You can get mad and jealous all you want, but *never* walk away from me."

My smile grows wide. "Never, Red. Never. I'm yours, too. If that wasn't clear before, I'm telling you now. I'm all yours. You're stuck with me."

I feel the relief wash over her as her body relaxes into mine. "Good. Because you're stuck with me too."

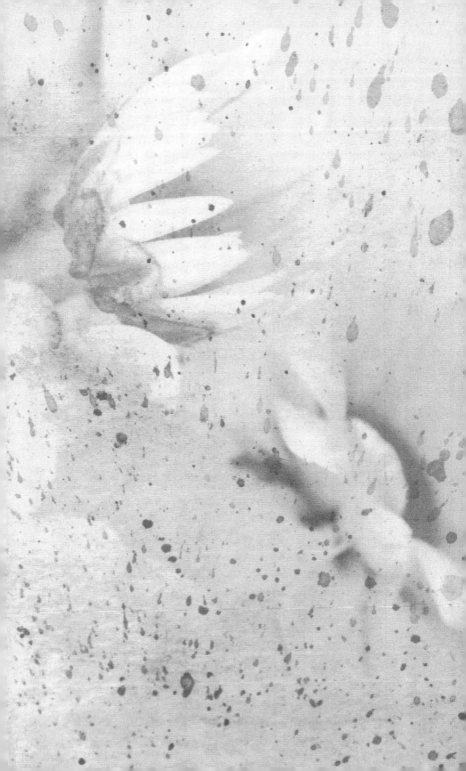

Chapter 30

Family knows no bounds and has no limits.

Sophia

"Mac, you really need to relax. Loosen your grip on the steering wheel before you break it."

We left for Circleville, a city an hour north of Beaver, about fifty minutes ago, and Mac has been mostly silent. He's anxious about meeting his other siblings for the first time, but his knuckles are white from how hard he's gripping the steering wheel. His hands have to hurt.

He lets out a deep exhale and flexes his fingers before he glances at me. "Can't help it. I'm nervous. What if they're just like Heidi?"

Translation ... What if they hate me?

At first, Mac wouldn't even talk about the news his mother dropped on him like a nuclear bomb. He tried to hide behind anger and apathy, but I saw through his armor. He may never truly get over the pain of his mom's abandonment. Finding out he has three half-siblings has only made it worse.

There's not much that means more to Mac than family. To any of the Mutters, really. He'd do anything for his brothers. If he'd known he had three more siblings, he'd have done anything to make them a part of his life too. But Heidi robbed him of that chance. She robbed him of so many things, and this secret is just one more nail in the coffin of their relationship.

His brothers tried to convince Mac to invite his new siblings to the house so they could meet them too. Mac refused. He's not ready to bring a part of his mother's world into his. He's scared that they'll be too much like Heidi, and they'll never have the chance to know each other the way siblings should.

I get it. He and I may have worked things out, but he still has trust issues.

He trusts me now—mostly, he's a continuous work-in-progress —but he's not ready to bring strangers into his close circle until he meets them first.

He refuses to let anyone close to his brothers that might cause them pain. The Mutters have suffered way more than any one family should. I can't fault him for wanting to spare his brothers more pain and suffering.

I smile and run my fingers through his hair. He leans into my touch and some of the tension leaves his body. "Today will be great. Millie seems like a really sweet girl. She says they're all excited to meet you."

He nods and keeps his eyes trained on the road.

Millie is the oldest of his half-siblings. She and I have exchanged a few phone conversations over the past couple of weeks as we worked together to set up this meeting. She's eager to meet Mac and be a part of his life. She says the same is true for the younger two, Greta and Ben.

We're about ten minutes away from the restaurant where we're meeting them for lunch. The closer we get, the more tension he holds in his jaw.

He reaches for my hand and laces our fingers together before he kisses my knuckles. "Thanks for doing this with me. I never would have reached out to them if you hadn't pushed."

"I know." I squeeze his hand. "And I know this isn't easy for you. I'm proud of you for taking this step."

He gives me a side eye glare. "You didn't exactly give me a choice, Red."

I chuckle, lean across the center dashboard, and kiss his cheek. "Just promise me you'll give them the benefit of doubt. Don't assume they're like Heidi."

He sighs and leans into my touch. "I'm trying. I really am."

My phone buzzes from where it's sitting in the cup holder and he tightens his grip on my hand. I grab it with my free hand to see who's calling. "Relax, Mac. It's my dad."

Ever since we set the date and time to meet, he's been waiting for them to cancel. He's holding his mother's transgressions against them. He doesn't mean to. He doesn't even realize he's doing it most of the time. He knows it's not their fault Heidi abandoned him, started a new family, and never told anyone he existed. But it's hard to squash a lifetime of pain.

I swipe to answer. "Hey, Dad."

"Pumpkin! How are you?"

"I'm good. Mac and I are driving to a lunch date in Circleville. We're almost there, so I don't have much time. What's up?"

"Your mom asked me to confirm your Christmas plans. You and Mac decide what day you're coming?"

"Yeah, I think so. We'll be there on the morning of twenty-fourth and stay until the twenty-sixth if that's okay."

"Of course. You two can stay as long as you like. Your mom is fixing up your room so it'll be ready."

"My room?"

Dad chuckles. "Yes. Your room. We know you're not a little girl anymore. You two can stay in the same room. This is the first boy you've been serious about. Your mom is beside herself with excitement."

"Even though he's a racecar driver and encourages my own dreams to race?"

"Yes, pumpkin. We just want you to be happy."

I glance over at Mac, and he gives me a wink. He may not be

able to hear everything my dad is saying, but he gets the gist of the conversation. "I am happy, Dad. Very happy. I'll see you soon."

We say our goodbyes, and I place my phone back in the center dash.

My parents aren't completely onboard with my racing aspirations, but they're coming around. To my surprise, they were happy when I decided to officially join the Mutter Truckers Auto & Racing team. They said being a part of a professional team seemed safer than the pieced-together approach I'd been operating under for the past several years. They're not wrong.

Shortly after Mac and I got back together, Liam called me into a meeting. He made it sound so serious, I was afraid he was letting me go. Business can get slow during the winter months, so it wouldn't have surprised me.

Instead, I walked into his family's kitchen to be greeted by Mac, Chase, Ash, and Liam. To say I was shocked and overjoyed they asked me to become a driver for them is an understatement.

Mac still plans on driving some, but he wants to step back and take on more of a recruiter and manager role. His goals and priorities have shifted.

Maybe neither of us will ever race in the Sprint Cup, but one day, the Mutter name will be known at the top of the ranks. And I'm excited to help them make that a reality.

Mac pulls into a parking space outside the restaurant, but he doesn't turn off the truck. Instead, he tugs me close and wraps his arms around me.

"I've never spent Christmas away from my family. This year will be the first."

"Never?"

He shakes his head. "We've always been together. Even Warren never misses a Christmas."

"Oh God!" I lean back and stare into his eyes. He looks calm and at peace. "Are you okay with that? I mean, missing all that time you could be spending with your brother. You hardly ever see him."

His smile grows and he gives me a light kiss. "It's fine. He's staying through New Year's Day. I'll get to spend plenty of time with him."

"If you're sure."

"I am." He kisses me again and clenches his hands at my sides.

"Ready to go in?" I ask before he deepens the kiss.

"No." He grumbles and drops his head to my chest.

I smile and hug him tighter. "Well, let's go inside anyway."

"Oh my God. It's him," a teenage boy says from a table just inside the entrance to the restaurant. The girl sitting next to him elbows and shushes him.

Mac tightens his grip on my hand while the older girl sitting with her back to the door stands and turns the gentlest smile on us.

"Oh, wow!" She beams. "You're so tall."

She leaps toward us and wraps her arms around Mac, causing his entire body to go ramrod straight. I try to extract my hand from his so he can hug her back, but he just pulls me closer as if I'm his lifeline.

The girl hugging him, whom I assume is Millie, is short. Maybe only five-feet-three or four. She's pretty with dark hair and a kind smile.

Mac finally relaxes and pats her back.

"Millie?" he croaks.

"Yeah." She releases him and steps back, wiping her eyes. "Sorry. I told myself not to get emotional on you, but clearly ..." She just smiles and points at her face with tears streaming down her cheeks.

Mac smiles and his own eyes glass over. He squeezes her

shoulder and says, "Don't apologize. It's not every day you get to meet a sibling for the first time."

"Oh, my gosh. Look at me crying, and I haven't even introduced myself. You must think I'm a silly girl. I'm not. I swear. It's just this is ... Well, a lot for us to take in. We thought we knew our mom, and then she threw this at us."

She turns around to her brother and sister who are still sitting at the table. They're both staring at us like they don't know what to say or do.

"I'm Millie in case you didn't already figure that out." Millie places her hand on her chest before she points to her siblings. "And this is Greta and Ben. We're all a little nervous."

Mac nods and gives them a smile. "I'm nervous too."

Silence falls over us as we all stare at each other, no one knowing what to say next. Ben and Greta have their heads down clearly unsure of how to navigate this. Millie smiles and Mac rubs the back of his neck.

"Why don't we sit? Maybe order some appetizers while we talk." I suggest.

"Yeah, good idea," Millie says as she slides back into her chair. Mac and I take the empty seats across from them. "So, Ben and Greta are racing fans. Turns out they watched you race lots of times with Dad. They were at the race a few months ago when Sophia beat you too. It was all they talked about for days. It's what finally broke Mom and got her to tell us you were her son. Things at home have been ... Well, there's been lots of fighting." Millie stops and takes a drink of her water. "God I'm sorry. I've said too much already, haven't I? I tend to ramble when I'm nervous."

Mac smiles and waves her concerns off like it doesn't matter. "Don't worry about it." Then he turns to Ben and Greta. "You're racing fans?"

They nod but don't look up.

"Ben's not just a fan. He's obsessed. Has posters all over his walls," Millie says.

"Millie!" Ben scolds his older sister. "You're embarrassing me."

Mac chuckles. "No need to be embarrassed. You wanna talk about embarrassing? My girlfriend hands my ass to me every day on the track. That's embarrassing."

"Hey!" I nudge him with my elbow. "What's that supposed to mean?"

He pulls me closer and kisses my cheek. "Just teasing, Red. But you are a better driver than me."

This makes Ben laugh which was what Mac wanted. "I want to race cars," Ben says quickly. "I mean, it looks like fun. I'd like to try it someday."

"Then you should." An easy smile covers Mac's face. The one that says he's perfectly at ease and comfortable with his surroundings. "You'll have to visit and come to the tracks with me. I'll teach you."

I look up at him in surprise and happiness. Pride swells in my chest at how he's opening up to them. He must see what I see. Three great kids who want nothing more than to get to know the older brother they never knew they had.

"You'd do that?" Ben asks.

"Of course. That's what big brothers are for."

"Will you teach me too?" Greta asks in a soft, barely audible tone. This is the first she's spoken since we arrived.

Mac turns his smile to her. "Absolutely. You'll all have to come for a visit. Make a weekend out of it or something."

"If Mom will let us," Greta whispers.

"You let me deal with Mom," Millie says in a stern voice that says she'll get what she wants, and she dares anyone to get in her way. It's in complete contrast to the sweet personality we've seen so far.

Mac clears his throat and takes a drink of his water. "Is your dad okay with you spending time with me?"

"Are you kidding?" Millie beams. "Dad is great with it. He's just as mad at Mom as we are. He's upset that he didn't get to be a part of your life sooner. Would've loved to be a part of your early racing days. Or worked on cars with you when you were young. He may be a lawyer by day, but he loves to tinker with cars. It's his hobby."

"Sounds like a good man." Mac's voice is heavy with emotion. I know he loves his dad, but their relationship is strained. All the Mutter brothers have issues with their dad.

"He is, and he'd like to meet you someday. If you're open to that?" Millie adds.

"Sure." Mac drops his head and fiddles with the button on his shirt. "Was she ..." He lets out a deep sigh and squeezes my hand. "Was she a good mom?"

Silence falls over our table. I glance between Millie, Greta, and Ben. They're all staring at Mac with sadness in their expression. I'm not sure what that means.

"Not the best," Greta says, surprising me. She's been so quiet. I didn't expect her to be the one to answer. "I mean, she's always been there, so I guess that means *something*. She's a selfish person. Always puts herself first, and only cares that we all make her look better."

Millie nods her agreement. "I think there's something wrong in her head. She didn't get the mom-gene. You know, the one that makes being a parent instinctual? She didn't get that. I'm sure she loves all of us in her own way, but she doesn't know how to show it. All of our love and affection comes from Dad."

"So you're saying I didn't miss much with her disappearing act when I was five?"

Greta snorts. "Not at all. In fact, she did you a favor."

I smile, even though nothing inside me feels warm and happy. Something tells me Greta's relationship with their mom is by far the worst.

Mac must sense it too because he leans forward and stares directly at her. She lifts her gaze to his and holds it. "She did you another favor by finally telling you about me. You have more family now. You didn't just get me as a brother. You got six more just like me. Some are grumpier than others but they're dying to meet you. And a Grams that will stuff your face full of all the best baked goods imaginable. That is … If you want that."

Greta nods, her eyes glassy. "I'd like that," she whispers.

"Good." Mac sits back and picks up his menu. "Now that the tough conversation is over, let's eat. Then we can make plans for you to meet the rest of your new family."

I look up at Mac and smile. I am in awe of this man. He may have been nervous about meeting them, but he recognizes they're nervous, too. These four need each other, and he's opening himself up to let them in.

I lean up close to his ear and whisper, "I love you."

He turns to me and smiles before he presses a light kiss to my lips. "I love you, too, Red. Thanks for helping me get here."

And by here, he doesn't mean in this restaurant meeting his new siblings for the first time. He means this place in his life where he's open himself up to love. Love for siblings he didn't know existed and love for a woman.

Love for *me*.

And I'm ready for a lifetime of whatever this growly-bear, overly protective, and jealous man has in store for me.

Because the love we share binds us together, and nothing will ever tear that bond apart.

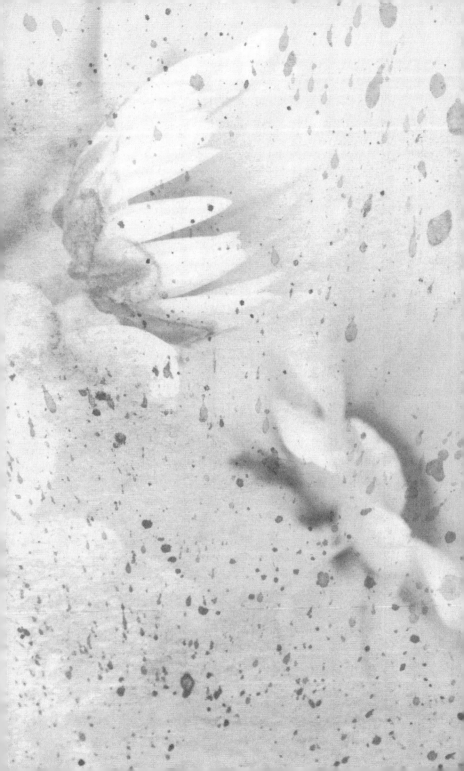

Epilogue

It began with a loss but ends in a win.
Mac

T*he following summer*
"Where are you taking me?" Sophia asks as I pull her through the crowd.

It's a warm summer day, and there are so many people around us that it feels like the entire county is here. The county fair is typically a busy event, but today is particularly crowded.

"You'll see. We're almost there."

I spot my brothers up ahead, and I can't contain my smile.

"Why are you so happy?" Sophia looks up at me with suspicion written all over her face.

I stop, causing a few people to knock into us and grumble as they stumble past. Not caring that we're blocking the flow of traffic, I cup her cheeks and plant a gentle kiss to her lips. "Because I've got *you*, Red. I'm happy because of *you*."

She wraps her arms around my waist and relaxes into me. "That's really sweet, Mac. But seriously, what is up with you today?"

I chuckle. "Why does something have to be up for me to be happy?"

She narrows her gaze as she looks up at me. "It doesn't, but you're acting weird."

"No, I'm not," I scoff.

"Yes, you are." This time she's the one that chuckles.

"Agree to disagree." I kiss her nose before I reach for her hand and take it in mine, lacing our fingers together. "Now stop distracting me, and let's go."

"Fine." She quirks a brow. "But I'm right."

I shake my head and continue leading her through the crowd. When the sign over the bumper cars track comes into view, Sophia stops.

"Are we racing?" she gasps.

I look down at her, the smile that lights up her face causes my chest to tighten. When I came up with the idea to challenge her at another bumper car race, I wasn't sure if it was the best idea. But seeing the excitement on her face tells me this is all kinds of right.

"We are. Now stop stalling so I can kick your ass."

"I am *not* stalling." She tugs at my hand, dragging me toward the entrance. "And you wish. Have you forgotten what happened the last time you challenged me at bumper cars?"

"How could I forget the day we met? Especially since you *never* let me forget about it."

"What can I say?" She gives me a sweet smile that I know is anything but sweet. "I like to win."

I pull her body flush with mine and cup my hand possessively around her neck. "So do I."

Then I kiss her hard and deep. I plunge my tongue into her mouth before she has a chance to stop me. It's a kiss that's much too indecent for public consumption but I don't give a shit. Sophia is mine, and I want everyone in this county to know it.

When I break away, she's breathless, and her pale cheeks are flushed the most adorable shade of pink. I love making my girl blush.

"You ready?" I tap her nose then let my finger follow the line of freckles on her cheek.

She blinks a few times before her eyes come into focus. She's off-kilter thanks to my kiss. That's exactly how I want her right now.

I learned a long time ago that if I want to surprise Sophia, I have to find a way to disorient her first. Kissing her like that seems to have done the trick.

The man operating the bumper cars gives me a huge smile and a wink before opening the gate to let us. I lead Sophia across the open track to two cars sitting on the opposite side.

"I assume you want the red one again?"

She shakes her head as if trying to bring herself back to the moment. Her eyes are glazed over with need, and I can't help but puff my chest out knowing that I did that to her.

"Umm, yes. The red one."

I hold her hand to help her in as she settles into the car. Then I slip into the blue one next to her. The two cars are lined up side-by-side with the noses perfectly in line with each other. All the other cars are in a cluster near the gate.

Once we're sitting in our cars, the operator lets a group of kids in to fill the remaining cars. Sophia is watching them with a serious look on her face. It's not one that suggests she's onto me, but rather like she's preparing to take me down.

"Why so serious, Red? This is supposed to be fun."

She shifts her stare to me, a tight smile on her face. "Oh, it will be fun. Especially when I kick your ass again."

I shrug and smile. "If you think you can, go ahead. Makes no difference to me."

"Who are you, and what have you done with Mac?"

I laugh. "Try to win and find out."

She turns her gaze back to the operator, and that's when she spots my brothers. They're all here, Liam, Garret, Ash, Christian, and Chase. Even Warren is here for one of his rare visits.

"Oh, look!" She points at them with a huge grin on her face. "Your brothers came to watch you lose."

"Looks like it," I say right as the buzzer sounds, signifying the start of the race.

Sophia takes off like a rocket, seemingly undistracted by seeing my brothers here to watch.

Me? I remain right where I'm at.

Sophia doesn't notice I don't move as she races away from me and toward the opposite side where all the kids are still clustered together. But just as she starts to round the first corner, the kids miraculously get untangled and head right for her. Within seconds, they surround her, stopping her from moving forward.

She lets out a loud growl. "Come on, kids. Move!"

The kids laugh and purposefully bump into her over and over again. It's beautiful and exactly how I planned it.

She finally pauses and takes a moment to glance over her shoulder to check where I'm at. When she sees I haven't moved, and I'm laughing my ass off at her, her shoulders drop and her eyes narrow.

"Mac! What is this? Some kind of prank?"

I cup my hand around my mouth and yell in response. "No, Red. No prank."

"Then what are you doing?" She turns around and tries to get unstuck, but it's no use. The kids are doing a great job at blocking her in.

"Laughing at you getting stuck in the middle of a bunch of kids racing bumper cars." I push up out of my car and make my way toward her. She's so focused on the task at hand that she doesn't hear or see me approach.

"So this is payback?" she calls out.

I drop to one knee beside her car and say, "No, it's not payback, babe."

She jumps in her seat and jerks around at the closeness of my voice. She presses her hand to her chest and sucks in a breath. "God you scared me."

Then her eyes meet mine before they bounce around my face, studying my expression. I'm nervous, and I can't hide even if I try. "Mac, what are you doing?"

Her eyes dart around us, focusing on where my brothers are gathered. If everything is going according to plan, my half siblings along with her parents and siblings are now gathered with them.

"Oh my God." Her eyes widen, and glisten with tears. Then she looks back at me, and all I see is love and joy. It's a look that makes my heart sing. "Why is my family here?"

"Sophia." My voice croaks as I pull a small box from my pocket. I pop it open and hold it out for her to see. Her tears break free and run down her cheeks, but her smile tells me they're all happy tears. "I love you. And I want to spend the rest of my life watching you win. You can beat me at every game or sport we play, and I'll love you more for it. Because as long as I have you, I can't lose. Please say you'll marry me and be my wife."

Her eyes shift between mine and the round solitaire diamond ring in the box. Then they settle on me, and she nods. "Yes. Yes, I'll marry you."

She lunges at me and somehow manages to get out of the car and settles into my lap. She's hugging me so tight that it almost pushes the air out of my chest.

"Oh my God, Mac. I can't believe you did this."

I lean back and cup her cheek. "I knew I wanted you from the moment you looked up at me and smiled. Beating me at bumper cars only confirmed you were made for me. I couldn't think of a better way to propose."

Her smile is so big and bright as I slip the ring on her finger. A perfect fit. "Now, you're mine forever."

"Was there ever really any doubt?" She chuckles.

"Not since the first time I kissed you, but now the world will know you're mine as well."

WANT MORE **MAC AND SOPHIA**? CLICK HERE (HTTPS:// ariabliss.com/bonus-content-sign-up/) to get your **FREE** *Truck You* bonus scene for sneak peek into their future.

DON'T STOP NOW. THE MUTTER BROTHER'S FAMILY SAGA continues in *Truck Me*: A Grumpy-Sunshine Small Town Romance with **Garret and Charlotte**. CLICK HERE (https:// www.amazon.com/dp/B0BSSJ5GW8) to grab it today. Garret Mutter is broody, grumpy, and always scowls. By all accounts, I'd say he hates me. But there's a fire burning deep in his eyes every time he looks at me that makes me shudder with desire.

STILL NOT ENOUGH? **SOPHIA AND MAC** FIRST MAKE appearances in Sophia's cousin's book *Aside From Me*: A Room-mates to Lovers Romance, Book 4 of A Drunk Love Contemporary Romance (**Trent and Persephone**). CLICK HERE (https:// www.amazon.com/dp/B0B1QSWKV5) to find out just how hard Trent falls in *Aside From Me*: A Roommates to Lovers Romance!

OR DIVE INTO MORE OF THE A DRUNK LOVE CONTEMPORARY Romance Series! In this sweeping family saga, you've met the four siblings, a few of their closest friends, and their sexy, irresistible counterparts. Start at the beginning with Aria's reader favorite.

Heath and Alicia fight for love in *Not for Me*: A Fake Dating Romance

A Drunk Love Contemporary Romance, Book 1.

CLICK HERE

(https://www.amazon.com/dp/B09FJ3GSWS) to grab your copy.

Books by Aria Bliss

The Mutter Brothers Series

Truck You: A Hate to Love Small Town Romance

Truck Me: A Grumpy-Sunshine Small Town Romance

A Drunk Love Contemporary Romance Series

Not for Me: A Fake Dating Romance

Let Me Stay: A Friends to Lovers, Best Friend's Sister Romance

Lead Me Here: A Grumpy-Sunshine Romance

Aside From Me: A Roommate to Lovers Romance

Make Me Go: An Age Gap Romance

Hearts of Watercress Falls Series

Healing Hearts: A Second Chance at Love Small Town Romance

Trusting Hearts: A Single Dad Small Town Romance

Falling Hearts: A Secret Marriage Small Town Romance

Laughing Hearts: A Best Friend's Sister Small Town Romance

Forgiving Hearts: A Hate to Love Small Town Romance

Standalone Novels

Good Wine & Bad Decisions: A Sexy Romance

An After-Hours Affair Series

In Charge: Book 1

One Drink: Book 2

You're Mine: Book 3

Charm Me: Book 4

Stuck Together: Book 5 (A Holiday Romance)

.

Connect with Me

Website: http://ariabliss.com
Subscribe to my Newsletter: https://ariabliss.com/sign-up/
Follow me on Amazon Author Central: http://www.amazon.com/author/ariabliss.author
Follow me on Instagram: http://www.instagram.com/ariabliss.author
Follow me on goodreads: http://www.goodreads.com/ariablissauthor
Follow me on Bookbub: https://www.bookbub.com/authors/aria-bliss
Join my Facebook Street Team: https://www.facebook.com/groups/SassySuperFans/
Follow me on Facebook: http://www.facebook.com/ariabliss.author/
Follow me on Twitter: http://www.twitter.com/ariablissauthor

Author Bio

Sexy & Fun Romance with a healthy dose of Real Life

Aria Bliss writes steamy, emotionally charged contemporary romance with humor, drama, and big feels. She has a soft spot for single dads, second chances, forbidden romance, and grumpy bad boys with sweet centers that are impossible not to love.